Cecelia Jackson's Last Chance is a mou[...] treat for any book reader who enjo[...] redemption and killer tuna fish sandwic[...].

~Mary DeMuth, author of *The Muir House*

This beautifully written tale from author Robbie Iobst offers more twists and turns than a food court pretzel, with equal parts salty and sweet. Highly recommended!

~Janice Thompson, author of the *Weddings by Bella* series

I laughed, I cried. *Cecelia Jackson's Last Chance* is a new take on the traditional buddy story—in this case, the three "inseparable" friends haven't been in touch for 20 years. Laced with southern flavor, Iobst's debut novel takes you on a journey punctuated with grief, grudges, and a dose of hope. I fell in love with the characters, their world, and the themes of forgiveness. Beautifully crafted, this is a novel not to be missed!

~Megan DiMaria, author of *Searching for Spice* and *Out of Her Hands*

Robbie Iobst has hit a homerun with her debut novel, *Cecelia Jackson's Last Chance*. It's been a long time since I've read a story where I so connected with the characters. Their life journeys were sometimes heart-breaking, but Robbie found that fine line of dealing with real issues without disheartening her readers. Yes, I cried. But I laughed, too. I cheered these women on, so engrossed in their stories that I had to remind myself not to pray for them-- they weren't really friends from down the street, they were fictional characters for heaven's sake! When I put the book down I felt joyous, hopeful, and empowered. What a great read!

~Paula Moldenhauer, author of *Titanic, Legacy of Betrayal*

In *Cecelia Jackson's Last Chance*, the characters introduce themselves much like new friends—one layer at a time. We begin to care about them as they reveal deeper and deeper things about themselves, and the emotions they evoke warm to rival a Texas summer. At one point I found myself tempted to pray for them. Author Robbie Iobst presents her breakout novel with wit and grit, which makes it one my favorite reads this year.

~Kathy Kovach, author of *Titanic, Legacy of Betrayal*

Robbie Iobst does an extraordinary job creating characters that seem so real you'll forget you're reading fiction. You'll find yourself shaking your head at some of the gals in *Cecelia Jackson's Last Chance*, roaring in laughter with others, crying with a few, and coming to love them all.

~Stacy Voss, **Eyes of Your Heart Ministries** director

Cecelia Jackson's Last Chance

- ROBBIE IOBST -

A Harpstring Book from Written World Communications

Cecelia Jackson's Last Chance

Brought to you by the creative team at Written-World.com:
Kristine Pratt, J. Christine Richards, Melissa Alicea

Cover Design: Lynda K. Arndt

Library of Congress Control Number: 2013919020
International Standard Book Number: 978-1-938679-07-0

Printed in the United States of America

FOR SALLY FLOYD, LUCILLE KELLUM, CAROL JO
MARLEY, MAXINE WILLIAMS
AND ALL THE OLDER WOMEN WHO HAVE POURED THEIR
LIVES INTO MINE AND OTHERS.

TITUS 2:3-4

AND FOR KAREN PRATT,
BELOVED SISTER AND BEST FRIEND.

Acknowledgements

Thank you Jesus for Your love, joy and guidance.

Thank you:

Noah – your "You can do it, Mom" fueled me.

Marriah, Sarah and Hannah – Being your step mama has taught me so much. I love you!

Perry and Kasey Floyd, Karen and Paul Pratt, Phil and Lory Floyd – my siblings are the best!

Loretta Oakes, Kay Day and Michele Cushatt – You are my critique group and my best friends!

Stacy Voss and Dianne Daniels – Our Masterminds group and the two of you have grown me in so many ways!

Chris Richards – Thank you for editing, believing and working hard for this story.

Kristine Pratt and all the folks at Harpstring and Written World Communications.

Susy Turnbull, Stacey Crutcher, Desha Crownover, Linda Crownover, Deborah Chapman and Laura Engelberg – Thank you for being the first readers of this story and telling me to go for it.

Sharen Watson – I'll never forget the day when I walked into Words for the Journey Christian Writers Guild – you are my mentor and friend.

Megan DiMaria, Denise Holmes, Jan Parrish, Danica McDonald, Lucille Zimmerman, Paula Moldenhauer and the many other writers who have taught me, encouraged me and supported me.

Every person who has read one of my "Joy-votions" and commented. Your words have meant the world.

Sandra Bishop, whose belief in my abilities gave me such hope.

All of my old students. Thank you for inspiring your teacher to dream and believe.

Those wonderful folks in Van Horn, Texas who taught me the invaluable good of living in a small town.

Finally, thank you to my best half, John. You listened to me read this each night after I wrote and you encouraged, challenged and loved me. I love you so much!

Chapter 1

Belinda

Wind Storm, Texas

Why in God's green earth did I show up to this fancy-shmancy shindig?

Oh, come on, Belinda, don't get the cows running. Just relax.

"Bee!" From my Honda Accord, I spot Sue on the sidewalk, waving me over. I take another puff before putting out my cigarette. I can't believe I'm going to a baby shower at Sandra Hood's house. I'm insane. Do I wanna get beat up?

"Come on, we don't want to be late." Sue holds a big 'ole present, covered in giraffe wrapping paper. I guess I'll need to chip in for that.

"I honestly do not like baby showers." I walk with Sue up to the huge wooden front door. This house is stately and proper, like something I'd find in an *Architectural Digest,* not in a podunk East Texas town like Wind Storm.

Sue nudges me in the shoulder. "You may not like baby showers but you like Rachel and it's about her baby-to-be. She invited you so she doesn't hate you. Probably hasn't had the privilege of knowing you long enough to hate you."

I love the Hood home as soon as I go in to the foyer. Expensive and tasteful and luxurious. All the things I ain't got the money for. The only out of place décor is the huge buffalo head mounted in the foyer.

"I know, it's awful, isn't it?" a voice beside me asks.

I turn to see Sandra Hood standing there, eyeing the monstrosity. Did I speak out loud? My purse hits the floor. Darnitt. She's the first person I have to see?

"I'm not a fan of taxidermy." I pick it up.

Sandra laughs loud and touches my arm. "I love honesty. Can't find that in everyone. 'Specially in Wind Storm, you know? My husband loves that thing and it's my dutiful wife compromise. Of course, I stand near the entrance and tell everyone who comes in to ignore it."

I feel a bit more comfortable. Most women don't cotton to me, so this is an unexpected surprise. Apparently she ain't got a clue as to who I am.

"I'm Sandra Hood, by the way." Her huge smile shows off her extra-white teeth. As she shakes my hand, I notice her wedding ring. Must weigh a ton. She's tall and blond, of course. As different from me as night and day. No wrinkles. Probably Botox. It's weird I've never seen her before, but well, I stay away from her part of town on purpose.

"I'm Belinda Kite." I try to smile back and watch her eyes. A flash, like a pocket lighter, fires then disappears in her eyes.

"I'm Sue Patterson." Sue shakes our hostess's hand.

"So glad you came, ladies. Everyone is in the living room through there." She points to a huge room off the foyer. She's wearing long sleeves on a hot day. I wonder if he 'loves' on her, too, like he does me.

My stomach somersaults with nausea. "Where is your restroom?" I use my polite voice, but I'm ready to scream and throw up at the same time. She points and I skedaddle. The bathroom is foo-foo too, with a porcelain doll on the back of the toilet. Who in the world puts a breakable doll on a toilet? She does, apparently. I breathe deep. In, slowly through the nose and out through the mouth, making a little cylinder of air.

I remember the reasons I came. First, I do like Rachel. Ever time she comes into the Silver Spoon she leaves great tips for Sue even if she ain't made of money. I wondered about the big tips for a while, thinking she might be trying to impress somebody. But frankly there ain't nobody to impress at the Silver Spoon. When I went over to the 'Cut and Curl' where she works, she gave me a manicure that made me feel like a rich woman. Treated me like I was something special. I wanna wish her well.

Second, I'm at this baby hoedown 'cause of *him*. If he's here, I'll get a kick outta seeing what he'll do. He'll get furious or turned on. If he's mad, I'll steer clear for a couple days. If he likes it, well, I'm up for that. Yep, I'll take the chance. My stomach says this is a mistake, but I ignore it.

And third, I wanna see what his wife is like. So far, it makes no sense whatsoever. She's a rich gal that has probably spent a paycheck or two on some kinda surgery on her face. I don't see them together at all. I breathe again, slow like and feel my heart calming down. I can do this.

When I walk out, Sue awaits. "Are you okay?" Sue don't miss a thing. At the Silver Spoon, I'm the cook and she's the head waitress. Great at her job, she remembers details and don't put up with anybody's guff.

"I'm fine."

"You're acting like you're sick or something." She eyes me like she's trying to pick out a good cantaloupe.

"I'm fine. Let's do some showering or whatever they do at these things."

The living room is gigantic, with Victorian décor and soft pink and brown chairs and sofas. I just can't see him sitting in this fancy room. It'd be like a big 'ole moose stomping through a beauty parlor. Sue and I sit on one of the sofas. At my house, this is called a couch. I bet here it's called a sofa or even a divan.

"I ain't playing no games," I whisper.

"You don't go to parties often, do you?" she teases.

I give her a look. Seriously? She knows me better than that.

The party officially starts when Sandra Hood invites us all to say a prayer for Rachel. I bow my head to be polite, but my eyes look up and around. I don't see any pictures of him and her. Just fancy paintings. And I've never seen so many coasters in one room. I wonder what she does when someone doesn't use one. I think about trying this experiment but the amen's of all these nice women interrupt my plan.

"Okay, everyone! We are going to have lunch outside on the patio since it is such a nice day." Sandra directs traffic as the twenty or thirty of us stroll to the backyard.

When I walk through the French doors that lead to the patio, I'm stunned. *He* owns this backyard? Looks like a TV commercial for garden fertilizer. The hedges are even and the grass is shiny green. The new May flowers all got orders to bloom at the same time and they obeyed. And there's a fountain beside the pool beside the Jacuzzi. Sue and I get in line at the buffet at the end of the patio.

"I didn't know the Hoods had money," I lower my voice.

Sue responds in kind. "Mr. Hood doesn't have money. Mrs. Hood has money."

Well, there you go.

The scents coming from the buffet table make enduring all this worth it. I smell spices and heat and deliciousness. The food is all tiny and beautiful. My estrogen level is on the rise just sniffing. I pick up some tiny quiches. I start analyzing each item and putting together the recipes in my head. I could do this. I could cater, if I needed to.

"Belinda, come on over." Sandra Hood waves me to her table. I'm confused. She is the hostess and she wants me to sit at her table?

I glance at Sue and she shrugs. I walk to Sandra's table and silently hope she meant Sue, too. Only one chair is empty. "I'm sorry, Sandra, but I came with Sue and I believe I need to sit with the one that brung me." I giggle at my stupid little joke.

"Sue's sitting somewhere else, honey." Sandra's smile shows all those pearly-white teeth but her eyes are squinting like she's planning something. Uh-oh.

I look over and sure enough, Sue sits beside the Pierce sisters. She looks my way and shrugs again like it's no big deal. Sue ain't got no idea. I sit beside Sandra Hood. Rachel and her mom Shirley sit here and so do two other women I don't know. A drop of sweat goes down my back.

"These are Rachel's aunts, Becky and Sarah. They're from Oklahoma, just came special."

Sandra doesn't introduce me. I reach over. "I'm Belinda."

"Oh, silly me, of course you are." Sandra's smiling weird.

The aunts ask Rachel questions. Good. The less I speak, the better. I concentrate on the food. The assortment of hors d'oeuvres is eclectic but fascinating. I see miniature Roman style pizzas with roasted cherry tomatoes. And then there are deviled chicken wings. Those will be messy but good. Interesting choice for this crowd. But the stand-alone favorite for me are the sweet potato gaufrettes with duck confit and cranberry jelly. Fancy food for sure. Makes me glad I read *Gourmet* religiously. I get to try food I've only seen in magazines. My taste buds are getting a banquet today.

"What do you think, Belinda?"

"I'm sorry?"

"I asked what you think is the most difficult thing about being a mom."

Sandra asks this innocently enough, but my insides know something's happening. My stomach goes back to gymnastics and I really want to enjoy the food. Not good.

"Well…" I pause hoping someone else will jump in. They don't. I look at Rachel, "I guess the most difficult thing would be managing time right." As soon as I say it, I know it is a stupid answer.

Sandra looks at me with questions in her eyes. "Okay. I guess that's one problem." She laughs a fake laugh. The aunts don't join in but look at me with compassion, bless 'em.

"When are you due?" I ask Rachel this, hoping the conversation will go back to her. It's her day.

"I guess time management would be especially difficult for you, being a single mom and all, right?"

I look at the hostess and return her steel smile. "Absolutely. When are you due, Rachel?"

"July 4th."

"If it's a boy, I told them they have to name him Sam, for Uncle Sam." Shirley says this through the crab tostada in her mouth.

"Mom. We'll name him when we see him, depending on what he looks like."

"That's what the Indians used to do, you know." One of the aunts says this.

I try to concentrate on the food again as Rachel and her family debate different names for the baby. My mind races and I know I need to calm down. I breathe in and out and pick up another treat. I am midway into a delicious smoked salmon barquette when I see Sandra looking at me again.

"Belinda, I think my husband goes to your restaurant often. The Silver Spoon, right?"

I start choking a little and grab my water glass to help get it down. Smooth, Belinda. Does she know me? I look around the lawn. Did someone tell her who I am? But no one knows. Wind Storm isn't a big town and we've been careful. Maybe she guessed or maybe she knew when I walked in. I take another drink, stalling.

Rachel comes to my rescue. "Mrs. Hood, Belinda is an incredible cook. More like a chef, I'd say. Have you ever tasted her food?"

"I'm afraid not." She ain't smiling now.

"I tell you, she makes the best fried chicken I've ever eaten. Jason thinks the same way. I can't believe you've never heard of her food. She's a legend in Wind Storm."

"All thirty thousand of us?" Sandra's snide little laugh has horns attached.

I try to steer the conversation *again*, away from me. "Thank you, Rachel. You're very kind and you do a mean manicure yourself." Shirley and the aunts laugh. Not Sandra.

"I guess I will have to drop in sometime. See what my husband loves so much." Sandra stares at me.

Coming was a huge mistake. "Excuse me," I stand. "I need to visit the restroom."

"Again?" Sandra's voice calls after I walk away.

I stay in the restroom for a few minutes. My purse is in the backyard, or I would leave. I return to find all the women moving to the patio doors. After I grab my purse, Sue locks arms with me.

"You have to stay until we give her our gift. Please."

I sigh and nod. Just a few more minutes. As we herd back to the living room for the opening of the presents, we pass through the dining room where the cake sits. Now this is a skill I don't have. I admire the precision of the cake decorator. A block with letters, a rattle in blue and a little teddy bear, all made of cake and icing, sits on the two-tier cake. Amazing to me. I'm looking forward to the taste. If I ain't gone when they serve it. The icing looks like your basic white butter cream. But I bet the inside is chocolate with Bavarian cream.

As I settle down on one of the couches, Sandra announces that we're going to play a game. I hear the front door close and I put my head down. Oh no.

"Oh come on, party pooper." Sue nudges me.

I glance up as one of the catering guys walks through the side hallway. I sit up. What was I thinking? He won't be turned on; he'll be furious. I need to leave.

Sandra brings out a tray of baby stuff and tells us to look at it for a minute and then she will hide it. Afterword, we write down as many items as we can remember seeing. I don't try hard, but I do participate because if I don't I'll never hear the end of it from Sue. For both of us to be off on Saturday is unheard of, so I want to make the best of it.

One of the aunts wins and we all clap and laugh. Politely. A little too pretentious for my tastes. Sandra uses a tone of voice that sounds like a perky Minnie Mouse. "Rachel, we have one more game if you want."

I fall in love with Rachel when she says, "How about we just skip that and open the presents?"

Sandra's face falls. "Oh, of course, honey."

We sit and ooh and ahh as Rachel opens up her presents. One of Rachel's friends sits across from me with a baby boy, about three months old. He stares at me with big brown eyes. I look away.

Memories smash my heart and start up my tear ducts. No, Bee. Not now. I don't cry. It's a sign of weakness and I've spent too much of my life being weak. Lookin' at all this baby stuff is fine, but seeing a little man with soft skin and dark hair is too much. He's a spitting image. I shake my head. No, Bee.

"Oh, thank you, Sue and Belinda." Rachel's voice slams the book of memories shut, bless her heart. I look over to see the diaper genie we gave Rachel. Wonder what it cost.

"Well, isn't that...something?" Sandra should've just said, "What a piece of crap." But she wouldn't. I can now say with assurance that Sandra Hood acts nice at first, but it's just an act. She's an angry, bitter woman. I've heard this verbatim.

"It's something I wanted very much. Thank you again." Rachel smiles as she sets it down with the rest of her loot.

My throat hurts. The baby boy is looking at me again. I swallow but my throat constricts a bit. I feel like I'm about to suffocate. I try to breathe slowly. If I don't look, I'll be okay. The baby reaches his hands out toward me. His mom, Rachel's friend, says, "He really likes you. Do you want to hold him?"

"No!" Uh-oh. That was too loud. "Um, I mean no thank you. I need to be going." I glance at Sue and she rolls her eyes.

"Oh you have to go?" Sandra stands with me. "I'll walk you out."

"Thank you for coming, Belinda," Rachel calls.

"Congratulations, Rachel." She's a sweet kid. I grin at her

and turn to walk out.

"See you at work." Sue calls. I nod to her.

Sandra meets me at the front door with a blue plastic plate with a piece of cake on it wrapped in cellophane. "You have to take a piece of cake, honey." She smiles and it reminds me to buy some new sunglasses.

"Thank you for having me." The cake looks delicious; I'll share it with Tracey. Like her mother, she loves cake.

"Oh, I'll walk you out." Something in her tone changes. She winks at me and I feel mocked. I don't like this woman. She has fake hair and a fake home and most of all, fake friendliness.

We walk out onto the front lawn. I need to get out of here. "Goodbye, Sandra. Thank you again for having me." I turn to walk to my car.

"Belinda."

I twist around. "Yes?"

"I know about you. And I don't care. At all." Hatred colors her face a splotchy red. The woman who greeted me when I came vanished. It's like some horror movie where the mask is lifted to reveal the monster.

"Lady, I ain't the Emily Post Office of manners but that ain't a nice way to say goodbye to your guest." I turn away from her. I want to run, but I walk to my car. Deliberate. She won't beat me.

"And this is the life you're living to teach morals to your daughter? Really?"

I want to spin around, run up to her and smash this cake in her face. But the thing is, she's right. I gotta get out of here. My head throbs and my throat closes. As my car pulls out of its space, I glance at her. She stands on the front lawn, shaking her head at me. Judge and jury. Guilty. I pull over to the first dumpster I see and throw away the cake.

Chapter 2

When I wake up I smell his scent.

'Fore I open my eyes or take a thought 'bout what the day holds, my nose twitches with familiarity. It's a mixture of gun cleaning liquid and Brute aftershave. Reminds me of strength and masculinity.

I love his smell, but I detest this man.

I let Hank stay over last night for the first time. It's a pathetic stab at Sandra. But not worth it. Without turning over, I can picture his corpse-like body. A six-foot three redwood. No stirring, no snoring; just sleeping on his back all night. He might as well have his hands crossed in front of him. If he died, they could just slip him into a casket.

I open my eyes when the sun makes a grand appearance through my window blinds. I try to soak in the warmth of an East Texas May morning.

"Why don't you get a curtain that actually blocks the sunlight?" Darnitt. He's awake. I close my eyes.

Maybe if I pretend I'm asleep, he'll just go.

"Belinda." He pushes on my back.

Are you kidding me? Not today. Not now.

"Belinda."

Uh-oh. I know that tone. "What?" I try to put a lilt at the end of this. It's hard to put a lilt on anything at 6:00 a.m.

"The sun is shining right on me. How am I supposed to sleep in?" His voice is gruff. Better be careful. I turn over to see he's sitting up on the side of the bed. His giant tattoo on his back is a shotgun with the words 'Keeping America Free.' Ever' time I see that I shake my head. He's more redneck than redwood. Figures.

"Wouldn't know. I never sleep in, Hank."

"Well, I wanted to and now I can't." He stands up in his whitey-tighties and turns to me. "Get up and make me some breakfast."

"Honey, tell you what." My voice sounds like syrup. "Come by the restaurant in an hour and I'll open it up and make you a special whatever-you-want meal that will dance on the plate in front of you."

"No." He ain't buying it. "Get out of bed and make it here and now."

I turn back over and shut my eyes. When we were at that Tyler motel, I ignored his ranting and he just left. Maybe it'll work today.

"Belinda, I said now."

I ain't gonna take his whiny power trip. I twist my neck and look up at him. "Hank, you know Tracey's here. So go on and I'll make you a meal later." I get up and put on my housecoat and turn to face him. I see a tiny flame in the pupils of his eyes. "Come on, sweetheart." I open up my robe and use the only power I have.

"I said," he walks around the bed to me, "make me a breakfast right now. Who do you think you are talking to me like that?" He grabs both my arms.

I try to bend my way out but his thick fingers dig in. "Hank, no. We gotta be quiet." My stomach tightens in a double knot.

"I won't get loud if you obey me."

Obey? Did he just say obey? "Let me go." I struggle again to free myself. He takes my arms and throws me on the bed. "Hank, no!"

He jumps on top of me and punches me in the gut at the same time.

"Mommy?"

Hank freezes. I look over his shoulder to see my eight-year-old standing in the doorway. I swallow the pain. "Tracey, go back to bed."

"Why is Mr. Hank here?"

Hank rolls over and doesn't even attempt to cover himself. "Tracey, get out of here!" He cusses and throws a pillow that hits the wall behind her.

Fear covers Tracey's eyes and she whips around and leaves.

Quick-like, I scoot over, stand up and grab the baseball bat I have in the corner. "Hank," my voice is like a dog growling, "don't you *ever* talk to my daughter like that again."

He stands and moves around the bed toward me. "Belinda, you aren't going to hit me."

I raise the bat to swinging position and he stops. "Try me. I'll knock your head off and it'll roll like a tumbleweed across Texas."

The flame in his eyes dies down. "I'm sorry, sweetie." His tone is sweet but I feel his anger. He reaches out. "Give me the bat."

"No. Get dressed and get out!" I push him in the gut with the bat and he stumbles backward just enough for me to get past him. I run out of the room and down the hall to Tracey's room. I lock the door and grab her desk chair and put it against the door.

Tracey's a little ball on the bed, curled up and hugging her knees. Her tangled red hair covers part of her legs.

"It's okay," I whisper. I sit on the end of the bed, bat still in my hands.

"Mommy, should we pray?"

"Be quiet."

"I'll pray for both of us."

I turn back to her and whisper. "If you're going to pray, then do it silently."

We wait. I hear the jingle of his keys.

He's putting on his pants.

Footsteps to the door.

Silence.

I watch the doorknob. It moves right to left.

His breath whistles through his teeth. "Belinda, you've gone and made me angry."

I know what that means. I don't move a whit.

The steps begin and he goes to the front door and leaves. I don't get up 'til I hear his car drive off. I stand up and move the chair away from the door.

"Okay, Tracey, we might as well get up. I'm gonna make your breakfast." I look back at her and she's crying without making any noise. "I'm so sorry you saw that but it's best you just learn now to toughen up. Life ain't easy." I should hold her. That's what a good mama would do.

She stares at me with her big green eyes swimming. "I wanna go to church. Why don't we go to church? Nana said you used to like it."

Nana. The name jars me and I ignore her question. She has no idea that I can't ever go back to church.

"You might as well stop your crying and get dressed. We'll have us an early breakfast." I go to the kitchen and open the fridge. Need to go shopping but I ain't gonna. I don't feel like cookin'. I wanna run away. What am I doing?

I shut the fridge and put my forehead against its door. I feel a magnet and I take it off. It's not holding anything up. No work or coloring from Tracey. One more thing a good mama would do. She deserves better than me.

How did I get myself into this? The first time Hank came into the restaurant he went on and on about my pancakes. Called Jack, the owner, over and told him he'd never tasted better. Loud and happy, Hank attracted attention and Jack loved him. Folks started ordering the pancakes left and right. Jack told me to go out of the kitchen and thank Hank for the compliment. I walked out and saw a tall handsome man. Black hair with streaks of gray and a smile that convinced me he was a mix of fun and ornery. I got it wrong. But he smelled so good, like potential.

When he discovered I'd flirt back, he went all out to impress me and make me laugh. Two days later we sealed the deal at Wind Storm's swankiest Holiday Inn.

Then I found out 'bout Sandra. Two weeks later, he yelled at me for the first time for being ten minutes late. His anger startled me. Two months later, I touched him in public at the restaurant. Nothing but a pat on his arm, but his eyes got all hot.

That night he hit me for the first time.

Almost two years has run away, and I'm for sure in a prison, no key in sight. If I left this town he'd find me and hurt me or Tracey or both of us. I know he would. I'm trapped.

"Mama, what are we having for breakfast?"

I turn to see Tracey still in her pajamas. I slam the magnet against the fridge. "Get dressed like I said." She shrinks right in front of me and goes to her room, obeying me.

Darnitt, Bee. I can't do nothing right.

We got tortillas so I'll make breakfast burritos. It's her favorite.

Chapter 3

Hank walks in the restaurant with his tail between his legs around two, after the lunch crowd's mostly gone home. He sits at his usual table, right where he can see me through the opening above the back counter. I glance at him once and sure enough, he stares at me like a puppy who can't find his bone. Well, let him look. I busy myself with serving the chicken fried steak, today's special. After a long while, I look back at his table and he's vamoosed.

I lock up after eight. I'm always the last to leave Sunday nights. I have to go to the bank, deposit the weekend's earnings, and then go pick up Tracey from Mrs. Hilfiger's house. She keeps Tracey on the weekends and nights I have to work late. I walk out the back to my car and Hank stands beside it. He's wearing jeans and a plaid shirt and that horrible looking black cowboy hat he owns. I hate that thing. Only real cowboys should wear cowboy hats.

As I walk up, he pulls out a bouquet of roses from behind him. He smiles.

"Those are pretty," I say. "I'm sure you know someone who will want them. It ain't me."

"Oh come on, sweetie. I'm sorry we fought."

We? "I will not have you yell at Tracey like you did."

His smile disappears. "You yell at her all the time. Being a bit of a hypocrite, aren't you?"

I grab his flowers and take a whiff. They smell like a grocery store. "Thank you." I smile at him before throwing the flowers to the ground.

Hank grabs me and pushes me up against my car. "You little slut. You think you're better than me, is that it?"

This is the real Hank. "I want out. It's no good anymore."

He shakes his head and looks at the ground. When his head comes up, it looks like his eyes are on fire. He slaps my face. My cheek burns. He takes my throat in his hands. "You are mine. You have been mine for two years and you will be mine until I am done with you. Don't ever forget that." He pushes my head back and it bumps into the roof of the car. With that, he turns and leaves.

Breathe, Belinda. Breathe. The side of my face stings. I reach into my purse to get a cigarette. My hands shake and tears come but I keep them back. He ain't worth crying over.

Before I leave, I pick up the roses off the ground. If they're here in the morning, it'll become a mystery at the Silver Spoon and a topic of discussion tomorrow. Small town folks like to make drama out of everything. I don't need that so I throw them into the dumpster.

I get in the car and peel out, gravel twisting in the air behind me. I take Main Street out to the Interstate and I drive. I head toward

Arkansas. I'll never go back. No one will ever find me. Tracey will be better off.

My cell phone rings. It's Mrs. Hilfiger, so I don't answer. She can take care of Tracey and my daughter will be better off than with me. I have to get away; I have to leave.

The red and blue lights fill up my rear view mirror. Shoot. I pull over and hit the steering wheel hard. My hand aches. Why did I do this to myself? I see myself younger, innocent and believing in my future. How did I not know he would die? Why did I believe God would work it all out? It never works out.

The officer gets out of the police car and I notice he's not in uniform. I see a plaid shirt. My gut wrenches and I slap the steering wheel. I look up and see Hank Hood.

The Wind Storm sheriff.

Chapter 4

Hank leans down with both his hands on the top of my car. I feel his gaze drilling hatred into my head. I stare straight ahead. Like a wounded rabbit, I am trapped. "What do you think you're doing?" His words come out as a snarl, like a dog's growl before they attack.

I ain't gonna speak. If I do, it'll just make him madder. If I keep my mouth shut, he'll still be mad but he won't drag me out of this car and beat me. Better to play possum.

"You know, Belinda..." He reaches in and turns my head toward him. I hate him and I don't trust the gentle act he's trying to pull. "I love you. Don't you understand how much I have invested in our relationship? You are my angel, my sweet lady. You are my woman."

His hand lingers on my cheek. A slideshow runs through my mind. Pictures of anger and violence and a picture of Sandra, a woman who doesn't fit with him, except for the matching evil jackets. I stare at him, pushing all my hatred into my eyes. I want him to see me, really see me.

"Oh sweetie, it's okay. I know you're sorry."

Tracey and I pull up to our home. Hank ended our love chat by telling me I could leave Wind Storm when he gave me permission. He followed me back into town until I got to Tracey's babysitter's house. I need to think about something good so I glance in the rear view mirror and look at my wonderful girl. Her long red hair is up in a ponytail and she's looking out the window and smiling. She is truly beautiful. "Mommy, guess what? Nana said she's going to call me tonight."

Cecelia. Great. I don't need this. "It's late. You probably missed her."

"No, she said she will keep calling no matter what time it is."

"Are you sure?" I grip the steering wheel a little too tight. My hand still hurts.

"Sure, I'm sure. It's my half-birthday."

"Tracey, there's no such thing as a half-birthday."

"Yes, there is." Her excitement leaks out like a poked balloon. "Nana says so."

She needs to learn. "Cecelia isn't always right. Now stop talking 'cause I have to think."

As soon as we enter the house, the phone in our kitchen rings. I don't even think about answering it.

"Hello?" Tracey's voice rises, thrilled. I sit down on the couch and light a cigarette. A cooking show on the Food Network is on. I keep it low so I can hear Tracey.

"Hi, Nana! …Thank you…I know. Eight and a half exactly…
Well, today we took a spelling test and I got the best grade in the
class."

I don't know why she didn't tell me that. On the other hand,
why would she? Ever' time they talk on the phone I learn something
about Tracey I don't know. I listen as she tells Cecelia all her news,
which ain't very much.

"She's here…she's okay…I think one of her friends was mean
to her today."

"Tracey." I stand up and look toward her. "It's time to get off
the phone."

"Mommy," she holds out the phone, "Nana wants to talk to
you."

Cecelia, why do you keep trying? "Tell her I said hi and then
you get off the phone." I sit back down and take another puff.

"Nana, she says hi and I have to get off the phone now…It's
next week…I haven't asked her yet…I will."

Tracey's voice lowers, and I can't hear the good-byes. What is she
going to ask? She sits on the stuffed chair across from the couch.
"Mama, can I ask you something?"

I turn up the cooking show I'm watching. They're making Beef
Wellington. "What is it?"

"Will you go with me to…?"

"Speak up, Tracey." Annoyed, I turn the TV down. "What did
you say?"

"There's a mother-daughter party at school in a week."

Oh, that's right. Mother's Day is coming. Sigh. "You want me
to go with you, Tracey?"

"Yes." Her eyes have hope bulging out of them.

Guilt pours over me like sauce. "I don't know. I probably won't
be able to get off work." I see the disappointment in her face. Again.

"Mama, please."

"Tracey, we'll see. But don't count on it." I turn my show back up.

Tracey gets up and stands right in front of me, arms crossed in front of her. Her eight-year-old war position. I don't say anything; I just lean and look around her to the TV.

"Mama, I really want you to come." I glance at her and her lips are pursed, her signature stubborn-Tracey move.

I return that move with a no-way-am-I-gonna-lose-this-battle stare. "Let it go, Tracey. Now." My daughter relents and goes back to the chair and falls in it with a loud sigh. She'll get over it.

I keep my eyes on the TV but I'm a-wondering how she's gonna turn out with a mama like me. I didn't have it great, either. Mama left and I think Daddy blamed me even if I was just a squirt. My ole' step mama never liked me a'tall. I did have Cecelia, though. Now Tracey has Cecelia, too. She'll be okay. The cooking show ends. I turn it off and tell Tracey to go to bed.

She don't move. "Do you have any pictures of my father?"

Apparently, it's the time for this conversation. Tracey's never asked about her father before. We sit in silence for a minute as I consider exactly what to tell her. The truth ain't pretty and she's only eight. But on the other hand, she doesn't see me as some saint. She knows her mama is well, stained, I guess.

"I don't have any pictures."

"What was he like?"

"Tracey, I didn't know him for very long."

"You never married him, right?"

"Right."

"Did you like him?"

Again, I wonder what to tell her. I met Rick on a trip to Tyler to do some shopping. Wind Storm got old after a couple of years and I thought 'bout moving to Tyler to save up and start my own café. After looking all day for a space, I met him in a bar that night. He made me laugh out loud. Not many people can do that. The next morning he kissed me and told me he would come back to the hotel with some coffee and breakfast. I never saw him again. "Tracey, his name was Rick and he made me laugh."

"What else?"

"That's all for now. Go to bed."

But of course, she's got one more question. "Mama, why don't you talk to Nana?"

"I've talked to her plenty, Tracey. Anyway she really doesn't want to talk to me. It's you she calls and writes and sends packages to."

"I think she loves you, Mommy." I don't think she should call me Mommy. It's a title I don't deserve.

"Go to bed, Tracey." I turn away from her. I'm tired of having this conversation. "And remember, she's really *not* your grandma."

I hear the closing of her bedroom door. I wish she would've slammed it. But she never does. I smoke for a minute more, thinking about what I should do. I put out my cigarette, go to her room and open the door. "Tracey, I'm so sorry." My daughter is already under the covers and hugging a big stuffed armadillo Cecelia sent her.

"It's okay, Mama. I know she's not my grandma. What happened to my real grandma?"

"My mama left me early in life and my step mama wasn't the nicest person in the world."

"So you don't know where they are?"

"No," I lie a little. Mama is who-knows-and-who-cares-where and my step mama and daddy live in California. They send a Christmas card once a year. I've never told 'em about Tracey.

"I think Jesus gave me Nana so I could have a grandma."

I bet Cecelia told her that along with all that other Bible nonsense. It's a sweet thought, though. "You're probably right. It's time for you to go to sleep now."

"Okay, Mama."

I shut off the light. She closes her eyes and I stand at the door for a moment looking at her. So peaceful and sweet. And she is mine. I want to hug her. I want to get in the bed and cozy up to her little body and hold her. I want to tell her that I do love her and I am proud of the little girl she's becoming. I want to say I'm sorry for being such a horrible mama. I want to move.

But I ain't gonna. I can't.

"Good night." I close the door.

Chapter 5

I should haul off and hit my boss Jack with a cookie sheet. He deserves to have a dent in his head. I know I screwed up school, marriage, and a kid, but I am a fantastic cook. Martha Stewart and all those fancy-dancy chefs in New York City ain't got nothing on me. So when that little runt makes a suggestion, I can't help but react.

"It needs a little salt, Belinda." Jack's hand reaches for the shaker. I pound his shoulder, probably a little too hard. "Ow!"

"Don't even think about it, Jack. Your tongue's been wagging so long about useless information, it's lost the ability to discern between good-tasting food and newspaper copy."

Jack owns the Wind Storm Advocate as well as this restaurant. I pick up the weekly paper on Tuesdays just to see what kind of food they're serving at the school, but I just skim the articles. The school lunch menu is the only thing good in that rag. Jack can't write worth spit. I ain't a brainiac but I know the difference between there, their, and they're. My boss don't.

I keep on stirring the soup. It's today's special and a crowd favorite, even though it's May and hot as a pistol that's just been fired. Homemade Chicken Soup and Blueberry Scones.

Jack backs away. "Just a suggestion. You are even testier than usual."

I ignore him, which is my favorite activity at work, and call out to the waitresses, "Soup's ready!" I hear a key turn and the jingle-jangle of the Silver Spoon's door opening, followed by folks rushing in. On Mondays, we don't serve breakfast, just lunch and dinner. It's confusing to me. Jack can never give me a straight answer about why we do it that way, but that's the way the pickle jar stacks. Jack leaves the kitchen to welcome ever'body with his fake smile and high voice. "Come on in, folks. Soup's on." He laughs through his nose at his own comment, making me think of what a rat in heat might sound like.

Seems like ever' day I tell myself to leave this restaurant and this town. But I'll probably die here. They'll find my body slumped over some freshly fried okra, or maybe some just-out-of-the-oven cornbread. When I get to daydreaming, it's always the same thing. How a restaurant of my own would look and feel. What the menu would be like. Nothing like the Silver Spoon, that's for sure. A black and white checkered floor gives this place a 50's feel, but the rest of the décor is western. Stools with leather fringe hanging off them scoot up to the counter. Brown and blue tablecloths cover the fifteen tables, two bucks' heads hang on either side of the door and cowboy hats dangle here and there around the brick walls. I've told Jack that it looks like a Yankee interior designer with dreams of being a cowboy came in here drunk and started fixing up the place.

I'm on my second batch of soup when the phone rings. Only one person ordered something besides the soup, so my assistant Franco helps me make some more scones. Franco is getting to where he can do the whole shift by himself. He follows my recipes pretty good, and occasionally has an idea all his own about some concoction. I like him most 'cause he's quiet and minds his own business.

"Phone for you, Belinda!" Sue holds up the cordless, reaching out to pass it over the counter and through the kitchen window.

"Tell 'em I'll call 'em back."

"It's Tracey."

"Tell her I'll call her back."

"She's crying."

I look at Sue. She's got a be-a-decent-mother look on her face. I hate that look. Her kids ain't no better. I wipe my hands on my apron and take the receiver.

"Mama, come get me." Tracey's bawling but I understand every word.

"What happened?"

"I'm not a murderer." A murderer? I have a drama queen for a daughter.

"Tracey, this is a horrible time, so pull yourself together and...."

"Mama, come get me!" I hear the little hiccupping sound she makes when she's crying and trying to breathe at the same time.

Shoot. "Okay, calm down. I'm coming." I toss the phone over the kitchen window and it scuttles across the floor.

"Hey, watch it." Sue gives me the be-a-better-coworker look.

"Jack, I gotta go." I call out, knowing he'll hear me. His ears are little bat ears. I take off my apron and throw it on the pile of dirty dishrags in the corner of the kitchen. "I probably won't be back today."

Jack pushes through the double doors to the kitchen and stands smack dab in front of me, his tiny hands on his tiny hips. "You can't go. This is three times in the last month you've deserted me in the middle of the lunch rush."

I glance at the clock. "It's 1:30. Franco can finish."

"What about the dinner shift?" The little rat blocks me when I walk back to get my purse.

"Franco can handle it and call Stan to help him. They can do this. Now let me go. It's Tracey." I inch closer to him so I can stare down on his little head.

"Listen, Belinda. If you leave, don't come back." I watch him grit his teeth and let out a little growl, like a cornered rabid Chihuahua. The inevitable has arrived. The five-foot-nothing is trying to stand up to me.

I suck in my breath and let the air come out slowly. Try to breathe, Belinda. *You need this job.* The only other restaurants in Wind Storm are dives, truck stops, and fast food places.

"Are you threatening me?" I say. "Or is this you making promises like you've promised to promote me to manager for eight years?"

The rabid Chihuahua takes a tiny step back. "How could you be manager if you have to hightail it outta here every time that brat of yours makes a sound?"

My hands make fists and I want to punch the little cur. But I'm not gonna. Instead I raise my voice so everyone within a mile can hear me.

"Good-bye, you lousy, good for nothing, penny-pinching, always belittling, treat-your workers-like dirt, desperate excuse for a itty bitty man." Silence throughout the restaurant. "And don't you ever call my child a brat again!" I hear a little bit of applause and I look through the kitchen window. Ever' body in the place is looking this way. Sue grins with a bit of shock added.

I walk past Jack to go get my things.

He doesn't follow me. He stands there, looking toward the customers. Showboating. "You aren't indispensable, Belinda! You can't even cook worth beans!"

"That's why the restaurant is empty, right?" I fling open the cabinet on the back wall and grab my purse. I see the red bag beside it. I forgot again. I look back towards Jack and sure enough he's standing at the double doors looking at Sue and his audience. I grab the red bag.

As I stomp out the back door, I hear the Chihuahua yapping, "No one in Wind Storm will hire you. I'll make sure of that!"

I start up my Honda Accord and I glance at the red bag on the floorboard. My heart is a timpani drum. Good riddance.

Wind Storm Elementary, the only elementary school in this dot on the Texas map, is a long rectangle with a dirt playground in the back and patches of dying grass in the front. It's a fitting symbol of this town: square, dirty, and dying. Trees are ever'where in East Texas, but seems like God poured something in the dirt here that made them sparse. I pull into the parking lot and stop. Before I get out, I practice my deep breathing. Peacefully.

The front desk is manned by Nancy Perkins, the worst secretary I've ever encountered. As usual, Nancy is standing away from the counter, back by the coffee machine, chatting with the PE teacher, Rex Woolf. There's a rumor about them two, but I don't pay no never mind. There's lots of rumors 'bout me too.

I clear my throat and Nancy looks over. "Just a sec, darlin'."

I feel my peace starting to leak out. "I'm not your darlin,' sweetie." As soon as I say it, I regret it.

Nancy looks at me and squints up her eyes. Her face is getting red. "Excuse me, Rex." Nancy smiles at the coach and turns to me. No smile. "May I help you, *Miss* Kite?"

She loves reminding me of my marital status. She's made it her personal little game for four years. I ignore the married tramp. "I received a call from my daughter. Apparently, her teacher yelled at her again. I'd like to see her."

"How did she call you? Does she have a cell phone? Students aren't allowed to use cell phones. You know that, right?" Her dark eyes dance.

I try to breathe in slowly, but I can't. "Just get my daughter for me now!"

"No need to get testy." She picks up the phone on her desk.

It occurs to me that twice in one day the word 'testy' has been used to describe me. They ain't seen testy yet.

"Mrs. Hume, Tracey Kite's mother would like Tracey to come to the office." Nancy glances my way and then turns giving me her back. She puts her hand over her mouth and whispers something I can't hear. She hangs up and turns to me. "She'll be right here." Nancy's smile is sweet apple pie, but her eyes are spoiled apples.

I walk out and stand in the long hallway. In the distance I see two silhouettes. A large woman and a young girl. As Mrs. Hume and Tracey get nearer, I see my girl's head drooping toward the floor. Mrs. Hume's big 'ole head rises high like a proud peacock. Her hand grips Tracey's shoulder. "Miss Kite, I am having a problem with this girl."

Tracey breaks from Mrs. Hume's grip and runs behind me, tugging at my shirt.

"Your daughter is out of control."

I sigh and remind myself that this woman is with Tracey ever' day and blowing up would only cause more trouble for my daughter. "Mrs. Hume, Tracey isn't a bad girl. But she's only eight. What happened today?"

"She killed our class hamster."

"What?"

"No, I d'nt." Tracey's head is glued to my back and I don't understand her. I reach around and pull her arm 'til her body follows.

"Tell me what happened."

Tears. "Mama, I didn't kill Mr. Whiskers. I wouldn't. I loved him."

I look into Tracey's green eyes filled with pain and my heart hurts something awful. "Mrs. Hume, why do you think she killed the hamster?"

"It died in her hands. I believe she squeezed it to death. When I took it from her, it was dead. This is a logical conclusion. When I announced that Mr. Whiskers died, some of Tracey's classmates pointed out that she probably killed him. Tracey proceeded to have a fit. We cannot have fits in our classroom."

Tracey speaks up. "I didn't kill him. I took him out of the cage and he didn't move or nothing. I pet him, Mama, and tried to wake him up cause I thought he was asleep. I didn't kill Mr. Whiskers." Sobbing follows and Tracey falls to the floor and curls up like a ball.

"This," Mrs. Hume points to Tracey, "is a child out of control."

I look up at Mrs. Hume and it occurs to me that even though Hume is taller and much larger, she probably ain't all that strong. She's flabby.

"You are an absolutely horrible teacher." I say this low.

"What did you say to me?" Mrs. Hume's voice is loud and I see a teacher down the hall poke her head out of the classroom.

I grit my teeth. "I said, 'You are an absolutely horrible teacher.'"

"Well, you're a horrible mother with a horrible daughter!"

I punch Mrs. Hume in the side of the face. She rocks to the right and falls to the ground.

Tracey's sobbing stops. For a moment, I freeze and realize that my daughter and this fat cow both lay on the ground at my feet. Mrs. Hume starts squirming like a crippled pig trying to haul herself off the floor. The teacher down the hall leaves her classroom and heads our way.

"Tracey, let's go." I grab her hand, pull her up and practically drag her to the front door.

"I will press charges!" For the second time today, I walk away from someone yelling at me.

Chapter 6

When we get out of the car at our house on Summer Street, Tracey spies something on the doorstep and runs to it. "Mama, it's from Nana!"

Great. "Well, take it in."

"Can I open it up now?" Her excitement annoys me. She bawled her eyes out a few minutes ago.

"Do you understand what just happened? I hit your teacher, Tracey. And I quit my job, too." I plop myself down on the couch and reach into my purse for a cigarette. "What am I gonna do now?"

Tracey's excitement disappears. "I'm sorry, Mama." After a few seconds she adds, "Can I open this?"

I light my cigarette and take a drag. "Go ahead."

Tracey rips off the brown paper to find a red and white polka dot box. Cecelia spoils my daughter. Carefully, as if it were glass, Tracey lifts the top of the box off.

"Oh, Mama, look." Tracey lifts up a plastic tiara. "It's so pretty."

Instead of commenting, I take another puff. If my daughter is a princess, doesn't that mean I'm a queen? Queen of what? Greasy Spoons? But when she puts the crown on her head, I smile. My girl shines.

"There's a note, too." Tracey unfolds the letter. "Can I read it to you?"

I feel my smile melt. "No. Go to your room and read it. The police will be here soon and they will take me away. But you go ahead and read your letter from perfect Cecelia."

"You're going to prison?" Tracey's eyes fill up.

Shoot. "I shouldn't have said that. Just go read your letter."

She doesn't move. "They're going to put you in jail 'cause you hit Mrs. Hume?"

"No, Tracey. Now go to your room and see what Cecelia says."

She turns and plods down the carpeted hall to her room, letter and tiara in hand.

Cecelia. I know the words the old woman wrote will be full of encouragement for Tracey. Maybe a poem or a song. But I ain't interested in anything Cecelia has to say. Religious dogma will be tucked in behind every word. Not my world anymore.

"Mama, wanna see what else she sent?" She calls this from her room.

"Well, come show me if you want." I take another drag.

"Look!" Tracey shoves a photograph in front of my face.

I sit up and stare at the faces.

"Nana said that's her and you and your friends in the picture. And you all have crowns on. I know they're made out of construction paper and not diamonds like mine, but you played princess when you were little, too? Did you have red hair like me?"

I can't say anything. I haven't seen this picture in over twenty years. Or those other faces.

"Mama, were they your best friends?"

Four faces smile brightly. One possesses long red hair and eyes that dare anyone not to smile back. I got rid of my red hair long ago. Was I ever that beautiful? Beside me a short brunette stands with tender blue eyes and a pleading smile. Donna. And then there is Maggie. Tall, blond, always in control, always confident. The fourth face has wise, twinkling eyes. Cecelia. Brown hair. Last time I saw her, silver streams framed her face.

Enough. I hand the picture back to Tracey. "I grew up with those girls, Tracey and yes, we did like to play princess some times."

"Nana said you went to church together."

Of course, she did.

"Mama, could we go to church sometime?"

My leg starts shaking. Can't she sense I'm having a bad day? "You know what, Tracey? I don't want to talk about church. I don't want to talk about Cecelia or the past." I hear myself again. Harsh. I soften. "Listen, Tracey, why don't you call Nana tonight and talk to her about the picture?"

Tracey smiles. "Could I?"

"Yes." I force a grin. "Now go back to your room."

"Can I call her now?"

"No. Later. Now go." I put out my cigarette, pick up my purse and the red bag and go into my bedroom. I sit on my bed and put the purse on the floor. I open the red bag and see the stacks of twenties and tens and fives. "What have I done?"

For the last four years, my job has included shutting down the restaurant on Sundays, two days before the Advocate comes out. Part of that duty is to count the weekend's profits, put the money into the red bag and make a deposit at the bank. Last night I left the Silver Spoon exhausted only to find Hank out in the parking lot. I told myself I'd deposit the money this morning. But I forgot. I planned to take it to the bank right after the lunch shift. Saturday the special was fried chicken and yesterday chicken fried steak, and it seems like half the town came out to eat. The red bag bulges.

We can finally get outta Wind Storm. Our start-up money is in my hands. My eyes dance over the cash again.

But what am I thinking? I have to give the money back. I have to apologize to Jack and Mrs. Hume and then we'll be stuck here forever. It's our fate. Or as Cecelia might say, it's God's will. Whatever. Anyway, Hank would never let me get away. Tracey deserves better than Wind Storm and that cow Mrs. Hume. And me, for that matter. What am I going to do? I light up and take a puff. The phone rings.

"Mama, the phone. Do you want me to get it?"

"No." Mrs. Hume has probably called Hank. I walk out into the hall and I see Tracey reaching for the phone. "No! Don't touch it!"

Tracey's eyes fill up with tears faster than a faucet filling a pitcher. Again. It's not like I enjoy yelling at her. "I'm sorry, but I told you not to get the phone."

With that, Tracey runs to the bedroom, her uncombed red hair chasing her. I hear her muffled sobs. But I don't care. I can't care. I'm a trapped caterpillar, wrapped in a tight cocoon. I'll never escape. I'll never fly. I hear my voice blurt out. The answering machine's message.

"We ain't here. Leave a message or not, your choice."

"Yep. Well, I reckon I choose to. I'm trying to getta hold of a Belinda Deltan."

I walk to the kitchen, wincing at the use of my married name. One I gave up a long time ago.

"Belinda, this here's Vern Jackson. I'm the husband of Cecelia May Jackson. She taught you at the First Baptist Church in Boots,

Texas and you and those other gals was over to our house a bunch of times. Cecelia talks to your young'un a lot."

I look down at the answering machine and feel dizzy. Why would he call me?

"Um, well, this is downright strange for me talking to a machine. We never did get one of these doodads. Always seemed a bit, well high-fallutin' and sure 'nough impersonal. 'Specially now."

Sadness covers his thick West Texas accent. "Yea, well, shoot fire, I don't know how to say this, but just to say it."

I think I hear a quiet sob. "Cecelia's gone. Passed this morning."

I smash the cigarette into an ashtray. My heart bangs on the floor like a dropped skillet. Cecelia?

"One of her wishes is for you to come home to Boots and help make the grub all of us'll be eating after the funeral. I know that sounds silly, but if you remember Sissy, well, pert near every notion was a bit off the cow path."

I hear a short moan, like someone belted him in the stomach.

"I have a couple round trip plane tickets for you and your little one from Dallas to El Paso. Seems you only need this here confirmation number to get it so if you'll call me we'll make sure you're all taken care of. Hope you can come. If you got work, well, I know that's life and all." He pauses. "But dadgum, Sissy wanted you to be here, so well, come on out. The funeral is Thursday, so we need to make a plan here pretty quick like. All right. Guess I'll say adios." The old man gives his phone number and hangs up.

I talked to Cecelia for the last time six years ago. And no way I'm going back there. It's been almost twenty-five years.

"Mommy?" I look over and Tracey is leaning against the doorway.

"Mommy, is Nana dead?"

My poor baby. My words are gonna hurt. "She's dead, Tracey.

I'm sorry."

Red hair covers Tracey's face as her head falls. "That was Vern, right? He invited us to the funeral. Are we going?"

"No."

"Please, Mama."

What if *they* go? They hate me. "Tracey, go to the bedroom to cry." Without looking at me, Tracey turns and goes to her bedroom and shuts the door. I hear loud, awful, little girl sobs.

I walk to my bedroom and lay on the bed. I don't know what to feel. I'm so tired. I wake up to the ringing of the doorbell. Insistent ringing. I sit up on the bed and shake my head to wake up.

"Hello, Mr. Hank."

No. NO! I get up and hurry into the living room to cut her off. It's too late.

"Nana died but Mama said we can't go to the funeral. Don't arrest my mom, okay? Mrs. Hume was mean to me, but we'll say sorry. I didn't kill Mr. Whiskers."

"Tracey, go to your room." I touch her shoulder.

"Mama, it's Mr. Hank."

I squeeze her harder. "I know. Thank you, now go to your room." I watch Tracey shut her door before I turn back to the sheriff. "Hank, you wouldn't believe how bad my day has been."

He stands in his uniform today, complete with badge and gun. "I think I might. I heard about your busy morning." Hank grins at me with his perfect teeth. I know he colors his hair and he has a little gut, but I still think he is the most handsome man in Wind Storm. And the meanest.

It's time to act. I move close to him and grin back. "Can you make all this go away?"

Hank puts his hands on my waist and pulls me in. "You know I can, honey. I don't like it when we quarrel. How 'bout you give me some sugar?"

I reach up and he kisses me. Hard and long. I want to throw up.

His face is still close to mine. "That's better, sweetie. It's going to be okay. I can square things with Mrs. Hume, you know that. I betcha there are people around here who want to give you an award for hitting that cow."

I smile at him. He will make this go away.

"But of course, you have to give back the money."

I jerk back. He knows about the money? "Jack called you?"

"Yep. Mrs. Hume and Jack both want to file charges."

I lean back against the wall. "What have I done?"

"Sweetie, I'll help you." He cups my head and pulls me in for another kiss. Then he whispers, "But give me the money."

"I don't have it."

He pulls back and gives me a look. "Well, where is it?"

"Not here."

Hank shifts, putting his hand on his gun. I know the move. He's telling me he has all the power. Again.

"I hid it. Away from the house. I'll go get it."

"Let's go now."

"No. I have to deal with Tracey. Our good friend just died and we're quite upset." I try to pull up tears, but I've never been good at that. "You could be a little sympathetic, Hank."

A sly grin covers his face and he pulls me in again. His breath smells of my chicken soup. He must have eaten after I left. "Well, if you take me back to your room, I'll show you some sympathy."

I shove him back. "Tracey is here."

"Hasn't stopped us before. Won't stop us in the future." He starts kissing my neck.

Again, I regret most of the choices I've ever made in my life. I push him back. "How is Sandra today, Hank?" I've said the one thing I'm never supposed to say. I know this will push his button; it's the only power play I have with my clothes on.

Hank's eyes darken and he gives me his official look-at-me-I'm-in-charge voice. "Belinda Kite, you have until 6 p.m. tonight to get me that bag. Otherwise, I am going to come back here and haul your butt to jail, and Tracey to Social Services. You know I'll do it."

And then he grabs me and kisses me again. It's a violent kiss and scares me. He leaves, a devil-smile on his face.

Jail wouldn't be so horrible. Maybe I could work in their kitchen. Maybe Social Services could find Tracey a good foster mom. I'm sure she'd be better than me. But I can't just give up. I'm not a horse, broken by Wind Storm's rotten whip.

I grab Tracey's backpack off the floor and call, "Tracey, come here." She walks in, her hair a mess and her eyes still red. "Come get your backpack and fill it with everything you can. Don't worry about clothes though. I'll do that. We're leaving."

"Where are we going, Mama?"

"I don't know."

Chapter 7

Donna
Denver, Colorado

The numbers do not lie. No matter if it's the scale or a spreadsheet, I know numbers will tell me the truth. That's why I love working with them. My fingers used to fly on my calculator. Now, a computer program adds and subtracts, reasons and applies. When I work with numbers, the world is just as it should be. I am a geek and my skill has led me to an extremely well paid position in an elite firm in Denver.

"Donna, I'm leaving and you should, too. It's 6:30."

Gina, my assistant, disrupts my nirvana of numbers; I don't look up from my computer. "I have to finish this spreadsheet and then I'll go."

"You work too hard." Gina comes into my office

and sits down across the desk from me.

I glance at her. "I really have to finish." She doesn't move. Giving my best friend the job as my secretary was not the best idea. She forgets I'm her boss.

"Why don't you go with me to The Falling Rock? I'm meeting Billy and a couple of his coworkers."

I put my laptop screen down so she can see I have my serious face on. "I have to work. So just go and have a great time for me."

"Since I'm your assistant, why don't you give me some of the work you need to do?" She stands as if she is ready to receive her assignment.

"There *is* something you can do for me."

"Whatever I need to do to get you out of this office, I will do."

"Leave me alone."

"Donna, there is more to life than work, you know."

"I like my work, Gina. How many times do I have to tell you that?"

"But you need to get out in the world and find a man."

I sigh. "There's more to life than getting a man."

I lie.

"Have you talked to the Saint today?" she teases.

"Gina." I throw a pen at her.

She ducks like someone who is skinny. She is skinny. "Good night, workaholic."

I respond, "See ya later, party girl." I don't hate her. I just resent her tremendously.

Get out in the world and find a man. Living under this banner exhausts me. At forty-two, hope is in my genes, thriving and growing as I get older. If only a menopause for hope existed and I could just tell myself the race was over. No hope of marriage. Alas, it is not to be. Every day I think *this* could be the day I meet *him*.

For Gina, it's never been difficult, but then again, Gina looks like a tall Reese Witherspoon. Well, an older Reese. Her divorce isn't two years old and she is out there. I don't have her looks but I am trying to find a man. Maybe I have.

After I'm sure she's gone, I open up my computer screen. I might as well take this interruption as a little break. I click on favorites and hit Facebook. The home page comes up and I see a little red number on the right top. I have a message. I click it and smile. William.

Hello, pretty lady! Thinking of you a few minutes ago, smiling, and a friend of mine asked what's the joke? I told him that a Colorado gal gets me to grinning all the time. Are you up for a phone call later? I'd love to hear that sexy voice.

My insides dance a little. He loves my voice.

William, thank you for the compliment. I like your voice, too. I am still at work but maybe we can talk later tonight. How about 9 p.m.?

I hit send and lean back in my chair, grinning. I wish I could tell Gina about William. She would just give me a big speech about resorting to love on my laptop instead of going to a downtown bar like she did when she met Billy. Once again, I'll have to listen to the story of their love. Blah, blah, blah. No, I will not be telling Gina. William is my secret for now, but only for a while. I go back to his page and click on photos. He only has a few pictures and every one of them shows a gorgeous tall cowboy. One is of him sitting on a horse and the other is him on a horse in the middle of two cows, out in a pasture. The third picture of him is a close up. He's suntanned and has hazel eyes, black hair and a black mustache. My own cowboy Tom Selleck with a little bit of Jude Law's eyes thrown in. Yum.

I should celebrate my internet love story. Where are they? Yes, I know. I get up, go over to the filing cabinet against the wall, and pull out the third drawer from the top. Behind the file folders marked April sales numbers, I see a slender unopened box.

My taste buds dance as I slip a green one in my mouth. I pour out a bunch of sweet-tarts onto my desk and begin separating the colors and lining them up. The purple ones are best so I will leave them for last. The green ones I will eat first. I like it when things are in order.

I suck on the sweet and acidy taste and look at my William's picture.

"You look happy."

I jump a little, look up and slam the top of my laptop down.

"I'm sorry; I didn't mean to scare you." My boss, Stuart, is standing at my office door with a smile on his face.

"Oh no, I'm fine." I almost choke on my candy. Instead, I swallow it whole.

"So what made you so happy?"

No words come to mind and I just stare at him. He has the best eyes I've ever seen. Dark, warm, and mesmerizing like the Halona Beach Cove I travelled to last year. I wish he'd been in Hawaii with me. His glasses make those eyes darker and warmer. Come on, Donna. Say something intelligent. I glance around trying to think of something. I spy the sweet-tarts in lines like a candy parking lot on my desk. I'm mortified. I lean up and put my elbows on my desk so my hands can cover the candy.

Oh no. I'm leaning up so much, my cleavage is hanging out. I bet he thinks I'm trying to show him my breasts. I know I must be scarlet and I feel like I'm having a hot flash. I actually feel sweat. If I switch positions, the sweet-tarts will go everywhere and he'll notice. If I don't move, I look like I'm a hussy, practically lying on my desk, telling him to come over.

I glance up and he is still standing by the door, waiting patiently like he always does. His little grin gives him a dimple in one cheek. He's grinning at me like he enjoys watching me. That can't be true. Not me. I don't look like Gina and I am not a kind-hearted woman. He, on the other hand, is a saint. So much so that behind his back he's called Saint Stuart. I love his bald head. Before he joined our company two years ago, I was ready to quit. Working for him is part of the reason I've turned down the two job offers I received last year. More money could not top his pure kindness and the way he treats all of his employees. Not just me.

I have to answer him but I can't think of anything. I hate how nervous he makes me. Say something, Donna.

"Numbers." Seriously, Donna? Numbers?

"Oh." His smile disappears. "I didn't expect that. Guess it's good that you're an accountant, right?" He winks at me and I melt. I smile at him and he smiles back.

I can't breathe. My tongue thickens and I can't speak. I can't move from this awkward position and I can't say anything either. I just stare at him. Sure enough, he finally begins to look uncomfortable.

"Well, goodnight, Donna. Don't stay here forever."

He leaves. I move and as I expected, the organized lines of tart get all mixed up. At once, I put them back into place. Gina tells me I'm probably a borderline obsessive compulsive. It's true. My disorder has made me a good deal of money.

Yet, I can't seem to get it together in front of my boss. He never complains and I don't see him that often anyway. Just office meetings mainly. I hate that I adore Stuart. He is too…nice. I'm, well…ample.

"Donna, it will never happen. Never." It is good to say this aloud. I breathe in slowly. As I let the air out, I shake off my boss's interruption like I do guilt, after a pint of Rocky Road. Back to my reality.

I check Facebook again and see that William has messaged me back.

9 sounds delicious. Like you.

I giggle and click off. Stuart is a fantasy but William is real. I might have a chance with him. Time to get back to crunching the numbers. I turn on my iPod and a country song comes on. Maybe someday, William and I will two-step together.

Maybe someday I'll actually meet him in person.

Chapter 8

"Would you like to sit at your usual table, Miss Dougans?"

"Yes, please."

I follow the waitress to a booth set in a quaint corner of the restaurant. Two small prints of Monet grace the walls behind the royal blue seats. I love Monet and I love royal blue. Perfect. I feel delicate and feminine. At least until I have to squeeze myself around the booth to sit in the middle. An inch separates my stomach from the table. They must have put in a different table since yesterday.

I open up the menu and peruse it with relish. My mouth waters. Choosing the perfect meal from an array of sumptuous dishes is an exhilarating moment for me, and this restaurant I've found to be exceptionally challenging. One of Denver's finest breakfast establishments is how the Finicky Eater's article described it. 5280 magazine listed it as one of the top ten breakfast places in Denver. When I saw the list, I knew this would be the perfect place for my next challenge. Each morning for the last two weeks, I've come here and sat in this same booth and with systematic profundity, I've ordered a different item from the menu. The eggs Florentine was delicious, the Belgium waffle sweet and utterly satisfying and the crape Suzette left me in a state of ecstasy. Really exquisite food.

The waitress returns. Every morning I wonder if she is an actress while off duty. She's blond and has a perfect body.

"Are you ready to order, Miss Dougans?"

"Yes. I believe I am in the mood for flapjacks." I've waited for this day.

"Excuse me?" The waitress's forehead crinkles, making her look even cuter. "I don't think we have flapjacks."

"I mean pancakes. I'm from Texas and sometimes the old terminology pops up."

"Oh, then I will get you a short stack." She turns to leave and the heat rises in my cheeks.

"Excuse me…" Hollywood turns around. "I would prefer the larger order."

"Of course. I'll get that going right now." Before she walks away, the waitress turns to me and flashes an awkward grin. It occurs to me I should have asked her name sometime during the last two weeks. But she is well, the waitress.

"May I ask you a question?"

"Of course." I answer politely, but I want to say 'You just did.'

"Are you a food critic?"

I'm glad I never asked her name.

"No, I'm an accountant." I stare at her purposefully. A food critic? Really?

After a moment of silence, the waitress returns to her job. "Okay, well, I will go put in the order for…flapjacks?"

I force a smile. "That's right."

I reach for my Droid X to check Facebook. William should've messaged me by now. Nothing. I click on his wall and it shows no new posts since Friday night. I read his last post for the fiftieth time: *I just talked to a beautiful Rocky Mountain girl.*

That's me. He's talking about me. Our phone chat was wonderful. He's not a deep person and when I tried to talk about relationships and goals, he changed the subject to how beautiful I am. Of course, he's only seen my Facebook photo. How many years ago did I pose for that? I love his voice and hearing a man say wonderful sweet nothings to me is not a bad way to spend my evening. I cut him off when he started talking dirty. I'm not into that. Especially with someone I've never met in person.

I close my FB app, reach into my briefcase, and place a stack of papers on the table. I look at them intently and notice that the information is from an old department meeting, literally yesterday's news. I don't care. I pore over them, even though the numbers are just a big blur.

I glance around the restaurant. People fill up the tables near me, but no one looks directly at me. However, I sense it; they're staring.

Better to immerse myself in imaginary work than deal with a look of pity or even disgust. I'm sure someone is talking about me. The same conversations come to mind.

Can you see the fat lady?

Don't make fun of the fat lady, honey.

Why doesn't she take care of herself?

I know I'm not attractive. I'm ample. No, the truth is I'm fat. No other word describes me. I'm not pleasantly plump or chubby or just carrying a little extra. I'm fat. I have a pretty smile and I take great care of my teeth, but I never know what to do with my shoulder-length brown hair. Therefore, I don't do much. My eyes are blue. Daddy used to say my eyes reminded him of the sky right before nightfall. I like remembering him saying that.

I notice a tiny little piece of lint on my red skirt and I brush it off. This suit is beautiful. Clothes are never a problem for me since I make a good deal of money. Upscale plus size stores cater to me. I even employed a tailor named Katherine who knew how to make clothes fit me perfectly while covering up what I wanted covered up. Of course, I let Katherine go when she brought up that diet idea. I smiled and thanked her. Then I emailed her and fired her. If I wanted her help in dieting, I would've asked her. I didn't pay her for her nutritional opinion.

No one in the restaurant is watching me, but I still feel uncomfortable. I reach for my phone to check again. William often changes his status in the morning.

Nothing. I click on my wall and read my last post: *Another day, another fifty cents. I'm exhausted.*

Two comments are underneath my post. One from Vanessa who lives in North Carolina, and one from Ed, my cousin from Mississippi. Nothing from William.

I click on his wall again. *I just talked to a beautiful Rocky Mountain girl.*

Wonder what he's doing. Maybe I'll instant message him. No, I shouldn't do that. Maybe I should. I start typing on the tiny keyboard. Experience has taught me to use my fingernails since my fingers are too big. *"Are you okay, William?"*

A response pops up. *"I'm fine, good looking. How 'bout you?"*

My heart races. Good looking? He's talking about me. *"I'm good. Just tired."*

"You need a vacation. Come see me."

I know that will never happen. He can't ever see me in person.

"Maybe someday we'll meet." It's a lie but a harmless one.

"I can't wait. I'm getting lonely hanging around cows every day."

"What, no cowgirls?"

"You're the only one."

We keep up the flirting and I feel myself blush. William is the one, I'm sure. I won't meet him until I've lost some weight. I'm going to start a diet next Monday. Then I'll get skinny, I'll meet him, we'll date and marry. Happiness is around the corner.

The waitress approaches so I write a quick goodbye and close the app. I met William Donovan through a writing group online. I've toyed with the idea of writing a novel and he is a cowboy poet. I giggle when I think of his profession and the connection to Cecelia. William lives an hour from her and Boots, the podunk town where I grew up. I wonder sometimes if William and Cecelia have ever met at a poetry meeting. Cecelia always claimed to be a cowboy poet.

I laugh aloud at the thought.

The pancakes look like a picture from a magazine. Plated perfectly. I apply tabs of margarine and watch the yellow butter-fall melt over them. I pour on the maple syrup slowly, enjoying the rich aroma.

I take my first bite and savor the taste. They're delicious. Almost as good as Cecelia's. She's been on my mind frequently the last few weeks. I haven't talked to her in over a decade and I don't plan on calling her anytime soon either. She's a nice memory. One of a woman who loved me like a mother. My own mom died in my ninth year of life.

However, with Cecelia's love came lies. She was wrong - vastly, horribly, and immeasurably wrong.

Soon, the pancakes disappear, save one last bite. I stab the final offering, ready to finish off the plate.

"Hello, Donna."

I look up. My fork falls on the plate and the clang reverberates throughout the restaurant.

"Stuart? Um, hi." Close mouth. Use napkin.

"I'm making a habit of startling you, Donna. I'm sorry. Do you come here often?"

Should I be honest and say yes? I reach for my coffee. I set it down with a thud. I pick it up. I set it down. Say something. I can't.

"I'm sorry. What a line, right? 'Do you come here often?'" Stuart laughs.

"Um, oh, yeah." *Come on, Donna. You sound like you have syrup on the brain.* Time passes like sliding molasses as I stare at my boss. I'm an idiot.

"Well, I'm having breakfast with Sheila." He points across the restaurant to the table where a thin strawberry blond sits. I know who she is and I give her a polite wave. The Director of Marketing smiles.

I wish he would leave. I wish he would stay.

More silence.

Stuart's words tumble out. "Listen, Donna, I'm not on a date with Sheila. It's a business thing. We're talking business. Firm business. I just want you to know that. It's all business. I'm still talking out loud, aren't I? I need to shut up now. It's just well, I've been meaning to ask you something for a while and…"

"I love my boss! He is so hot!"

Oh no! My ring tone continues as I lean down to grab my bag. My head hits the corner of the table. I ignore the sudden pain and search frantically for my phone that is always in the side pocket. Today, of all days, it is in the middle section.

My recorded voice continues to the tune of *I'm So Excited*. "I know, I know, I know, I know I want him, want him!"

This is not happening. I find the phone and hit the mute button.

I stare at the phone, willing myself never to look at Stuart again. I will quit this afternoon. I can find a job. If I don't die right now, right here.

"I like your ring tone."

I glance up to see Stuart grinning.

"I'm sorry but I have to go now." I don't return his smile. Instead, I stare at him, silently pleading with him to end the torture and leave.

His grin vanishes. "Okay, good talk. Um, I'm going to go talk to the Hunter now."

I can't help but grin when I hear Stuart refer to Sheila using her nickname, a well-earned title describing her dating life.

"I saw that." Stuart's smile reappears. Then he turns and walks away.

I look at the one lone bite of flapjack. It beckons me. I leave it, and carefully calculate the tip. I glance over at Stuart and the Hunter. She's laughing. I wonder what about. Me? I put cash down for the tip and I gobble up the last bite. Delicious.

Denver's May morning air cools my now sweaty face as I start the two-block walk to the office. That did not just happen. It did, didn't it?

As I turn the corner on Seventeenth Street, I grin. Stuart Brown, my wonderful boss, expressed interest. In me. My heart quickens at the thought. Maybe *he* is the one. Maybe it isn't William. The old fantasy flashes through my mind. The white dress I've already picked out. The music and flowers. The joy of having a man's arms around me. In eight years, I'll reach the big fifty. Half of a century. I sigh and feel the old pang of heartache that comes with the fantasy. Maybe it's all about to change. He likes me. Even after that ring tone.

I have to change that. Gina dared me to do it. Why did I cave?

As I walk, I get my phone, now in the side pocket where it belongs, and put in the numbers that will retrieve messages. None. I hit a button and look at the last phone number. 915 area code?

Isn't that from Texas?

"I love my boss!"

I hit the answer button.

"Hello."

"Well, hey, is this little Donna Gail Dougans?"

The voice sounds familiar. "Yes, this is she. To whom am I speaking?"

"This here's Vern Jackson from Boots, Texas."

His thick accent transports me to my childhood. "Mr. Jackson?"

"Yep. You sound all growed up, Donna Gail."

No one's called me Donna Gail in forever. "Yes sir. How are you, Mr. Jackson?" Why in the world is he calling me?

"I'm 'bout as bad as bad can get." The sudden silence confuses me. "Donna Gail, Sissy died."

"What?" I stop walking.

"Sissy died."

"Oh, I am so sorry, Mr. Jackson." I feel sick. The pancakes begin to stir.

"Sissy wanted you to come home and help make her funeral fixins'."

"She what?" Now I'm nauseous.

"I have a confirmation number that will get you a round trip ticket to El Paso. We'll pick you up and then you can come on to Boots. The funeral is this Thursday."

"She's really dead?" I'm dizzy. Cecelia can't be gone. Mr. Jackson wants me to come back to Boots? Never. I swore never to go back. I need excuses. Work is busy, calendar is full, isn't there a wedding

I have to attend? Stuart might need me?

Wait.

William lives in Texas. Maybe I should meet him. No, I can't; I haven't lost weight yet. However, if he doesn't like me as I am, well, then there's Stuart. I have choices now, right?

"Donna Gail? Whaddya think?"

Mr. Jackson. I have to give him an answer. I can't go back there. What if *they* come? I have absolutely no interest in ever speaking to them. There's no way *both* of them would come. It's been two decades. Surely what happened is a thing of the past. Think, Donna.

I could meet William.

"Mr. Jackson, I'll be there, but I have to go right now. I will call you back." I close my phone and look up to see I'm standing in front of a restaurant. I fly in to find a restroom.

Chapter 9

Maggie
Tucson, Arizona

God, is he okay? You've got him, right?

It's a quarter past eight and Noah hasn't called yet. He told me he'd call me tonight. I sit by the phone in our living room, trying to read a book as I wait. I've been staring at the same pages for a long while.

The phone rings and I grab it. "Hello?"

"Hi, Mom. Can I come home at 9:30 instead of 9:00? We're not finished with the civics project yet."

It's Jeremy, my fifteen-year-old. I sigh. "Is that okay with Doug's mom? She's bringing you home, right?"

"Yeah, she said it was cool."

"Okay, but not one minute longer than 9:30."

"Okay." He hangs up and I do the same.

Noah is nineteen and a freshman in college. Almost a sophomore. He's my baby and he said he would call tonight. I want him to call every day, but he doesn't. Frank says it's unreasonable to expect that of a man.

Man? Noah is not a man. Not yet. Right, Lord? *Oh, please Jesus, keep him safe.*

The phone rings.

"Hi Mom."

I breathe out. "Hi Noah. How are you?"

"Good."

We talk for thirty minutes about school, his brothers, his dad and Noah's new girlfriend, Becka. This is precious time to me. I find myself tearing up at the end of our conversation.

"So tell Dad I said hey."

"I will." A lump forms in my throat.

"Mom?"

I try to collect myself. I hear him chuckle.

"I'll be home in a few weeks. You need to get it together, you know?"

"I know." I say this through a cloud of wetness. "Noah, are you making good choices?"

Silence.

"Mom, do you trust me?"

What? I've asked him the same question for years as I have his brothers. He's never answered me with a question.

"Of course, I do. But are you making good choices?"

"I've gotta go."

"Noah?"

"I'll call you next week."

"I love you."

"I love you, too, Mom."

He hangs up and I freak out. Visions of college debauchery dance in my head. Noah in the middle of those visions causes me to start crying. I hate that he's growing up and I have no control. In five short years, Jeremy and Michael will be gone, too. It goes too fast. Just yesterday, three little boys played in a stand up pool in the back yard, asking me to come in with them. Now Noah is gone, Jeremy is getting home late, and Michael is upstairs in his room doing who knows what. I sniffle and I feel arms around me. Frank.

"How's Noah doing?"

"He wouldn't answer me when I asked him if he was making good choices. You know what that means, right?"

"He's tired of answering the question?"

"Frank, he could be into anything."

Frank sits beside me on the couch and pulls me into his chest. My place. I cry freely now. He doesn't say anything, just holds me and the comfort that is my husband seeps into my heart. Thank you Jesus, for this man.

"It scares me. The world is an evil place, Frank, and if Noah doesn't make good choices then the enemy will eat him up."

"Maggie, Noah is a great kid and you need to trust him. And trust God."

"When we make bad choices, bad things happen. Period."

Frank sighs and I sit up. "It's true, honey. I know what I'm talking about. I've followed Christ most of my life and I know how God works."

"Really? *You know?*"

I scoot over on the couch. He mocks me but I know. I'm the one that reads my Bible and prays every day. I'm the one that leads the women's council at church. Frank's the one who told me he was going to be a preacher and then backed out of it after we got married. He sensed God wanted him to sell insurance. Seriously? God wanted Frank in the pulpit. If Frank's Christianity looked like mine, he'd be better off. We all would.

"Maggie, I have my own personal relationship with Christ, as does Noah. You have to deal with that."

I grab a pillow to hold onto to and I squeeze it hard. Sometimes I wonder what it would've been like to marry someone else. Someone actually called to preach. I would be an excellent preacher's wife. My destiny proved to be an insurance seller's wife. Pul-lease.

The phone rings again.

"Frank?"

He grabs it and says hello. A smile breaks out on his face. "Yes, she's right here, Cecelia. I think she'd love to talk to you."

I sniff and sit up. A talk with her is just what I need.

Frank hands me the phone, kisses my forehead and leaves the room.

"Hello?"

"Maggie May, hello darlin'!"

"Hi Cecelia May." It's our little joke, having the same middle name. I sniffle.

"What are you crying about?"

I tell her about Noah and the tug-of-war going on in my heart.

"Sweetie, it's hard to let your little ones go, but that is the way of life. You wouldn't want him staying home with you forever now would you?"

"No." Of course, she's right. Cecelia has never had kids, but you would never know that from all the wisdom she has for me.

"What's going on in Boots?"

"Imogene and Lola Bee and I had our Scrabble club tonight."

I laugh. "Scrabble? I thought you were having a book club."

"Imogene and Lola Bee got into a big uproar about that book that Oprah recommended a few years ago, you know the one called…well, I plum forgot what it's called, but our discussion turned into an old lady cat fight so we ended the book club."

"Cooking club and sewing club didn't last long, did they?"

Now she giggles. "It doesn't look very good for us, does it?"

"Well, how was Scrabble club?"

"We were playing fine and then Lola Bee played the word G-O-R-M-A. So Imogene told her, 'Lola Bee, that ain't a word.' And then Lola Bee got all heated and said, 'Imogene, you sit there using the word "ain't" and you say my word is fictional?' Imogene asked Lola Bee to say it in a sentence and Lola Bee said, 'G-O-R-M-A is a way you cook.' And then Imogene said, 'Lola Bee, have you been dipping into Dr. Dwyer's Novocain again? You spell that word G-O-R-M-A- E.' Lola Bee fired back, 'I work for the doctor not the dentist and you know that!'

"So of course, words started to fly back and forth and none of them had any point value at all. By the end, we decided that a Scrabble Club is not for us."

Cecelia always makes me laugh. "Maybe a club-of-the-month is not such a good idea for you three."

"Maybe. But we keep trying."

"How is Mr. Jackson?"

"He's just about the most wonderful man on the planet. That is if you don't count Engelbert Humperdinck. That man is just sex on a stick."

"Cecelia!" I laugh out of shock. She loves to do that to me. Says things that no one would ever guess she would say.

"Heh-heh." Her little laugh tells me she knows exactly what she just did. "Maggie May, you know I love Vern and wouldn't trade him for a trip to the circus."

"I know, Cecelia."

"Now tell me what has the good Lord been teaching you lately?"

She asks this question every time we talk. I share with her what God has shown me through my life as a mom and wife and then she shares with me. She's not just my friend, but she's my spiritual mentor, and has been since I was six years old. After we talk a while, Cecelia starts to say something and then stops. Awkward silences never occur when I talk to her.

"Cecelia, what is it?"

"I've been thinking about Belinda and Donna."

My heart runs a lap. This is a taboo topic and she knows that. "What about them?"

"Do you pray for your old friends, Maggie May?"

I think about lying, but she would see right through it. "No, I don't."

"Would you do me a favor and pray for them?"

Curiosity lands atop my heart. "Why?"

"Because I asked you."

I don't want to know the answer but I push anyway. "What's going on with them?"

"Maggie, if you want to know you can ask them. I have their phone numbers."

She knows their phone numbers? Since when? Now it's time for me to contribute an awkward silence. Cecelia knows the entire story and she asks me to pray for them? I've forgiven, I think. I don't feel bitterness anymore, just emptiness. It's been twenty-five years. I am a woman who loves Jesus and her family and I am a woman happy to be alive. I don't know why I can't pray for them.

No, I know exactly why. They betrayed a friendship that lasted longer than a decade. The old anger pops up in me and tries to come out my tear ducts. I won't let it. "Okay. I have a date tomorrow and I'll make sure to pray then."

"Are you okay, Maggie?"

"I'm okay. Just over emotional lately. I'll pray for them, Cecelia." I mean it.

"I do love your dates. It's such a great idea."

"I'm excited." I change the subject. "Listen, Frank and I were talking about you and Vern and we were thinking since you are both retired now, you might want to come visit us for a while."

"Oh, that sounds fun. Course it'll take some talking 'cause Vern hates to travel."

"Does he miss working?"

"No, he has a pretty strict routine. Between keeping up the gardens and having coffee with his cohorts, and of course, seeing to it that he has a happy wife, well, he keeps busy."

"Do you miss the cafeteria?"

"Oh, yes. I drop in on them every once in a while just to give 'em what for. I don't know any of the children anymore, except every once in a while I'll see a spitting image of one of the kids I used to know and I'll go up to them and sure enough, they are the child or grandchild of someone I fed."

"I've never heard of a lunch lady having such a wonderful legacy."

"I wasn't a lunch lady, sweetie, I was a cafeteria manager, specializing in good food." She laughs at her own joke.

"Cecelia, you have so many people who you've touched for the Lord, you know that, right?"

"I do, honey. But…"

Is that a sniffle?

"Cecelia?"

"Oh, don't you pay me no never mind. Just pray for those two, okay?"

"I will."

"Call me tomorrow, Maggie."

"I love you, Cecelia May."

"Oh and I love you Maggie May."

Chapter 10

"Jeremy, Michael, good morning! It's time to get up!"

I knock on the two doors that face each other in the upstairs hallway. Leaning into one, I wait for any sound of teenage movement. A muffled thump. A deep yawn. I step over to the other door. Silence.

"Jeremy!" I knock again. "Good morning."

"Mom, please."

I smile, head downstairs and take each step lightly. "Today is the day!" I say to no one in particular. "God, I can't wait!"

Frank sits at our kitchen table, coffee cup in his hand and his calendar open before him.

"So you said Michael's Boy Scout Court of Honor is tonight?"

"Yes, at 6:30. We're all going."

Frank stands up and approaches me as I put breakfast burritos on two plates. "I might be a little late but I'll be there."

I hit the microwave to heat up the breakfast. "What? Frank, I told you about this two weeks ago. I also emailed you and put it on your calendar. And today is the day you said you were going to come home early."

"What? Why early?" He pours the rest of the coffee into the sink.

"I'm going to Saint Benet's so you need to be here and make sure Michael is all ready for the Court of Honor." I pick up the plates and take them to the kitchen table. "Don't tell me you forgot." As soon as I put the plates down, I feel Frank's arms curl around my waist.

"I might've forgotten." He kisses my neck. "But now that I remember, I'll be home early."

I turn my body to face him. "I love you, Frank." Our kisses still delight me, even after twenty-two years. I adore this man, even if he sells insurance.

"My eyes. I've been blinded." Michael, our thirteen-year-old delivers this in a dry monotone.

"I'm blinded by love." Frank kisses me again.

"It's too early for porn." Jeremy follows Michael to the table.

"Jeremy." I slap his head affectionately. "You both should be grateful you have parents who love each other."

Frank lets go of me and grabs his jacket off the chair. "Okay, so Michael, I'll be here at five o'clock sharp and Jeremy, your mom will pick you up from practice at 5:30."

I add to our troops, "We'll meet here, get ready and go to Michael's Boy Scout Meeting. They're serving dinner there."

"Sounds good, sweetie. Have a blessed date." Frank winks at me and leaves for work.

"You have a date, Mom? Cheating on Dad?" The burrito muffles

Jeremy's words but I understand every word.

"He doesn't mind this date, Jeremy. You guys don't be late for the bus. I'm going to go get ready."

One errand. Only one errand. I am giddy as I pull out of the driveway. The post office is crowded. I count eight people in front of me so I set my package down, knowing it will be a while before I make it to the front. I see that my next-door neighbor, Isabel, is number eight, standing in front of me.

"Isabel." No movement. I speak louder. "Isabel."

My friend turns to me with a blank expression on her face. "Maggie, how are you?" I can tell she doesn't want an answer.

"Isabel, what's wrong?"

She leans toward me and speaks in hushed tones. "I guess I didn't tell you. I thought I did. Dave has cancer."

I feel my stomach fall. "Oh sweetie." We stand there, looking at each other. Silence. I pick up my package and we move up in line.

Isabel turns to me, her eyes pleading. "Maggie, there is hope, right?"

"Of course. I should know."

"We were talking about you last night. We would love to have you and Frank over and talk about this. Dave starts chemo in two weeks. We only found out yesterday."

We move quickly to be customers four and five. I glance over at a noise and I see a man using a huge package to shove the door open. He walks in and scowls at everyone. "Only two people working? Come on."

I look back at Isabel "We would love to talk to you guys. Remember how sudden it all happened for me? There's hope,

Isabel. I'm going to start praying immediately."

"It'll be a long road. We watched you and Frank go through this and we know it doesn't have to end in death."

"Of course not. What kind of cancer is it?"

"Prostate."

It's time to move ahead in line, but Isabel doesn't budge, her eyes watering as she stares at me. I feel my own tears forming. "Isabel, I'm so sorry." I put my package on the floor and wrap my arms around her. I remember Isabel's kindness during my bouts with cancer. I squeeze tighter.

"Lady, did you hear him?" The impatient man in the back is barking at me.

"What?" I ask.

"I can help the next customer."

I realize we're next and I release Isabel. She grins and shakes her head as if to change topics. "Is that for Noah?" She asks as she moves toward the postal employee.

I grin back at her. "Of course. An end of the year care package." It's my turn. I finish earlier than Isabel does and I wait for her. As we walk out of the post office, I grab her hand. "We will help, you know? I'll be there."

Isabel stops near the parking lot "It was horrible, wasn't it Maggie?"

I want to encourage my neighbor but scenes of my fear and hopelessness play throughout my mind like a quick trailer for a horrible movie. The chemo almost killed me. I have to be honest. "Yes. Pretty awful. But God never, ever left me. He poured strength into me."

"Okay." Isabel squeezes my hand and then starts toward her car, shaking her head again. "Can you believe you're sending care packages? Before you know it Jeremy will leave and then Michael.

Time flies doesn't it?"

"It does." I watch my friend get into her car and drive away. I can't move. *Oh Lord, no.*

Saint Benet's is a sprawling retreat center run by nuns. I'm not Catholic, but this place feels like home to me. The grounds are beautiful, marked by trees, cactus and sculptures. The prayer chapel's stained glass windows always move me and God's presence descends on me even as I get out of my car in the parking lot. I walk up the stone path to a small building labeled "Office."

When I go in, the office looks deserted. "Hello? Is anyone here?"

"Is that you, dear?" A tiny voice laden with cracks calls, "Maggie, is that you?"

"Yes, Sister Loretta. It's Maggie, and I was hoping to hang out here today."

A woman just slightly over four feet comes out from the back. Sister Loretta's face tells a story of pain and hope and deep contentment. I love looking at her.

"Maggie, I'm so glad you called yesterday. It's good to see you." She reaches for my hands with both of hers. "Of course, you may stay here as long as you like. The weatherman said it would rain today, but it looks beautiful to me. As Tucson always does."

"Thank you, Sister." I pull back to leave but she holds tight to my hands.

"Maggie, He wants me to tell you something."

Sister Loretta has spoken this way to me before. It's as if she's some sort of Pentecostal prophet, but she's Catholic. "What is it, Sister?"

"The pruning of rose bushes is a necessity to a season of growth and beauty."

I wait for more but she just stands there, holding my hands tightly, looking at me as if she's examining my soul.

"Thank you, Sister." I guess. I'm not a gardener. We employ a wonderful man who takes care of our yard as well as Isabel's.

"Maggie, don't fight the pruning. Forgive."

I cock my head like a puppy, wondering what she means. Before I can ask, she pulls me in for an embrace and then turns and leaves.

My date with Jesus begins the same way each time. I take a long walk through the tree-lined path that curves its way through the grounds. A few tiny cabins dot the grounds but only two large buildings occupy this land. The chapel and the café/office. Benches and statues mark the places to stop and contemplate or rest. Flower and cactus gardens surround each 'rest stop.'

This is my favorite place to come and simply be alone in God's presence when I am away from my house. I've called them 'dates' for years and I plan each one as if it was a not-to-be-missed appointment.

"Father, I am here. If there be any wicked way in me, show me, Lord." I continue to walk, asking for forgiveness for my sins as I make my way around the winding path. At a statue of St Francis of Assisi, I sit down.

"Father grant me the serenity to accept the things I cannot change, the courage to change the things I can and the wisdom to know the difference."

Forgive. Let go.

This thought surprises me. I'm asking for forgiveness. I've

learned to recognize the voice of my Shepherd.

"Is that You, God?" I wait.

Forgive. Let go.

"Forgive who?"

Belinda and Donna.

"What?" Cecelia asked me to pray for them and now God brings them to mind. To forgive them? They are the ones who should be asking me for forgiveness. My heart starts pounding. I've come to know this means I should listen carefully.

Forgive. Let go.

I notice a yellow rose bush across from me in a garden of flowers and cacti. It's the only bush. I remember Sister Loretta's words. "The pruning of rose bushes is a necessity to a season of growth and beauty. Don't fight the pruning. Forgive."

I am confused.

My pastor's words from last Sunday come to mind. "If you can't truly forgive someone, it hurts you more than whoever offended you. If you want to serve God, an unforgiving spirit will block your path."

"God, I've let it all go. Isn't that enough? I don't wish either of them any harm." I sit and listen, but the voice in my heart is silent. I breathe in and out quietly. Deliberately. I haven't seen Belinda or Donna for years. Over twenty. I've moved on. This is silly. "I've let it go, haven't I, God?"

The silence of the King answers my question.

I stomp my feet like a child. "What's wrong with me?"

Cecelia told me to pray for them. Maybe if I pray for them I will find a way to forgive them. How will I know I've forgiven them? I thought I had. Oh God, this day is about You and me. Not them. I just want to curl up in the Father's lap and rest, not think about Belinda and Donna. Their betrayal is like an old scab that never seems to heal fully.

This is ridiculous.

My eyes follow a tree limb from its genesis sprouting at a trunk into a tangle of branches. When I reach the end, a tapering of twigs and leaves, I breathe in and out again. "Lord, I praise you as Creator, Elohim, the One who designed that branch." I take the next hour or so to sit and praise God for His wondrous traits. Then, a prayer of thanksgiving.

Next, I hunt for one of my favorite spots. I smile when I see it - a little fountain with a kneeling bench beside it. I get on my knees and plead for Dave and Isabel, for my friend Katie, and for Frank's joy at work. I pray for my boys to be good and to follow Jesus. I ask God to help them stay on the path of righteousness, like I have.

Forgive them!

I sigh and I begin. "God, I have no idea what to pray for them. I guess I ask you Lord to bless their paths and show them You. Cause them to develop intimacy with You and make right choices in their lives."

Forgive them!

"Okay, I hear You. Help me to truly forgive them, Lord." Whatever that means.

After a while, I reach into the bag I brought and take out a sketchbook. I love to draw. "Show me, Jesus." I see a single dandelion dancing in the wind between two gray rocks. When my picture is finished, I put on my iPod and walk until I find a secluded spot. Making sure no one is around, I dance between two trees, my hands raised to God in joy. I stop when my heart is racing. I need to get in better shape. "I still got it, right, God?" I laugh aloud and look around to see if anyone heard me. No one is in sight. "Maggie, you silly girl."

Time to eat the picnic I brought.

The phone rings. Oh shoot, I forgot to turn the phone off. I reach to shut it off but when I see the caller ID, I know I have to answer. "Hello?"

Rain pelts on the windshield of the SUV. It never rains in Tucson but today a deluge has hit. My own personal flood of tears won't stop streaming down my face. How life can change in a matter of minutes.

I can't move. I don't want to move. Putting the key in the ignition is not an option. A knock startles me. I look up and realize I fell asleep. Outside my SUV window, Sister Loretta is standing under an umbrella.

I roll down the window. "Sister Loretta, what are you doing? You're getting soaked."

"He told me to tell you to go home."

"I'm sorry?"

The nun's smile breaks across her face as she points up. "He's had me praying for you for a couple of hours. You've just been sitting out here for a long time. I don't know what's wrong, Maggie, but it is time for you to go home." With that, the tiny nun turns on her heel and leaves.

I flip open my cell phone to check the time. 5:15. "Oh no. Jeremy." I put the key in the ignition. It's time to move on.

The rhythm of the windshield wipers somehow comforts me. No surprises. Steady. Dependable. I'll tell Frank when I get home. I'll also have to tell him about Dave. "Oh Father, why all at once?"

A horn honks behind me. I look up and see the light is green. I grab a tissue, wipe my eyes and hit the gas. I feel like my SUV is on autopilot. I realize I'm now at my son's high school. I don't remember how I got here. I stop and stare at the campus without seeing anything. The sliding door opens and startles me.

"Mom, you're late." Jeremy and two other sweaty teenage boys climb into the back.

"How was the scrimmage?" I ask. I don't care about the answer. I wish I did but I don't.

"We won. No thanks to that ref."

"That's for sure. Did you see...?" his friend Greg begins.

As the boys launch full throttle into a discussion of the basketball game, I drive home. I hear their voices and I'm grateful. I have three healthy boys and a husband who adores me. I love my home. I am truly blessed. The tears come again and I take another turn into my mind's journey. I visit places I haven't gone to in a while. The caverns of death and its impacts on family and friends are locations I do not want to think about and now, I must.

Again, a voice tells me what to do; it compels me. "I need to read Psalms tonight," I speak aloud to no one in particular.

"What? Mom, are you listening? I just asked you if Greg and Brandon can come over tomorrow night for dinner to watch the game."

I glance in the rear view mirror and see Jeremy's confused face.

"Oh. Well, of course, if their moms say it's okay."

I need time to process the news. What do I think about this? Feel? I'm scared of all it means. God, help me lean on You.

A knock scares me again. This time it's Frank outside the SUV. His face tells me he's worried.

"Honey, are you okay?" His voice is muffled through the car window.

I'm in the driveway of my home, sitting in my car. No teenage boys in sight. I turn the key to shut down the engine and I climb out of the SUV.

"Hi." Tears again. "I'm so glad to see you."

I wrap my arms around Frank and bury my head in his shoulder. This is my best friend.

"Maggie, I love you and I am so sorry. I'll take Michael to Scouts tonight. You can stay home. I sent Jeremy's friends home."

I jerk back.

"What?" My mind is racing. He's sorry? He knows?

"I am so sorry. I know you loved her a lot."

"Who?"

"Didn't you get your messages? I thought that was why you were sitting out here alone. Jeremy and the boys came in five minutes ago."

"I have no idea what you're talking about, Frank."

"Cecelia Jackson died, honey. I've already started packing for you."

"What did you say?"

"Cecelia Jackson died."

I look up into the sky and feel the rain flick my face as if to wake me up.

"Honey, let's get you inside," Frank says. "We're getting soaked."

Chapter 11

Belinda

On the road in East Texas

My Honda Accord ain't pretty but it runs well.
I like the sound of it purring as we cruise down
Highway 175, a lonely road hedged in by brush and
trees fighting for the same space. Tonight the dark
shape of leaves dancing in the wind is all that's visible
to the sides of us. I imagine the wind is shaking the
branches in celebration of me high-tailing out of a
life wrecked by failure. I also imagine I see a police
car behind me. But no, I've only seen a couple of
semis and a station wagon with somebody's feet
hanging out the passenger window.

"What about my friends?"

"Tracey, you make friends easy."

"Can you tell me where we're going, Mama?"

"I don't know. We'll know when we get there.

Think of this as an adventure."

An adventure with your criminal mother.

I slug down more Red Bull and once again glance in the rear view mirror. No Hank. No posse of horse-riding cowboys out to see me hang for leaving their brother-in-arms. After Hank left, still trying to look powerful with his hand on his gun, I packed us up quick-like. Nobody saw us load the car with two small suitcases, Tracey's backpack and a whole bunch of money.

We left at 5:30, thirty minutes before Hank would've rung the bell. Sandra always puts supper on the table at 5:00 sharp so I knew he wouldn't be early. She insists Hank be home for supper ever' day. Like that will make their marriage something other than a big 'ole sham.

Dallas and I-20 are thirty minutes away. Decision time. Do I go north on I-35 to Oklahoma City? Living outside of Texas ain't appealing to me, but maybe it's time for me to change my opinions of what's best. I let Hank sweet-talk me, and that ended in sham-ville. Something's wrong with my man-meter. Need to put it out of business for a while. Maybe I should just pick a place I'd never choose normally. Oklahoma's bound to need a good cook. We could stay for a year or two. Tracey may like it.

I sneak a peek in the backseat and my eight year old is staring out the window. Bet she's dreaming of a real life. One where she gets a daddy and a mama who don't hit teachers or steal money.

Course, I could go I-20 East and travel back to Boots. Pay my respects to Cecelia. But what if Maggie and Donna go? It'd be like paying good money to see an old movie you hated. And I was the villain in that show. Nope, I think Oklahoma is it.

"Mama, I'm hungry."

"We're fixin' to eat."

Just outside of Seagoville, Texas, I pull over to a gas station.

We use the bathroom, I let Tracey get some snacks, and I pick up another Red Bull. It's 9:15 at night and no one else is in the store. The cashier is an old woman with granny glasses and a flowered apron on. She looks like she should be in a kitchen making fried okra, not in a little Gas and Go on Freeway 175.

"Hello, little one. What beautiful red hair you have. But you look hungry." She slides Tracey's snacks over the scanner.

"I am hungry." Tracey gathers up each snack after the lady prices it. Too much food but I don't care.

"And you look tired, Mama."

The lady's eyes reflect genuine concern. I want to tell her to mind her own business, but there ain't nothing wrong with small talk.

"I am." I don't smile and I don't look at her. Not in the mood for a whole conversation.

"Are you okay?"

"I will be." Life in prison flashes through my mind and I wanna hurry up and get outta here.

"Nana died and so we're sad." Tracey unwraps a chocolate cupcake.

"I'm sorry." The lady takes my money and then hesitates. She hands it back to me. "How about this one being on the house?"

What's the catch? "Lady, I got money." If only she knew.

"You know this doesn't happen very often to me, but I feel an overwhelming sense to tell you to go home and don't worry about the money."

She's crazy.

"We just left home," Tracey offers.

"Take this money, sweetie, and go on home."

Her smile reminds me of Cecelia's. I take the money, knowing that she is just some old sentimental sucker who has no idea she's giving money to someone who ain't broke by a long shot.

"Thank you." I put the money back in my purse.

"Jesus adores you."

I stop cold. You've got to be kidding me. In the middle of nowhere and I run into Cecelia's twin. Come on.

"He loves you, too." Tracey sports a big smile with chocolate covered teeth.

"Let's go, Tracey." I corral her to the door.

"Ma'am." The old lady calls me and I turn to look at her. She's walking toward me and I see her apron goes all the way to the floor.

"Take this." She hands me a hundred dollar bill.

"No, thank you." I don't take it and she shoves it into my hand.

"Please, for me. You go home, Bee."

"How do you know my name?"

"Go home, Bee and don't worry about the money." She turns around.

Tracey and me walk out the door and get into the car. Weird. I look down to see if my name is on my shirt. It's not. Weird. I shake it off. We ain't going back to Wind Storm. Just a crazy lady.

A sign says the I-20 is coming up. I pull my car over to the shoulder of the freeway.

"You okay, Mama?"

"Tracey, eat your snacks. I just need a break."

"Should I get out?"

"Stay in the car. I'm gonna stretch my legs for just a second."

The crisp air wakes me up more than the Red Bull. I look up and see a black carpet of diamonds, each winking at me like they know this joke. I love Texas, especially the sky. No other place on earth has stars so intense and dazzling as Texas. When life gets rotten, I wait 'til the sun goes down and then I sit outside just to look up. Going east on I-20 to Boots is crazy. Oklahoma makes sense.

Something behind me calls. I jerk around and don't see nothing but the shoulder of the highway and some brush. Kinda sounded like Cecelia calling me. I shake it off. Probably just a car in the distance or a coyote with a weak howl. Cecelia used to call us in for dinner when we were at her house playing games in the Visiting Room. Nostalgia warms me a bit but I can't go. I'm sure Cecelia's cronies are still kicking. Imogene and Lola Bee will get nosy and ask me questions I don't want to answer. I'll have to be rude to them or lie to them.

Worse than that, if I go back for Cecelia's funeral, Donna and Maggie might show up. They probably still hate me. It's been over two decades but I bet they still don't want anything to do with me. Mean teenage girls live in grown women's hearts.

Two cars pass me. Wonder where they're going? When I picture Boots, I think of wooden buckets of homemade ice cream on a million hot summer days in front of Cecelia's house. I think of Imogene's pool and endless swimming sessions playing Gilligan's Island and Miss America and Marco Polo. I see me, Donna, and Maggie all piled into Maggie's mom's LTD driving around getting a coke from the Dairy Queen. Us and the other kids from youth group.

But then I remember that old dilapidated castle looking so out of place in the middle of Boots. The memories turn into painful recollections bringing with them a U Haul of bitterness.

I can't go. I pick up a rock and chuck it into the brush off the side of the highway. Cecelia can't be dead. Who is gonna write letters or call Tracey on her birthday and Christmas? And half-birthdays? Who's gonna send tiaras?

I sure can't. I don't know how to be a mother. I buy the food and the clothes and sign the report cards but Cecelia does the extra lovin' and the teachin.' When I showed her Tracey as a baby, I knew the Jesus-talk came with Cecelia. Just part of the deal. I grew up listening to all of it and going to Sunday School and the whole bit. Didn't really hurt me. Just didn't take. And Cecelia loved me more than my father's wife ever tried.

And now she's gone?

I have to go to the funeral. Cecelia was Tracey's Nana. It's the right thing, the decent thing to let Tracey say goodbye. If only she'd been Tracey's mother and not me. Her life would be so much better with a new mom. Somebody who didn't have such a temper. Somebody who knew how to pick out dresses and wanted to go to mother/daughter get-togethers. It just ain't me.

Wait a second. What if...?

I know what I need to do. Boots is full of ghosts and stupid decisions, but it's the perfect place for a child to grow up. Just a horrible one to grow old. Tracey will love it. She'll be sad at first, but after a while she'll be super glad at how it all worked out.

I look up at those stars and I grin. This is the right thing to do. And I ain't taken that path a lot in my life. I'll pay my respects to Cecelia and cook 'em up a great meal. And then I'll give Tracey the best gift I could ever give her.

Freedom from me.

I glance over at a billboard with the Texas flag on it and the slogan, "Don't Mess with Texas." As I open the car door I say aloud, "You don't mess with me."

"Mess with who?"

"Tracey, we're gonna go to Cecelia's funeral. It's a long drive so we may stop in an hour or so at a motel."

"Can we swim?"

"In the morning before we hit the road, you and I will take a swim."

"Oh Mama, that will be great. And then we get to go and

meet Vern? I've never met him."

"I know."

"And weren't you born in that town we're going to?"

"Yep. Born and raised."

"So we'll go to your home? Hey, Mama, maybe that old lady was right. We're going to your home."

"Just sit back and be quiet." My voice cracks when I say this and I glance in the rear view mirror to see my eight year old, all emotion and adventure. That cuckoo of a lady wasn't right, just religious. This is the best way. I take a deep breath and spill it out in little circles.

Phone rings. Hank. Does he expect me to answer and tell him where I am? That ain't gonna happen. He will never see me again. I turn it off and throw it out the window. Hank may try to hunt me down but by the time he figures out where to look, I'll be in Mexico. The idea of freedom flows from my heart down to my feet. I step on the gas.

Chapter 12

Maggie
Boots, Texas

Forgive me for lying, God.

Just a little lie. In the rush of packing and working out all the details with schedules and dinner plans, I didn't tell Frank. He asked me why I was upset in the driveway if I didn't know about Cecelia. I told him about Dave's cancer. I can't tell him the truth. Not yet.

Now everything is surreal. After landing in El Paso, I rented a car and began the two-hour drive to Boots, Texas. Interstate 10 looks the same, and yet everything looks different. The speed limit is 80 miles an hour on this lonely road, but I can't enjoy the thrill of speeding. Tears of grief over Cecelia keep springing up and spilling out with no warning. I'm glad I'm alone.

As I near Boots, the sadness mixes with excitement. I loved growing up here. Dad's reputation didn't spoil that. My hometown comes into view on the horizon and I smile. Boots lies in a valley surrounded by brown hills that want to be mountains. Desert brush and dirt surround it – the nearest town is 92 miles away. I see the Boots city limit sign and I grin at the population. 2,899 people lived in Boots in the 70's. Now they have a thriving population of 2,949. Fifty new people. Population explosion. I'll probably meet them all while I'm here.

I slow down the car to a crawl so I can see every old and new building on Main Street. So much looks exactly the same as it did twenty-five years earlier. But it's different. It's Tuesday late afternoon and I can almost feel my blood slowing down so it can match the pace of Boots. There is the Rambling Rock store. That was here way back when. I see some people walking between Coulters Groceries and Munn's Pharmacy and Ice Cream Parlor, which is across the street from the Boots Bank. Munn's is closed down. What a shame. Boots Movie Theater is adjacent to the ice cream parlor but appears to be no longer in business. It's a salon now? How many movies did I see in that theatre? I hope the drive-in is still open. Across from the salon, I see a small building with a neon sign saying "Videos, DVDs and Blue Rays." That's new. Seems weird that Boots has entered the twenty-first century. And there is Ortega's. Same bright pink and green paint. Such great food. I will have to stop by there while I'm here. My mouth waters thinking of it.

Oh my goodness, Boots has a traffic light? Why? I obey the red light and look around but the lack of traffic makes this stoplight some kind of embellishment. I can't help but giggle. Décor for Boots? Things have changed. But the post office is still the same. As I continue down Main Street, I pass Gloria's Flower shop, the Dairy Queen and Eddie's Auto. Most of these buildings hold memories.

Stewart's Hardware Store has been there forever and is still the same. A few new stores pepper the street, but most are exactly as I remember. Toward the end of the long drag is the doctor's office and Bell's Café, the place where I worked as a waitress forever ago. Across from Bell's is the Sewing and Going, Mrs. Friesen's fabric store, looking exactly as it did twenty-five years ago. Maybe new paint. Next to it is Harry's Hair. I think a friend of Cecelia's owns that. But it's new. At least not since I left twenty-five years ago.

I can't stop smiling as I make a U-turn and drive to the middle of Main Street, where the stoplight hangs. It would've been nice if Frank or the boys could've come and witnessed my past life. They'd get a kick out of this. At least Frank would. I make a right, pass the post office, and cross the railroad tracks.

My hands are shaking. No smile now. I'm close. "Maggie, you are forty-two-years old. Stop this."

I could go another way to get to the Jackson home. I could drive over by the pool and pass the high school. It wouldn't add any time. But I've known I needed to do this ever since landing in El Paso.

I see the tall structure looming up ahead on the left side of the road. It looks exactly like I remember it, but older and smaller. I pull over and park on the dry yellow grass in front. Of every building in Boots, this one looks the most out of place. It is an unfinished two-story castle, built with bricks. The first floor has arched windows and an arched doorway. An unfinished turret is atop the second story. Most of the roof is gone. The story I've always heard is that a count born in Poland came to Boots and decided to build a castle that resembled his home somewhere in Europe. Adults told us the castle was haunted and housed trap doors throughout. A wire fence surrounds the West Texas castle. Talk about not fitting into its surroundings. This place scared me as a child. And here, twenty-five years ago, my heart shattered.Now my stomach is churning.

Why can't I just let it go? "Father, I don't know how to forgive them. Help." My eyes tear up and then I think of Cecelia. I turn off the car to sob for a while. I loved her so much. For the first time, it occurs to me they may come back for this. Cecelia did have their numbers so she probably kept in contact. "God, help me. If they come back for this funeral, help me."

"Land sakes Alive! Magdalene May Curry! My goodness, look at you! I would've knowed you anywhere! Come here and hug my neck!"

Cecelia's best friend stands in the middle of the Jackson front yard. She looks exactly as I remember. Imogene Friesen is a big woman who waddles when she walks. She hugs me hard and although it is a little painful, I feel comfort. The smell of fresh cotton off a fabric roll and homemade fried chicken combines to fill my memories. As I keep holding on, I know I am home.

Mrs. Friesen attempts to whisper in my ear but it comes out as a yell. She only has one volume on her controls. "Cecelia loved you with a fever!"

I step back and try to smile. "I loved her. It's Maggie Shanks these days."

"That's right. Cecelia told me you got married. I think she showed us the wedding pictures, too."

"How are you?"

"Oh honey, I am fine as can be expected at seventy-five-years of age, but I am plum darned depressed about the reason I am seeing you. How is your family, child?"

"I have a husband and three sons and they're all well."

"No, I meant your Boots family."

I sigh. "Mom lives with my brother's family in Little Rock, Arkansas. Daddy died about eight years ago."

"I am sorry to hear that. Your daddy did the best he could."

My father was a drunk and she knows this. Instead of explaining to Mrs. Friesen how Daddy died alone and homeless, I change the subject.

"When I drove in, I saw the Sewing and Going. You still own it?"

"I own it but I have a lady that runs it all now. I go in every once in a while to check on everything. But I'm officially re-tired. They have a Joann's Fabric Store in El Paso so some women in Boots drive the two hours to get their fabric there, but I don't understand that one bit. I have all the best materials." Mrs. Friesen starts shaking her head. "Don't get me started about that, I'll tell you what."

I don't want to get her started. "How is Mr. Friesen?"

"Oh, now Wilbur is still about the sweetest thing on earth. 'Course he doesn't say a lot, since the surgery. He had his tongue removed due to mouth cancer. All that chewing and spitting caught up with him, that's what Dr. Hobbs said. But I guess his silence kind of adds to his sweetness." She cackles and slaps her thigh. "Wilbur used to say that a word fitly spoken is a delicious apple, but silence is piping hot peach cobbler."

I laugh and the pain of my crying headache disappears for a minute. Mrs. Friesen looks the same except for gray hair and some wrinkles. She still has a hint of a mustache above her upper lip. Her presence has always reminded me of a mama bear, large and foreboding, which is completely misleading. She's more like a teddy bear that envelops any around her who might need snuggling or safety. Memories of the First Baptist Church's fellowship hall whisk me away to scenes where people visited, sang, and ate. I hear the sound of Mrs. Friesen's deep cackle floating above it all.

"Maggie, you said you have babies?"

"I have three boys, Mrs. Friesen. Thirteen, fifteen and nineteen."

She laughs again. "Those must have been some good years." She winks and the mole on her cheek seems to dance. "Well, honey, now you get on inside. Don't ring the bell, just go on in. People been coming and going all day. Cecelia was sure loved, I'll tell you that much." She pauses and I can see she's about to cry. "I lost my best friend."

We stand in silence and I am afraid to speak. I don't want to start bawling again but I need to know something. "How did she die?"

"Apparently, a heart attack. Dr. Hobbs said she probably went sudden. She was at the house. Vern found her."

"Oh, my word. I talked to her Sunday night. We laughed and talked." Mrs. Friesen and I stare at each other, not saying anything.

She cuts the silence. "Well, I'm going home to check on Wilbur's supper. He don't have no tongue, but still loves to eat. You'd think at seventy-nine the man could fix himself a little something but getting Wilbur to cook is like pulling teeth out of a cat's behind."

I start cackling now. The language of my upbringing is a delight.

She laughs and begins to waddle away but then stops and turns, a serious look on her face. "I heard about your job fixing the grub. You know, Cecelia meant to show me that recipe but just never got around to it. If you girls want me to help with that tuna fish, you call anytime day or night."

You girls? Tuna fish? "I don't know what you're talking about."

"Have you talked to Vern? I thought he told all three of you."

My headache returns as if I stepped in front of a semi. "All three of you? Who do you mean?"

"Well, landsakes, it ain't my chore to tell you what Cecelia wanted so…"

"Tell me." My toe starts tapping.

"Cecelia wrote out exactly what she wanted for her funeral a few years ago. Real specific-like. She left instructions that the three of you gals, you, Belinda and Donna Gail, was to come on back here and fix tuna fish sandwiches for everybody after the service."

"She told me she left the tuna fish recipe to me," I state a fact. "Just to me."

Mrs. Friesen looks at me long and hard. "Maggie, not just to you. To them, too."

"They aren't coming, are they?"

"Sweetie, I'm so sorry, I thought you knew all this. Didn't Cecelia mention them to you? And weren't you three thick as thieves in school?"

My suitcase and purse weigh a ton now so I put them down. "So they are both coming?"

"I believe so."

This is absolutely ridiculous. Have they seen Cecelia more than once or twice in two decades? Have they talked to her every day and sent her packages? Did they fly her to Las Vegas for her seventieth birthday? Have they looked at her as Nana to their kids? I kick my suitcase over. "This is ridiculous."

"You wanna come over for some coffee? Settle down a bit before you see Vern?"

Mrs. Friesen is telling me to get it together. I breathe in deep and then out slowly. "I'm okay. I honestly didn't think they were a part of her life. Least not like I was." She gives me a little pity grin. "So we have to make tuna sandwiches for the whole town?"

"No. Just most of the town." She winks again and it looks like her mole is winking, too. "And as I stated, I think in her heart Cecelia wanted me to have that recipe. Just didn't get around to it."

Cecelia wrote me that her tuna fish recipe is a big 'ole secret in

Boots. It's won awards and even got a write up in the magazine *Texas Tastin'*. She told me that Mrs. Friesen and some other women have asked for it several times. But only I would get it. Only me. Father, why in the world did she do this? "I guess she's leaving the recipe to…" I spit out the word, "us."

"Well, we'll see about that, girly."

I laugh aloud at the sudden seriousness of the woman. "It's just tuna fish."

Now she turns her large body and faces me full on, shaking her head. She stands staring at me as if she is going to say something and then changes her mind. She grins. "Well, if you need any help whatsoever, you call me."

"Thank you, Mrs. Friesen."

"Please, you are a grown woman as much as me now. Call me Imogene."

"Will do, Imogene."

As I watch Mama Bear amble across the street to her house, I realize I just spoke with a Texas twang. My goodness, the Texas acclimation has begun.

I walk into the Jackson home and hear voices in the Visiting Room. Memories from childhood flood my heart and I feel like I'm swimming in nostalgia. The Jackson Visiting Room was the biggest living room I can ever remember seeing, even in the Parade of Homes in Tucson. I take a deep breath and go down the hall. I peek in and gasp a little. I expected it to look smaller than my memories from childhood. It's still huge.

Inside I see five people congregating. Mr. Jackson is sitting on a couch with his back to me. I take in the moment until a woman I've never seen catches my eye and says, "Hello. Can we help you?"

Vern stands up and turns. His eyes are red and puffy and he looks old. But then he smiles this huge smile showing his crooked teeth and he looks just as I remember. He's six feet something, broad shouldered and rough like John Wayne. He's deep brown and I remember he loves nothing more than being outside in his garden.

With no words, Vern comes to me and embraces me. I smell the fresh dirt on his plaid shirt underneath his overalls. He's been in the garden today. He draws away and looks into my eyes, "Thank you kindly, young 'un, for being here. Sissy loved you like you was hers."

"I am so sorry, Vern. She meant the world to me. I can't believe she's gone." A moment of silence slips by and then I add, "Frank and the boys send their love."

"How are those scooters?" Vern asked. "I expect they are all tall as Washington pine trees by now."

"Absolutely. I am the shortest in the house, believe it or not."

"We gotta go, Vern, but we'll see you later." Two men, close to Vern's age, are standing beside us.

"Maggie, this is Joe and Mac, two friends of mine."

We shake hands and they move toward the door. Mac says, "Vern, come have coffee with us in the morning."

"I 'spect I will. I've done it for the last thirty years of Wednesday mornings. Don't see why that should change." The men leave and Vern points me to two people sitting across from the couch. The man stands and puts out his hand. He is tall and has a kind smile. I walk around the couch and take his hand. I wince at the grip.

"Hello, Maggie, my name is um, Ben Flanders. Uh, you being here is just wonderful."

Vern steps in. "This is our new preacher, Maggie. He and Sissy were right friendly. And this sweet woman is Mabel Worthers. She is Mark Kildwell's assistant at the funeral home."

Mark Kildwell is still here? Memories of the mortician and

music leader make me grin.

Vern shakes his head at me. "I can't get over the fact that a gal puts on funerals. You ever heard such a thing?"

I glance at Mabel, still sitting, and notice a fake smile, surely a must for the job.

"Actually Vern, women now-a-days do most anything men do," I say this and glance at Mabel, whose fake smile turns into a sarcastic grin.

"Well, I know Sissy had more smarts than me and could do most anything she wanted." He stops cold and looks away for a moment. Sadness washes over me and I reach out and touch his arm. He looks down at me and grins, eyes wet. "But putting on a funeral?"

Mabel's grin is melting so I change the subject. "So Pastor Ben, you're new? How long have you been in Boots?"

"Um, well, fifteen years." He says it matter-a-factly with a deep bass voice.

"How long have you been the pastor at First Baptist?"

"Um, well, fifteen years." Ben looks at the floor.

I feel an awkward silence in the room. I glance up at Vern.

"He's doing a fine job, Maggie. But you know Brother Joe preached at First Baptist going on forty-one years when he died. Fell over flat right there in the middle of a sermon. I didn't go that day, but Sissy said it felt as if Jesus Himself came in and grabbed Brother Joe's chest and gave him a bear hug to come on home."

"Wow." I look at Ben. I'm beginning to understand. "Hard act to follow?"

Ben nods his head and grins a little. "You have no idea. Well, um, Vern, I think we can talk some more tomorrow if you'd like. Uh, make sure the service is just as you, uh, want it."

"Thank you kindly, Ben."

Mabel stands. "I think I will go, too."

After they leave, Vern and I go to the kitchen and he pours me a glass of iced tea. We sit at the Formica table with the steel chairs and white cushions. I've sat at this table many times. The rest of the kitchen looks different. "You've redone some of this room, haven't you, Vern? All I really remember is this white Formica table. I don't think they make these anymore."

Vern doesn't answer me but just stares at me. "I'm so glad you're here, Maggie. So glad. I remember many nights the three of you sat at this table with Sissy, eating and playing gin rummy or scrabble." He sniffs again and stands. "I'm gonna go get a little shut eye. Go on up and pick a room. Donna Gail is in one of 'em."

I almost spill my iced tea. "She's here?"

"Yep, she got here an hour ago. Seems a lot quieter than she used to be, but she's a grown woman and maybe she just don't have a lot to say. You need help with your bags?"

I stand up. "Vern, I'll see Donna later. I have to go check into the Ramada first anyway." Anything to put off the inevitable.

"No, you're not, young lady," Vern interjects. "Part of Sissy's plan was for you three to stay here."

My head pounds. "Is Belinda here too?"

"No, she'll be in later tonight. Bringin' her young'un. So you need some help?"

I sit down. So they had a child.

"No sir. I don't have that much luggage."

"Donna Gail's been up there an hour or so. She'll probably be down pretty quick and you can say hey to your old friend. She's probably tickled twelve shades of pink to see you."

I doubt that. Jesus, help me. I don't think I can do this.

Vern leaves. I don't move.

Chapter 13

Donna

My Facebook status says it all: *I can't believe I'm in my hometown of Boots, Texas. Surreal. Weird.* I close the app on my phone and look up at the words on the wall.

"Do not be anxious about anything, but in every situation, by prayer and petition, with thanksgiving, present your requests to God." Philippians 4:6

I recognize this one as a piece painted by an artist in Mexico. I stood by Cecelia when she bought it. We went on a mission trip to Mexico and worked at an orphanage. On a day when we went into a city to walk around, Cecelia saw it, clapped, and yelled. "Donna Gail, look at that. I have to buy it."

So much of the Jackson house seems different. When I arrived, several people were in here talking to Mr. Jackson. I excused myself quickly and walked around the house, sniffing for some good memories. Boots was the place of my mother's death, my father's depression and that horrible castle the night of graduation. The Jackson home was a refuge. Now I see changes everywhere. Many of the rooms shine with new carpet, wallpaper, or furniture. After exploring a bit, I took a nap and came back here. The Visiting Room remains just as I remember. It's more like a banquet room or a great hall. In fact, I remember Mr. Jackson moving the furniture back so square dancing and fiddle playing could fill this place. I loved those nights because I got the chance to dance with so many different boys. Mr. Jackson made us switch partners every dance.

I grin. I have found a good memory.

The décor is still all blue and brown with rose accents. I don't see any television, and the Jacksons arranged the furniture so that several groups can sit and visit within this one room. Back then, the expansive front window let the sunshine in during the day when not guarded by the heavy blue and brown draperies. Today the curtains are closed. In one corner, Cecelia's rolltop desk sits. I don't go near it, for fear that I will be intrusive. We weren't to sit at her desk; it was her place to write and dream big dreams. This room reminds me a bit of a hotel lobby, only cozier. I think of San Francisco's Hyatt Regency.

But no hotel lobby would cover the walls with Bible. All sizes of frames cover the walls. Some are pictures that are cross-stitched, some are painted and some are photographs. But each of them contains Scripture. The one from the Mexico mission trip is a watercolor painting of a peaceful ocean. I love this room and I hate this room. In here, we three met so often to talk. We'd have sleepovers and Cecelia would walk in as we talked and bring food. She always pointed to a wall, read the Scripture aloud and applied it to whatever we were discussing.

Now I know it was like library-reading time for children, all made up stories. Cecelia's wisdom based itself on fairy tales that accompanied my innocent dreams of childhood. The Bible simply does not fit into my adult real world experience. The words are still pretty like old poetry or art, but to base a life on such words is to live a naïve lie.

I wonder if I'm the only one coming. I doubted they would come for this, but someone has to help me with the meal. Women in Boots will help if Maggie and Belinda don't come.

I open up my phone, to see if William has left a message. I texted him last night and told him I would arrive in Boots today. The thought of meeting him face to face scares me to death. Will he like me? Will he even come? Will he make up some excuse not to drive the fifty miles to see me? No message but his Facebook status is different.

Received some wonderful news.

Is he talking about my text?

"Hello, Donna."

I jump and shut my phone. I look up to see Maggie Curry standing in the doorway.

"When did you get here?" Oh no. That sounded mean.

Maggie doesn't flinch. "A couple of hours ago. Vern told me you were upstairs napping. I didn't want to disturb you."

My old friend sounds cold, distant. Of course she does.

"It's been a long time. Twenty-five years, right?"

"Yes." Maggie moves toward me and sits in the chair opposite me. She is tall and slender with blond hair and looks as pretty as she always did. I've always admired her violet eyes. Now crinkles surround those eyes as if life has wadded her up like a piece of foil. Feels good to think I'm not the only one who's changed.

"I didn't mean to startle you, Donna."

"I'm easily startled, it seems. Is Belinda here, too?"

She doesn't answer immediately. "Vern said she's supposed to get here tonight."

Was that a flash of anger I just saw? So Belinda is coming. This will be interesting. "You look exactly the same, Maggie. I've gained weight." As soon as I say it, I feel stupid. My confidence has vanished. I'm an accomplished high-paid Denver accountant, I belong to some exclusive clubs and I've seen my name in the Post more than once. Sitting here, I am an insecure sixteen-year-old girl.

"We have all gained weight and lost weight and gained it back. Wouldn't it be great to have a seventeen-year-old's metabolism again?" Maggie was always sweet but her accompanying smile doesn't look genuine.

I shoot back, "As long as we don't have to have her hormones."

Maggie chuckles and I laugh with a nervous giggle. It occurs to me we didn't hug hello. Were we supposed to?

Silence.

After a moment Maggie blurts, "Oh my word. This room is exactly the same." She gets up and walks around the room looking at the Scripture covered walls. When she turns around, I notice tears in her eyes. "I can't believe she's gone," Maggie whispers.

I nod.

She walks to Cecelia's desk and runs her hand along the roll-top. Apparently, she doesn't care about intrusiveness. I am quiet, watching her grieve.

"So how are you, Donna?" She asks this but is still looking at the desk.

"I'm fine." I know the reply is curt and unbelievable. "And you?"

"I guess I've been better."

"I guess we all have."

"Did you fly in and get a rental car?"

"Yes. And you?"

"Me too. Vern offered to pick me up but I wouldn't hear of it."

"Was your drive okay?"

For an eternity we, who once told each other our darkest fears and biggest secrets, engage in rapid-fire small talk that could bore the most desperate for entertainment. Will we ever talk about what happened graduation night? Maybe we should let it evaporate into the Texas air. We are grown women and there is no reason to bring up the past.

I notice that neither of us have exchanged any personal information and that is fine with me, thank you very much.

"Are you married?" Maggie asks, as she sits back down across from me.

And there it is. The question I hate more than any three words on the planet. Even if I came up with the cure for cancer, people would still see me as incomplete without a man in my life. I wish I could be honest and say, *Of course, I'm not, Maggie. I am fat. Can't you see that?*

"No," I answer politely. "Still single. How about you?"

"I'm married. For twenty-two years now."

"Figures."

"What?"

"Well, hot-diggity, you both grew up!" A tall woman whose dyed rust hair looks exactly like Princess Leia, buns included, walks into the room.

I look at Maggie and she glances at me. We both shrug at the same time.

"You don't know who I am? Are you kidding me? I'm Lola Bee Turner. Now get over here both of you and gimme a Yankee dime."

Lola Bee Turner? Really?

"The Sunday School Director. Of course!" Maggie laughs.

"You look different, though." I observe. When I get to Mrs. Turner, she kisses me right on the mouth. The smack of her lips and the smell of a heavy dose of Aqua Net cause me to remember. She was one of Cecelia's best friends. She kisses everybody on the lips. I thought it somewhat creepy as a child. I still do.

"It's my weight. I lost near almost 100 pounds; just plumb fell off." She gives Maggie a big smooch.

I turn away slightly to hide the fact I am wiping my mouth.

"You lost 75, you old heifer." Mrs. Friesen is suddenly in the room with us. I completely remember her.

"You weren't there every day looking at those numbers, Imogene, so you can just keep your mouth zipped."

I'm a little overwhelmed. Mrs. Friesen looks grayer but otherwise, exactly the same. A big woman who loves to laugh loudly. I glance at Maggie and see her giggling.

"Lola Bee, how did you do it?" Maggie asks.

"Do what?"

"She wants to know how you," Mrs. Friesen starts to yell, "lost the weight!"

"I am not deaf, Imogene. You know I hate it when you do that."

Mrs. Friesen giggles and Mrs. Turner turns away from her. "I made up my own diet." She looks at me. "I can sell it to you ladies."

Great. I've only been here a few hours, and someone is offering me a way to lose weight. Just seems to follow me everywhere I go. Blah, blah, blah.

"She didn't 'make up' anything," Mrs. Friesen interjects. "She went to Weight Watchers meetings and stole their show is what she did."

"I did not." Mrs. Turner turns on her heel and stomps to the door. "I came over here to invite you gals to supper tonight at my house, but maybe I will just go home."

"Lola Bee, is your program like Weight Watchers?" Maggie asks.

Mrs. Turner turns back. "It's nothing like it."

Mrs. Friesen shakes her head. "You ever been in Weight Watchers, Maggie?"

"Hasn't everyone?"

"You count points, right?" Mrs. Friesen asks Maggie but looks at Mrs. Turner.

"I don't count points, Imogene. I've told you that a million times."

"Do you count something, Lola Bee?" Maggie asks.

"Well, yes. I count dots."

Mrs. Friesen snorts and Maggie laughs aloud but I don't find any of it funny. I need to get out of here.

Time to make an excuse. "Listen, it's good to see you all, but I need to lie down for a moment. I'm tired from the travel."

"I thought you already took a nap." Maggie looks at me innocently but I can tell she is trying to dig at me.

"I just read. I need to sleep now." That's somewhat true.

"I'm sorry we've gone on and on, Donna Gail." Mrs. Friesen reaches out and grabs my hand. "We're so glad to see you girls and we were honestly hoping you could have supper with us at Lola Bee's tonight. Maybe first you two could come over to my house and swim like you did when you was little."

"I'd love to come, Imogene. Just have to change," Maggie replies.

"You brought your swimsuit to a funeral?" I can dig back with the best of them.

Maggie gives me a curious look. "I still love to swim, Donna."

"Oh, you do?" As I say this, I reach into my pocket and thumb the button on the side of my Droid X. It rings.

"Excuse me." I say to the women and walk away. "Hello?" I hear nothing as my imaginary conversation develops. "Really?

Okay. I'll send it now."

I turn back. "I have to go email some documents to my work. I'll see you later."

"What do you do, Donna Gail?" Mrs. Friesen uses my old name.

"I'm an accountant. I go by just Donna now."

"You were an A student, if I remember right." She's smiling and I notice a big mole on her cheek. I try to remember if she's always had that.

"Yes, Mrs. Friesen. I have to go now. I'll see you later."

"Well, when you wake up if you wanna have supper at my house, just call me," Mrs. Turner says. "My number's on the fridge." She shakes her head and continues telling Maggie, "When you get to be our age, phone numbers can be a little tricky. We write them all down."

I walk out of the Visiting Room and up the stairs. Rodeo pictures, cowboy hats and even a bed with horseshoe posts decorate my room. A huge framed picture covers most of one wall. I look at it closer than I did earlier and I notice a poem penned in the picture. A cowboy poem written by Cecelia.

"Oh, Cecelia." I smile and for the first time I feel I might cry.

It's just exhaustion. I am here to pay respects to this woman I haven't seen in ages and I meet up with a bunch of strangers. She's acting like it's a vacation. Swimming? Maggie doesn't know me anymore. What a fake attitude, too. I know she's angry even if she went off and got married. This is exactly why I never go to reunions. Everyone is fake. I came for William. The rest is just obligation.

The feelings inside me twist like a pile of old necklaces tangled in a jewelry box.

I'm nervous and tired and angry. I wonder if Maggie is guessing how much I weigh. What do I care? I pick up my suitcase and put in on the bed. I find the bag tucked in the corner where I neatly packed it. I sit and breathe in and out and begin unwrapping each of the golden covered delights. The taste of peanut butter and chocolate reminds me of home and gives me much needed energy. I do not care how many dots these beauties might be.

I open my laptop and remember Vern doesn't have Wi-Fi. I click on Facebook on my phone. Wi-Fi works on there. No new messages. William hasn't changed his status since this morning. I hope I am his wonderful news. But maybe he got other news and had to leave town. Maybe he just posted so he would have an excuse not to see me. He could tell me he is busy with ranch work and couldn't come meet me. I check my email and I see I have one from Stuart.

Donna, we miss you already. Okay, I miss you already. I felt like we achieved a little breakthrough at that restaurant, you know? And then you left. Come back quickly. I would love to talk to you. Not about business. I'm really sorry about your friend. Praying for you.

My skin lights up like a match. Can he really like me? Is this some joke? Two men at once? I close my phone and shake my head. Look at me. I'm like Cecelia, filling my mind with fairy tales. I stand up and walk to the window. I look out and see the Friesen's house directly across the street. I met Belinda and Maggie at First Baptist, but we spent most of our childhood here or over at Mrs. Friesen's. We all loved swimming. I haven't swam in years. No way am I going to show this body in a swimsuit. Maggie and Belinda were always better swimmers, anyway. They never almost drown like I did. Goodness, that was thirty-five years ago. We were all eight. My mom would die that year.

Mrs. Jackson's words interrupted my terror. "I've got you, little one."

I splashed with one hand and with the other, I clung to Mrs. Jackson. I scrambled out of the pool and lay down on the cement. Tears came mixed with pool water. My throat burned and my lungs fought as I coughed up my fear.

"It's okay, Donna." Maggie stood beside me, towel in hand. She started wiping my legs.

"She all right?" Belinda stood a few feet away.

"She'll be fine." Mrs. Jackson sat me up, and put one arm around me.

"I thought you was gonna die," Belinda blurted.

I started sobbing.

"There, there dear. You're okay." As Mrs. Jackson spoke, I laid my head on her shoulder.

"Donna, you know how to swim. What happened?" Maggie asked.

Mrs. Jackson answered for me. "Maggie, sometimes things happen and fear gets a hold of us and clamps on us like a clothespin on a flapping sheet and we just forget what we've learned. Happens to everybody. Trick is to keep your lessons close and then you'll be less likely to forget."

I tried to stop crying, but the tears made me gasp more.

"Girls, I want to teach you how to breathe."

"We know how to breathe," Belinda remarked.

"Breathing right is the best way to calm down when you're afraid or stressed or you just forgot how to swim." For a few minutes, she taught us to breathe in deep through our nose and let it out slowly through our mouths, pretending we were blowing straight little tunnels of air.

Sure enough, my breathing slowed down and I announced to all of them, "Mrs. Jackson's right. I just forgot how to swim. I want to go home now."

"We still have a little time left, Donna. I think you should get back

in."

"No, Mrs. Jackson, I don't want to." I glared at her. "If I don't want to, then I am not going to."

"Maybe we should go home," Maggie suggested.

"Maggie, you and Belinda go ahead and swim some more. Dive down for pennies or something. I'm going to talk to Donna."

"Now?" Belinda asked.

"Now." Mrs. Jackson used her serious voice.

"I want to go home, Mrs. Jackson."

"No, I don't think so, Donna. You should go back in again and swim. You won't be scared next time. And when you get back in, you'll keep your lessons close, just you watch. You won't forget anything anymore."

I looked away from her and muttered, "I am not going back in."

"There is absolutely no need for you to be scared."

I snapped back, "I am not scared." No one got away with calling me scared. Even if I was always terrified.

"Then show us. Get back in."

"Just watch me."

To prove Mrs. Jackson wrong, I jumped in and challenged Belinda to a race.

A knock at the door interrupts my thoughts.

"Who is it?"

"It's Vern. Just wanted to tell you to help yourself to anything in the fridge. Towels are in the closet by the bathroom down the hall. I probably won't eat much tonight but you go ahead. I'll talk to you in the morning."

"Thank you." I wait until I hear the old man shuffle away and I sit on the bed. Straight ahead of me, sitting on the dresser, is a framed photo. Three little girls in bathing suits, all holding their hands like fake guns, positioned to look like the Charlie's Angels pose. I grin at our cuteness. My brown hair used to be so curly. Maggie stands in the middle, pretty and bossy, as always. Belinda's long red hair was gorgeous, even when it fell in one long red rope. We were ten in that picture, probably around 1980. We loved playing Charlie's Angels in the Friesen pool along with Marco Polo and beauty pageants. Bittersweet pangs come and I sigh. We'd been so innocent in that pool. So carefree. I stand and pick up the photo. I can almost hear Belinda and me arguing.

"Do you ever think I could marry Willie Ames? He is such a dream on Eight is Enough."

"Belinda, you can have them. I have Shaun Cassidy. Donna and Shaun – it's perfect," I replied.

"Maybe I just could date Tommy Bradford on the show. I'd be his girlfriend."

"Two minutes, ladies," Mrs. Jackson called.

"It's time!" Maggie yelled and began running in a circle trying not to splash.

Belinda and I quickly followed suit and soon we three were making a circle of water and laughter and energy. We ended each swimming time with a rushing whirlpool. The best part of the water flight was when Maggie yelled, "Now!"

We did an about face and fought through the motion of the water. Fighting the current we'd created brought squeals and more laughter. Our battle quickly rescinded and we made our way to the steps of the pool, sighs filled with sweet disappointment at the ending of another good swim. On the steps, we stood in a circle and put our hands together. Maggie guided us. "One, two, three..." With our hands flying up, we yelled, "Jesus Girls!" The same mantra we would use hundreds of times growing up.

So long ago. I put the picture back on the dresser and move to the window again. I wonder if Maggie is over there in the pool by now. I wish I were thinner and able to slip into any swimsuit and go. I'm not and I wouldn't. I'm definitely not a Jesus Girl anymore. Just like I'm not a Girl Scout or a musician. Not anymore. This is going to be much more difficult that I thought it would be. And when Belinda gets here, the tension is going to be unbearable.

I find the bag of peanut butter delights and see that a few are left. I sit on the bed and start unwrapping. As I taste the sweet chocolate comfort, I remember the sight that always greeted us at the end of those swims years ago.

Mrs. Jackson stood at the edge of the pool, waiting for us with warm beach towels.

Chapter 14

Belinda

"Mama, I'm tired."

Even in the dark, I see the mop of bright red hair in the back seat. She is adorable like that cartoon character Annie with long hair. Course Annie had a perm gone crazy. No way Tracey'll ever get a perm as long as I have anything to say about it. I won't let her cut it. Sometimes she wants to chop it all off and we have a fight about it. But I win. I couldn't give a rip about what she wears, but darnitt, she's keeping that hair. People everywhere, from that weird apron-wearing woman at the Gas and Go to the foreign fella at the motel in Abilene to that teenager at the fast food place has commented on Tracey's pretty red hair. I agree but I also know just how annoying she can be. And whiny like now.

"Tracey, I'm tired, too. You're not the one

driving. Just go to sleep."

"Mama," she whispers, "I can't sleep with the music so loud."

"Well, that music is the only thing that's keeping me awake. And if I go to sleep we both end up dead in a ditch." Darnitt. That helps, Belinda. Just scare your kid to death. For an hour, George Strait has serenaded us. Cecelia loved George.

Right after Tracey's birth, we listened to George croon. Cecelia said her three loves in life were Jesus, Vern, and George. I remember thinking "Oh no, a Jesus speech," and then Cecelia quipped, "Course, not always in that order. Sometimes, Vern and George switch places, especially if Vern's in the outhouse. That's worse than the doghouse."

Right now George's singing about all his exes. I see the Boots, Texas city sign. "Anyway, Tracey, we're here."

The billboard is lit up with the words *Boots - In our town, you'll never use your boots for leaving. Population 2,949.* I grin. Seems I missed a population explosion.

"Where's the town, Mama?"

I can't help but chuckle. "It's those bunch of lights up there. It's small, even smaller than Wind Storm."

"Can we go to your old house?" Tracey says.

"Nope. Now be quiet so I can remember how to get to Cecelia's."

I turn off the CD player and slow down to the posted speed limit. I light a cigarette and take a long drag. So weird.

"Look at that," I say aloud. "This crappy town seems just the same. Same old run down stores and backward hick restaurants. Stupid movie-theater that only showed one movie looks closed. A salon? Seriously? Somebody in Boots uses a salon? Used to be just plain ole beauty shop. Dairy Queen? I worked there for two years. The Dilly Bars are the best ice cream treat anywhere. That's the only good thing about the place. Tracey, you should thank me daily that I don't raise you in a place like this. Nothing to do, ever'body knows your business, gossip is a sport. I hated this place."

"Don't you say those things about Wind Storm, Mama?"

"Be quiet."

I shouldn't say bad stuff about Boots. She's gonna be stuck here for a long time. Boots is a ghost town to me but the spirits are in the car with me as I drive around. I learned to drive on this street. Coach Stemson taught Driver's Ed and history, and we always got a coke at the Dairy Queen before practicing. Eddie's Auto still in business? Eddie's son, Roberto, was the first boy I let kiss me. I shake my head. Weird. I turn off Main Street and over the railroad tracks. I know where I want to go. Best spot in this entire town.

I pass the old castle and glance at it. I remember.

"What a waste."

The First Baptist Church comes into view. The night sky darkens the old beige building, but I can see that the outline is the same. A tall white steeple with a slender cross atop of it lights up the black West Texas sky. It looks simple and pretty. I loved this place. I park in the front.

"Mama, are we there?"

"Not yet." Doesn't look any different.

"What is this place, Mama? Is this a church?"

I shouldn't smoke here so I put out my cigarette. So easy to stare at that shining steeple.

"Mama..."I cover myself with the warmth of the goodness this church brings me. I ain't for being sentimental but I can't help it. Memories hit me as if those spirits in my car are showing a drive-in-movie of my youth. We used to sing around a piano, Donna playing, for hours. And those youth group nights were so fun. I remember the night we played Romans and Christians with the Methodists. We went all over town hiding. I remember the Boots

Chili Cook Off and how our youth group won it for the Baptist Church. Me and Cecelia did most of the cooking.

Good times were had. Plenty of 'em. The faces of my childhood play across that movie screen. Mrs. Wright played piano for years and she always smiled at me from her piano bench when she saw me watching her. I see Mr. Bakers, who drove the church bus that picked me up on Sundays. He used to say to me, "Belinda, God's got a wonderful plan for your life." He's probably dead by now. There's Mrs. Cusher who always got on us when we whispered in church. Of course, there's Lola Bee Turner and Imogene Friesen arguing, and Cecelia playing referee.

Cecelia. She taught us in the six-year-old Sunbeam class at church. Cecelia led Girls in Action when we were in elementary. And she watched us and listened to us in her house when we were teenagers. What a great place. And then I threw it all away.

"Mama, answer me please. Is this Cecelia's church?"

I flare up at her voice. "Cecelia went here yes, are you satisfied?" With that, the spirits are gone and the movie ends. No more good feelings and memories. Just a job to do.

"Can I help you?"

I jump.

"Mommy!" Tracey screams at the man standing beside our car.

A tall man in a button down shirt and slacks stands a few feet from the car. He looks harmless. I roll down the window.

"We're just looking." He's gorgeous, even in the dark.

"Um, well, uh, are you shopping for a church?" His voice reminds me of Barry White. A stumbling Barry White.

"No. I'm not the church-going type." I smile at him, wondering if he could be a little distraction while I'm in Boots.

"I like church." Tracey's head pokes up through the seats, straining to see around me.

"Well, hello, uh, little lady."

As soon as he talks to Tracey, I know he won't be a distraction. He's a good boy, I can tell.

"Hi." Tracey says brightly.

"Thank you anyway, mister, but we need to get somewhere."

"Need directions?" He gazes at me as if he's looking right through me. It's unnerving.

"We're fine." I start up the car. He backs up to the sidewalk of the church. He never bent down to the window. I notice and I'm impressed. Nice guy didn't want to get too close at night and invade my personal space. Too bad though. Doesn't know what he missed.

I pull out and drive only a little before stopping. I tell Tracey to wait 'til I tell her to get out of the car. I hop out and open up the trunk. I check the red bag. The cash is real. Wasn't a dream. I cover it up securely with an old blanket and shut the trunk.

I open the back door for Tracey to climb out.

"Well, hello there, Bee!" Imogene Friesen waddles across the street toward me. I chuckle at her. No woman existed as friendly to ever'body as Imogene Friesen.

"This is Mrs. Friesen, Tracey."

The old woman comes up to me, grabs me and hugs me hard. Mrs. Friesen has no concept of personal space. I smile to myself as she continues to squeeze. No use arguing with this one.

She lets me go and looks down at Tracey. "Landsakes alive! Are you Tracey?"

Tracey moves to hide behind me. It occurs to me this big lady might remind her of that cow, Mrs. Hume.

"Answer her," I say.

"Yes," Tracey whispers.

Imogene performs an on the spot maneuver I didn't think

possible for a woman her size and age. She bends down and sits on the street. Right on the street, in front of Tracey. We might need a crane to get her up and it's late.

"Tracey, I happen to be the best friend of Cecelia."

Tracey comes out from behind me. "You know Nana?"

She smiles a huge smile and I see her mole poke out from her face. "Yes, sweetie. I knew your Nana and I tell you what, she loved to talk about her dear little Tracey."

"She did?" Tracey takes a step toward Imogene.

"Yes. And I have so wanted to meet you for so long. You are even prettier than your pictures, you know that?"

"Thank you." Tracey's head drops a little. "Did you know that Nana died, Mrs. Friesen?"

Imogene doesn't respond for a minute. "I do, honey. I already miss her. But I know she's in Heaven with Jesus."

Yep, I'm back in the Bible Belt of my childhood. Yeesh.

The old woman holds out her arms and Tracey just falls into them and sits in her big lap. Imogene hugs her, but gently and starts rocking her right there in the street. Tracey starts to cry and then sob and the old woman joins her.

I don't belong in this scene. I back up to the car and get our two suitcases out. It's better for me to stand by the car and watch them from a few feet away. I feel like I'm watching a moment that should've happened in my own home. I'm annoyed at their crying and I wonder when it will be over. Tracey and Mrs. Friesen are quite a pair.

Wait.

Yes! She's the one I can leave Tracey with. Mrs. Friesen will live to be a hundred and she will be a better mom than I could ever be. Mrs. Friesen whispers something to Tracey and Tracey nods and then stands up. "Bee, get over here and help me up."

I set the suitcases down and extend a hand.

"Oh no, child. You need to get behind me and push me forward so I can be on my knees and then you bend down and push up on my bottom."

I stare at the old woman. "Are you serious?"

"Yes, honey, I am. This here is a delicate procedure that Wilbur and I have conducted together for years." Her laugh comes out as a cackle and I wonder how many neighbors are going to wake up. But I don't care. Imogene Friesen is comfortable in her own shoes and I admire her. I join her in the laughter and do as instructed. After a couple of heaves and grunts, she's on her feet.

"Vern hit the hay early so I kept watch for you tonight. Go on in the front door and up the stairs and your room's the third one on the left."

"Are we sharing a room?" I ask.

Imogene looks at me for a blink of a second with curious eyes, then says, "Well for tonight, yes. But if you girlfriends don't want to be roomies you can have separate bedrooms tomorrow."

"Good night, Mrs. Friesen."

"Good night, sweet Tracey. We'll talk some more tomorrow, okay?"

"Okay."

Nerves attack me as I watch Imogene waddle back to her house. Once she reaches her yard, I turn to Tracey and move her head where her eyes are locked on mine. "Tracey, do not talk unless spoken to. And do not, under any circumstances, embarrass me or I will tan your hide."

Chapter 15

Maggie

Good morning, Lord.

It takes me a second to remember where I am. My heart is racing and I'm breathing fast so I try to slow it down. In and out. One thing at a time. Today, Cecelia.

I tiptoe down the stairs and into the kitchen. The coffee pot is on and full but no one is around. I pour myself a cup and head out the back door. A rocking chair with a baby blue cushion sitting on the back porch is a perfect place to start the day. I sit and sip the coffee slowly and examine the huge back yard. I never appreciated it as a child, but now, with my own backyard and garden, I see the hours of work Vern and Cecelia have put in to make this place Eden-like. Three huge pecan trees and two apricot trees stand tall lining either side of the expansive yard. Just beyond the porch is a picnic table. I see the arch-shaped gate at the back of the lawn and the flower and vegetable garden beyond it. Tall sunflowers seem to wave and beckon me come talk to them. That flower garden has been Vern's baby for years. Roses, daffodils, gardenias, and cornflowers fill it. I'll find the bench later, if it's still there. It was there I used to sit and pour out my heart to Cecelia. I told her about my father's drinking and how Mother loved my brother Barry more than me. Cecelia listened. She understood my love for Alan. She held me on that horrible day. And now Cecelia is gone.

Father, I come to you this morning for faith and guidance. Maybe I should call Frank today and tell him the news. But I can't. Not yet. I have to deal with what is right in front of me. Right now, it's Cecelia's funeral, Donna, and Belinda. *Oh God, help me. Hold me and help me forgive truly and deeply.* Why did Cecelia do this? She knows how they hurt me. Apparently, she forgave them for what they did to me. I'm not Cecelia. I don't know if I can. And how can I say good-bye to my Cecelia May? She mothered me through heartbreak and cancer. What will I do without her? I push the grief back. I can't just feel sad, because I have to deal with them, too.

God, where are you? Haven't I done right by You? I don't deserve all this. I sit for a long time, hoping my emotions will change. They don't. I'm going to run into Belinda sooner or later. I want to get it over with. As I approach the back door, I smell a heavenly scent. Blueberry Pancakes. Imogene must have come over early but no one is in the kitchen.

On the Formica table a plate of pancakes stand high, with a jar of maple syrup beside it. Plates, silverware and glasses are out on the cabinet beside the oven.

"You're a cook, too?" Donna walks in and notices the breakfast fare.

"Not me. But it smells and looks like Cecelia's pancakes."

"Flapjacks." Donna corrects with a smile. Much better mood than yesterday.

We grab plates and serve ourselves. I notice that Donna is well dressed again. She wears expensive clothes. Designer labels. I'm in my blue jeans and a white tank top I bought at Marshalls. Donna has on navy blue pedal pushers that look new and an off-white lacy blouse that is striking. She might have gained a little weight, but she is beautiful and has great fashion sense.

It must be nice to have money for designer clothes.

"You really look nice, Donna." I am going to be kind to her no matter the past and besides, what I'm saying is the truth.

"Thanks. Is that so surprising?"

Oh my word, that sounded abrupt. I want to be nice and try to accept and forgive. She's going to make it difficult. This is ridiculous.

"Good morning, ladies." Vern shuffles through the kitchen to the back door. "I'm going down to Bells. I'll be back in an hour or so and we'll talk about a plan."

"Thank you for the pancakes, Mr. Jackson." Donna says this as if she's trying hard to be polite.

"Wasn't me. She still cooks like Sissy." Vern grins and leaves.

Oh no. I look at Donna and she's giving me a curious look.

"He can only be talking about one person." I sit at the Formica table and look at my plate. My appetite is suddenly waning.

"Belinda?"

"Of course."

We sit and I wonder if she wants me to pray. I'm starving. I skipped supper last night and went to bed early. The swimming did me in.

I'm about to ask Donna about praying but she looks past me, toward the doorway to the kitchen. I breathe in and turn around, ready to see Belinda. Instead, I spy a red-haired little girl looking lost.

After a moment, Donna speaks. "Belinda?"

I am looking at a face from our past. "It must be Belinda's daughter. Is that right, honey?" The little girl nods.

"It is truly amazing how much you look like your mom." Donna says what I'm thinking.

"Thank you. I'm Tracey." With that, she gets a plate and walks to the table.

"Let me serve you." I reach for the spatula.

"She can do that herself."

I turn again to the doorway to see a thin, ragged-looking woman with an unlit cigarette in her hand. Her large brown eyes are bloodshot and her obviously bleached blond hair is uncombed. I can't believe I'm looking at Belinda.

"So, we meet again." Bitterness laces her words. What does *she* have to be bitter about?

"Belinda, how are you?" Donna asks. "We can't believe how much your daughter looks like you did at that age."

"Yeah, she looks like me." Belinda stares at me and then Donna. Then she holds up her cigarette to us. "I smoke but Mr. Vern Jackson informed me that I can't light up in this exquisite palace." Her words are biting.

I consciously shut my wide-open mouth.

"You gained weight, Donna."

My mouth opens again and I look at Belinda, horrified, to see that she is grinning. Donna looks hurt. "Belinda." I feel like

I'm talking to one of my sons.

"Oops. I'm mean as a one-eyed cat 'fore I have my coffee. Sorry, Donna."

Belinda doesn't sound sorry. I look at Donna and see that she has her phone out and is texting or reading or something to keep from looking at this mean woman.

"Doesn't take much these days for me to be nasty. Just ask my daughter." Belinda walks to the coffee pot and pours herself a cup. Her Texas twang surprises me.

As if Donna reads my mind she asks, "Wow. I haven't heard an accent like that in quite a while. I mean, it's worse than Vern." Knife thrown.

Belinda smirks and picks up her coffee mug. "Spent most of my adult life in East Texas and people who don't talk like me ain't real Texas if you ask me."

"Ain't? "Donna looks back at her phone and shakes her head. "Didn't we go to the same English class in high school?"

Belinda sips her coffee, glaring over the rim. "What's your favorite recipe, Donna? I'm sure you eat a whole lot of it ever day."

Donna slams her phone down. This is truly stupid. I change the subject quickly. "Belinda, are you going to eat?"

"Nope. I think I'll just have a cup of Joe."

"You made these pancakes?" I ask.

"Yep."

A moment of awkward silence passes.

I ask Donna, "Should we pray?"

More silence.

"If you want to pray, go ahead, Maggie. I don't really pray that much anymore." Donna puts her phone on the table and fills her mouth with pancakes.

Belinda gives a little laugh like a chicken squawking. "You

still pray, little Miss Maggie? I will not be joining you under any circumstances. Might as well talk to the air." Belinda delivers her words with that same sardonic smile.

I didn't expect this. I knew there might be, would be, tension but anger and apathy towards God?

"I'll pray with you," a tiny voice says.

"Tracey, be quiet. She wasn't talking to you." With that, Belinda sits down with us, and stares into her cup of coffee.

No one says anything. I look at Tracey and smile and wink at this small girl whose eyes plead for kindness. I pray silently. *Father, help. Bless my food and be with my words and actions. Comfort dear Vern. Please show me what in the world Cecelia thought when inviting these two to her funeral. Amen.*

I begin to eat and search for something nice to say, but instead I find a pocket of old anger. How could they have turned away from God? The three of us were self-proclaimed Jesus Girls. So many times, we sat at this very table and talked about Jesus and our hope in Him and our love for Him. We were going to change the world for Jesus! Now they won't even pray? Belinda and Donna have no right to be angry with God. I was crushed, not them. I am the one who loved Cecelia like my mother. Not them. At least I don't think they did. Why did they walk away from Christ?

The pancakes are beyond delicious. I don't want to like them, but I've never tasted better.

Donna finishes her plate and reaches for more. "Belinda, you may be extremely rude and bitter but you can cook."

Belinda laughs like Donna said something hysterical. "Now I like that. To the point. And liking my cooking is a way to my heart."

After a couple more bites, I put my fork down. Timpani drums are playing inside me, but I need to do this. It's time just to get it all out.

"Belinda, how is your husband?"

Donna makes a choking sound and says, "Talk about to the point."

"What husband?" Tracey asks.

"She said it all, little Miss Maggie." Belinda stands up and takes her coffee cup to the sink, keeping her back turned away.

"Did you get married? Divorced?" Donna asks.

"Mama, what are they talking about?"

Belinda turns to face us. "Listen, if we really need to talk about this, I'm just gonna tell you once and for all."

Oh no. I stand up quickly and rush out of the room. The hall bathroom is close and easily accessible. Afterward, I sit on the floor with my head to the door. I can't believe that just happened.

"Maggie, are you okay?" Donna is outside the door.

"I'm fine, thank you. I'll be out in a minute."

Belinda's voice is low and a bit muffled but I hear every word. "See, Donna. Just talking about the past makes her sick." She gives out another hard laugh. "Let's just let it all go."

Later that morning, Vern knocks on my bedroom door. "I need to see all you squirts out in the backyard in just a minute." He knocks on my door but it he is talking to all three of us. Are they in their rooms, too?

The backyard is hotter than earlier, but still beautiful. When I walk out the back door, I see Vern and Donna sitting at the picnic table. As I approach them, Belinda comes from behind me and walks past me.

"Well, Mr. Jackson, here we are." Belinda declares holding a cigarette. "Is it okay if I smoke out here?"

"Go ahead, Belinda. How you holding up there, Maggie?"

"I'm fine, Vern. Just a little upset stomach I think." I sit down at the picnic table.

"I want ya'll to know it would've meant the world to Sissy to know you came. She loved the three of you gals more than pig's feet. I guess ya'll know that from all that's happened over the years with each of you."

What does he mean by that? Did Cecelia tell them about my cancer? If Belinda got divorced, why didn't Cecelia tell me? Of course, I probably would've cut her off.

"And she wanted you to come back and make the fixin's for tomorrow's funeral. It's tuna fish sandwiches, one of her specialties. I was partial to her cobbler, but most folks 'round here love that tuna. 'Course I don't think Sissy ever met a meal she couldn't make terrific."

He stops and fishes for a handkerchief from his jeans pocket. Wiping his eyes, he starts again. "Seems I'm pretty much a blubbering ole cuss these days. Sissy always loved it when I cried at movies. Don't know when I've cried like this though. Anyway, I don't mean to burden you, but the whole town'll probably show up for the funeral. We'll have most of 'em come through here afterwards. Lots of folks been bringing grub already, so it's not like we need tons and tons of tuna fish sandwiches, but Sissy wanted it to be the main 'un-tray.' And she specifically wanted you three to make them."

I grin at Vern's mispronunciation. It takes me back to a childhood filled with Vern's own dictionary of words.

"Why?" Belinda asks the question aloud that I've asked myself since Vern's first call.

"Don't know. I guess...well, I don't know. I was married to her fifty-four years and I never fully understood the woman. She always said a little mystery added to the spice of our marriage, like paprika to deviled eggs. And I know there are only two theories to arguing with a woman. Neither of 'em work." He chuckles. "I don't know what I'm going to do without that sweet ..."

We sit in silence for several minutes.

"So," Vern comes back, "how 'bout we make a plan? I have shopping lists for you. Each of 'em have different ingredients and they include things that aren't even in the sandwich. This recipe is a pretty guarded secret. So much so that if you all go to the store, there'll probably be ladies watching what you buy. That's why we all have to be spy-like and go to the store like that feller James Bond and buy ingredients you won't use."

Donna laughs. "You're kidding. This is just tuna fish, right?"

"Donna Gail, you will find that a few old women in this town want this recipe real bad. Been bribing my wife for years. But Sissy left it to the three of you. I hope you have fun with the secret agent part of it despite circumstances. It'll be work, but maybe Sissy did this so you gals could get together again for a laugh. And of course you know, Sissy didn't want you to share this particular recipe. So never miss a chance to shut up about it." He grins. "Letting the cat outta the bag is a whole lot easier than putting it back."

"We don't have to spend our own money, right, Vern? I don't have the kind of cash it'll take to buy all that tuna and what not." Belinda's bluntness again surprises me.

"Belinda, I have enough money to cover it." I offer. Did Cecelia know *this* Belinda?

"Now it's all right, Maggie. Belinda, I appreciate your honesty. We got plenty of cash for you to do all the shopping.

This entire trip is on me. You hear that? If you have any other expenses, well, you just let me know."

I turn and stare at Belinda. Maybe this is how she's always been and I just didn't know. She doesn't deserve the recipe.

"Well, that's the plan, ladies. On the dining room table is the three shopping lists and each has some money for you to shop with. This afternoon you can do the shopping and start making it later on after I give you the recipe. I suspect that making this many sandwiches is gonna take a while, so you might want to take a nap. You might be up late tonight." Vern looks old and exhausted. He excuses himself and walks back to the house in his own time and rhythm. We don't move. I don't want to be the first to say something. Belinda would probably bite my head off anyway. Donna beats me to it.

"You know what, Belinda, this is going to be so much fun," she remarks sarcastically. "It is just delightful to see you again after all these years."

Belinda is silent for a moment and then begins to laugh. For the first time, I recognize the giggling. It's neither hard nor sarcastic. "I am a walking party to be around, aren't I?" Her tone is apologetic. "We have to be around each other for the next 24 hours so why don't we make the best of it."

I still don't believe Belinda will make the best of anything.

"Anyway, I can't nap," Belinda quips. "Before we hit Coulters on our top secret mission, how 'bout we go for a ride and see the old haunts?" She sounds almost enthusiastic.

"Will you be pleasant to be around?" Donna inquires.

"I tell you, if we eat tacos at Ortega's like we've done a million times, and get Dilly Bars from Dairy Queen, I will be the most delightful of company." Belinda rubs her cigarette butt into the sole of one of her shoes.

"Ah, Ortega's – best Mexican food in town! Is it still here?" Donna asks.

"I asked Vern this morning. Still the same location and everything," Belinda responds.

"I believe it was the site of the last supper for us." Belinda looks at me with a curious look. I know exactly what meal to which she is referring but I say nothing.

Donna gets excited. "Oh I can taste their salsa. They always had great salsa. I can't get Tex-Mex in Denver. Not like here."

"Yep." Belinda continues staring at me. "So what do you think, Magpie, you wanna cruise around town with me?"

I grin slightly at my old nickname. We're grown women, not teenagers. We can do this civilly. What choice do I have? *God, are you here? Help!* "Let's do it. Where's Tracey?" I ask as we all stand up. "Shouldn't we take her?"

"Oh, yeah." Belinda's entire countenance drops. She sighs and says, "We could just leave her here. Vern won't mind. I'll go ask him if he'll deal with her." With this, she turns on her heel and heads toward the house. "I'll meet you both out front in a few minutes."

I watch her go through the back door. *Cecelia, why are you rewarding them? What happened? What happened to the Jesus Girls?*

Chapter 16

Belinda

"I suppose you want to drive, Belinda?" Donna's shoots nails at me with her eyes.

I'm already getting into my car. "I ain't gonna let nobody else, Miss Dougans."

"Shotgun," Maggie yells.

"Fine." Donna crawls into the back seat like a pouty toddler.

"You wanna sit in Tracey's car seat?"

"Very funny." She looks out the window.

I like driving and no way am I gonna let these two be in control of where we go. Maggie would end up taking us on a tour of the high school where she was queen of everything, and Donna would probably want to go to the cemetery where her mom's buried. No thank you to both of those bad ideas.

"I know our first stop." I skid off the curb onto the street.

"Belinda!" Donna's white knuckling the handhold above the passenger door.

I laugh. She's too easy. Maggie joins me and I'm a little surprised. But I remember when we used to look for thrills in this one-horse town while Donna always told us to stop. She still came along though.

"Remember that night we drove up and down Main Street asking for directions, Maggie?"

"With spray bottles?" Maggie giggles.

"I still can't believe we didn't get into more trouble." Donna's still holding on.

"We?" I ask. "If my memory serves me right you didn't join in."

At sixteen after I got my driver's license, I suggested the three of us drive up to fellow townspeople and ask for directions. After we got directions, we'd all yell, "Thank you," and then spray that person with water and drive off.

"I am amazed that people gave us directions, knowing we'd all lived here forever," Maggie quips.

"I participated," Donna says like she's four.

Maggie looks back at Donna. "Well, if hiding in the floor of the back seat pleading to go home is participating."

This is familiar. I remember us laughing and poking fun at Donna.

"Shut up." When I park she says, "The church, Belinda?"

We get out of the car and stand in front of the First Baptist Church. "I came by here last night. Looks even better in daylight."

"I'm surprised you want to come here, Belinda. Didn't you say talking to God was like talking to the air?"

"You pay attention, Magpie. That's good. Let's just say I look at this place like I would a museum dedicated to our childhood.

Great memories, but ain't nothing alive in there." I giggle a little. Maggie ignores me and looks at the church. I can tell she's trying to hide a bit of shock.

"Do you think anyone's here?" She walks up to the middle doors of the sanctuary and gives a push. They open.

We walk in and I swear I've walked into the past. It's kinda like I'm all color but entering a black and white TV. The sanctuary is beautiful with ten or so rows of pews and an altar with a huge podium on it in the middle. On the ground below, an ivory table stands with an inscription – 'In Remembrance of Me." The choir loft and its two rows of chairs are behind the pulpit. And located above the choir loft, set into the wall, is the baptismal. We stand in silence. I betcha the both of them are in that black and white TV set, too, seeing scenes from the 70's and 80'swhen we practically lived in this building.

"It looks the same as I remember." Donna sits in the back pew.

"The um, carpet has, uh, changed." The Barry White voice stands up from the front pew on the right and turns toward us. He's the man from last night. "Everything else is the sorta, well, kinda, uh the same."

"Pastor Ben, how are you?" Maggie leads us up the aisle. "Pastor, this is Donna and Belinda. They're here for Cecelia's funeral, too."

"I'm sorry. Um, for your loss." Mr. Gorgeous shakes hands with Donna first and when he takes my hand, a shock of electricity strikes me.

"Oh!" I say and laugh at the realization that the carpet caused the static.

"Um, maybe we need new uh, well, new carpet."

Our eyes meet and I like what I see. He has brown eyes that naturally glisten. He seems unsure of himself or maybe he just can't talk. A sorta stutter? I like his smile and he smells good. Probably married, though, and he's a preacher. I'd never go for a preacher. I have a couple of standards. At least two.

"Where are you from, um…? Belinda, uh, is it?" The deep and soothing voice. Oh my. "East Texas."

"Of course. That um, accent gives you away. Where, well, about in East Texas?"

Mr. Gorgeous is a little nosy, too. Wind Storm is probably buzzing about their local felon who flew the coop. I'm sure Jack made me a headline already.

"A tiny town. You ain't never heard of it." I change the subject. "You lived in Boots long?"

"Fifteen years."

He's staring at me. I know when a man is staring. I glance at Maggie and she's got a tiny grin on her smug face. We need to keep this moving. "Can we see the Sunbeam room?" I ask.

"Great idea," Donna chimes in.

"Absolutely. I think it's open." Ben shows us to the side door. "It's uh, just across the courtyard. I think, I guess, it's where it used to be. I don't know."

"Thank you," Maggie says.

"No problem." I glance back at him. He's still looking at me and says, "You need anything else, just let me know. And I'm truly, um truly sorry for your loss." With that, he goes back into the sanctuary.

"Wow. Talk about smitten," Maggie says, with that same grin stuck on her face. "He kept staring at you, Belinda."

"I get that a lot." I grin back.

"What happened to Brother Joe?" Donna asks.

Maggie explains the story to us as we walk into the Sunbeam Sunday School class.

The first thing I notice is the small colorful chairs parked in a semi circle at the back of the room. Different board games like Candy Land and Chutes and Ladders are in each corner and a craft table by the wall overflows with supplies.

"Wow. This brings back memories," Maggie says. "I can almost hear *Deep and Wide*."

"I remember that song. Mrs. Jackson played that piano right?" Donna points to an old stand up against a wall.

"She did. Donna, play something." Maggie asks.

"I don't play anymore," Donna states and picks up a paintbrush off a cabinet.

"Why not?" I walk toward her. There's a story there, I bet.

"I just don't, that's why."

Her eyes look like she's daring me to ask more. "Okay, just asking." I walk over to the wall with all the musical instruments. "Remember once a month we would get to play with Cecelia with sticks and tambourines and what not?"

"I don't remember that," Donna replies, "but I do remember stomping and clapping."

"We met in this room, didn't we?" Maggie sits in a tiny blue chair.

"No, we met at Mrs. Jackson's."

"Donna, you're wrong. We met right here under smiling Jesus." I see the spot by the door. "Right there."

"Oh, I remember that. But we'd already met before that," Maggie argues.

"The compromise." I point to the back wall. A huge picture of Jesus's face is painted.

"I don't remember what you're talking about," Donna says.

A memory comes clearly to mind. I have always possessed incredible recall. Doesn't pay the bills, but it helps with recipes. "Dad dropped me off at Cecelia's for baby-sitting. I was six, I think.

Lola Bee and Imogene came over and they argued about smiling Jesus."

I sat in the corner of the Visiting Room, pretending to cook a king and queen a meal. They got loud so I watched the conversation and heard ever' word.

"Even the very idea of a smile. I mean, that's just not gosher." Lola Bee shot her remark at Cecelia.

"Lola Bee, don't you mean kosher?" Imogene countered. "You ain't a Jew and you probably don't know any Jews so just keep kosher and gosher out of your vocabulary."

"Imogene, Jesus was a Jew, so I know a Jew, thank you very much. But not a smiling Jew, that's just not right."

"A smile, for your information, Lola Bee, is an expression. In this case, it communicates love," Cecelia argued.

"It is downright disrespectful is what it is." Lola Bee crossed her arms.

"You know what, Lola Bee, maybe we could get an artist to make a statue of you smiling. That might be a first." Imogene cackled.

Lola Bee stood up. "Cecelia, we are never told about Jesus smiling in the Bible. Do you know why? Because the Son of God is not a clown or some Jewish comedian!"

Silence.

"Lola Bee," Cecelia asserted, "I believe God inspired this idea in me and I am going to see it through. A Jesus who smiles will attract children to Christ. Brother Joe loves the idea."

"And Samuel Gomez? You know he is the only atheist in Boots. You got the only atheist in town to sculpt the SON OF GOD!"

"Lola Bee, he is also the only man who can sculpt anything in town." Cecelia offered.

"What about Floyd Harper? If you're gonna make this thing, get

a Christian to do it."

"Floyd Harper?" Imogene asked. "He's a welder, who works at the mine and makes misshaped animals out of iron on the side."

"You old heifer, Imogene! You are siding with Cecelia on this? Well, you both are a couple of blasphemers!" Lola Bee stomped out and I walked over to Cecelia.

"It's okay, Belinda. We're just arguing." And then to Imogene, "You know I saw the sculpture the other day and I think Samuel might get converted through this. I mean it looked Savior-worthy. Beautiful."

"We were in this very class when they unveiled the statue right by the door," I tell Donna. "We sat in those colored chairs and over there was a cloth-covered mountain."

"This is kind of coming back to me." Donna walks to the spot. "I think I remember."

"When Cecelia removed the cloth, a life-size Jesus stood there. He looked like a Middle Eastern Jesus, like those pictures we always see in a white gown and sandals. But He smiled at us. I remember smiling back at Him, He looked so real. Cecelia told us that Jesus knew how to have a good time. Adults came by during our class and after and ever'body voiced an opinion."

"Jesus should not be portrayed smiling!" Carol Fox spewed. "It takes away from the respect that we should instill in our children for God."

Guy Matthews agreed. "Why in the world do we want an atheist creating a statue of Jesus smiling? Did anyone ask Gomez if Jesus is laughing? 'Cause maybe he made Him that way to make fun of Baptists!"

When class ended, Imogene came in and told Cecelia that she heard that Jesus in the Sunbeam room was too Catholic for the Baptist church, and that He was too Charismatic for any self-respecting Southern Baptist. Lola Bee came and started arguing with Cecelia 'cause she heard someone say, "I heard that He is raising His hands."

"How do you remember all this, Belinda?" Donna scrunches up her forehead.

"I've always possessed an incredible memory for details. Don't you remember that?" I grin at her. "A while after smiling Jesus arrived here, Cecelia taught us about Noah and we sat over there in a circle for story time. Cecelia put up some picture on the flannel graph board and then, 'Shwaaap!'"

"What happened?" Donna asks.

Maggie snaps her fingers. "You're talking about that bird."

"Remember?" I ask.

"Mrs. Jackson, did you see the bird?" I pointed it out.

"What?" Cecelia walked to the front door to check out the noise.

SHWAAAP! This time, Cecelia shrieked, and when she screamed we all started screaming. She tried to calm us down but we kept yelling. SHWAAAP! The screams turned into crying. All of us sun-beamers poured rain.

"Okay, okay, let's all calm down. I know, let's listen to some music." Cecelia turned on the record player, and June Carter Cash started singing, "I'll Fly Away."

Then this big, black crow swept through the open window and flew in here and it started diving down and soaring up trying to find a way out. We stopped screaming and crying and started laughing and running. We tried to chase the bird out the window. When it finally left, we all cheered.

"What does that have to do with the smiling Jesus statue?" Donna looks at me and I realize she truly has no memory whatsoever of this.

"The day after the crow incident was the first day of Vacation Bible School. The three of us stood in front of the statue singing *I'll Fly Away* when Brother Joe and Cecelia and Lola Bee walked in the room."

Maggie starts laughing. "Oh, I remember."

Lola Bee yelled, "Are they singing to that thing? Brother Joe, it is an idol!"

We stopped singing and turned to look at the adults.

Cecelia said, "Girls, how lovely. You can sing really well."

Brother Joe grabbed a little chair, sat right in front of us, and said, "Young ladies, I want to ask you a question, okay?" Lola Bee came and stood beside him. He continued, "You know this isn't really Jesus, right? This is just a statue of Him. You know that, don't you?"

We all nodded and I said, "Of course, silly. We know it isn't the real Jesus."

"But you know," Maggie said, "we think this Jesus could be real."

I looked at Maggie and giggled.

"How's that?" Brother Joe asked.

"We can't tell," Donna whispered. "He might be embarrassed."

"Are you saying that Jesus might possess shame?" Lola Bee pointed out, as if her observation won the argument.

"I would be embarrassed. My mom would get mad at me," Maggie grinned and covered her mouth with her hands.

"Girls," Cecelia said gently, "what are you talking about?"

"Well," I began and I paused, trying not to laugh, "He poops!" We pointed to the statue and started squealing.

"Oh my Lord!!" Lola Bee pointed at smiling Jesus.

On the side of the upper thigh of the Savior of the world, a huge glob of nothing else but black crow dung clung.

Two business meetings later, the non-smiling Jesus contention won the vote. In a secret ballot deemed the most important vote of the seventies, the First Baptist Church decided to get rid of Jesus.

We all laugh.

"They tried to sell it to the Catholics but they wouldn't take it," Maggie comments, making us laugh more.

"That bird poop scared Lola Bee to death," I offer.

"Whatever happened to that statue?" Donna asks.

"A travelling evangelist bought it. A Methodist." Maggie giggles.

"I don't remember that," I remark.

"Cecelia told me a few years ago." Maggie looks at the mural of Jesus. "She loved telling me that story."

Oh. Apparently, Maggie has continued to be close to Cecelia. Just as always, Maggie did the right thing and remained the nicest, sweetest and purest girl in the room. I don't want to think about that. I turn to go.

"So you kept in touch with Cecelia all these years, Maggie?" Donna asks.

"Yes." Maggie follows me to the door. "We talked often." Her voice cracks a bit.

I stop and look back at Maggie. I have to ask Miss Little Goodie. "How can you still believe all this, Maggie? Smiling Jesus, Pooping Jesus, Jesus the one Son of God, supposedly. The Jesus who asks *way* too much of ever'one." I don't wait for an answer. It would probably be a Bible verse anyway. She ain't really lived in the real world. "I just don't get how you can still believe at your age." I turn and walk out, quick-like. I don't want to hear her sermon.

As I reach the car to get in, I hear Maggie mumbling as she walks across the courtyard. "I don't see how you can't."

Chapter 17

Donna

Wonderful. I'm with the religious right and the liberal left. Can't we just live in the middle? It's all blah, blah, blah anyway. I need some chocolate.

"Can we stop by the cemetery?" I should probably go although I don't want to. It's been twenty-five years since I saw her grave.

Belinda lets out a long sigh. "Donna, I don't mean to be insensitive. Well, maybe." She laughs her hard little laugh. "I'm just hungry, that's all."

I look out the window and stare at the little houses in this desert town. Lunch sounds perfect, but I don't want to act too interested. Belinda is downright mean. Maggie will say something anyway. Let her be rude.

"Belinda, we could stop by for just a minute. We have time." Maggie as always, comes to the rescue.

Perfect.

"It's okay, Maggie. I can go later." I'm serious. Food sounds fantastic. I look toward the front seat, Maggie is staring at Belinda, and Belinda is glancing at me in her mirror. She's taking my temperature. "Really, Maggie. I'm fine. Let's go to Ortega's."

Belinda grins a little and takes a turn that will take us toward the restaurant.

Maggie looks back at me with compassion. "Are you okay?"

Please. She is so fake. "Maggie, let it go. We happen to be here for a funeral so I will be visiting the cemetery tomorrow anyway." I know I offended her when she turns away. I don't care. I'm hungry.

Ortega's looks different but I don't know why. We walk through the restaurant and I see no one looks even a little familiar. We're seated and my mouth waters looking at the menu. I've missed genuine Tex-Mex cuisine. Denver has Mexican food, but it resembles the New Mexican kind with tons of sauce smothering everything. I order tacos, Belinda enchiladas, and Maggie asks for a burrito.

"I'm gonna go out for a smoke. I'll be back in a bit." Belinda stands and leaves.

Maggie and I sit in silence. I really don't know her at all but I know Belinda even less. "She is so abrasive. I don't remember her being that way. Funny, yes. Bitter, no."

Maggie shrugs her shoulders. Nothing. Fine with me.

Belinda returns just as the waitress delivers the food. As she leaves, another woman approaches our table. "Oh my goodness! I can't believe my eyes."

"Alana!" Maggie stands up and gives the woman a big hug. It's Alana Rodarte, a fellow graduate of the class of 1987. Belinda and I take turns hugging her. I didn't know Alana well, but Belinda and she were both in volleyball.

"You still live here?" Belinda asks.

"I married Robert Ortega. So I own Ortega's now." Alana gives a look to the waitress and she comes over to fill our water glasses.

"No kidding?" Maggie asks. "We are back for Cecelia Jackson's funeral and of course, we had to eat here."

"So sorry to hear about that. What a loss for us, but what a gain for God, right?" Alana smiles at Maggie.

"Absolutely," Maggie agrees.

Alana Rodarte, um Ortega, believes in God? Wasn't she a hell-raiser?

"Wait a second, Alana. When did you get all religious?" Of course, Belinda would be so blunt as to ask. However, I am interested, too.

"I made a lot of mistakes growing up but the grace of God protected me and a few years ago I decided to follow Christ. You all are Christians, right?"

"This food looks delicious," I change the subject.

"Thank you for coming in." Alana doesn't push anything. "Enjoy your food and it's so good to see you." She leaves.

Maggie glares at me but I ignore her and concentrate on the food. The tacos bring back the spicy tastes and smells of Boots' cuisine to me. We eat silently and that is fine with me. If I ask about Maggie's family or Belinda's life in East Texas, they will ask me questions. I don't want these two in my world at all. I ask for more chips and salsa and I don't care what Maggie and Belinda think. It all tastes so wonderful.

The two sticks I'm eating with finish and the waitress approaches. "Can I get you ladies take-out containers?"

Belinda and Maggie refuse. I don't even look up. I intend to enjoy every bite.

"We have to go through the Dairy Queen." I suggest this when we get back into Belinda's Honda.

"Are you still hungry?"

I can't tell if Belinda says this because she is full or because she wants to dig at me. Probably a dig. So I'm fat? So what? I want to say this.

Maggie speaks before I can answer, "I would love to go through the Dairy Queen. Belinda, you are outvoted on this one." Her tone is challenging as if she is daring Belinda to fight with her.

"Hey, settle down. I would love a Dilly Bar, Miss Thing. I told you that before." Her smile is as unreal as her hair.

Going through the drive through is surreal. I have glimpses of the three of us talking over each other reaching to get coke floats. Today we quietly take our Dilly Bars and Belinda drives to Boots High. At the school, we get out of the car, Dilly Bars in hand and head to the benches on the front grass.

"Let's finish our ice cream out here and then look inside," Maggie suggests and we sit.

"You'd think they would've improved this old school. Looks like the same one hall building of twenty-five years ago. I wonder what they use taxes for in this God-forsaken backwards town." Belinda remarks.

She was always outspoken, that I remember.

"And that football field we passed. It looks exactly the same. Seems they could've improved it over the years."

"Why don't we each say our favorite memory of being at this school?" Maggie suggests.

I don't mind Maggie's fakeness right now. Anything to get Belinda to stop whining.

"But what party game will we play next?" Belinda snarls.

I ignore Belinda. "I remember the night we came to watch a basketball game in the gym and Tommy Duncan drove me home after." I giggle. "We dated for three or four months after that. "

"Tommy Duncan adored you." Maggie leans into me and nudges me with her shoulder. I look at her and see the chocolate on her lip.

"Did you dump him or he you? I don't remember." Belinda remarks.

I squint at her. "Yeah, right. You with the great memory? You know he dumped me. He wanted to date Sally Cudgeon."

"But those months you were with him you were so happy. I couldn't believe he broke it off. It didn't last with Sally, you know." Maggie smiles and wipes her face.

"What about you, Maggie? What's your favorite memory?" I really want to know. Will she mention Alan?

She smiles. "I think it's Mr. Donaway's Civics class. We laughed so much."

Belinda stands up. "Mr. Donaway was a great teacher. Remember his Friday jokes?"

I can't believe she's smiling. A real smile.

"And remember when we snuck into the school for the senior prank?" Belinda continues. "And we took everything out of his room and put it on the roof."

I laugh. It is a great memory.

"My mom got so mad when she heard about that," Maggie adds. "But I didn't care."

"So mine is Tommy Duncan and Maggie's is Mr. Donaway's class. What's yours, Belinda? You probably have lots to pick from with your memory skills."

"Hmm." She licks the last of the ice cream off her stick. "I think I'm gonna say Mr. Fuentes." Her eyebrows go up and down as she says the name.

Maggie and I burst out laughing and stand up simultaneously.

"Oh remember his shirts?" I say, walking towards the trashcan.

"They were always unbuttoned just enough for all of us to see his black chest hair curling up and peeking out," Belinda points out.

Maggie nods. "I still think he used a curling iron on that hair before he came to school."

I join in, "So good looking."

Belinda elbows my arm. "I think he was too good looking."

"What do you mean by that?"

"Well, gorgeous and single, he curled his chest hair, he moved away to New York City. And his favorite singer - Barbra Streisand." There go the eyebrows again.

"No way!" Maggie and I yell. I feel like a teenager.

Before we go in, I ask, "Do either one of you know what happened to Tommy Duncan?"

"He married Sally Cudgeon and they have seven kids," Belinda replies.

"No. Really?"

"She's just kidding you, Donna," Maggie says while Belinda laughs again. "Tommy Duncan is a preacher. He has a church in Phoenix of about 2000 people. Never would have guessed it from all of his days here, huh? Didn't we pray for him? I can't remember exactly but I think we did."

I chuckle. Yeah, like our prayers had anything to do with it. My phone plays the jingle that tells me I have an incoming text message. "Just a second." I walk away, pull out my phone, and read it.

Very excited to see you Donna. Text address and I will come meet you tonight.

It's from William.

"Do tell, Donna. Secret lover?"

I look up and catch Belinda's wink. I feel my face go hot and I quickly close the phone. "No, nothing like that. It's work."

Belinda tilts her head. "Well, work must be pretty good right now."

"You are on your phone a lot, Donna. Do you have to be for work?" Maggie asks.

"Excuse me for a second. I need to text back." I ignore Maggie's question and think about my reply.

7400 Summer Street in Boots. Come at 7 p.m. sharp and call me before you arrive and I will meet you out front. Important that you call first.

As soon as I hit send, I feel regret. What am I going to tell Belinda and Maggie? What if he hates the way I look? But then again, what if William is *the one* and this is the beginning to a passionate love story? This is a good thing. I join my old friends as we walk to the front door of the high school. Belinda and Maggie are staring at me.

"So, are you going to tell us what happened?" Maggie asks.

"What?"

"Well, Donna your face absolutely lit up. Does work really do that for you?" Maggie has a point.

"What do you do for a living anyway?" Belinda pushes.

I stare back at the two ladies. They are like strangers to me. So why not tell them? After tomorrow, I'll never see them again.

"I'm an accountant. A friend of mine named William lives in Marshall."

"So it wasn't work." Belinda says this as if she's solved a murder mystery.

"The Marshall near here?" Maggie asks.

"Yes. And he is going to come meet or rather see me tonight."

"You're gonna still help make the meal, right?" Belinda jabs.

"Of course. I'll just take an hour-long break. No big deal." Even as I speak, I know that this is, in fact, a very big deal. I've been corresponding online with William for months. Now I'll finally get to meet him face to face.

"How long have you known him, Donna? Did you come out here before?" Maggie is beginning an interrogation.

"Let's go in and check out the old alma mater, shall we?" I grab the door handle to the Boots High entrance. The future with William smells sweet, scented with hope of love and companionship. But first, I have to deal with Boots, Belinda, and Maggie. Here, walking in nostalgia smells like overwhelming perfume. Nice, but part of it chokes.

Chapter 18

Belinda

As we tour the school, we find very little that reminds us of the old days. The trophy case by the front door only contains one of the trophies won during the years we attended. According to the current yearbook we found and looked through in the office, all the administration and teachers are new. Except one. "Well, I'll be, look at that. It's Mrs. Morris." The picture shows me she's older but remarkably the same. "I thought she would've kicked the bucket by now. Let's go see her."

We walk into the library and see a hunched-over old woman shelving books in the corner. We see her and all three of us start to giggle. The sound of our laughter, as we stand in this place, moves me. I gotta keep it together. But I feel like I'm in a movie made twenty-five years ago.

"Shhh!" Mrs. Morris turns and glares. And then recognition comes into her eyes. "My oh my!" She walks closer to us. "If it isn't those three little troublemakers I used to make leave my library! You all grew up!"

I lead the way and we give Mrs. Morris a group hug.

"Tell me your names again, ladies. Don't be offended that I don't remember either. At my age, remembering the Dewey decimal system is an award-winning feat."

"I'm Maggie Shanks, Mrs. Morris. I used to be Maggie Curry."

"Yes, I remember your brother Barry. How is he? He was such a fine, young man."

"He is a judge in Arkansas and he's doing really well. I'll tell him you said hi."

"I'm Belinda Kite, Mrs. Morris."

"Belinda. Oh, honey, you were voted homecoming queen, right?"

"You remember that?"

"It is a peculiar thing, the memory. Yes, I remember your smile. You had the most beautiful smile. And didn't you have red hair?"

"It's been so long, I don't know what my original hair color is." I grin, hoping Mrs. Morris will stop talking about how I used to look. I think about reproducing that old smile for her but I can't. I just don't have much to smile about.

"Honey, I think all of our bodies age, but a smile...well, that never grows old. Belinda, tell me about your family. You had two younger brothers, right? Where are they?"

I look at the floor, desperate for a way to change the subject. I don't like talking about the past. Any of it. It's irrelevant. No topic comes to mind and I keep staring at the floor. Maybe the old woman will have a lapse in short term memory and ask Donna a question.

"Well, sweetie, what's the story? This room is full of them, go ahead and tell me another." Mrs. Morris is direct.

I don't want to tell the truth. None of her business that my father, stepmother, and half-brothers don't talk to me anymore.

"I think they're in Dallas. I'm not sure." I look up and the woman, though shorter and tinier than me is hovering over me.

"Belinda Kite, you find your family and give them a call."

Mrs. Morris was always kind to me, but no one gets to talk to me as if I'm a child. I decide to tell her what she can do with her librarian order.

"Mrs. Morris, do you know who I am?" Donna blurts out.

Mrs. Morris turns her gaze to Donna. "I remember your face, but what is your name?"

"I'm Donna Dougans, Mrs. Morris," Donna yells.

Mrs. Morris peers at her. "Sweetheart, I'm old, but I am not deaf."

"Sorry," Donna says.

"What?" Mrs. Morris says. Donna begins to yell again, but Mrs. Morris stops her. "I'm kidding, sweetie."

Maggie and me laugh, but I don't think Donna appreciates the old woman's humor.

"Now, I bet you are all in town for the funeral, right? Cecelia was a friend of mine. I never met a better Canasta player."

"That's right. I haven't played Canasta since I left here. We have to play during one of our tuna fish breaks." Donna offers.

"I play quite often with my boys. I force them. It improves their memory," Maggie says.

"Did you all play with Cecelia?" Mrs. Morris asks.

"We used to play for hours." My thoughts turn to many an afternoon at the Formica white table in Cecelia's kitchen. Those were wonderful afternoons.

"I know she will be missed. Thank you, Jesus, I'll get to see her again. Maybe soon."

Donna pipes up abruptly, "I am going to look for a book," and walks away.

Miss Little Goodie warms up at the mention of Jesus and touches Mrs. Morris's arm. "I think that's what helps me the most right now. Knowing I will still see her, and who knows, maybe play Canasta with her in heaven. She loved Jesus so much."

"He definitely got a kick out of her. I bet He welcomed her like an old friend with a kiss and a long hug," The librarian adds. Mrs. Morris's eyes get misty and so do Maggie's.

I head toward Donna. Gooeyness makes me uncomfortable. And especially religious gooeyness. Cecelia is just gone. No heaven. No hell. Just gone.

From a bookshelf in the corner, Donna calls out, "Hey, look, I found one! It's a yearbook from 1986-87." We all gather at a table and Donna opens it up.

"This'll be a hoot, Donna." I sit down and genuine excitement bubbles. I don't feel this emotion much.

"Excuse us, okay, Mrs. Morris?" asks Maggie.

"Have a wonderful trip down memory lane, ladies. You know I just remembered what we teachers used to call you three."

I look up and ask, "What was that?"

"Bee, Dee, and Magpie." She smiles and her wrinkles all move like a flock of birds going in the other direction. "I'm going to the office and I'll be back in a while. Library is closed to the students right now."

I feel icecaps melting. Maybe we'll get through these couple of days without pulling off the scabs of old wounds. Maggie brought it up but she got sick so she won't talk about it again. We had ourselves some good times. It'd sure be nice if we can just remember those, leave and never see each other again. I hope.

We laugh at the old photos and the fashions and the hairdos. Our laughter is the kind that only happens cause of years of private jokes and tears and petty fights and make-ups. It's a laughter born of old friends and it's a laughter that tastes good kinda like my personal recipe for blueberry pie.

"Remember Audrey Forsythe? Whatever happened to her?"

"She still lives here. Maybe she'll be at the funeral. I believe she teaches fourth grade." Maggie fills us in.

"How do you know about everyone?" I ask.

"Well, not everyone. But Cecelia and I wrote letters and called each other all the time."

Shoot. We all get quiet.

"Did she write to you about me?" Donna inquires.

"No, she never talked to me about you or Belinda." After a long pause, she asks, "Did you talk to her about me?"

"I only talked to Cecelia a few times over the years. She wrote my kid a lot, but I only talked to her twice. We never talked about the two of you."

"That's funny. She wrote me a lot, too. I'm not much of a letter writer. I talked to her once a week during college, but only one time after that," Donna says.

"What did you talk about?" Maggie asks.

"Nothing."

An awkwardness sits with us. But darnitt, we was having fun. I chase it away. "We have to find a picture of Hughford Crave!" I suggest.

"Yes!" Maggie and Donna break out in big ole smiles. Once we find it, Hughford's picture brings another memory to my mind.

"The three of us and Hu in Trigonometry, remember?"

"I loved him so much," Donna gushes.

"You did not," Maggie counters.

"Kind of," Donna shoots back.

"We all loved him," I settle the matter.

As if twenty-five years haven't passed, we look at each other and in perfect unison say the line that had made us laugh countless times in high school.

"I Crave Hu!"

The icy walls between us tumble down like a glacier in a National Geographic video.

Maggie stands up. "You know what, ladies? We have a job to do."

"That's right. We got some tuna fish to create." Donna adds a touch of a southern accent.

"Isn't it something that in just a matter of hours we will become privy to a recipe held in top secret form for years?" Maggie is excited.

"I guess you don't remember anything about me and tuna, huh?" I follow the ladies as they walk to the exit of the library.

"What are you talking about? Oh, that's right." Donna giggles.

"I don't remember. What is it?" Maggie asks.

"Belinda hates tuna fish."

"Did you hate it back then?"

"I have always hated tuna fish. Cecelia tried to convert me to it, but it just never took. It was the only dish she prepared that I hated with a capital H."

"Please tell me you can still help, though," Maggie asks.

"Of course, I don't have to eat it. I'm a great cook, but I never cook with tuna."

"Your pancakes were delicious." Donna holds the door of the library open for us.

"You have Cecelia's gift, Belinda. You should lead us in the tuna making." Maggie offers.

"I think you should have a sandwich in Cecelia's honor," Donna teases.

Maggie joins in the sentiment, "I think so, too. It would be like lighting a candle for a Catholic, or throwing a sailor's ashes into the sea."

"Maybe I'll write her a wonderfully thought out cowboy poem." Donna giggles.

Memories of bad cowboy poetry hit me. Cecelia wrote horrible poetry and always thought ever' line was wonderful and award winning. I laugh at the thought. "She could rhyme, though."

As we walk the high school hallway of our youth, Maggie asks, "Do you two remember what we used to say about her poetry?"

"Oh, my gosh, that's right." I remember another one of our private jokes. "Poetry so good you can smell the cow patties!"

Our laughter carries us to the office to say goodbye to Mrs. Morris. We're still giggling like schoolgirls when we get back into my car. I really loved these ladies once upon a time. My heart is happy and that ain't happened for quite a spell.

"Belinda, what is it?" Maggie asks me, still laughing.

"What?"

"You look like you remember something funny. Tell us."

"Nothing. I'm just happy." Soon as I say it, guilt comes a calling. I'm about to abandon my daughter and leave the country, a felon. But I gotta do what I gotta do. As we leave the high school, I think of Hank and how I'll never see his miserable face, or that dust cloud of a town again. I can't help it. I laugh out loud.

Chapter 19

Maggie

Riding in the car with these two fills me up with nostalgia that tastes like hot chocolate. Warm and satisfying. *Father, what a hoot, visiting Boots High.* Hoot? Oh my word, I sound like Bee. I used to love these ladies. Maybe it is time to forgive and forget and just get on with life. We are adults, after all. That's what you want right, Lord? I bet that's what Cecelia had in mind.

"Boots could use a Wal-Mart. Why don't we just drive over to Marshall and shop? I bet you they have one." Donna suggests this as Belinda parks in the little parking lot behind Coulters Grocery Store.

I open the door to get out. "We can't do that Donna. A few years ago, Vern and Cecelia led a campaign against having one placed in Boots. They were very anti-mega-superstore."

"You just want to get closer to Mr. Fabulous. What's his name again, Donna?" Belinda winks at me.

"You can just call him Mr. None of Belinda's Business."

Coulters is the only grocery store in Boots and has been for as long as I can remember. It is a good size, nothing like the huge supermarkets of Tucson, but much bigger than a gas stop or a 7-11. I dated the Coulters' youngest, Don, for a month in ninth grade. I remember going to their house and really liking Mrs. Coulter. She was a Methodist and made great cookies.

Donna giggles as we go inside. "Do you think we should call Charlie after this, Angels?"

To which Belinda replies, "That reminds me. I have to buy three cans of Aqua Net hairspray for my Texas bouffant hairdo. And some bikini wax."

I give her a tiny shove. "Do not tell me they sell bikini wax in Boots!"

We are under strict instructions from Vern to not shop together. He gave us three separate lists with different items on each one. Before we split up, I notice I forgot my list. "Oh shoot. Belinda is your car open? I left my list."

"Here are my keys."

I go and get my list and walk back in. I look around at all the aisles. This place is just as I remember. Well, almost. There is an ATM, a Redbox video dispensary, and a magazine rack up front. I know they never sold magazines back then because I always bought my *Sixteen* magazine in El Paso.

Tuna is on aisle four out of twelve aisles. I walk to it and find the particular brand Cecelia specified and start putting the ones marked "packed in oil" into my basket.

A few years ago, Cecelia called to tell me a story. That year the media acclaimed spring water tuna as the healthy tuna that prevented heart failure. Cecelia said she succumbed to the pressure and tried an oil-free can. She and Vern both took one bite and then silently and simultaneously, spit said bites into their napkins. In one accord they stood up, and took the bowl of tuna fish and their individual plates to the trashcan.

The next day Cecelia marched into Coulters Grocer and explained to Mr. Coulter that the spring water tuna fish tasted like cardboard. She spread the word throughout Boots that her sandwiches consisted only of oily tuna. Elsewhere, folks might consider a discussion of tuna fish silly, but in Boots, where eating a Jackson tuna fish sandwich was like eating a New York City hot dog or a Philadelphia cheese steak, the announcement possessed merit.

Cecelia sent me a copy of 'Nancy's News,' a weekly column in the *Boots Advocate*:

"*It has been reported to this particular reporter that the culinary delight known to all Boots inhabitants as Cecelia's tuna fish sandwiches, will heretofore and forever only contain tuna packed in oil. As this announcement comes in the middle of the national trend toward healthier spring water packed tuna, the tension of controversy filled the room at a discussion of this decision at Ortega's this week. While dining on an Ortega's favorite, the chicken enchiladas topped with sour cream finished with hot sopapillas and honey,* (Nancy Ortega, the original owner's daughter, often dropped their menu specials into her column) *Mrs. Jackson was asked why she couldn't adapt to the changing times. Cecelia replied, 'Sugar, the changing times will never change the taste of my tuna.'*"

So the tuna fish sandwiches remained delicious and oily.

Sighing at the health implications of this, I continue stacking tuna cans into my shopping cart. As I do this, I am overwhelmed with the memory of my mother and me in this store. We talked here, really talked. My father never came into this place, on account of a grudge against Stanley Coulter that he preserved with great care for years. Something to do with a conversation about drinking. I don't know the details. I feel the same warmth for my mother right now as I did in those days when we shopped here. No resentment or bitterness hung in the air between us when we went shopping.

"Why lookie here. Maggie Curry, what in blue-blazes are you doing here?"

The loud voice of Imogene Friesen startles me. I look to my right and there she stands. "Hello, Imogene. It's Maggie Shanks now. I'm shopping for the tuna fish sandwiches."

"That's right, you told me your new name. I just went and forgot. You're shopping, dear?" It's obvious she knows I'm shopping for the tuna fish. "Really?" she continues feigning surprise. "Can I help you gather anything?"

The sad attempt at manipulation is obvious. Two can play this. "You know what? You could go get me a couple things."

"Sweetie, you name it." Imogene whips out a pad and pen from her large brown purse.

"I need some razor blades, a People magazine and some candy bars."

Imogene is halfway into writing the list when she looks up and sees my grin. Her loud laugh fills up the store like a sudden burst of smoke out of a chimney. "Wilbur says, well actually he used to say, he doesn't talk much anymore, seeing as how he got the mouth cancer and all, did I tell you this?"

"Yes, ma'am."

"So you know he's a bit on the quiet side, well, he used to tell me all the time that I was a bad liar. I just don't have the acting abilities it takes. Although I did try out for the Boots Rodeo One Act Theatre and Mr. Portubena, he's an I –talian feller that ran the movie theatre and wants to start a real theatre in Marshall some time. Right now he owns the DVD store. He's married, he says, but I don't know anyone who knows his wife. Weird, ain't it? Well, he said, I possessed great potential for neighbor roles, but in the play they was doing at the time, they didn't need no neighbors."

It occurs to me I've never run across a woman like Imogene in Tucson. She is unique.

"You see, you know and I know, if this here was a play, then the audience probably done got up and left cause of my bad acting. But movie star or not, I feel it would be a huge injustice to just take that recipe out of Boots. There, I said my piece! It just ain't right, Maggie Curry. Um, I mean Hanks. Hanks, right?"

I let it go.

"Your mama and daddy raised you right. If they was standing here they'd say the exact same thing. You know that recipe should stay here in our little community."

"Imogene, my father, the town drunk, beat my mom and she lived in terror and ignored me." The words just tumble out and immediately I am embarrassed about my outburst.

Imogene's face softens. A moment passes before she offers, "You turned out just fine, it seems. Nobody has to hang on to the past, that's for sure. It's your choice to let it go and kill it off if you want to."

"I'm sorry, Imogene. Coming back here has raised some feelings, that's all."

"Girl, you listen to me. I knew your daddy was a drunk. Whole town pretty much knew that. And I knew your poor 'ole mama raised you and your brother with wide-eyed fear all the time. But I think she feared *for* you, not *of* him. She's still living, right? You ought to talk to her about it."

"I couldn't do that." I'm suddenly aware that we are having this personal conversation between the tuna fish and the peanut butter. "My mother doesn't want to talk to me. She never really liked me that much. I think she gave most of her love to my brother and I don't blame her. He took care of her. When he finished college, she and my father went to Arkansas to live by him. They never even asked me to come. Anyway, I got some counseling about this, and I really thought Jesus had healed those wounds. Maybe not, though. She did finally put him out. Or maybe my brother did, I don't know. Daddy died on the streets a few years ago."

Imogene touches my arm. "I am so sorry. Maybe Jesus is telling you to go talk to your mama. He's just using tuna as a way to get your attention."

"You know, Imogene, Cecelia never asked me questions about Mother. Sometimes I would go to her house in the middle of the night. She would just direct me to a bedroom. I have wondered more than once why she didn't ask."

"Honey, Cecelia knew everything. She talked to your mama all the time."

"She did?"

"Absolutely. She tried to get your mama to leave your daddy. But your mama wouldn't have none of that. Cecelia offered to have you and your brother live with her, so you could always be safe, just in case your daddy ever got a hankering to beat up on you two. But your mama said no."

I am shocked. "Imogene, I have stayed in touch with Cecelia for years since I left here. She didn't tell me she stayed in touch with Belinda and Donna and she certainly never mentioned anything about talking to my mother."

"Magdalene May, you and I both know that Cecelia would never tell you. She told me 'cause I am nosy and happened to be her best friend. But what was between your mama and her wadn't your business. You were her daughter, not her friend."

"Imogene, did she tell you about my cancer?"

Imogene's rough exterior completely transforms to the softness of an angel. "Yes, she did, Maggie." I realize that Imogene is now holding my hand. "But now, you do have the chance to ask your mama about all this, seeing as how you are now fully informed."

I consider what it might be like to go to Arkansas and see Barry and Mother. The thought is uncomfortable. But maybe if Frank went with me. Maybe someday.

"Now, let's get back to something real deep and personal." Imogene smiles big, and her mole looks like a chocolate chip on her cheek. "Let's talk tuna."

"Imogene, you know that I cannot tell you anything about the recipe." I can't help but be a bit impressed with her determination.

"What if I told you what you just said could send me to counseling?"

Now my laugh fills the air. "I'd say maybe Jesus is telling you to go talk to someone you haven't in a while. Maybe He's using tuna fish to get your attention."

Imogene's cackle erupts. "This is not over, young lady. God has a way of working mysteriously. And I and a bunch of old women who've been talking to Him for years are currently praying that tuna fish recipe stays here in Boots."

"We'll see, Imogene. Right now I have some shopping to do." I push my cart past Imogene and go around the corner to the pickles.

God, You do work in mysterious ways. A divine appointment in Coulters? Thank You.

Even as I pray this in my heart, I spy a pair of eyes between the ketchup bottles watching my every move. Lola Bee Turner. As I check out, I hear four women whispering by the magazines.

"Did you get anything?"

"Donna is buying toilet paper for goodness sakes."

"Belinda bought some produce but most of it will not go into tuna fish."

"Calm down ladies, write down everything they bought. We'll figure it out."

My word, they are determined. I giggle as I push my cart out to Belinda's car. She and Donna aren't out yet so I take Belinda's keys out of my purse and open up the trunk. There are a couple of bags in it, but still plenty of room for all of our groceries. Soon Donna appears beside me, her shopping cart full of drinks and toilet paper and spices.

"Did you see Imogene and Lola Bee and their cronies in there?" Donna asks.

"Yes. But I don't think anyone could figure out a recipe with all this stuff." I begin putting bags in and Donna helps me. An old blanket is near the back of the trunk and Donna shoves it up a bit so we can have more room for bags. After she moves it, I see a twenty-dollar bill.

"Belinda would want to know about this money." I pick it up.

"Finders keepers, losers' weepers," Donna jokes.

I notice another bill and I reach down to lift up the blanket. Several twenty-dollar bills are sticking out of a red bag.

"What in the world?" Donna asks, reaching down for the bag.

"Donna, that's none of our business." But Donna has the bag in her hands and opens it up. It is full of cash.

Chapter 20

Belinda

When I mosey out of Coulters, I see Maggie and Donna standing by the trunk of my car staring at the red bag. No! Darnitt, they can't see that. How dare they put their sweet little non-snot noses into my business. Nothing's changed. I run my cart to the car and try to bump into Donna.

She dodges and yells, "Belinda!"

I grab the red bag and I let 'em have it. "We ain't little girls who share ever'thing anymore. We ain't teenagers who get all sappy about religion. We're grown women and basic strangers so let's mind our own business. How dare you guys snoop around in my belongings?"

I lean over the trunk and stuff the bag into the back of it. I start chucking my groceries into the trunk on top of the other sacks.

"Hey!" Donna says, "You're going to break the eggs."

"Belinda, I'm sorry…" Maggie begins.

"Shut up, little Miss Perfect. Guess you ain't so perfect after all, huh?" I slam the trunk.

I'm so furious I can't say a word. I start driving like a roadrunner streaking 'cross the desert. I aim for every pothole and I fly cross the railroad tracks, hoping their heads crash on the roof. I swerve around corners, just begging them to say something. *Say something, you phony cows.* How could they do that? Snoop at my private business. And how could I be so stupid? Didn't I realize we'd have to use the trunk for the groceries? They don't say a word. I consider running a couple of stop signs just to scare 'em. Hurt 'em.

At the Jackson's, I open up the trunk and we start unloading the groceries. Nobody says nothing. They ain't got the guts to speak to me. Vern comes into the kitchen just as I set down the last bag.

"So, how'd our double-0-7 mission go?"

I glance at Maggie and Donna and then say, "Fine. Snoopers were there but I would say we successfully diverted their attempts at the secret ingredients." I force a smile. It's not Vern's fault that I'm stuck with two buttinskis.

"Well, little ladies, I'll go get the actual recipe. Believe it or not, it's at the Boots Bank in our safety deposit box. You can put up everything and get some shut-eye. You're probably going to be up all night. After you sleep, come on in here, have some supper and then start this here process. I'll put the recipe in the silverware drawer. While I'm out, I'm gonna meet the new preacher at Bells and talk 'bout the funeral tomorrow. Then I'll turn in early. We have a TV in our room so I'll probably watch an old western and fall asleep. So I probably won't see you three again 'til the morning."

Vern grabs his keys off the counter and turns to us, "Belinda, your young'un is a sweet little lady. I think she's in the visiting room or somewhere 'round here. You did a good job with that one."

I stare at Vern as he leaves. A good job? He is a blind ole' man. We start unbagging groceries in silence and then Donna speaks.

"Did you rob a bank, Belinda?"

I stop putting the butter up and stare. "Donna Gail, you ain't got no idea what you're starting here, so I'd just stop right now if I were you."

Donna is stupid enough to keep going. "We don't know each other anymore, Belinda. You're right about that. But I would never guess in my wildest dreams that you were a criminal."

"Just 'cause I have money in a bag don't make me no criminal, Donna. Maybe that's how I bank. And anyway it's none of your business."

The idiot keeps pushing me. "I think it is. I'm an accountant and I could tell by looking into that bag that you were carrying a great deal of money in there. So if it is stolen property, by seeing it, I just became an accessory to your crime."

I feel hot and start to breathe hard. I look down at the butter in my hand and I try to slow down my breathing. In and out. In and out. It don't work. "You big 'ole sanctimonious fat cow. You don't dare threaten me—"

"Listen, ladies, let's just take a minute and calm..." Maggie injects.

"And you shut up, Sister Maggie!" I turn to her. "You stand there like you're a saint, but you're the one I loaned my keys to, *only* to get your list. Not to snoop around in my trunk."

"Belinda, if I am a fat cow then you are a little bleached blond hooker!"

I take the butter and throw it at that fat cow's face. Donna dodges it but it hits her shoulder.

"Ow!" she cries out.

I walk out and up the stairs to my room. My suitcase is under the bed and I pull it out and throw it on the bed. I open it and start grabbing my clothes from the chest of drawers. This rodeo is over and I'm outta here. Can't they see? Can't Vern and all of 'em see I have no idea what I'm doing? Cecelia's gone. Tracey's real mama's gone and she needs somebody better. Imogene will do. I ain't staying here one minute longer.

"Mommy?"

I stop and look over at the little red-headed girl standing in the doorway. I want to grab Tracey and hold her and cry into her mop of red. But I can't. She deserves so much better than a hot-headed blond hooker-thief-liar.

"Get out of here!" I shout and walk to the door. Tracey backs up and looks up at me with wide-eyed hurt. I slam the door in her face. *Darnitt, Bee. I am one horrible Mama.* I pull out a cigarette and light up. That old man can deal with it.

Chapter 21

Maggie

Father, please help me, guide me. What do I do? Belinda is so angry, Donna is so bitter, and I am just lost right now, Lord. Is Belinda some kind of felon? Sure, she stole from me, but never money. Help me to...

A door slams upstairs. I look up and hear little girl sobs. I leave the dining room and go to the hallway and look up. Tracey is at the top of the stairs curled up on the floor. My heart breaks and I run up and kneel down. I take her in my arms and she clings to me.

"It's okay, sweetie. It's going to be okay," I whisper as I stroke her hair.

These are not the same women I grew up with. What happened to them? We never fought in this house. This was our sanctuary. I came to get away from my father, Belinda to get away from her stepmother, and Donna came to get away from her house of grief.

What would Cecelia do right now? Probably go in and talk to Belinda. I won't do that. She doesn't deserve a sweet little thing like Tracey. Maybe she's in there seeing the truth in her behavior. She's always been stubborn from the moment I met her when we were little, 'til the last time I saw her at Ortega's. Twenty-five years ago, the day after graduation.

My eyes burned from crying. Fury. That's all I felt.

"Ain't it a hoot that we all still came today?" Belinda's words dripped with sarcasm and anger. "What a wonderful high school graduation lunch."

"I think we should all talk this out." Donna stuffed a taco in her mouth.

"You gonna say something to me, Magpie?" Belinda asked. She didn't touch her coke and like me, she didn't order anything.

I stared at her. How could I say anything? What could I possibly say to someone who murdered my heart? So I stayed silent.

"This is stupid. Maggie, I betcha think I owe you some kind of heartfelt apology, right?"

"Right," Donna muttered through a mouthful.

"I ain't apologizing. I ain't. At least not until you talk to me."

I looked at Belinda, but no words came. Just another teardrop. I hated that I started to cry. She saw my tears, but her face remained tight, like a mask of plastered anger.

"Fine. Cry all you want. You two have good lives, full of whatever. I'm so sick of this place and I'm so sick of both of you. See you in another life!" Belinda stood up, her long red hair dancing behind her like fire flames.

It fit. I wished her a life in hell.

"Belinda, don't go. You are the one in the wrong here." Donna wiped her mouth.

"Shut up, Donna. I don't care if we ever see each other again." Belinda stormed out of the restaurant.

"Great. We're leaving and she's acting like that? What a hussy, right?" Donna said.

My heart burst and I wanted to fly away. From Boots, from my drunken father, and my mother who hated me, from Belinda and even from Donna.

I stood up. "Donna," I spit out through tears, *"you were not a friend to me last night either. I don't ever want to see you or Belinda again. Ever."*

I left that restaurant and I left Boots. I would never return.

And here I am, stroking the red hair of Belinda's little one. *God, I know You're here. I know You are. Please rescue Tracey.* I watch Belinda's door down the hall. I smell cigarette smoke. She has some nerve. Tracey's tears stop, followed by sniffing. "Tracey, let's get you a tissue and then maybe you can lay down for a while. Do you like to read?"

Her eyes are swollen and her nose is messy. But she looks at me and nods.

"Well, come on." I lead Tracey to my room where she sits on the bed. I hand her a tissue.

"Why don't you lay down and I'll find you a book?" Tracey curls up and I cover her with a blanket and hand her a book. "This was in here in the bookshelf. Cecelia loved this story, and I read it when I was little. You should try it."

Tracey takes *The Secret Garden* and starts reading.

"I'll come check on you later, okay?" I ask.

"Okay."

I am so angry with Belinda. Doesn't she see she has a gift in that child? Is she that selfish? I head downstairs and find Donna in the visiting room, texting on her phone. I take the seat across from her.

Donna looks up. "Drama, right?" She rolls her eyes.

"Yes." I glare at her.

"What?" Donna asks. "Do *you* want to be associated with a criminal? I think we ought to look into this. What town in East Texas is she from?"

"Donna, what are you thinking?"

"We make one call to the police there and we find out if she's on the run."

"Your imagination is working overtime."

"Maggie, how can you defend her after what she did?"

"We don't know she stole that money."

"I'm not talking about the money."

I can't believe she's using that memory in this conversation. "Twenty-five years ago, Donna."

"I can tell it still bothers you. You aren't perfect, you know."

"I didn't say I was. But I'm not dragging up the past. I'm saying we can't accuse her of something we have no proof of and doesn't concern us. I'm much more worried about Tracey than the money."

"Oh, I know what you mean." Donna hits some button on her phone. "It's like she doesn't even like her own child."

Regret hits me. I shouldn't have said anything about Tracey. Donna continues badmouthing Belinda's mothering abilities. I agree with her, but I'm not going to join in. Donna pauses, waiting for me to continue the rampage. I change the subject. "So who are you texting? The guy in Marshall?"

"Speaking of something not being any of your concern." Donna grins. "But yes, it's the guy from Marshall. I can't believe he's coming in just a couple of hours. I wish I had time to get my hair done."

"You look great."

"Yeah, right."

I watch as Donna continues typing on her phone. It reminds me of my own sons and their obsession with phones and the internet. *God, please help Donna. Please help Belinda and Tracey. What do you want me to do? I feel so powerless, Father. I don't know how to help anyone. They both seem so distant. And can't you see I'm right? Look at them. Why in the world should I forgive them? They don't deserve it. They made the choices they made. And they weren't good.*

I hear a door open and close.

"Was that the front door?" I ask. Donna ignores me and continues reading and typing.

I get up, walk to the curtains, and peek through. I see Belinda, suitcase in hand. She wouldn't just leave, would she?

"Donna." She ignores me so I speak louder. "Donna."

"What?" She finally looks up.

I walk out of the Visiting Room. "Belinda is leaving."

"Where to?" Donna joins me and we walk to the front door and out.

"What are you doing?" Belinda jumps a little at my question and turns to me. She's standing by her car with the trunk open.

"Um…I'm leaving."

"Right now?" Donna asks.

"What do you care?" Belinda throws her suitcase in the trunk.

"Belinda, you can't leave. Not now and not like this," I plead.

"I ain't gonna stay where I'm accused of things I never did." Belinda stares at Donna.

"You have to stay and help us." Donna sighs. "You're the cook for goodness sake."

"Goodbye." Belinda slams her trunk.

"Donna, apologize," I whisper.

"But I didn't do—"

"It doesn't matter."

"Belinda, I'm sorry," she calls out. "It's not my business and I have no right to accuse you of something I don't know anything about."

She doesn't respond. She's staring at her closed trunk.

"We came to pay our respects to Cecelia and honor her final wish. We have to finish that, right?" I ask.

Her bleached blond head turns to face us. "Not another word about that money?"

"Your business, not ours," I assure her.

"Absolutely," Donna agrees.

She stands there and I sense she is trying to make a decision. I get the sense she's thinking about more than just leaving.

"Okay." Belinda puts her key in, opens the trunk and grabs her suitcase. "I need to sleep. I'll see you guys in the kitchen in a while." She closes the trunk and then walks past us.

Donna follows her. "I'll sleep later. I have something to do first."

We go back in the house and I see Donna go toward the Visiting Room. She's going to go text some more probably. Something occurs to me. I look up to Belinda at the top of the stairs. "Belinda?"

She stops and looks down. "What?"

"Tracey?"

"Um, yeah. Where is she?"

"She's sleeping on my bed."

Belinda looks around and then back at me. "Well, thank you."

Nothing more. She turns to go to her room and I stop her with "Belinda?"

"What?" Impatience colors her eyes.

"You weren't going to leave without Tracey, right?"

Belinda's eyes look down and search the stairs. For the life of me, I can't figure her out. And then after a moment, she looks at me and gives me that hard grin of hers. "What kind of mother would I be to leave her, Maggie? And just wait, she gets over things quickly." With that, she turns and goes to her room.

I stand frozen. God, I hate this woman.

Chapter 22

Donna

I cannot wait to leave this mad house. Belinda's hissy fit infuriates me. No class whatsoever. I see through Maggie. She's about to lose it herself with all that buried anger behind the religious act. Now it's 6:45 and the house is quiet as a still life painting. Everyone's asleep. I'd hoped we would start making the tuna fish earlier but everyone spread out like syrup on a short stack. I don't care. I played *Words with Friends* and calmed down after the scene Belinda made. But now I'm nervous again.

William will be here in forty-five minutes. I took a shower and I'm all ready. I think I'm as dressed up as I'm going to get. I look in the mirror for the eighteenth time. I have black pants and a beautiful black shirt with cherry red flecks in it. I went to a stylist in Denver and paid a lot of money to look like this. I even hired a make-up artist to teach me how to look perfect. I look in the mirror for the nineteenth time.

I can do this. I am a highly paid accomplished woman with confidence, pretty eyes and a beautiful smile. Great, I feel like Stuart Smalley. 'I'm good enough, I'm smart enough, and doggone it, people like me.' I hope William will.

My leg is shaking and I can swear I have some sort of eye twitch. He still hasn't called; I told him it was very important to call. I go to my suitcase and find a bag of chocolate kisses. I sit on the edge of the bed and suck on one. This will help. Of course, I'm going to have to brush my teeth again.

"Good morning all!"

A voice in the hall is sounding excessively perky.

"It's time to get cooking!" It's Belinda. Seriously? She wants to start now?

I open the door and step out into the hall. Belinda and Tracey are at the end near the stairs. "Belinda, I can't..."

"Wow, Donna!" Belinda adds a wolf whistle. "You look good, girl."

"Thank you."

Maggie opens up her bedroom door and peeks out. "Oh my goodness, Donna. You're going to make tuna sandwiches in that?"

"No. That's what I'm trying to say—I am going out for a while."

"That's right," Belinda teases. "The Marshall man."

Maggie comes out and shuts her door. Black circles are under her eyes. "When are you planning on coming back?"

"I don't know. 10:00 o'clock, maybe?"

"We have a lot of work to do." Maggie says this gently, but I can tell she's a little peeved at me.

"Maggie, I'll be back soon enough. Just leave me work to do, okay?"

"That's not possible, Donna," Belinda says. "In the instructions Vern gave us, we are to do one ingredient at a time, so we can't leave anything for you. You're just gonna get to do three hours less than us."

I will not let them ruin this for me. "Then I will do three hours less." I walk past Belinda and Tracey and head downstairs. Maybe I'll wait outside. The three of them follow me. I reach for the door handle.

"He's going to pick you up, right, Donna?" Maggie asks.

"Yes, but I'm going to wait outside. I'll be back soon." I walk through the door and try to shut it behind me. Belinda keeps it open.

"Well, I want to meet your Mystery Date." She giggles. "Remember that game?"

They all follow me out to the porch. Wonderful. Must they really do this?

"Didn't we play that for one entire summer?" Maggie joins in.

Why won't they leave? "Do you mind going inside? I'm nervous enough as it is."

A little hand grabs mine. I look down to see sweet Tracey smiling up at me. "Miss Donna, you are beautiful." My heart melts looking at her, a replica of Belinda when she was little. But much sweeter. Much.

"Thank you Tracey." I squeeze her hand and look up to see a brown pickup truck pulling up to the curb. I can't see his face, but I do see a black cowboy hat.

"Well, he didn't rent a limo, did he?" Belinda mutters.

I scowl at her and then look toward the pickup with my best I'm-the-one-you've-been-waiting-for smile. Oh wonderful. I forgot to brush my teeth after the chocolate kisses.

"At least he didn't ride a horse." Maggie whispers but I hear her and Belinda's muffled laughing. "I'm sorry, Donna." I want to scowl at Maggie too, but he's getting out of the pickup.

The first thing I notice is his height. Apparently, the horses in his Facebook pictures were Shetland ponies. But I shake that off. Hey, I'm not exactly a prize catch. So what if I wore heels tonight just to be taller. Should I go change to flats? No, no, I'm fine.

He's looking at the ground as he approaches. Finally, he gets to the sidewalk and looks up at the three of us. It occurs to me he might like Maggie or Belinda more and my heart churns like old butter. But no, he's looking at me. That's when I notice his face.

"Wow." Belinda has no self-control at all.

"Donna?" Maggie wonders aloud, too. Can't they both just be quiet?

"Well, hello gorgeous." He comes up the couple of stairs to the porch, takes my hand, and kisses it. Very gallant.

"Hello, William. It's so good to finally meet you." I have to be polite. This could work. Maybe. "Did you have any trouble finding the place?"

"Oh no, I got myself a GPS." He extends his hand to Tracey. "Hi, little lady. Your red hair is just pert near like our Texas sky after a dust storm. I'm William."

I make the introductions to Tracey and Maggie and when I get to Belinda, I notice she has a look on her face that spells trouble. Oh no.

"How old are you?" Belinda just blurts it out. I can't believe her. But I do want to hear his answer.

William doesn't say anything for a second but looks at the ground as if his birth certificate fell out from his pocket and landed down there. Finally, he looks up at me. "It's true, my pictures on that there Facebook was a wee bit old. I am, well, I am seventy-one years of age. But I am young at heart."

Confusion. His voice sounds like it did on the phone, but not this old. At all. He has kind blue eyes but everything else is white. The tufts of hair coming out the side of his cowboy hat, his mustache and even the hairs on his arms. He's wearing a blue sports jacket with a plaid shirt underneath. And is that? An ascot? Wonderful. I'm going out with Robert Goulet, the cowboy version.

"It's okay." I think I say this aloud. "We should be going." I'm disappointed but I would never be so mean as to just tell him to go home after he drove an hour to see me. Anyway, I like him. The man I've gotten to know online and over the phone is a wonderful man. Of course, he might have lied about a couple of things. He grabs my hand and we walk down the steps. I can actually see the top of his hat.

"Just a second," Belinda calls. "I have one more question for you, mister."

I try to ignore her but William stops and turns around. "We can just go." I whisper to him as I scowl back at Belinda.

"Donna Gail, I'm one of your oldest friends and whether you like me or not, I'm not gonna let you just go off with a stranger who happens to be a liar."

"Belinda." Maggie grabs her arm. "Let's go inside." Belinda shakes her off.

I am dying of humiliation. I just want to go and enjoy a free meal and a nice conversation. Women marry older men all the time. I could do this.

Belinda walks down the steps and comes up to us.

William lets go of my hand and takes a step toward her. "I don't know what the problem is little lady, but I won't have any woman calling me a liar."

"Any woman?" Belinda glances at me and glares back at him.

"Oh that's right. You're old enough to have lived when women couldn't even vote, right?"

Now she's just being flat out rude. "William, ignore her. She's a criminal anyway." I say this and immediately regret it because Tracey can hear me. William turns around, grabs my hand and we start walking to his truck.

"Donna, you might be desperate but you ain't desperate enough to date a married man, are you?"

I stop. How dare she?

"Sweetie pie, let's just go and let your PMSing friend go back and switch pads."

I look at William. What? Is this the same man I talked to on the phone? I let go of his hand and turn back to Belinda. I don't think I've ever hated her more. "Belinda, you have no right to say such things."

"Look at his left hand, Donna." Belinda points and I look down. No ring, but a tan line that looks recent. Really recent.

I lower my eyes to meet his. I need to know the truth. "Are you married?"

He puts his hand on my back, leans near me, and whispers. "Sugar, you're only going to be here one night, right? Let's go have some fun."

I want to throw up. My skin is crawling. I jerk away from him and run past Belinda to the porch. Maggie reaches for my arm but I pass her and go inside. I shut the door and lean on it. Of course, this is happening to me. Of course.

I hear Belinda yelling at William. I want to watch him shrink even shorter at her words, but I can't go back out there. I feel the tears running just as I hear his truck peel away. The door opens behind me and I step away. I don't know what to do, so I just stand. Frozen.

"Donna, I am so sorry." Maggie wraps her arms around me and I feel Tracey putting her arms around me, too. I keep crying but I step out of their arms.

"I should have known. I am so stupid."

"Don't say that, Donna." Compassion is written all over Maggie's face. "This could happen to anyone."

Belinda comes in from the porch. "Listen, girlie, I know of what I speak when I say Maggie is right on the money. It could happen to anybody." She's looking at me with her bleached blond hooker hair and her wrinkled face that makes her look like a witch hag. And she's trying to be nice to me? My tears turn to anger. Red hot anger.

"I bet you enjoyed that, didn't you, Belinda? You love breaking up people's chances at hope, don't you?" I know I've pushed another button and I'm glad. "You are the meanest and most selfish person on this earth and I want you to stay out of my business, you hear?"

"You don't seem to be very good at staying out of my mine, do you? I was honestly trying to look out for you. You ain't supposed to end up with an old married fart like that."

"Maybe I am! How do you know? You don't know anything about me so don't you ever presume to know anything about what I think or do. Leave me alone!" I turn and start climbing the stairs. Belinda calls after me.

"You're still going to help us cook, right?"

Maggie talks before I can yell back. "Belinda, give her a second. Come on."

I go to my room and shut the door. I look in the mirror and my beautiful make-up is streaked. How could I be so stupid to pay money to look like this for him? I open up my phone and click on Facebook. I find his name on my friend list and *un-friend* him. *Good riddance, you ugly, dirty-old-man liar.*

I sit on the bed, crying again. Adrenaline is pumping through me. How dare Belinda? It's her fault, of course. He never actually said he was married anyway. And who is she to try to think she knows better than I do? She's probably a wanted felon.

I'll show her.

I click on Google and start searching. It only takes me fifteen minutes to find her. Wind Storm, Texas? I just bet someone is looking for her.

"Donna? Are you okay?" Maggie's outside my door.

"I'm okay, Maggie. Really. I just need a minute to change and I'll be down to help, okay?"

"Okay."

I turn back and find the phone number to the sheriff's department in Wind Storm. Yep, I will show Belinda that I know what's best for her, too.

Chapter 23

Belinda

Ain't nothing like the smell of Cecelia's pickles. They're a wonderful mixture of tart like a divorcee who just don't care, and sweet like a little girl at her first square dance. I open up a jar just to sniff and then take a bite. Delicious.

Me and Maggie put jar after jar of them out on the Formica table as we wait for Donna to come down. If Maggie asks me to apologize to Donna, heck if I will. I just saved her from who knows what. She just don't see it.

"This is silly," Maggie starts, and I know what's coming.

"I ain't gonna say sorry for something I ain't sorry about, Maggie."

She rolls her eyes at me and continues, "Belinda I was going to say that how we are preparing this is silly. It would be much more efficient if we just divided up the ingredients and each of us be in charge of a few."

"Oh. Well, read this yourself. Specific instructions. And a bit paranoid if you ask me." I pick up the papers off the counter and give them to Maggie. Cecelia left clear instructions that ever'thing was to be done in a certain order. "And look at the bottom, Magpie. Cecelia left us a doozy of an order." I watch Maggie's eyes as she peruses.

"You're kidding me. We aren't to talk aloud about the instructions?" Her face is priceless. "Even in here?"

"I guess so. Vern said to not deviate one iota from that piece of paper."

"Hey, Donna." Maggie looks past me so I turn around.

Donna stands in sweats and a t-shirt. She wiped all that make-up off, too. It didn't suit her if you ask me. But by the looks of it, she won't be asking me a thing.

"What is that smell?" Donna asks.

"It's these." I wave my hand Vanna White-like to display all the mason jars on the table. "These are all Cecelia's pickles home-grown and home-canned."

Maggie hands Donna the papers. "Donna, you need to read this to yourself before we begin." She giggles. "It's thorough, that's for sure."

"Seriously?" Donna's eyes are still reading.

"As a dead woman." Darnitt, I can be clever.

"Not funny, Belinda." She looks at me with a grin. But it's a weird grin. "Tracey in bed?"

"Yep, she's reading and playing on her DS. She'll crash soon. We won't hear a word from her 'til morning 'cause she can sleep through a hailstorm." I've always admired this about Tracey and I know if I decide to leave at night, her waking up won't be a problem.

"I guess she's probably slept through many of your adventures, hasn't she?" Donna's grin is annoying me.

I take a step toward her. "What do you mean by that?"

Maggie steps between us. "I am so sorry for what happened to you Donna, but I have to tell you I am glad the three of us can get after it. This is going to take a while."

"Great. I'm ready." Donna says and steps away to open a drawer. She takes out an apron. I guess she doesn't want to get her pretty t-shirt and sweats dirty. Please.

We get knives and bowls and we each pick a station and a cutting board. Soon we are silent, except for the sound of knives hitting cutting boards and pickle juice flying. I love the efficiency of chopping and the pure pleasure of preparing food. I finally feel completely comfortable.

"You chop really quickly, Bee," Maggie says.

"Why, thank you kindly. It's a tool of the trade." I pause. "This feels right, you know?" I say to no one in particular.

"We spent a lot of nights in this room, but I don't think any of them were chopping pickles." Donna's tone is friendly but she sure is chopping hard.

"Nope, just playing scrabble or canasta, eating and laughing." My mind plays a scene of the four of us sitting around the Formica, arguing over words, and Donna always wanting to use the dictionary. "Remember how Cecelia never let you look up words?" I ask, my eyes still on my growing deposit of sliced pickles.

"I only wanted the dictionary because you made up words." She laughs and I find myself suspicious. Why is she being so nice to me?

I look over at Maggie and she ain't cutting. Her head is on her hand, which is being held up by the handle end of the butcher knife she's cutting with. "Maggie, you okay?"

She lifts her head up. She looks a little peaked. "I'm fine. Just a little tired."

That ain't the truth. Something is up with both of them. Apparently, I just wrecked Donna's night and she is sweet as a big ole lump of chocolate chip cookie dough. And Maggie doesn't look like she's feeling well a'tall. "Okey-dokie." I say. She better not get sick and leave all this work to us. Maybe if I bring up an interesting subject she'll perk up. It's time anyway.

"Maggie, are you gonna ever ask me?" I ask the question while keeping my eyes on my pickles. I can sense Donna jerking her head around to stare. "Well?" I let a minute pass of silence and I look over at her. Maggie knows exactly what I'm talking about.

She slowly wipes her forehead with the back of her arm, puts her knife down and turns to me. Her eyes are tired. "Belinda, tell me, what ever happened to Alan Deltan?"

There it is. The question I wanted. I thought we'd get it out of the way earlier but Maggie ended up depositing her cookies in the bathroom. She didn't ask when we went through the town. It needs to be said. Old bones are cluttering up the room—good idea to clean them up.

"I think it started a week before graduation. I've thought about this. Do you remember us having a conversation at Cecelia's?" I stop chopping.

"Seriously? We had millions of conversations." Maggie sits down.

"Probably a week before graduation and Donna was consumed with her hair."

"I have never been consumed with how I look."

Maggie and I both stare at Donna and in unison we say, "Oh yes, you have." We look at each other and smile. But Maggie's smile disappears quickly.

"Whatever." Donna says.

"That night we were in the Visiting Room and Cecelia made us grilled cheese and we were talking about our futures. And I remember very clearly, just being done, you know? Done with Boots and with small town life and with you guys, to be honest."

"I am so sick of the place." The carpet of the Visiting Room could've been a bed, it was so comfy. Red strands of hair covered my face as my blood pumped with restlessness.

"It won't be long now," Donna said. "Are you wearing your hair up or down with the graduation cap?" Donna sat in a beanbag with a compact mirror held to her face. "I think I might turn Tommy Duncan's eye if I wore it up inside and then, just at the right moment." She lowered the compact dramatically to act out her plan. "I take off my cap and my long brown hair falls past my shoulders and I do a three-quarter hair toss." She moved her head and hair around as if she were the Charlie perfume commercial gal. I laughed.

Maggie, who also sat in a beanbag, commented, "Donna, I am really tired of you always trying to please guys. Why don't you just be yourself? You're leaving for Texas Tech soon anyway."

I took up arms for Donna. "Be quiet, Maggie. You have been dating one guy for seven months, most of our entire senior year in high school, one of the most important years ever to have a boyfriend. You don't know how Donna feels."

"Like you do, Bee? When is the last time you sat alone waiting for the phone to ring like Donna does?" Maggie snapped back.

"Wow, this is really encouraging me," Donna quipped. "Neither of you have any room to talk about what it's like to be me. So both of you," she pointed for emphasis, "You Miss-I'm-dating-the-church-youth-group-leader-and-he's-perfect-and-we'll-get-married, and you

Bee, Miss-I-was-voted-most-beautiful-two-years-in-a-row-and-I-never-have-to-look-for-a-date!" She had yelled her tirade but now was perfectly calm. "So, should I put my hair up or what?"

I looked at Donna and resolved to leave Boots as soon as possible. "I am so sick and tired of this place."

"How many times do you have to say that, Bee? You think either of us wants to stay in this hick town?" Maggie asked.

"You don't want to leave like I do. And you both know where you're headed. I ain't got no ide," Belinda answered.

"I hate it when you use 'ain't'."

"Too bad."

"Your lack of plans isn't our fault. So what about my hair?" Donna pleaded.

With each moment, I became more fed up. We were all drifting and wanted to fly. No more clinging to each other. Instead, we held our scissors ready to cut the strings.

"Wear it up, wear it down, who cares?" I snapped.

"Belinda," Donna spoke, "don't be so mean."

My plans weren't solid and it made me restless. The summer would be lonely. Donna and Maggie were both leaving the day after graduation. Sometimes I thought of being a chef. Cecelia noticed my culinary bent and spent extra time with me in the kitchen, showing me the secrets of cooking and the delights of certain spices and ingredients. I liked the idea of food being a career for me, but I didn't think it could happen.

"When I get to Texas Tech," Donna said, "I am going to have plans all the time. I am going to constantly do interesting things and meet interesting people."

"What about studying?" Margie countered. "If you're going to be an accountant, you'll need to keep your head in those books."

"Yes, but when I am not studying, I will be having fun. I really think I'm going to meet a Red Raider and fall in love and get married.

You guys will have to fly out to be in my wedding."

"I'll be there, Donna," Belinda said. "But don't you want to get married in Boots?"

"I don't know," Donna replied. "I'd like to have a big city wedding."

"What about you, Maggie? Do you think Alan and you will get married here?" I loved bringing up her favorite topic.

"I have been accepted to Baylor and I am going to Baylor. I've told you guys a million times. Before I walk down the aisle, my degree in English will be in my hand." Maggie smiled slowly. "But I wouldn't mind having a long engagement, if someone asked me. Alan's going to Hardin Simmons, not too far away from Waco."

"He's so cute," Donna commented.

"I just think it's incredible that he wants to be a preacher. Our Maggie, a preacher's wife." Jealousy colored my words. We each dreamed of marrying a preacher. As self-proclaimed Jesus Girls, nothing could be better than marrying a godly man who wanted to be a minister.

"His heart is good," Maggie said quietly.

"A good heart? Maggie, he is the youth group leader and loves Jesus so much! His testimony last Sunday made me want to cry," Donna said.

"Do you think he'll ask you pretty soon?" Belinda asked.

"Graduation is next week." Maggie looked out the windows. "Who knows?"

"You're being too quiet, Maggie. What's up?" I knew her inside and out.

"If I tell you guys something, will you please not say anything to anyone?"

"Of course." Donna and I said.

"You know how we promised each other we would wait until our wedding nights?" Maggie gave us a questioning look.

"For what?" Donna asked, looking in her compact.

"Donna, think," I urged her.

She put down her compact. "Oh! I know what you're talking about. Did you…do something, Maggie?"

"Um, well, no, not yet. But Alan…Alan told me he thinks it would be fine if we were engaged. And I think he's going to ask me soon." Maggie bit a fingernail. "I don't want to."

"Don't want to get engaged?" Donna asked.

"Seriously, Donna?" I glared at her.

"Oh. You mean the other thing." Donna looked in her compact again.

"If you don't want to, then don't, Maggie," I said.

"Ladies, would you like some tuna sandwiches?" We looked up and Cecelia stood at the door of the Visiting Room.

"They look good." Donna jumped up.

"Here you go."

Donna and I got our sandwiches and sat back down. Maggie stood in front of Cecelia, sandwich in hand. "Cecelia, please don't tell anyone what you just heard."

"I won't, sweetie." Cecelia sat on a couch facing us and led us in prayer. "Have you ladies ever noticed that one?" She pointed to a medium frame in a corner with a cross-stitched hand reaching down to smaller hands.

"Therefore, I urge you, brothers and sisters, in view of God's mercy, to offer your bodies as a living sacrifice, holy and pleasing to God—this is your true and proper worship." Romans 12: 1

"I know it's about time for graduation and college and even wedding plans possibly. Like that verse says, I want to urge the three of you. Give your bodies to Christ always. Make sure in all you do, be it graduation hair, college plans, or walking down the aisle that you give God your body and your life first before you give it to any plan or any man."

Donna giggled. "Any plan or any man. I like that phrase, Cecelia."

"Make that 'Give yourself to God's hand, before any plan or any man.'" Cecelia smiled. *"I could use that in my poetry."*

We laughed and kept eating.

"Resentment toward you started right then, Maggie. This incredible godly guy and future preacher loved you and just wanted sex after you got engaged. I thought you were crazy to say no if it meant losing him. You guys remember, don't you? All we used to talk about was becoming preachers' wives." I dump a cup full of pickles into the bowl I have. "So, Maggie, everything started in me a week before graduation night. Resentment and restlessness." I look at Maggie willing her to see why I did it. Hindsight and all.

"So you were resentful and restless. We all feel that way from time to time. Doesn't mean we hurt our friends." Maggie's chopping the pickles like they're my limbs.

"She's right, Belinda. You can't make excuses for betraying a friend," Donna says this with a glance to me and then a quick glance down at her pickles. She looks guilty. I have no idea why.

"You still haven't answered my question, Belinda? What happened to Alan?"

"Do you remember what happened on graduation night, Maggie?"

She narrows her eyes into slits and stares at me. "Yes, I remember that. Pain acts like superglue with memories."

"That night resentment and restlessness grew into silent fury."

"So what, Belinda? You're trying to justify stealing my future fiancé because you were angry with me?"

"Maggie, just listen to my point of view."

"What a disappointment," I said as I climbed into Maggie's car. "I expected more from our graduation ceremony."

"I loved it. I think wearing my hair down was the perfect choice." Donna sat up front.

"Let's make a plan," Maggie said. "Alan is going to pick me up in two hours and we'll come get you both and we'll ride around and celebrate. That way we'll have time to hang with our families and then get together." Maggie orchestrated us even as she started driving.

"Fine. Another night of riding around in Boots. Sounds like a party to me."

"It could be, Bee. And just think, this will be our last night as people who live here."

"That does sound like it's worth celebrating," Donna added.

"You have a point," I conceded.

Two hours later, Alan came up to my door and rang the doorbell. Surprised me. Most of the guys in Boots honked.

"Are you ready, Miss Graduate?" He smiled at me and something in my heart twitched.

Maggie sat in the front seat and I climbed in back. We picked up Donna and she joined us. First stop, the Dairy Queen. After coke floats and the review of all of the ceremony's details, we began the process of riding around, our number one past time.

"Okay, guys, every time we pass a place with a memory, shout it out the window." Maggie suggested.

I rolled my eyes "You've got to be kidding. We have memories everywhere. Boots is a small town, Miss Maggie."

"Come on, Bee, it'll be fun," Maggie retorted.

"I'm in," Donna offered.

"It does sound a bit childish, Maggie. We're graduates now, not some high school kids anymore," Alan remarked.

Maggie got silent and I knew that meant hurt feelings but I didn't care. So what if our last night didn't include some silly walk down memory lane?

"So what are we going to do?" Donna asked. "Should we try to find some other grads?"

"Fine. That sounds good," Maggie said. "Let's just go to a party. Isn't Shelly Dodson having one at her house?"

"Absolutely. I think Tommy Duncan might be there." Donna sat up and started shaking her hair.

I looked out the window and shook my head. "Donna, you still like him after he broke up with you. You're leaving tomorrow. Forget about Tommy. You guys are acting like you're not getting out of this place. I say let's not go to some stupid party. Let's just ride around and talk about the future. That's where it's at!" I knew they didn't like my little outburst and I didn't care. I just wanted something new.

After an awkward moment of silence, Alan spoke up. "Sounds good to me, Belinda. I've spent four years of my life in this town. It is time to get my head out of Boots and on to the world out there. Let's talk about the future."

Alan and I started laughing and dreaming. Donna talked a little but Maggie didn't say a cotton-pickin' thing. At 3:15 a.m. we were still driving. We'd turned philosophical.

"I just want to be somebody, you know. Someone who makes a difference for God." Alan spoke earnestly.

"You will, Alan," Maggie finally contributed something, but she whispered it.

"I can't wait to be around people who have no idea who I am or what I did last Saturday," I said. "That is freedom."

"Absolutely," Alan agreed.

Donna spoke up, "Alan, drive me home. I still have to pack some and I am exhausted."

"Okay," Alan answered and then looked to Maggie, "Do you need to go home, too?"

Alan's question made my eyebrows rise. He conspicuously asked Maggie and not me.

Maggie answered him in a voice of doubt. "Um, in a while... Belinda probably wants to go home, though."

"I'm fine, Alan. I am wide-awake. Let's keep talking. "As soon as I said the words, I knew I'd made a mistake. The mood in the car grew tense. But I didn't care.

Alan asked me about my caffeine intake and I giggled. I enjoyed the attention. I thought the soon-to-be preacher never really saw me. But he did and to me, he looked like a juicy future I didn't think I could ever taste.

Donna got out of the car with a sympathetic look to Maggie and a questioning one to me.

I responded to her look. "I'll see you tomorrow. Donna. Our goodbye lunch at Ortega's, okay?" As we drove away from Donna's house, I looked at Maggie. Tears formed in her eyes.

"I think I need to go home, Alan," she said.

"Are you okay, Maggie?" I asked it to be polite.

"I'm fine."

My thoughts began to race as Alan drove to Maggie's house. I asked myself if I really wanted to do this. To my friend? But I didn't know if anything was going to happen, anyway. And if it did, well, we were all leaving anyway. Maggie got out of the car and jogged to the steps of her home without a word to me. Alan made no attempt to chase her to the door.

"So, what do you want to do, beautiful?" Alan asked, looking back at me.

"Let's keep riding." I winked at Alan and hopped over into the front seat, ready for anything.

I put down my knife and turn around to look at Maggie straight on. "We talked for about an hour and then Alan got the crazy idea of sneaking around the old castle. He had a couple of flashlights in his car and a couple of blankets in the trunk. We climbed over the fence and through an empty window. We didn't do a lot of searching around because I just knew the rumors about the booby-traps were real. So instead, we found the first empty spot we could find and laid the blankets down." A moment of silence settles into our pickle duties. "Maggie, I was young, stupid and resentful. I didn't want it to happen, believe it or not."

Silence.

So I ask something I've wondered about. "How did you come to find us?"

Maggie glances at Donna and then back at me. "Does it matter?"

"I did it." Donna jumps in. "I knew something was going to happen between you and Alan and it upset me, so after you dropped me off I waited a while and went over to Maggie's. I talked her into it. We drove around to find you."

I smirk. "Seriously? Well, I'll be, Donna Gail."

"Not proud of it. But I had no idea we'd be walking into what we did."

Maggie looks at me straight on now. "We drove around and spotted Alan's car on a side street next to the castle. We started searching and heard noises." She glances at her pickles.

"I lost my virginity to that idiot, Maggie. I figure you think I owe you an apology, but the way I look at it I saved you from a real jerk."

Maggie stares at me and I don't see any so called Christian love.

"And since you asked, Maggie…I married Alan Deltan."

"I know." Maggie's words are frozen ice.

"You married him?" Donna puts her knife down and sits at the table. "Is he the father of Tracey?"

"Nope." I watch Maggie as I say it. Her eyes blink.

"Oh. I thought…" Maggie starts.

"Alan turned out to be such a wonderful, caring man. Did you know that I supported him throughout most of college? His dad gave him an itty-bitty bit of money, but I waited tables and cooked and paid for his degree. Just so he could become a preacher." The memory hurts.

"What happened, Belinda?" Ice again.

"One day he ordered me to get rid of the red hair and go blond. Like someone else." Maggie winces but she ain't got no idea. "I actually started to believe him when he said I wasn't pretty enough or fun enough. Before I knew it he brought home guys ever night unannounced to watch sports or sit around and talk or study. College students who thought they were smarter than anybody 'cause they were paying to listen to some professor talk about a history book. Of course, Alan ordered me to cook and entertain for them. Once I did four guys' laundry while they sat and watched football."

"What a jerk," Donna announces. "It just doesn't make sense. Our youth leader?"

"Well, Donna, we change, don't we? And they hide who they are. You don't even know the kicker. That came on a Tuesday night. Funny I remember the day of the week. I cooked macaroni and cheese for dinner."

"What are we having tonight?" Alan threw his books down on the couch.

"We, my good husband, are having "ze cheese of ze macaroni." I thought if I brought some silly humor to the house, Alan might lighten up a bit. Wrong.

"Mac and Cheese, again? Can't you add some variety to our meals?

I mean you have time, so use it. You are so stupid." As he yelled at me, he flung open the refrigerator door and put peanut butter and jelly jars out on the counter.

"What are you doing?" I asked. "Are you actually going to have peanut butter?"

"Yes, I am. Will you please leave me alone? And you know what? You look horrible as a blond. Why don't you just be a red head like God made you?"

I got so angry I took the macaroni and cheese off the stove, shoved it onto the counter and left the room. Alan followed me.

"Where are you going? I am talking to you. Listen, I failed a test in applied math today because you wouldn't help me study last night!"

"I was working!" I could yell, too. "Someone has to pay for applied math!" As soon as I said it, I knew I'd pushed a button.

Alan grabbed me by the arm and swung me around just as I'd entered our bedroom. He put his face near mine and screamed, "I don't owe you anything! You're the one who stole your best friend's boyfriend and wrecked your entire life!"

"I hate you, you worthless little preacher boy!"

Pain shocked me. I covered my face in protection against another blow.

"I'm out of here!" Alan yelled as he slammed the front door.

I walked to the bathroom and looked into the mirror. The side of my face burned. A red welt grew right as I watched.

I've shocked the two Miss Perfects 'cause their mouths are wide open.

"He apologized profusely that night and bought me presents the next day. For a while, he even treated me like a queen. But then, it happened again and again and…."

Maggie puts her knife down and stands up. Her eyes are shining.

If she touches me, I am ready to shake any of her pity off. But she doesn't.

"I had no idea, Belinda. Sometimes…" Her eyes search the floor like she's looking for words to pick up. "I wondered about his anger sometimes. Maybe I should've said something."

I glare at her. Even now, she thinks she has the answers. She's so wrong. "You think you could have saved me, Miss Maggie? You have that kind of power just 'cause you've lived a perfect life? Jesus didn't, but you think you could have?"

Silence. That shut her up.

"So you divorced him?" Donna's mousy voice asks.

I hear the question. I've told them the truth. I ain't no liar. Not gonna start now. "No, he left me. Years later."

"Why?"

"A dead baby."

Chapter 24

Maggie

Oh Father, forgive me. Why didn't I tell her what happened with Alan and me? I can't. Was I wrong about her? No. She deserved what she got. She made a choice to take him from me, her best friend. Yes, I was right. If you obey God, things like that don't happen. What am I talking about? Look at me. Betrayal. Cancer. And I've obeyed You. God, where are you? I stare at Belinda, shocked. Pickle juice drips from my fingers and I rub it on my apron. Belinda locks eyes with me for a second and then begins furiously chopping again.

"Of course, that's an entirely different story for another time," she says.

"Belinda." I'm supposed to forgive her. That's part of the reason I'm here.

"What?" She keeps chopping.

Maybe forgiveness begins with me telling her the whole story.

"Ladies! We have come a'calling!" Imogene's unmistakable cackle fills the air outside the kitchen. "It's late we know, but we thought you might need a bit of help."

Belinda laughs like she's glad for the interruption. "Is she serious?"

"Extremely." I answer after wiping my eyes. Horrible timing but I feel relief, too. "But we can't let them in, girls. Cecelia said specifically - just us." I'm annoyed at Imogene. She's acting like a teenager, not a grown woman.

"It would be great to have some help," Donna comments.

I put my knife down and give Donna my best no-nonsense look. "We cannot let them in."

"Ladies!" Imogene is just outside the kitchen door now. "I'm not alone. Please open up."

Belinda walks toward the back door.

"Belinda, don't," I insist.

"I'm just gonna talk to them," Belinda replies with a wink.

Donna joins her at the back door so I go, too.

Imogene is complete with blue denim flowered apron and hair in a black hair net. She looks as if she were about to engage in a full on Olympic cooking battle. Lola Bee and two other ladies stand with her.

"You three haven't met Barbara and Maxine. Well, this is Barbara Harry. She owns Harry's Hair and she was a good friend to Cecelia, too."

Barbara's hair is a up in a perfect and rather high bouffant bun. She smiles very sweetly and I'd swear she was one of those polygamist sect women if she had a long dress on. She's probably in her late sixties and wears a sweater and capris, quite modern and cute.

"It's a real pleasure to meet you ladies. I've heard so many lovely stories about ya'll."

Her accent is pure Georgia. "I love tuna fish."

I glance at Belinda and grin. After a couple of seconds of silence, I respond. "I do, too."

Imogene continues her introductions. "This here is Maxine Massey, another one of our cohorts. She's about our caliber and she loved Cecelia right along with us."

Maxine Massey grins and nods her head but says nothing. Her cat eyed glasses and short white hair make me think she's stuck in the fifties. She wears an apron, too. The four old ladies look like cocked shotguns ready to fire.

"So nice to meet you. It's really nice of you to come here and be so helpful, but you simply cannot come in," Belinda's tone is cotton candy sweet.

"Belinda Kite!" Imogene is not shy. "It seems we haven't had a good sit down since you been here. Let's have some Folgers and talk a spell."

"Imoge...." Belinda begins.

Maxine interrupts. "Ladies, you know you have something we really need. Now, God rest her wonderful soul, Cecelia May and I were friends forever and I would never be so callous as to be indelicate...."

"but our friend is dead." Barbara Harry jumps in with her Georgian accent. "She is meeting Jesus and enjoying a banquet of whatever she wants. Where she is, there is simply no calling for a silly tuna fish sandwich recipe. I feel certain she would be obliged if you lovely ladies would do the kind thing, dare I say the Christian thing, and give us her recipe as a last act of friendship."

My goodness, with that smooth accent Barbara Harry could make the telephone book sound like Shakespeare.

"Oh come on now!" Lola Bee is less cultured. "It is just selfish to keep that recipe to yourselves. We know you are going to leave Boots day after tomorrow and we will not let that recipe leave, too. In the name of peace, you should let us, the elder ladies of Boots, have that recipe. It is the right thing to do. You three are city dwellers now, mind you, and that there recipe is Boots and Boots alone."

I feel I should explain. "Ladies, Cecelia left instructions with Vern, specific instructions, and we are just trying to follow them."

Donna adds, "It's just a recipe, anyway. In the name of peace." She looks at Lola Bee. "Why don't you go home and you can eat these tomorrow after the funeral."

"Well, Donna, you were always such a sweet little peacemaker, weren't you? But sweetie, do you really need another recipe?" Lola Bee attacks.

I see Donna's mouth fly open but nothing comes out.

Maxine Massey quickly utters, "Donna, that is a lovely shirt you have on."

"Lola Bee, you're being as helpful as a trap door on a canoe!" Imogene's steely-eyed gaze makes Lola Bee back down.

"I'm sorry, Donna." Lola Bee insists. "That was wrong. I just can't see never eating another Jackson sandwich again. You girls have no idea how much she and her recipes mean to this town. She's gone, and Lord knows she's not coming back, but her recipe should stay put."

The seven of us are all standing at the back door facing each other showdown style. Maxine fills the silence again.

"You are grown women and most of you have children of your own, so maybe if we put it this way. We want our children and their children to have those sandwiches, too. It's silly, but it's a little piece of Boots history, and we're proud of it."

This needs to end. "We respect the four of you more than you know. Lola Bee and Imogene, you were a part of our childhood and you loved the woman that we came to know as our second mama, but we are not going to budge. You cannot come into this house." I start to giggle. I can't help it. "And if I have to take drastic measures to insure the top secret recipe stays in this room, then," I do my best impression of Scarlet O'Hara, "as God is my witness, I will do whatever it takes!"

The women stare at me but Belinda ducks back into the kitchen to laugh out loud. Donna begins mock applause for the performance.

"Please excuse me, but you do not seem to be taking us seriously," Barbara states this as if she is making a speech to Congress. "Please think carefully about this. In fact, I think it is only fair and civil to grant you some time to ponder what the right thing to do might be."

"That's a good idea, Barbara. Maggie, we'll be right here on the back lawn." Imogene leads the way to the picnic bench in the backyard.

"And don't think we will leave with the recipe!" Lola Bee yells as she takes her place on the picnic bench.

"You mean without the recipe," Imogene corrected.

"I said that."

"No you said, 'with' the recipe. That makes no sense."

"Imogene, for once can you act like we are on the same team?"

I close the door and smile at my partners.

"So, what do we do about them?" Donna asks. "It's dark, but it's not cold at all, so they just might be able to stay out there for a while."

A light bulb blinks to life atop my head. "I have a great idea!" I go over my plan with my conspirators.

"I'm not sure, Maggie. We are talking about seventy-year-olds," Donna questions.

"None of them even have a cane," Belinda urges. "They're in great shape."

"It would be a hoot!" I plead with Donna.

Donna sighs. "I don't know."

"Oh, and we should call Mark Kildwell," Belinda interjects. "Vern told me this morning that Mark hasn't changed a bit so I bet he's as funny as ever and would love this."

"It would be like a Texas made tribute to Cecelia, wouldn't it?" Donna is coming around.

"She is looking at us right now and I bet she is hooting and hollering…and these are her friends," I exclaim.

Belinda finds Mark Kildwell's phone number on the fridge and calls him. After she hangs up, she tells us, "He loves the idea of a replay of history and he'll be over a little while."

"Without the water, right?" Donna asked. "I mean, they're old ladies."

"We won't use water." I assure her. "But I know just what to use. It's somewhat poetic, in a way. A tribute to a great memory."

At sixteen, I hauled Bee and Donna around all the time because I got my driver's license first. One of those Friday nights, I cruised to Belinda and Donna's houses, gave them our secret-friend honk and away we went. We were going to ride around and listen to music for a while and then go over to Cecelia's for a sleepover. Belinda came up with the idea.

"Ain't it our turn with Mark Kildwell?" she asked.

"Yes, I think it is," Donna replied.

Mark Kildwell worked as the one and only mortician of Boots, Texas. He and his wife Cathy lived in Boots for close to ten years and served as the music minister and pianist at the Baptist Church. A little boy in a grown man's body, Mark was a master of practical jokes. His business' title, *Kildwell Funeral Home*, provided a source of humor for him and even landed a mini-spot on a T.V. show that highlighted quirky and unique personalities around the United States. Mark often played jokes on the three of us and the other youth in the church. His lawn got toilet papered often in retaliation, a badge of honor to Mark, and a pain to Cathy.

"Let's do the car thing. We've talked about it, but none of us have ever had a car," Belinda suggested.

The plan hatched and the three set of us off to the Kildwell home. At 10 p.m. I parked my car while Donna and Belinda took their 'supplies' and hid quickly in the bushes on the sides of Mark's home. Cathy answered the door. She eyed me suspiciously. "What are you up to this time of night, Maggie?"

"Hello, Mrs. Kildwell. My car stalled across the street. I just want to use your phone and call my mom."

"Um-hmm." She continued peering at me.

"Honestly, that's all. I just want to use the phone." I won Best Actress at the U.I.L. Area One Act Play contest.

"Well, okay. You know where it is." I came in and walked to the phone and I noticed Mrs. Kildwell leaned out the door and looked around. Apparently, she saw nothing because she shut the door and looked at me. As I picked up the phone to dial, Mark walked into the room.

"Hey there, Maggie, what's going on?" He spoke with the ultra twangy accent from East Texas. The Kildwells were both from Tyler, Texas.

I put the receiver back and looked at Mark. "My car. This is the very first night I've been able to drive by myself and my car broke down across the street. I need to call my mom and she'll come help me." My *approach included part damsel in distress and part matter of fact.*

Mark took the bait completely. "Well, don't call her yet. Let me take a look-see at your automobile and maybe I can help you out."

"Mark." Mrs. Kildwell's tone was obviously suspicious. "Are you sure?"

"Just being a good neighbor, honey." Mark led the way out the door and strode to my car. As soon as he walked past me, I took a right and ran to my station at the water hose. Donna and Belinda began the assault.

"AAH!" We all yelled our war cry as the onslaught of water balloons streaked through the sky. Being veterans of many hours of practice, Donna and Belinda knew how to reach the desired target.

"What are you doing?" Mark yelled and then began to laugh and run. The bullets of water followed him and soon he stood soaked, not only by the balloons but from the dousing of water he took from the water hose I commandeered. Finally Mark ran out of shooting distance, taking cover behind the left side of the house. I turned off the hose, Belinda and Donna each grabbed a bucket and the three of us ran to the car stumbling and laughing.

As we got in the car, Mark called, "You girls are gonna get it big-time," in his twangy Texas way.

For the next hour and a half, we rode around, stopped at the truck stop for nachos, listened to music, and all the while told the story of our prank over and over. At midnight we decided to go to Cecelia's. She told us that we could come in late, but to notify her as soon as we got there. When we reached the stately house, we crossed the front yard, each of us carrying our overnight bags.

"That's weird." Donna remarked after shaking the front door knob. "It's locked."

"No, it's not. It's never locked," I said, leaning in to have a go. But I couldn't open it. "You're right, it is." The house was completely dark.

"Ring the doorbell." Belinda suggested.

"What if they're asleep?" Donna said.

"We're supposed to wake Cecelia up anyway," Belinda argued.

"How about we knock and yell for Cecelia? That won't be quite as loud as the doorbell." Donna began knocking. "Cecelia," she whispered.

"Come on, Donna. Cecelia!" Belinda yelled.

The inside entryway light went on. A calm voice came through the door. "Who is it?"

"Cecelia," Donna answered, "it's us."

"Us who?" Cecelia said seriously.

Belinda and I exchanged puzzled glances. "Cecelia," I called, "it's Maggie, Donna and Belinda. You said we could have a sleepover here tonight."

"Oh, yes, that's right." A moment of silence filled the night.

"Well," Belinda said, "Can we come in?"

"No, I don't think so." Cecelia's voice showed no emotion.

"Why not?" Donna asked.

"Because," Cecelia began talking loudly and in a very twangy accent, "you girls are gonna get it big time."

We turned to run. At the same moment, a floodlight from Mark Kildwell's truck, hidden until now on the side of the house, hit us. Bathed in light, we stood for a moment like three deer facing a car. The next moment we were soaked from head to toe. Mark's funeral home assistant, Fred Walters, stood in the pickup bed, shining the lights on us as we ran around, frantically dodging the water. Mrs. Kildwell held the Jackson's water hose in her hand on the east side of the house, while Mark stood at the west side. Both smiled and giggled as the ambush raged on. We laughed and screamed. As suddenly as the assault started, it ended. Fred killed the light and Cathy and Mark jogged to the truck and hopped in and drove off. We were now wet rags fresh out of a washer whose spin cycle doesn't work. We stood in the middle of *the Jackson yard, giggling. The front door creaked open and I turned to look. A hand come out and plopped three towels down on the front porch. Cecelia giggled from inside and then told us in a quiet, calm voice, "Dry off best you can. Then come on in."*

"It's gonna take a little while for us to get ready. Do you think they'll wait?" I ask as I bring in two buckets I'd found in the laundry room.

"Are you kidding? Those old women are stubborn as mules. They aren't going anywhere." Belinda replies.

"You know, it is kind of a shame that we can't give them the recipe. It really wouldn't hurt to leave it here in Boots, would it?" Donna suggests as she brings in to the kitchen a big box from the pantry.

"It was Cecelia's right to do this. It's her recipe." I know how to construct the kind of doohickey we need to execute our plan. Raising three boys teaches you certain information. Like a pie in the face, this trick never gets old to me. The phone rings and Mark tells me he is ready with his part. I open a window to listen to the ladies as Belinda and Donna finish setting up.

"Exactly how long are we supposed to wait?" Lola Bee complains.

"Lola Bee, we have to show them that we are women of our word. Even if we don't get the recipe tonight, we will have planted a seed." Barbara explains to her friends the big picture. "One of them will see the error of their ways and end up giving one of us the recipe. Mark my words, ladies."

"So, Barbara, as I said, how late?"

"I don't want to miss the late, late movie tonight. It's *Stella Dallas*. The one with Barbara Stanwyck," remarks Maxine.

"I like the Bette Midler version better," Lola Bee remarks.

"Really?" Maxine responds.

"Just a little while longer, girls," says Imogene, loudly. "I feel something is bound to happen. We are, you know, four poor old senior citizens, feeble and all."

The quartet laughs at this.

Belinda signals to me that everything is ready and in place. "Okay, I opened up the window to let some of the heat out," I call out nice and loud.

"Did you hear that?" Lola Bee asks.

"Shhh! We can hear what they're saying now," Imogene orders.

"Can we please take a break?" Donna pleads. "I'm tired. Let's go sit in the Visiting Room for a while."

"Sounds good," I agree. I lean in to the window to hear how the old ladies react.

"Now is our chance, women. We have to do something." Imogene sounds as if she has stood up.

"Heat? Do you think she's cooking something for the tuna fish recipe?" Maxine wonders.

"Let's just go in there and find out," Lola Bee barks in a large whisper.

"We have to have a plan, ladies. Let's get organized." Barbara adds.

"Okay," Imogene says, "I'll go in, go right, and search all of the right side of the kitchen. Barbara you go left and Maxine, you search in the middle. Lola Bee, you go right over to the door that leads to the hallway to the Visiting Room. If you hear anything you whistle."

"Imogene Friesen, you know I can't whistle. Why on God's green planet do you bring up my shortcomings at a time like this?"

"You can't whistle? I never knew that. Didn't you see that Bogart and Bacall movie? You just put your lips together and blow."

"Imogene, I cannot whistle, I just told you that. And no

amount of movie watching is gonna help me." Her tone is getting angry.

"Ladies," Barbara interrupts. "Please, we are wasting valuable time. Lola Bee, why don't you just snap your fingers?"

"Now that I can do," she says, "and I never learned it from a movie neither."

"You certainly are testy tonight," Imogene counters.

"LADIES," Maxine yells, "ARE WE GOING TO GO ON OUR COVERT MISSION OR NOT?"

I look over at Belinda and Donna and we are all trying hard not to laugh out loud. "Desperate measures and all that," Maxine whispers.

I hear the four seniors attempt to tiptoe up the back porch stairs. We are all watching the door. It opens and the four quickly move through. "Go, go, go." All of them are barking orders.

"AAAAAAAAAAAA!" Lola Bee cries and begins to wipe at her body as if spiders were crawling on her.

Barbara and Maxine both jump forward and turn around quickly, brushing out something from their hair.

Imogene yells, "WHAT IN THE WORLD?" as she ducks and covers in genuine surprise.

Looking at each other and the floor around them in shock, the ladies find themselves surrounded by tiny goldfish crackers, some of which are still in each lady's gray and white hair.

"LADIES!" Mark Kildwell turns on the back porch light. The screen door is held open by Nancy of *Nancy's News*. She looks much older than I remember.

CLICK! Nancy takes the photo and the four old women stand in astonishment.

I proudly announce, "Ladies, you can't have the tuna, but how 'bout the goldfish?"

"Well, I never...." Lola Bee says, furiously.

"I cannot believe this!" shouts Barbara.

"What were they thinking?" begins Imogene in mock anger, "We are just four old feeble senior citizens!" And then her laugh sounds and fills the house.

Maxine joins in, "They got us, that's for sure."

Belinda, Donna and I are laughing.

Lola Bee is still upset. "I can't believe you ladies, who are not teenagers anymore, would stoop to such an inane trick just because we are trying to uphold a long standing tradition for our community." She accentuates her tirade with an audible huff. "And on the eve of Cecelia's funeral!" Her eyes are angry but they are darting around looking at the pickles in the bowls.

I'm still smirking but I'm trying not to laugh out loud.

"Mrs. Turner, we didn't mean any harm," Donna says.

"Oh, Lola Bee, it was all in fun. And you know Cecelia would have loved it," Barbara agrees.

"I just have one question for you, ladies," Imogene remarks. "Do you have the recipe for these goldfish crackers? They look pretty good." With that, she takes one from her hair and eats it and we all laugh except Lola Bee who is still snarling.

"Now you have to leave," I say and Belinda, Donna and I usher them out.

Before Nancy and Mark leave, Nancy tells us she will write about the incident and put it in the next week's paper. Later, I read the article:

Fishing for Fish Recipe ends in Fish Fallout

This last week saw Boots celebrating the life of one of our dearest loved members, Cecelia May Jackson. In honor of her memory, four of her dearest friends attempted to pry the long celebrated top-secret Jackson tuna fish recipe from the hands of its new owners. But as many of us know, crime never pays and the four lovely ladies, shown here in Cecelia's kitchen, fell prey to a practical joke involving the elements of surprise and snack crackers. Everyone laughed and forgave. A reconciliatory lunch at Ortega's was planned, including this week's special, soft chicken tacos with a guacamole salad.

Chapter 25

Donna

As I stand on the back porch watching the old women shuffle off home, I can't seem to stuff enough goldfish crackers into my mouth. I hope that witch, Mrs. Turner, is seeing this. Of course, she made another crack about my weight. It hurt. And I did nothing but stand there. I should've told her off. I should've said something horribly mean. But I just went blank. I am better than this. Why this backward town has this effect on me, I don't know. Of course, Mrs. Turner left angry and muttering. I'm glad. The rest of her cohorts laughed it all off.

At the side gate, Mrs. Friesen stops and turns around, "Donna Gail, consider yourself and your friends winners of this battle, but know that the war is still on!" Her cackle echoes through the night air and I turn to go back into the kitchen.

"So where were we?" Maggie is still laughing.

"We just finished the pickles," Belinda instructs. "Now on to the onions, while we boil all the eggs."

I'm tired and after the saltiness of the crackers, I need something sweet to balance them out. I plop down at the Formica table and reach into my pocket. I pull out a couple of wrapped pieces of chocolate, unwrap them and pop them in my mouth.

"Come on Donna, look alive!" Maggie puts bags of onions on the counter. "We just got the better of four of the sweetest battle-axes Texas has ever seen."

"That was a truly priceless moment," says Belinda. "I wish Tracey could have seen it."

I'm surprised at this. Belinda has proven to me in just a short amount of time that mothering is not her forte. She doesn't care about that child.

"You know, Belinda, you could've asked your daughter to help us prepare the food. It wouldn't have hurt her to stay up for a while."

Belinda is still smiling. "Donna, no offense, but I can tell you ain't raised a child."

"Well, do me a favor and don't attempt to teach any parenting classes, okay?" I snap this out and I immediately regret my choice of words. I'm just hungry and hurt by Mrs. Turner. A moment of awkward silence enters the kitchen. I watch Belinda's face turn from fun to anger.

"Don't ever talk to me about being a mother, Donna. You ain't got no idea what it's like to have a family."

I stand up and get in her face. "Apparently you don't either by the way you treat that little girl." My aggressiveness surprises me but I like the feeling.

"Come on ladies." Maggie separates us. "We are not kids

anymore. Settle down. We were having so much fun so let's not spoil it. Let's just cut some onions and try not to cry."

I walk over, get my cutting board and knife, and sit at the table. Maggie gets three big pots, fills them with water and turns on the burners. In silence, Maggie and Belinda set up their stations and begin chopping along with me. I am tired and hungry. Belinda thinks she is the only one who has had trouble? Really? My hands start to shake and I put my knife down. Well, she is about to pay for her troubles. At least I'm not a criminal. I have absolutely no regrets about making that call. She deserves everything she is going to get.

I glare at her and words just tumble out. "Listen, you do not have the corner on the market in tragic life events, okay? We each have lived twenty-five years outside of this bubble. Life beyond the Visiting Room proved difficult for me too, and just because I didn't get the joy or privilege of raising kids, and it is a joy and privilege since you seem to have forgotten, that doesn't mean I am less of a woman than you or that I haven't shed a few tears myself!" I never raise my voice. But it feels good, even freeing. "So please excuse me for daring to insult your precious mothering skills!" I pick up my knife.

Belinda mumbles something but I can't understand it.

"Donna, do you want to take a break or go take a nap or something?" Maggie's kindness irritates me.

"Were you always so stinking nice, Maggie?" I ask.

Belinda laughs at this.

Maggie's eyebrows rise. "Of course, I was always this stinking nice. I was also the best dancer of the three of us, the best cook, the best dressed, and the friendliest."

Belinda sticks her knife into her cutting board. "Now, just watch it there, Missy. I was definitely the best cook."

"I was the best dancer," I say. This is a true statement.

"Wasn't I voted best dressed?" Belinda adds.

"I believe I got most friendly," I continue. I'm grinning at Belinda.

"Fine! But I was always this nice," Maggie said. This time, I appreciate Maggie's sneak attack at humor.

"Point taken," I concede. "But I don't need a break. I too, will chop my share of onions."

For a moment, the only sound in Cecelia's kitchen is the thumping of my knife, the clockwork beat of Maggie's knife and the rat-a-tat machine gun chopping of Belinda's knife.

"So, tell me, Donna, what tragedy has life given you? Please don't be offended, but if your tragedy is an insufficient amount of dates or not enough marriage proposals, then honey, you don't know the meaning of tragedy," Belinda comments.

I stop cutting. "Do you really want to know what happened to me when I left Boots?"

"I would really like to know," Belinda answers.

"I would, too," adds Maggie.

I regret asking. If I tell them, what will they think? I just couldn't deal with 'Poor Donna' looks. Not here. Then again, what do I care? They're just two old acquaintances that I will never see again after this weekend.

"Okay. I've never told anyone except Cecelia. And if you cry, I won't know if it's my sad life or the onions. That'll be fine with me."

I begin in the Visiting Room, my favorite place as a child, underneath my favorite verse.

"Take delight in the Lord and He will give you the desires of your hearts." Psalm 37:4

"Remember that one? It's still in there. I looked for it when I arrived. I wanted to know if I made it up in my mind. But it's hanging in there, painted in oils. Cecelia's walls always inspired me, but that verse was special. Just for me. And so I took it with me, in my heart, when I went to Texas Tech." I laugh with bitterness. "I dreamed of being an accountant who shined for Jesus. That was the plan or should I say God's will, Maggie?" I don't wait for an answer. "And as I delighted in Christ, He would give me the desire of my heart - a husband and a family."

I look down at the onions and I feel the old shame creeping up my spine. "Turns out, I just didn't delight enough, I guess. I didn't have the strength." I chop some more in silence, preparing my words. "So, I took classes at Texas Tech and I loved college. I went to the Baptist Student Union, met many friends, and even dated some great guys. No one special, but I felt like they were 'prep' men, getting me ready for the one, right? And then my junior year, my dad died. Just like that." Twenty-two years ago. The grief is still a stealth monster in my heart that causes a throbbing pain when I don't expect it. "At forty-four, he died of a heart attack in his sleep. Ridiculous."

"I'm so sorry, Donna," Maggie whispers.

Belinda joins in, "Me too."

"I thought about calling you both but we had written each other off. But you know, since I'm an only child I found myself with no parents and no family. Incredibly difficult time. I talked to Cecelia almost daily for a long time. A close friend at Tech helped me, but I just…just wanted something more. And I didn't know how to get it from God. I tried. Cecelia helped me the best she could. My senior year, I got a job at a small Baptist church there in Lubbock as the pianist. I quit the large church I attended to take the job. I really loved the big church but I felt that I needed the extra money, because I wanted to get a new car. Seems Daddy used his savings for my college, so no inheritance. We rented our house in Boots, so no money from that. I always loved playing the piano, and this church was small and they didn't need any fancy playing, just hymns for worship and accompanying the special music. Each week I prepared a solo for the offering time, and I loved that. They required me to be the pianist for the choir, too. And that meant rehearsals every Thursday night." My eyes mist up. "Darn onions."

"I loved the people in the choir. Only about twenty of them, but they each befriended me and made me feel like family. I really felt loved and accepted. And then there was the music minister, Dennis."

I haven't said that name aloud in years. I stop talking and look at the pans of water on the stove. The steam is rising as the water boils. "It's time to put the eggs in, ladies."

"Hold your thought," Belinda says. Belinda and Maggie quickly put the eggs in to boil. As soon as they finish, they once again go back to chopping.

"Continue, Donna," Maggie says.

"I guess the rest of what happened occurred on those Thursday nights. It's strange to talk about this. It was…." I can't believe the math. "Twenty-two years ago."

I want to tell this story. I want to say the words aloud. But what if Belinda, who has apparently become so angry over time, makes light of what happened? And what if Maggie, who seems exactly the same and has probably never experienced any real tragedy, glosses over it by calling it God's will or some other hellish Christian cliché? I just don't know if I can do this. I don't know these women any longer. I look up and see their faces, glancing at me and then back to their onions. Patiently. They aren't hurrying me or asking me questions. They're just waiting.

These are the soulmates of my youth, not just old

acquaintances. I can tell them.

I travel back to that little church in Lubbock, Texas and see those faces of people who lifted me up after Dad died. I also see my own face, young and hopeful. A face so different than the one I see in a mirror today.

"Is there any way we could transpose that entire song to the key of B flat?" His voice reminded me of a local deejay's and I always blushed when I heard it directed towards me.

"Sure, whatever you want."

Choir practice started in five minutes. As my newfound friends showed up and took their places in the choir loft, Dennis and I plowed through the notes for the upcoming rehearsal's songs. "During He Lives, I think we surprise everyone in the entire Baptist community and sing verse three. It's a dramatic departure but I feel we as modern Baptists can handle it."

"Sure, whatever you want." Quit saying the same thing, Donna. I looked up from the pages of music to see his twinkling eyes looking at me.

"Joke, Donna." Dennis's smile told me he wasn't laughing at me but at a joke he'd made.

"What?" I fumbled and felt embarrassed again.

"The third verse? Don't you feel it's time we made our mark on church history? No self-respecting Baptist choir ever seems to sing the third verse."

"Oh, that." I giggled but it was the kind of laugh that pops up after the joke has already had its moment.

"Are you okay?" His voice produced warm and soft inflections. Music to my ears. It made me even more nervous.

"I'm fine. Are there any more notes for me?" I wanted this conversation to end.

"Yes," he said, but looked at me unsurely. "I believe that will do for tonight."

Soon, everyone arrived and choir practice began. I felt sure of myself, happy and loved. I joined in on the laughter between songs and even added a comment or two about the arrangements. The joy of singing filled the atmosphere.

Later that night, I made the same call I made every Thursday night. "Cecelia, I just love playing for them and singing with them. And if I make a mistake, which I do a lot, they don't seem to care."

"Donna, they probably don't even notice."

"Maybe not. I don't care, really. I just feel like I'm in a family again. Like I did at our church and like I did in your house in the Visiting Room."

"How are you doing?"

The question might seem out of place in the middle of a conversation, but I knew exactly what she meant. One year, one month, two weeks and three days since Dad died. I loved numbers, and counting the days seemed to help me make sense of it all. "I miss him so much."

"I know, honey."

"Most of the time I'm fine. But then someone brings up their family and for some reason, I just want to crawl into a hole and cry for days."

"Donna, you have to remember, sweetie, you are not alone. You always have me and Vern, and more importantly, you always have Christ. Always."

"I know. I know He's here, Cecelia. I just don't seem to feel Him a lot."

"You know what? Some times in life I think all that we are required to do by Christ is to hang on to Him. Nothing else. Just hang on, little one."

"What about the rest of the time? What's required then?"

"To find someone who is just hanging on - and encourage them to not let go."

The next Thursday night my hands shook as I sat down on the piano bench. Dennis wore a blue button down I loved. I told myself over and over, Come on, Donna, he's married. He's married. He's married. He's married.

"Let's get started, everyone," Dennis announced.

Thank God. After the amens, Charlotte Goosby made an announcement. "Everyone is invited to come over to our house Saturday night. We are having a choir get together!"

Her husband, Merle, echoed, "We have invited every other choir in town, but none of them can make it, so you're what we're ending up with."

"Oh Merle," Charlotte said with a look to her husband. "Anyway, we will have a barbeque, so bring a side dish and we'll provide the meat. We'll have some good barbeque and play some games or something fun."

"I promise to not let Charlotte show you videos of the grandkids," Merle added.

"Oh, Merle!" Charlotte gave him the look again, but he squeezed her close and she smiled. They were an adorable older couple that minded me of Cecelia and Mr. Jackson. After choir practice, I gathered up my music while everyone made their way out.

"Donna," Charlotte Goosby approached me, "you were once again wonderful. It's as if Van Cliburn himself graced our midst. We are so thankful you're here."

I laughed at the comparison. "Thank you. It's a blessing in my life."

"You are coming Saturday, right?"

"Absolutely. It sounds like fun," I answered, "What should I bring?"

"Bring your boyfriend." This came from Amanda Peterson, Dennis's wife, who had walked up to us.

"I would if I had one." I giggled and Charlotte joined me, but Amanda just walked away. When I called Cecelia, I told her about it.

"Do you think she wants to set you up with someone?" Cecelia inquired.

"No, in fact, she doesn't ever really talk to me."

"Hmm. You said she's married to the music minister?"

"Yes. I talk to him, but only right before practice. He makes me blush and I always feel nervous around him."

"Well, there it is, sugar."

"What? She was kind of mean because her husband makes me nervous?"

"Donna, you are the most innocent thing I have ever met. I love it! But, goodness, you are an adult out in the world now, and you have to know that wives don't like to see their husbands flirting."

"What?" I felt the heat rising to my cheeks. "Cecelia, he's married, I told you that!"

"Yes."

"I do not flirt with him. All we talk about is the music. That's all."

"Well, maybe I am wrong, Donna. Lord knows it wouldn't be the first time. But just to make sure, you steer clear of him at that party. Okay?"

"Fine with me. I tell you he makes me nervous." After we hung up, I asked God to help me. This was trouble.

At the party, I walked away any time Dennis came near me. I only talked to him when we were in a crowd. But I started getting nervous again when I noticed Amanda looking at me. More than once. I decided to leave early.

"You can't leave now, sweetie. It's only nine," Charlotte implored.

"I'm so sorry, Charlotte. This headache is just killing me." With that, I dodged out to my car. As I opened the door to my Maroon Chevette, I heard his voice.

"Donna. Wait a minute." Dennis stood in front of me, my open car door between us.

"Hi, Dennis. I'm going home." Get in the car. Get in the car.

"What's wrong? Are you angry with me?" His face filled with concern and I noticed dark blue eyes. With the streetlight hitting us, those eyes looked royal blue, my favorite color. The Lubbock wind tossed his black hair around. I couldn't breathe.

"I have to go, Dennis. I don't feel well." I should have gotten in the car. But I stood there. My legs wouldn't move.

"Did Amanda say something to you? Did she hurt your feelings?" He cared about me.

"She didn't say anything to me."

"Well, then what is it? You seem like you avoided me all night."

I couldn't tell him the truth. I felt silly and stupid. Why had Cecelia planted the thought in my mind? "Listen, I just need to go home, okay?" I forced myself to get in the car and leave.

I told Cecelia I would call after the party. I didn't.

The next day at church, I felt waves of melancholy hit me as if I was sitting in a rocky boat. I'd created this ridiculous drama and now I didn't know how to end it. I tried to avoid Dennis but he came right up to me after church ended. "Donna, wonderful playing today. I really liked the offertory. Count Your Many Blessings never sounded so good."

"I found a new arrangement." I used my most nonchalant voice.

"Listen, can you stay for a while today and talk? I want your opinion on some choices for special music for Mother's Day."

I sighed. I'd created my own little silly soap opera. This couldn't affect my job. And Mother's Day's was a big day for our church. "Yes, I'll stay."

He smiled a gorgeous smile and said, "Okay, I have to go mingle a bit and tell Amanda, but I'll meet you back here at the piano in ten minutes."

An hour later, we finished going through the Mother's Day pieces. "Okay, then we will do this one for special music and then this for the offertory."

"Sounds good." Nothing felt weird. Finally, I could relax.

"Thank you, Donna. You know, I never seem to have a chance to tell you this, but you are an incredibly special woman."

Relaxation left as I tensed up. Woman? Did he just call me a woman? No man had ever called me a woman. "Thank you, Dennis," I said quietly. "You are very sweet."

"You think so? I wish my wife did."

I don't know why but I felt my heart thumping like a bass drum. All I could think of was how crazy his wife must be not to see Dennis for the incredible man I knew him to be. I stood up from the bench and gathered my music. I needed to tell him. "I don't know what she's thinking. You're a great man, Dennis. The way you lead our choir and the way you always seem to know what's going on in everyone's lives. You care, you really do. You are extremely sweet." I meant every word.

In slow motion, it happened. I felt his arms around me in an embrace.

"Thank you, Donna," he whispered in my ear. "Thank you."

My stomach did flip-flops and I left. But I played the moment repeatedly in my mind. I had never felt this way. The phone rang that night. I answered it, with a silly hope that it might be Dennis.

"Donna, it's Cecelia. How are you?"

I kept it to small talk, even when Cecelia probed me. The hug, the relationship with Dennis belonged to me. Only me.

Thursdays began to start earlier. I arrived a little sooner hoping he would be there. And he usually was. For two months, we talked and talked. Not about music anymore but about life and what we wanted from it. Dennis understood me. He lost his mother, too. Amanda didn't appreciate what he did for their family and she always nagged him about making more money. Dennis and I talked about how life meant having joy and love. Not money. He couldn't believe no one had 'snatched me up.'

Every week we stayed after choir rehearsal, usually for a half hour. Amanda drove separately. Our talks always ended in wonderful hugs. I loved it when his arms were around me. A truly great man appreciating me. He became my best friend.

Sometime after the fourth of July, we stayed after rehearsal and talked. But this time, longer than usual. When he embraced me for our normal hug, he held on for longer than he'd ever held me. I melted. He leaned me back but didn't let go. His eyes looked at my eyes and then my mouth. And we kissed. I fell in love. I'd never felt like that.

"Amanda is out of town. Would you like to go somewhere with me?" His lips were on my ear kissing me.

I pulled back. "Why?"

"Donna, I want to be with you. I love you and I want to marry you. I am going to leave Amanda. She doesn't love me anymore. I'll have to leave this church, but for you, it's worth it."

My hands trembled. I couldn't do this. But I loved him. Maybe God's plan included him and me together. I tried to think logically. I remembered I'd vowed not to have sex before marriage. I told myself to apply the same reasoning to this decision as I would to an accounting problem. But the pulsating of my heart drummed out the logic.

"Where should we go?" The words just came out.

We drove separately to a hotel. On the way, I found myself wanting to call Cecelia. But I didn't. She would only try to talk me out of it. But she didn't know Dennis. She couldn't know how much he loved me and how much I loved him.

I thought of the three of us as girls swearing that we would wait until we married. And I thought of Belinda and Alan Deltan. I tried to remember the reasons for waiting until marriage, but I couldn't remember even one. All I could think of was Dennis and how glorious *our life would be together.*

At the hotel, he checked us in as Mr. and Mrs. Peterson. I couldn't stop smiling.

The next morning, we said goodbye in the parking lot. He smiled at me with a promise. He told me he would tell Amanda that night when she came home.

I thought he would call me that night but he didn't. I figured he had to wait until after Sunday. I knew church would be difficult, but I would face the world, if necessary, to stand by his side. When I got to church, I couldn't find him. He came in just as the choir sat in the loft. I looked for his eyes. Nothing.

After church, I caught him alone in the choir room. "Dennis, are you okay?"

He glanced toward me and turned back to a pile of music on a table. "I have some music sheets to get and then I need to go home. I think Amanda invited some people over."

Amanda? "Did I do something wrong?"

"I'm sorry?"

"I asked you if I did something wrong?"

He didn't turn to look at me. "I think you played quite well, Donna. Although you did hit a wrong note in the middle of Amazing Grace. *Seems like you would know that one by heart."*

He was talking about music?

"Dennis, what are you doing? After Thursday night?"

He jerked around to look at me. Cold. "Thursday night? Nothing happened Thursday night. Amanda and I were home. I love her so much. God gave me a gift when he gave me her. No one else in the world could ever hold a candle to that woman, you know?"

My body went numb and I sat in the closest chair. Dennis turned back to the pile of music sheets. "Dennis?" I whispered.

The man I gave my heart and my body to gathered some music and left the room without another look or word.

One week later, I quit my job at the church, amidst several objections by choir members, and amidst nothing but silence from the music minister.

My call to Cecelia would be my last.

"Donna, honey? Did you get my messages? I haven't heard from you in five weeks. I tell you, I have been worried."

"Cecelia, I'm moving to Denver."

"Denver? Why Denver?"

"I have a chance for a great job. And it's a way to leave Texas behind me."

"Donna, talk to me. What happened?"

The sobs came easily and then the torrent of what happened soon followed. I spared no detail and confessed all. "I'm no good, Cecelia. That's the bottom line."

"Sweetie, listen to me. You are human. You made a mistake. But there is forgiveness. You just have to ask and receive. And by the way, that music minister is a snake in the grass."

"I'm so stupid. Afterwards, he wouldn't look at me. He ignored me. I am so ashamed, Cecelia. I didn't think I would ever do something like that. I really meant it when I said I loved Jesus and I would save myself for marriage. I did. I really loved him."

"Donna, giving into temptation is just a lack of trust in God's providence. It is a lack of trusting that God, and only God can take care of your loneliness. But we all give in to temptation. All of us. Just makes you like everyone else – human."

"It's too late now."

"No, it's not, honey. It's never too late. Christ is right there with you right now. Just look to Him and talk to Him."

"No, I'm just not good enough, Cecelia. I mean, I knew better. I was raised in church and I sat through endless hours of you pouring God's

Word into us. I made a choice, Cecelia. And now I have to live with it. That's all."

"Seems to me you have another choice to make. Talk to Jesus. Or not."

"Not."

I spoke the word as a frozen testament engraved with letters that would never melt away.

"Donna, I'm coming to see you."

"No, Cecelia. I'm leaving in a week anyway."

"I'll be there tomorrow."

"She came, too. Spent the last week in Texas with me. Loved me and held me." I sigh and stop chopping. Maggie and Belinda are both sniffing. I don't know whether the cause is my story or the onions.

"Men are pigs, Donna," Belinda pronounces judgment as if the final word.

"Not all are, Belinda." Maggie finishes her last onion.

"Maggie, go out there and really live and then tell me if you know so much. Diapers and church teas have filled your life, right? Donna will tell you, Christ was a great man to live for in Boots, but out there in the real world, Jesus Christ is not real and all the men to choose from are rolling around in the mud and living for the slop pigs."

"Belinda, are you forgetting I grew up with a drunken wife-beater?" Maggie points out.

"Point made, then," Belinda shoots back.

I don't agree. "Belinda, my father was not a pig. Mr. Jackson isn't a pig. And I wouldn't call Dennis a pig. Speak for yourself, okay?"

"Are you kidding me? Sounds like Dennis took up residence in the trough like a pig with a capital P," Belinda replies and keeps cutting.

After a moment of silence, I add, "Cecelia did something I will never forget when she visited. A very Cecelia thing to do, too. Do you both remember when my mom died?"

"Yes, I think. We were little but I don't remember how old," Maggie answers.

"I was nine. I loved my mother very much, and I don't know if I ever told you this, but she had a serious problem."

"Who doesn't?" Belinda asks.

"I know, but my mom gambled. Did I ever tell you that?" After the girls shake their heads, I continue, "She would gamble and she would take money from wherever she found it. It didn't matter. My mother acted differently when she planned to go out to gamble. I remember so clearly. She became another person, very Jekyll and Hyde-like. My father started to give me silver dollars when I was four or five. I collected them. Those coins were like my secret treasures. One day my mother needed money, and she came to my room and took my twelve silver dollars. Said she would pay me back, but she never did."

"You never told me that," Maggie interjects.

"I felt so ashamed. And when she died, I just kind of let it go."

"What did Cecelia have to do with that?" Belinda asks.

"I told her about it at the time. But we hardly ever talked about it after that. Until she came to Lubbock. We talked for a long time, then, about everything. I told Cecelia it was time for me to grow up. A day or so before she left and I moved to Denver, she drove me to a bank.

"If you want to grow up, here is a great way to do it." Cecelia turned off the ignition and turned in her seat to me.

241

I looked at the bank. "I cleared out my account already. Why are we are here?"

"It is time for you to take ownership of who you are."

"You are going to have to speak English if you want me to understand."

"Dennis did not make you sin; you made that choice."

I felt my anger rise. "Cecelia, I know that. I am the one who sinned."

"It takes two to tango, sweetie and that Dennis is a dirt-bag filled up with pond muck. It wasn't all your fault but you need to own your part. But you also need to own the fact that you are not the only sinner in the world. You are not unique in that way. You need to own up to the fact that people hurt you, including Dennis. Including your mom."

I open the car door. "Why are you bringing her up? What do you want from me?"

"Donna, I want you to love who you are. I want you to see God made you who you are and that you are a redeemed, wonderful woman. I want you to take back the parts of you that you seem to have lost because other people hurt you. Their wounds are stealing from you."

"Cecelia, how exactly do I do that?"

"Give God a chance to lead you, first and foremost."

"We've talked about that. I need a break from God, okay?"

"Secondly, go in that bank and ask the teller for twelve silver dollars."

The memory flew in the car and hit me in the heart. Why did Cecelia do this?

"Do it, Donna. Take back part of what you lost."

With no other words to Cecelia, I got out of the car, as much to escape as to do what she asked. I exchanged a ten and two ones for twelve shiny silver dollars.

"I kept those coins for years. They helped me, in some way, to reestablish who I wanted to be in Denver. But I'm not sure where they are now." I finish my pile of onions and wipe my eyes. "I think I lost them in a move somewhere over the years."

"What an empowering thing to do, Donna," Maggie says through tears.

"I guess so," I reply.

"Have you ever forgiven yourself, Donna?" Maggie's voice oozes sympathy but she is missing her target.

"Come on Magpie, she doesn't need to forgive anybody, especially herself."

I ignore Belinda and stare at Maggie. "It just doesn't matter anymore. Listen, I need a minute." I stand up and walk down the hall to the Visiting Room to find my purse. I look around and glance at all the verses surrounding me. Lies. Stupid lies that set me up for failure in the world. Tears cloud my vision as I locate my purse and sit beside it.

I look on my phone and check Facebook and see that I have a message. It's from the old geezer. Apparently, he can still message me even if I've deleted him from my list of friends. I click on his message.

Your loss, sweetheart. I believe those hips of yours are a bit big for my taste, anyway.

I hit reply.

My gain. I refuse to have anything to do with a lying sack of short bones on his way to the grave.

I hit send and regret it as soon as I click. No need to stoop to his level. And that's a pretty short level. How could I not see through him? What is wrong with me?

I check email and see I have 21 messages, mostly from organizations I've signed up for or from Gina. But there is one from Stuart:

Donna,

I am so sorry for the loss of your Texas friend. Two years ago, I lost my favorite aunt and I still miss her kindness and banana nut bread. I'm praying for you.

When you get back, I'd like to talk to you. Not office stuff.

Take care of yourself,

Stuart

I read it three more times. No. No, I am not going to start thinking he is interested in me. There's no way, anyway. He's too good. And he's praying? Please.

I pick up my purse and I find the bag of candy corn in the lower left pocket. They taste good. Sweet. I lean back to relax and breathe. Maybe I shouldn't have told them what happened. I don't know. My eyes zero in on the painting directly in front of me. It's that verse, Psalm 37:4.

Leave me alone! I grab another handful of candy.

Chapter 26

Maggie

God, are you seeing this? Please help Donna.

Belinda and I drain the hot water from the pans and run cool water over the eggs. We each take a pan to the table and begin peeling, a trashcan on the floor between us.

"Well, I guess it goes to show you. Religious training just brings guilt." Belinda's comment is callous.

"Whatever, Belinda." I don't feel like arguing.

"So, Maggie, what about you?"

I look up at Belinda, startled and annoyed. "I'm sorry?"

"Has anything real happened to you? Probably not. You got your precious God to protect you, right?"

I am just too tired to talk to her. *Lord. Please*

help her shut up.

"You don't have an answer, Miss Maggie?"

"Belinda, I'm tired, okay? Let's not talk."

"I'm right, aren't I? You've got yourself a pretty easy life. I know, I know, your dad was the Boots drunk, but besides that, I bet you've had a cakewalk right through your church parking lots and potlucks."

I stop peeling and glare at her. "Why are you so mean-spirited?"

"Me? Why, darlin' I just tell it like I see it."

I keep peeling and look away from her. I don't understand women like this that just can't seem to see good in anything. She made her own bed. We would never be friends today. I couldn't take all of her negativity.

Forgive.

What? I have, God. Leave me alone. The thought shakes me. *Now* You're talking to me. What about giving me a little help here, Jesus?

"So, what about it?" Belinda's words. I look at her and see she is grinning a little malevolent grin.

"What about what?" I don't smile back.

"You. We know you're happily married with three boys and you still love doing the church and God thing, but all that's pretty boring, ain't it?"

I've had it. She has no idea and no way am I going to tell her. Forgive her, God? Where do I start? She is obnoxious and cruel. I stand up and put the peeled egg I have in the bowl. I leave the kitchen and walk out the back door. I need some air.

"Little rude for a Christian!" Belinda calls.

The stars are sparkling like beautiful tiny diamonds in the vast ebony sky. I love the night sky in West Texas more than anywhere in the world. Frank and I moved frequently during our first ten years of marriage. Took him a while to find the right job in the insurance business. I've looked up into many a night sky, and none can astound me like this.

Through memory and moonlight, I go through the arched gate and find the bench at the back of the expansive garden. Even in the dark, I recognize different colors trying to shine through the flower petals. The smells fill me up and the silence is deep and encompassing. As I sit, I do the one thing that seems the most natural. I talk to the Father.

God, he beat her. The man who I thought would be my husband and a pastor beat her. I have to tell her, don't I, Lord? Oh, help me! You are God above all and You know what's going on inside of me. Lord, this is Your work. You allow everything. Nothing happens without it being sifted through Your loving hands. I know if I tell myself truth, it might sink in.

So, help me be honest. Help me forgive. Really, truly, honestly, completely forgive. I miss Frank so much. It seems like weeks since I've seen him and it's only been a couple of days. I know You will give him guidance when I tell him. Please show him how to lead our family with Your wisdom.

I look up and try to find the Big Dipper and the Little Dipper. I stare at the moon.

Jesus, guide me in how to love these two. Should I tell them what's going on with me right now? They act as if they don't even know You, God. How can I share this with them if I don't think they'll give me Godly counsel?

Donna, Belinda, and I all loved You. You were our foundation. Lord, what's happened to them? We three were Jesus Girls who wanted to save the world. I thought the deal was forever for all of us.

"Maggie, are you okay?" It's Donna's voice.

"I'm fine, Donna. I needed a minute, that's all."

"I understand that completely." Donna sits beside me. "Belinda's taking a smoke break right now. This is a beautiful spot, isn't it?"

"Absolutely. Remember we used to sit here and pray together, the three of us?"

"I remember that, Maggie. Seems like forever ago."

"It was." I feel a comfortable space between us. No awkwardness. I look up at the moon. "Donna, we all made mistakes, you know. Frank and I did things before we were married that I'm not proud of."

I feel Donna's eyes glaring at me. "Really? You? What happened?"

"Just things." I want to relate to her, but I can't.

Donna leans back. "Oh. But you were still a virgin, right?" I feel her rolling her eyes. "How horrible, Maggie."

"Sin is sin. And Jesus forgave me just like He has forgiven you and that music minister."

"I know He has. But you remember me when we were young. Jesus Girls and all that? I loved the Bible and praying. It filled me up and gave me joy."

"I know that. It still does the same for me."

"Well, I threw it all away the first time I thought someone really loved me. Don't you see that? The first time any real temptation came my way, I laid down for it, no pun intended. It just proved to me that what I felt as a kid was just some childhood affection, you know? Like a crush you have on a teacher or something. And because you and Belinda had the same crush on Jesus, I loved Him easily. The minute I didn't have you, I just walked away, that's all." Donna stands up and looks at me. "I don't see myself as someone who wants to be part of that particular club, that's all. I'm over it."

"Are you? We all need to make the right choices. You made a wrong choice. You can start today and make a better choice, Donna. Jesus loves you so much."

"Okay, Maggie, don't start with the witnessing. I went to the same training you did, remember? I know the four spiritual laws. I've read the pamphlets. No, I am not interested. It's not as if I'm an atheist. I'll always believe in God. I just have no need of the whole Jesus thing in my life."

She reaches out her hand to me. "We have tuna to prepare, my dear Maggie. Let's go."

I take her hand. I loved this girl so much long ago. *Why can't she see You are the answer?* I stand up and truth occurs to me. To forgive her, I need to ask for forgiveness.

"Donna, I'm so sorry I resented you for what happened with Belinda and Alan. It wasn't your fault. It was just easier to group you two together in some kind of conspiracy betrayal. Forgive me."

"I'm sorry too, Maggie. We were stupid kids then."

I reach out and we embrace. Not like strangers or children, but two women whose connection is real. Forgiveness for my old friend comes easily.

Chapter 27

Belinda

I divvy up the celery into three piles beside the three stations we got going. They're taking their merry time doing whatever it is they're doing. I had to finish the eggs myself. I hear laughter and the back door opens. Both of 'em seem to be in a better mood. Why does Maggie have to take everything so seriously? Apparently, asking honest questions is against little Miss Christian's religion. I ain't gonna make a thing of it. Even if she practically stomped out. "Okay, you two, we just need celery to make this precious tuna concoction complete. We can mix the tuna fish with it all in the morning, right before we make the sandwiches."

Donna puts her apron back on. "Good. So all we have to do is slice and dice these and we can go to bed?"

"Yep. That's the plan," I concur.

As the ceremonious hacking begins, I bring up an old love from our days in Boots – movies. My old friends jump into the discussion.

"I loved *The Godfather*."

"So violent."

"I thought the third one was a bit boring."

"Did you all see *Splash*? I loved it."

"Everything Tom Hanks does is wonderful."

"I agree. I saw *Forrest Gump* four times."

"Four times? You really must have liked it."

"Oh, I did. 'Life is like a box of chocolates.'"

"Maggie, don't become an impressionist."

"'Barbeque shrimp, fried shrimp, boiled shrimp…'"

"Please!"

"Hey, let's play movie lines. I play this with Frank all the time."

"How do you play?"

"I say a line from a movie and you guess the movie. Easy, right? I'll go first. 'I love you.' 'I know.'"

"No idea."

"Me neither."

"*Star Wars*."

"That's from *Star Wars*?"

"Yes, Princess Leia says I love you to Hans Solo and then he says 'I know.' It's a classic."

"Ain't that from *The Empire Strikes Back*?"

"Didn't we see it together?"

"Remember it was the first movie any of us stood in line for. We saw it in Marshall."

"I have one. 'See ya, Hubbell.'"

"*The Way We Were!*" We all sigh.

"Here is a classic. 'This is the beginning'...."

"...of a beautiful friendship. *Casa Blanca*!"

"Did you ladies know that Lola Bee is a movie aficionado?" Maggie asks randomly.

"Remember when she and Cecelia used to take us to the drive-in when we were little and see all those Disney films?" Donna adds.

"That's right. And then we'd go back to Lola Bee's house for cookies," I remember.

Maggie starts laughing loudly.

Donna and I look at her. "What?"

"Do you remember her ever asking if we wanted some iced tea? And Cecelia always saying we were only to drink milk?"

"I think so. What's so funny about that?"

"Cecelia told me, just a few years ago, that Lola Bee always added a little something to her iced tea."

Donna stops chopping and looks at Maggie. "You don't mean...?"

"Yes I do. Jack Daniels."

"You're kidding!" I start to convulse. "The Sunday School Director?"

"Cecelia said she never got drunk and only drank Jack Daniels and only a little in her iced tea. Said it made it taste so much better." We all burst out laughing until tears appear.

"Well I'll be," Donna says in an exaggerated twang.

We keep going 'til the celery is finished and put away. All we need to do is clean up a bit. I glance over and the clock shows 2:35 a.m.

"We need to start making sandwiches at seven," I declare. "The funeral starts at ten and ever'body will get here between eleven-thirty and noon."

Maggie starts to wobble right in front of me. "Whoa, girl."

"I better sit down for a minute." She stumbles to a stool.

"Maggie, you are pale." Donna pulls up a chair and sits by Maggie.

"I'm fine, I'm just tired. We're not seventeen anymore."

"That's the sweet smelling truth, sugar. But you do look a wee bit peak-ed, you know? You sick?" Her eyes look weird to me.

"Nothing some sleep won't cure," Maggie insists. "Let me sit for a second while you all clean up and then I'll go to bed." She winks at us.

"I see those wheels working now!" She ain't too sick. "We do all the work while you sit on your hiney and supervise?"

"A minute ago you were very concerned for my well-being, Belinda."

"Please!" Donna adds, "It is getting pretty deep in here."

Maggie stands up. "I can help. But just a little."

We clean the counters and put the Tupperware in the fridge.

"You know," Maggie remarks as she puts the remaining jar of pickles back into the refrigerator, "we didn't find out a super-secret ingredient, did we?"

"I thought that myself but I didn't want to admit it," confesses Donna. "Everything we put in there is normal, everyday, put-into-tuna-fish ingredients."

I'm surprised. "You serious? I picked up on the 'secret.' I just didn't say anything because we ain't supposed to say anything out loud. Even this minute, Imogene may be just outside that door. It's top level clearance kind of information, you know."

Donna chuckles as she wipes the Formica table. "You know it wouldn't surprise me if Imogene and her band of brewers bugged this room."

Maggie sits down. "If you know the secret, tell us."

"It's nothing new. Actually it's pretty old," I reply.

"So tell us, already!" Maggie mumbles.

"It's the …"

Maggie falls and hits the ground before Donna or I can get to her. She smacks her head on the floor and I see blood spots beside her.

"Maggie!" Donna kneels beside Maggie and rolls her over on her back. She's out. I go to the sink and open the drawer beside it and get out a clean kitchen rag and wet it. Donna barks at Maggie while I dap at the cut on her chin. Within a few minutes, she opens her eyes.

"I'm going to call Imogene. Doesn't Boots have a hospital?" Donna asks.

"I'm okay." Maggie mumbles.

"No you ain't. I have no idea, Donna. Call her."

Donna picks up Cecelia's phone on the counter by the stove and dials.

"I'm okay. Let me sit up," Maggie orders and I help her sit up a bit.

"Do you want some water, Maggie?" I ask.

"No, I really am okay." She notices her own blood and reaches up to touch it. "What happened?"

"You fainted. You were out cold." Donna is kneeling beside her. "Imogene said she just needs to put on some clothes and she'll be right over."

"You called Imogene? In the middle of the night?" Maggie is wiping her chin.

"Yes, I did." Donna surprises me with her tone. She is in charge. "And I don't want you to move until I see some color in your face." It occurs to me that Donna would be a terrific mama.

"Are you on any medication, Maggie? Is there some kinda pill I can fetch?" I should do something for her. "I'll go to your room or even the store, if you want."

"What store?" Donna asks. "We're in Boots, Belinda. Stores close at seven."

"Imogene can call the Coulters." I fire back. I notice Maggie's color ain't getting much better. "Maggie, is there any medication in your room?"

"Please don't yell, Belinda. There is something you could get me to relax."

"Name it."

"In my suitcase there is an iPod and some earphones. I'd love to listen to some music right now. That will help me more than you know."

"Music? Are you into holistic medicine?" Donna asks.

Maggie replies, "No, but praise music always gives me peace." She grabs her stomach in pain. "I just need to relax."

Donna sits closer to Maggie. "Listen, we don't really know each other that well anymore, but if you need to go to the hospital, you need to be honest and tell us. We could drive you to wherever the nearest hospital is or call 9-1-1. You look….weird. And not just overtired. Is your stomach hurting, too?"

"Donna, believe me, I would know if I needed to go to the hospital. I don't. This will pass." With that, Maggie closes her eyes and doubles over a bit.

"I'll be right back." I hustle upstairs and into Maggie's room. An expensive piece of luggage is on the floor in the corner of the room. I think of my old shoddy black bag. Of course, she owns nicer luggage. A perfect life would include a fancy suitcase. I kneel down, open it, and see expensive clothes. Maggie's perfume smells wonderful. I need to find a new scent. Designer clothes, designer perfume. Well I'll give her God that much. He's given little Miss Maggie a designer life. Must be nice.

I dig around for Maggie's iPod. I see the earphones and pull them out. I'm about to shut the lid on the suitcase and I notice the corner of a picture sticking out from an unzipped compartment on the suitcase top. I pull it out.

I stare.

It's a family portrait. An adult man with thinning hair, glasses and a warm smile stands tall in the middle. I wonder if he is the real deal. Three young boys group around their dad. They all look like their father, with the exception of the eyes. All are genetic matches to the violet black eyes of their mother. Nice family.

But what stops my heart is Maggie. She sits in the middle of her men, looking like a queen bee. On top of her head is a beautiful scarf tied up turban style. It's royal blue like her husband's tie. I see she ain't got no hair and her face, despite perfect make up, shows shadows and a gaunt edge. I'm sick to my stomach. An easy life? I just knew Maggie fit into that group of disgustingly sweet Christians who never face anything difficult. Looking into the eyes of the woman in the photo, I know I ain't right.

Cancer got to Maggie. Is it attacking her now?

Chapter 28

Donna

Maggie looks like she is bad pain. Mrs. Friesen had better show up soon. I don't know if 9-1-1 works in Boots. "Maggie, stay with me, okay?" She keeps closing her eyes. "Maggie." Without opening her eyes, she holds her stomach again. There is blood on the floor beside her. Not from her head. "Belinda!" I scream. I know I'm going to wake up Mr. Jackson and Tracey but I don't care.

"What's going on?" I look up and Mrs. Friesen is there and Mrs. Turner behind her. They're both in bathrobes.

"She's bleeding now. We need a doctor!"

"I'll call Dr. Samuels." Mrs. Turner steps over to Cecelia's phone.

Belinda appears with an iPod. "Oh no." She looks at the blood.

"Belinda, go get a pillow and a couple of blankets." I order. "We don't want her going into shock."

Mrs. Friesen pulls up a chair by Maggie and bends down to stroke her hair. "Lord Jesus, we ask you to protect your girl."

She keeps praying but I tune her out.

"Samuels is on his way. Be here in about three minutes."

"Wow." I say. "That's fast."

"He lives next door to Imogene across the street."

I can't help but smile. Of course, he does.

Belinda brings the pillow and blankets and we make a bed for Maggie. Belinda stands up and asks, "Is there a hospital in this town, Imogene?"

"There is going to be, but not yet." Mrs. Friesen sends Mrs. Turner a look. "There is an emergency clinic, though."

Mrs. Turner huffs. "It is not my personal responsibility to make sure Boots has a working hospital, Imogene. I was on the city council for about five minutes and you still blame me for every darn thing that's wrong with this town."

Dr. Samuels walks in, dressed in pajamas, and kneels down by Maggie and takes her vitals. "She's in no imminent danger but I need to examine her and I'm not going to do it on the kitchen floor."

As if ordered by a genie to appear, Mr. Jackson is now standing with us in the kitchen. "I can take the little'un to the back bedroom. That be okay, Doc?"

He swoops down and picks up Maggie. She opens her eyes when he does.

"Vern? Oh, I'm sorry. I fainted again, didn't I?"

"It's okay, little'un. Doc'll get you fixed up in a jiffy." Mr. Jackson takes her down the side hall into the first floor guest room that Cecelia used as a craft room. It has a twin bed in it. We all follow

but when we get there, Dr. Samuels shoos us out. So we go back to the Visiting Room and sit down.

"She's going to be fine." Mrs. Turner announces this as if she has the final word.

I don't know about that. The blood looked serious. No one is saying anything and it occurs to me that the recipe may be sitting out on the counter in the kitchen. I excuse myself to go hide it. Silly as it is, we have a responsibility. It is out in the open, sitting by the sink. I feel guilty as if I'd been a part of leaking top-secret material to Soviet Spies. I grab it, fold it, and put it into the dishtowel drawer.

"Donna, I'm really worried." Belinda makes me jump a little bit. She is sitting at the Formica, tapping her fingers. Haven't seen her like this since we arrived. She really looks nervous. "I think I'm gonna go outside and have a cigarette. But first, I need to tell you something. Something I know about Maggie."

"What?" I sit down beside her and have a notion to grab her hand. But I don't.

"I feel as mean as a junkyard dog."

What? Despite her words, this is the first softness I've seen in her. I grab her hand, but she jerks it away. There. That's the Belinda I know.

"Just give me a sec."

I watch her stare at the table. Something is really upsetting her. Maybe I was wrong to think she doesn't have a heart at all. None of us are incapable of feeling. It's not like she's a sociopath or something. I get up and get two glasses of water. Guilt attacks me. Did I make a mistake? I think calling the Wind Storm Sheriff was probably an overreaction. But she got me so angry. He, I think Henry is his name, seemed nice enough. He told me they were looking for Belinda to question her about some criminal activity.

He thanked me for the information. That was it. Should I tell her? I sit with her again and give her the water. She takes it and drinks a big gulp. "Belinda, I have something I need to tell you, too. I really need to apologize because I did something I don't think I had any right to do."

She looks at me curiously and takes another drink. "What did you do?"

"Mommy, what's going on?"

I turn and see Tracey, her red hair all messed up. She's holding what looks like a stuffed porcupine. No, it's an armadillo. She looks so precious and little.

"Get back to your room." Belinda's growling voice startles me. She grabs Tracey's shoulder and turns her around.

"Ow." Tracey groans.

I hear Belinda's low and harsh words as she walks her daughter up the stairs. "This is adult business down here and you know you are not to leave your bedroom unless I say so and I didn't say so."

My pity runs out of the room and I am once again resolved that I did the right thing. Belinda needs a good lesson in humility and parenting and decent kindness. Maybe that sheriff will be a good teacher.

Chapter 29

Belinda

"Stay in here, Tracey." I tuck her back in and give her the armadillo to hold. I can see her face twists up with worry like a baby pug but I ain't gonna add to it by telling her Maggie is probably dying. I stand at the door and look at her. She'll be better off with Imogene. She will. I'm impatient and hateful with her. She deserves better. I'm doing the right thing.

Lola Bee, Imogene, Vern, and Donna all congregate in the Visiting Room. I look toward Donna but she looks away. Wonder what she wanted to tell me? It doesn't matter much right now. Not when Maggie has cancer. I stand at the doorway but I don't want to join them. I need a cigarette in the worst way.

Outside, I sit in the homemade swing under the

pecan tree. I can't believe she's dying. I feel absolutely rotten about all the things I've said to her. Stealing that rat Alan Deltan away from her changed her life for the better. But Lord knows what she's been through with cancer. In Wind Storm, I watched my neighbor Sylvia go through ovarian cancer and die. Horrible way to go. I shudder and take a puff.

And to think that Maggie relies on Jesus? Where is God right now? Where was He when she was going through who-knows-what? What a waste. Where was He when Alan beat me up?

"Or when Isaiah…?"

I did it. I said his name aloud. It's hard to breathe. Oh crap, I feel like I'm gonna cry. "No!"

"You okay?" Donna stands on the porch ogling me.

"I'm fine." I take another puff. "Just worried about Maggie."

"Me, too." Donna comes over and sits across from me at the picnic table. In the light of the back porch, I notice she's pretty in her own way. Obviously makes good money. She looks city-fied and confident. I try to smile at her, but it won't come.

"She'll be okay, Bee. She just fainted."

"Donna, you saw the blood."

"I'm sure there is a logical explanation for that."

"Donna, Maggie has cancer." There it is. I said it. Donna should know.

"What?" She's staring at me with her mouth open.

"Maggie has had cancer in the past and I bet she has it again."

"How do you know this?"

"I just know, okay?"

"What kind?"

"I don't know."

"When?"

"I don't know."

"Well, it could be anything then. Some cancer isn't lethal at all if you treat it quickly."

"Donna, she could be dying right now." I twist my cigarette out on the ground beneath the swing. We sit in silence. I look up and Donna is staring at me in pity. I hate that. I look up at the stars.

"Belinda, I need to tell you something."

Here it is again. "So, tell me." I look at her and she looks plum pitiful like she let out the chickens when the foxes were visiting. "Donna, just tell me. In light of what's happening with Maggie, it ain't that bad, right?"

Donna takes a deep breath and lets it out slow like I do. Cecelia taught us both how to breathe and get your heart to slow down when something's worrying you. "Belinda, I got so mad at you after William left."

"Hey, that old geezer just wanted a night in bed, you realize that don't you? I did you a favor."

"Listen to me. You did me a favor like you did Maggie a favor in stealing her boyfriend that night. It wasn't noble, just downright mean."

"Whatever, Donna. Water under the bridge." Ain't she ever gonna let that go?

"In my anger, Belinda, I did something I don't think I should have done."

Uh-oh. My heart thumps wildly and it's my turn to breathe deep. "What did you do?"

"I am so sorry, Belinda."

"What did you do?" I stand up.

"That money looked extremely suspicious. In a bag and hidden."

"What did you do?" I walk over to her and look down at her. I can't believe this. She ain't that stupid.

She stands up. "I Googled you and I dug up that you live in

Wind Storm, Texas…"

"YOU DIDN'T!"

"I called the sheriff of Wind Storm." She stares at the ground. "And I asked if there had been any recent crimes involving a bunch of money and…"

"Donna, what exactly did you tell him?" I'm in her face.

"I told him you were here in Boots. I'm so sorry, Belinda."

"You have no idea what you've done, you stupid cow!"

She scoots away from me and the picnic table. "Well, I can't believe you're a criminal!"

I push her down and she falls on the grass. Hard.

"Ow! What are you doing? Stop it!"

She jumps up faster than I think she will so I push her back down.

"Belinda! Grow up. We're not kids anymore and that hurt." She stands up.

I can't see straight. She's gonna ruin everything. I grab her hair and pull.

"Ow!"

She reaches for mine and pulls harder. It hurts. "Stop it!"

"Bee, you're not as tough as you think!"

I'm gonna hurt this heifer once and for all. I feel her knee in my stomach so I take her hair and pull her to the ground "You want tough, you roly-poly sissy!"

She bites my arm and slaps my face. "Shut up, you Texas ho!"

I get on top of her to pin her down but she uses her body weight and rolls me over. I put my nails into her arm and dig in. She takes my hand and bends it back and it hurts something awful. I lean forward and bite her arm. We roll around again and she kicks me and I try to kick back. I wiggle free from her arms and stand up. She flings her legs out and trips me and I fall down again. I notice a rotten apricot near me and I pick it up and smash it into her face.

She growls low like a rabid dog and punches me in the side of my face. I fall over and I feel an apricot shoved in my mouth. I roll away and spit out the fruit. I scramble to my feet and pick up another apricot to chuck it at her.

She's up and walking away. The apricot gets her in the shoulder.

"What the...?" She turns around, picks up an apricot, and throws it at me.

We commence an apricot war and I find I'm a better shot than this Denver dog. I hit her square in the eyes.

"Ladies."

"Stop it, you idiot!" She rushes me like a bull in a bullfight. We both hit the ground hard.

"Ladies!"

I feel something scratching my back. "Ladies!"

We both freeze and look up. Imogene is standing near us with an old broom in her hands.

She's smiling. "It's been a while since I swept up a grown woman fight." She cackles but I don't think nothing's funny. "Maggie is awake and much better. She wants to see you both but only for a minute. She's as weak as a cat's fart." Imogene turns to leave and then looks back at us. "Do you all need me to call the doctor again?" She don't wait for an answer. Just cackles and goes into the house.

I'm breathing hard. I can't wait to leave this place. I have to leave soon. We untangle and stand up. I brush myself off and glare at Donna. I ain't gonna tell her about the apricot gunk in her hair.

As we walk up the back porch stairs, I ask her, "When did you talk to that sheriff?"

She growls, "At about 9 this evening."

I need to leave before the funeral. But first, Maggie.

Chapter 30

Maggie

"Thank you, Dr. Samuels." *Thank you Father, for this man.* His eyes carry wisdom and compassion. An honest to goodness small town doctor. "No one makes house calls in Tucson." I try to giggle, but I'm so tired.

"You'll be fine. But you have to take it easy for a while. For a long while." He pats my hand like Cecelia used to and leaves with his little black bag in tow.

Lola Bee smiles down at me. "You need to rest now, but your gal friends are coming into say hello in just a minute."

"Do you want to stay, Lola Bee?"

"Maggie May, I would, but I think you're gonna be sound asleep in a matter of minutes. I'll see you in the morning light." She walks to the door.

"Why did this happen?" I ask her without thinking.

Lola Bee turns. "I don't know. God knows but He ain't telling."

"I think I'm wrong about God, Lola Bee." I have to say it. Aloud. And she just happens to be here. "I thought pleasing Him was about making the right choices. But I don't know anymore."

She sits on the side of the bed and looks down at me. "I'll tell you a secret Maggie May. You don't need to worry about pleasing Him. You just be you and keep talking to Him. He just wants to part of your life."

"But bad things keep happening. Like what if..."

"All you got is this minute, sweetie. This minute. And right now, He loves you and He could give a rat's hiney if you are 'good' or 'bad.' God just wants to be with you."

"But I can't just go to God and talk about anything unless I've made choices that please him. This is how I've lived my life."

"Oh child. Don't you know you're loved 'cause of who God is, not 'cause of what you do or don't do? Look at me. I made plenty of bad choices and God is still sweet on me. I don't think 'fore I speak and sometimes my fuse is shorter than a crippled pig's tail. But Jesus loves me completely and walks with me every day. Just think of those three boys you got. When they mess up, you still love 'em, right?"

"Of course. But I want their lives to go smoothly and if they choose the wrong things, well..."

"The way I see it, God uses those bumps in the roads to make us more like Him. Nobody's life goes perfect. No matter what happens, God loves completely. You don't know how much He gets a kick out of you, do you Maggie?"

My eyes fill. "Maybe I don't."

"I guess I know how to pray for you then." She smiles.

I've never seen her look this beautiful. "You are wise, Lola Bee. You know that?"

She stands. "Of course, I do. Now if we can just get that old heifer Imogene to concede to that fact, well, then we'd all be in a better place." I laugh and watch her leave.

"How are you feeling?" Donna walks in and sits on my bed.

"Better, thank you." I notice some yellow orange stuff in her messed up hair. "I gave you guys a little scare, huh?"

"Yes, but that's okay."

"What happened to you, Donna? Did you fall or something?"

"Um, nope. I'm just a mess."

I don't believe her, especially when Bee comes in. She looks pretty messed up, too. Belinda sits in a chair on the opposite side of the bed from Donna. Did they have a fight? They wouldn't, would they? But something's going on, I can tell.

"I need to explain something to you two…" I begin.

"You don't have to," Belinda says and I notice she's shooting red anger out of her eyes. "We know you have…well, we know."

"Know what?" Now I'm confused.

Belinda looks at Donna and Donna glances back. I see compassion mixed with a lot of anger running between them. Father, what is going on here?

"About the.…" Donna starts.

"Cancer," Belinda finishes. "We know you have cancer, Maggie."

"What? How?"

"I saw the picture of you with your family in your suitcase."

I giggle a tiny little laugh. I'm so tired but I can't help it. "I had cancer. Had. But I don't have cancer now. Haven't for six years."

Belinda looks angry.

"I'm sorry Belinda, but I don't have it." I draw up the covers a little.

"Well, then what is wrong with you?" Donna asks.

"I'm pregnant." I watch their faces register my news.

After a moment, Donna whispers, "The blood. Are you okay? Is the baby okay?"

"I'm okay. I'll have to get an ultrasound when I get back to Tucson, but Dr. Samuels said he thinks everything is fine."

"So, is this good news?" Belinda asks.

I sigh. "I don't know. New life is always good news. But I am scared, I have to tell you. I haven't told Frank about this. I mean I'm forty-two years old. My youngest is almost fourteen. I thought I was finished. And I didn't know I could have a baby, because of the cancer." I feel the tears on my cheeks.

"How long did you have cancer?" Donna asks as she lays her hand on my leg.

"I battled it for six years." I wipe my face. My eyelids are heavy.

"Six years?" Belinda whispered with a wince.

"I've gone through two operations and two remissions and of course, a lot of chemo and radiation. It seems to have dragged itself into six years of my life."

"What kind of cancer?" Donna asked.

"Breast cancer. I have had two partial mastectomies. But, of course, I never really was the buxom one anyway, right?" My attempt at humor is lost. "If I have a baby, I won't be able to breastfeed it." I expect more questions but no one speaks. We sit in silence and I notice Belinda won't look at me. "I've been in remission for six years, Belinda."

Donna asks, "Did you throw up the other day because of the pregnancy or the cancer?"

"Donna," Belinda retorts, "Maggie said she's pregnant and she doesn't have cancer. Listen to her."

The anger in Belinda's voice shocks me. "It's okay, Belinda. It really is. I think I'm fine. I just don't know for certain, that's all. Of course, I never know, really. The thing about cancer is it can return anytime. My doctor says the longer I am in remission, the better chance I have for it not to return. But what if it returns and I'm pregnant?" Tears rush out again. Donna grabs my hand and squeezes hard.

I look around the room and see all of Cecelia's crafting items. She thought she wanted to be a scrap-booker, but quit. Then she thought she wanted to learn to knit and bought tons of yarn and then quit.

"I called Cecelia first after I found out my lump was malignant. Except Frank, of course. He's an incredible man. I wish you both could meet him." I miss Frank so much. If he were here, he would hold me and I could fall asleep in his arms. But I can't call him. I want to tell him face to face.

"What did she do?" Belinda whispers again, without looking at me.

"She prayed. And then she said she would call back and tell me when she would be in Tucson. Sure enough, two hours later, she called with flight times."

"That's Cecelia for you. Always running to help," Donna says this and I wonder if she meant it to sound so sarcastic.

"She stayed with me for four months that first time. The first three months of chemo were the worst days of my life. And Cecelia, I don't know how she did it, always found energy to help me with dinner or making beds or whatever. My own mother only called me. She has never come out to Tucson. We've gone to Arkansas to see her. Once."

I think about Imogene's words to me in Coulters. Maybe I will call my mom. Maybe. "But Cecelia came. During the worst of it, she stayed with me. She was my own personal angel."

"*Cecelia, I need a rag.*" I spoke urgently as I moved from a kneeling position to sit on the floor of the bathroom.

"*Comin' right up!*" She handed me a damp rag and took a seat on the edge of the bathtub.

I wiped my mouth and looked at her. Cecelia knew just when to speak and when to shut up. What a gift. After all the preceding sounds of discomfort, precious silence reigned. I broke the quiet. "*Aren't you glad you don't have to hold my hair back anymore? Such a hassle.*"

"*Yessiree. I think I broke a nail once,*" Cecelia replied straight-faced.

I grinned and added, "*Complain, complain, complain. That's all you do these days, old woman.*"

Cecelia smiled.

"*I guess I should get up, huh?*" I questioned.

"*Honey, you do whatever you need to do.*"

"*Then I will just stay right here.*" I felt so exhausted all of the time. The most minute of everyday actions sapped me of strength.

"*So, I was thinking, Magpie,*" Cecelia said, using her pet name for me, "*and you know thinking is a bit dangerous for one like me, but I was thinking that we ought to go to a store – a special store with wigs.*"

"*Cecelia, I can't go out. I am exhausted.*"

"*I thought you might say that. So I just happened to make some calls. Do you remember Pauline Ferguson in Boots?*"

"*Did she work at the post office?*"

"*Still does. Well, her husband Mac had a bout with prostate cancer, which he survived by the way, a few years ago.*"

"*Yeah, so is Mac going to go to the store for me?*"

"*Hold your horses, I'm getting there. You see, Pauline, because of Mac, got really involved in the American Cancer Society. They do all sorts of things for people. I called Pauline last week and we talked and of course the Lord showed up in our conversation, because she happens to know a gal who is part of a chapter of the American*

Cancer Society right here in Tucson."

"What do they do?"

"Everything from giving rides to offering home medical equipment to explaining the ins and outs of the disease. But I thought you might be interested in one particular aspect of the Tucson's chapter."

"You called the girl Pauline told you about?"

"Last week. And she put me in touch with a gal who can come over today, this afternoon, if you are up to it, and give you a little makeover. And she brings with her all sorts of scarves or wigs that you can buy. Course that part is my treat. The makeover is totally funded by the American Cancer Society."

I started to cry.

"Sweetie, I didn't mean to make you all blubbery."

"Yes you did! You know how I have been feeling about the way I look. Oh, Cecelia, I think I even have energy! She can come today? Are you sure?"

"I talked to her last night. She'll be here in an hour if you are up to it."

I found the strength to get up, be it slowly, and hug Cecelia's neck. The makeover gave me energy and cheered up my heart. Cecelia cooked a fancy meal that night and then took the boys to a fast food restaurant. Frank and I had a date in our own home.

"That day Cecelia bought me that scarf that you saw in that picture, Belinda."

"I would like to see that photograph," comments Donna through tears.

Belinda just stares at the floor.

"But I have to tell you my favorite moment was when I saw her crying and she didn't know. One morning in, I don't know, year four, I guess, and my remission ended and I had chemo again and what a rotten time. The boys were little balls of energy. Cecelia came out again and helped me. She got up early and got the boys off to school and preschool and she wanted me to sleep in. But I got out of bed and went out to the back yard. Cecelia sat on our back patio swing, swaying in the breeze, before it got hot. On her face was such a look of sadness. And then she just started crying. I don't know if I ever saw her cry before."

"She cried with me when I left Lubbock," Donna says, tears in her eyes.

Belinda whispers, "Cecelia cried with me once, too."

I wait for Belinda to explain but she doesn't so I go on. "I saw her crying and it just killed me. So I said, 'Cecelia Jackson, you must not cry for me, Argentina!' Corny thing to say, I know. She looked at me, startled at first and then waved me over to sit by her. Didn't say a thing, just motioned me over. And then, she put her arm around me and just started sobbing. Pretty soon I joined her." I feel the tears in my eyes as I tell it. "The best cry I have ever experienced. Afterwards, I felt so exhausted, but cleansed, sort of."

Donna is crying softly and Belinda is still staring at the floor.

"What an old broad she was, huh?" I ask rhetorically.

It's the first time I've talked to these two about Cecelia without either of them being sarcastic or mean, so I go on. "Do you gals remember a tiny black and white photo of a bottle framed by the front window of the Visiting Room?

"Record my misery; list my tears on your scroll — are they not in your record. Psalm 56:8"

I laugh. Donna is looking at me and Belinda continues her fascination with the floor. "Cecelia explained that some translations say wineskin instead of scroll and wineskin is like a bottle. Isn't it funny that up in Heaven right now, she may be taking a tour and going into the Warehouse of Bottled Tears? I bet you it is a huge, very well lit, tremendously lavish mansion that has these intricate and beautifully hand carved shelves everywhere filled with exotic bottles of every color. And I bet that Cecelia is in the room with her tears. All the tears she shed that God collected. Isn't that a beautiful thought?"

Donna whispers, "I am going to lay down a while before we put the sandwiches together. Maggie, you don't have to help us. Belinda and I can put them all together by ourselves." She stands up and glances at Belinda, "See you at 7:00 a.m." She leaves the room.

I watch her leave and then look at my other friend. Belinda's face is hard, like jagged rock and her eyes are steely, staring at the carpet. She suddenly rises but doesn't look at me. "I am sorry about your bad luck, Maggie. I really am. I hope, well, I hope everything goes well for you." She quickly leaves the room, too.

Father, whatever You want, Lord. I surrender. Please be with this little one in me. And be with those two ladies You adore. Lola Bee was right. I have been wrong. I've been praying for Noah and my boys to do well and make good choices. I've been so wrapped up in my own righteousness. Forgive me, God. I pray that my sons, Frank and me will live in Your presence and keep in close touch with You. Begin to show me how much You love me. Thank You for dear Cecelia. I think of that ornate palace filled with the tears of the compassionate. I begin to drift.

Chapter 31

Belinda

I make a beeline for the backyard and I light up.
It's time to get outta Dodge. Maggie will be fine,
Donna can take a flying leap into whatever hole of
quicksand she scrambled out of, and Imogene will
scoop up Tracey and be a right good mama to her.
Mexico is where I'll start. I can find a job cooking
and save up enough money to go to England. Always
wanted to see that place.

The stars are still bright. I click on my watch and
it lights up to say 3:30. I throw the butt down and
twist it out under my shoe.

Goodbye sorry, sad existence for a life. Hello
possibilities.

Tracey is a little carne asada burrito on the bed,
her head peeking out under the tunnel of quilt. She's
completely out. I grab my bag and put my clothes

into it, careful not to take any of her belongings. I put it on the bed to zip it up and she stirs. I freeze, but her eyes are awake, looking at me.

"Mama, what are you doing?" Her words are slurred like she's almost sleep talking.

"Just doing some pre-packing for our trip home. Go on back to sleep."

"Okay." She shuts her eyes. I wait a minute and her breath slows to practically nothing.

I stop at the door and look back at her. This is the best decision. This is the only decision.

"I'm sorry, Tracey," I say it aloud but in a whisper. I feel a lump in my throat. What am I doing? I don't need to apologize. She'll thank me later.

I sneak out quietly. The house is dark and silent and I open and close the front door as gentle as I've ever been. My Honda is unlocked and I gingerly get in putting my bag down softly, too, as if anybody would ever hear that.

The streets of Boots are quiet and dark. Streetlights guard the sleepy town. I open the windows and listen to the silence. It's beautiful. And so sad. A dog's bark startles me as I make my way out of Cecelia's neighborhood. I think about stopping at the church, saying farewell and take care of Tracey, but I don't. And if for some insane reason that good looking preacher was there, well, I might be tempted to stay. Instead, I cross the railroad tracks and turn right. Time to get back on the freeway and head south.

When I turn, I see headlights far behind me. I'm barely doing the speed limit but that car is racing. Their headlights are inching closer to me. Really? Seriously? Tailgating in the middle of the night in this one horse town? Must be some crazy teenagers, maybe a little drunk.

I feel a jerk and I look in my rear view mirror. They bumped me? Are you kidding me? I don't know if I should stop. Might be a crazy person with a shotgun. This is Texas. I think it's a law that you have to be armed at all times.

I decide to speed up and just leave town. I feel a hard bump. What? Again? Oh no, they didn't. I pull over and my boiling blood starts writing my 'Who do you think you are?' speech. The idiot pulls over behind me. I get out of my car and slam the door. They messed with the wrong woman is what they did.

I stop cold. It's Imogene. She gets out of her car and looks at me as if I'm crazy.

"Imogene, are you insane? You could've killed us both!"

"Oh landsakes alive! Don't be a sugar baby, Belinda. It was just a couple of taps. And you are the insane one if you ask me. What are you doing out here?"

I pause to think of something she might buy. "I needed to take a little drive, that's all."

"Uh huh." Imogene puts her hands on her hips. She is still wearing a daisy yellow bathrobe with matching house shoes. "I don't believe that for a moment."

"I don't care if you don't believe it. It's the truth." I don't enjoy lying, but it's needed at the moment. We stand in silence with Imogene looking at me as if she's trying to figure me out. Well, good luck, old woman.

"Belinda Kite, you listen to me. Your daughter needs you. She adores you like no one else. Do you understand *that*?" She over-enunciates her last word and the "t" sound shoots across at me.

I can't say anything. She doesn't understand what she's saying.

"Raising my four boys was pure difficulty. I don't have a boatload of Brady Bunch or Walton stories. Most days, I just thanked God I didn't kill any of them or do any real damage to their psyches.

Course maybe I did. Wilbur used to tell me I said things nobody should utter to their young uns."

I wonder if she ever left in the middle of the night because she knew her boys were better off without her. Probably not. I cross my arms and lean against my Honda. I need to get going.

Imogene walks over and leans beside me against the Honda. We're both facing *The Rambling Rock Store*. It's all dark but the sign is lit up. Do people actually come to Boots to buy rocks?

Imogene speaks again. "And you might not know this about me, but I was an honest to goodness thief."

I need a cigarette. Did Donna tell her, too? Is my history going to be in the Boots Advocate next week?

I turn to her. "Listen, Imogene, I don't know what you're doing, but you need to just let things be, okay?"

She puts her face right in my face. "Belinda Kite, act like you got some raising. I knowed you since you was just a little thing and I think I got something to say to you so you best just get comfortable and let *me* be. Now you wait right here for a second."

I open the passenger car door and reach in and get my cigarettes. As I do this, Imogene goes to the trunk of her Impala and brings back an iron-folding chair. She sets it down and sits in it. It's a strong chair.

I light up, scoot back, and sit on my hood. I'll let her do her talking and then I'm gone. Maybe I should hint that she could have Tracey. Maybe not.

"Cecelia used to talk about you to me, like you were her own kid. When Lola Bee starting talking about her boy Peter and I would tell the news of my four, well, Cecelia always chimed in about you, Tracey, Donna, and Maggie. So I've heard about your life from time to time."

"I'm sorry about that. Must have disappointed you, too."

"Shut up."

Now this surprises me. I flick my ashes on the ground so I don't have to look into Mrs. Potato Head's angry eyes.

"Belinda, you got to quit feeling so sorry for yourself and grow up and be a Mama to that girl. You have the ability and you got the love, too. You just need to find it."

"Imogene, it's late. I'm tired."

"And I know you are a tired thief, too."

Donna did tell her. "That sanctimonious witch," I growl.

"Don't you talk about your daughter that way."

"Tracey? Tracey told you?"

"She just talked and I put one and one together. And like any self-respecting Boots Baptist, I eavesdropped when you and Donna had your words in the back yard. It all added up."

"So what are you going to do? Turn me in, too? If you just leave me be, I'll get outta here and you never have to be associated with a criminal again."

"I knew it. You are flying the coop. But what about Tracey?"

I pause and take a drag. I don't how to say this but just to say it. I look Imogene straight in the face, using my own angry eyes. I blow out smoke. "She's better off without me, the criminal. I've never known how to be a Mama. You should take her."

Imogene starts cackling and I look around. She's going to wake up all of Boots.

"That's not exactly the response I hoped for, Imogene."

"Tracey living with an old man with no tongue and an old woman that talks too much is not exactly what I'd call a fairy tale childhood. And like I told you before, I am a criminal, too."

I throw the butt to the ground, hop down and twist it out with my shoe. "I can't believe that you actually stole something,

Imogene." I scoot back on the hood. "What, a candy bar from Coulters?"

"How about First Baptist's offering?"

I look at her to see if she's lying. "No way."

"In my late thirties, four kids and Wilbur got laid off from the sulfur mine. I sewed part time but raising four kids took most of my time. I was a wreck. I thought Wilbur was going to up and leave me. We got into some yelling fights that woke the neighbors."

"Cecelia and Vern?"

"They came over a couple of times and got the kids and let 'em stay overnight at their house. By the morning, we were always better. Well, we weren't throwing things. But it was a bad time."

"So what happened?"

"I deposited the offering every Monday morning. Lola Bee did it for me occasionally but it was my job. One Monday I drove home with the little bag by me in my car. It totaled a little over $200 on account of a special guest singer and preacher. They always brought in more money than Brother Joe did. I looked at it on the way to the bank and I didn't see no offering to Jesus, I saw an answer to some of our problems. We needed that money something awful. So I turned the car around and went home. In that bag, no checks. All cash. Most Sundays that didn't happen."

Imogene stole from the church? Well, I'll be. I never woulda thunk it. "Did anyone find out?"

"Yes, they did. Brother Joe asked me about it the next week and I just lied through my teeth. Lola Bee and I counted the money together every Sunday, so I knew she would tell Brother Joe it added up to 200 and something dollars, but I didn't care. I just lied and said I didn't know what happened. Put on an academy award winning performance. Next business meeting, the finance report came out and everyone looked at it and saw the discrepancy, in black and white. I didn't say a thing. I just hoped no one would notice."

I can't believe what I'm hearing. This is an Imogene I ain't never heard of.

"The funny thing is no one said a word until the last five minutes of the meeting. Then Olive Stauber brought it up and I just sat there, ready for the firing line. I was so down, I just didn't care. And then the unbelievable happened."

I lean up. "What?"

"Lola Bee up and said, 'It's my fault.' Said she couldn't believe she forgot to make the deposit but she'd do it the next morning. Everyone forgave her. She put $200 dollars of her own money in the bank the next day."

"What did you say to her?"

Imogene looks at me with a sad face. "Right then, not a thing, Belinda. And she knew it was me. I just know she did. But she never brought it up to me. We left church that night not looking at each other."

"How did you keep that from her?"

"I didn't. I confessed to her a week later. She looked at me and I'll never forget, she looked at me and she said, 'Imogene Friesen, I have no idea what you're talking about. You trying to rub it in that I forgot?' I looked at her and I started blubbering and she told me 'You go take care of those kids and stop bringing up all my faults.' That was it."

"You lucked out, Imogene."

Imogene pauses and looks at me with what I think is pity. "Belinda, God gives us friends and friends can provide the best of luck. You got some friends here, too, you know that?"

I sigh. I don't know nothing anymore. "Imogene, the sheriff from my home is going to be here soon and he is a jerk. A jerk that I happened to sleep with for two miserable years. And did I mention he's married? So you may have stolen from the church, but I'm a harlot and a thief. Just let me go." I'm so tired I just let it all out. I can't believe I just told her about Hank and me.

"Did his wife know about you two?"

"I don't know for sure, but I think she does. It was pretty much a town secret. If it ever came out, well it would be spun so that I, a cook and a slut, seduced the squeaky-clean hero lawman. I'm totally trapped. I have to go."

"Belinda, you can't go. You just can't."

I lie on the trunk of the car and wish I could just sleep this all away.

"Belinda, just stay for the funeral. You have the time."

I'm too tired to fight anymore. "You win, Imogene. I'll go back and I'll stay for the funeral but then I am hightailing it outta here."

"With Tracey, right?"

I sit up. "Yep." I know I don't sound convincing.

"Belinda, I stole something else, too." Imogene stands up and folds her chair.

"Are you on the FBI Most Wanted list?" I snicker. I can't produce a belly laugh. "What did you steal?"

"The tuna fish recipe."

She says it so casually it startles me. Energy kicks in and I laugh aloud. "What? You stole the recipe? *The* recipe?"

"I did. It lay on her kitchen counter once when I visited. Cecelia went to the bathroom and I grabbed a piece of paper and copied it."

I slide off the hood. "Well, if you know the recipe why do you and Lola Bee go on and on about getting it?"

She opens the trunk and puts in her chair, closes the trunk and turns to me. "Soon after I stole it, I felt so bad about it, I crumpled it up and asked God for forgiveness and I've never stole a thing since. Cecelia and Lola Bee and me ate those tuna fish sandwiches one day after and I had it all planned out to just 'guess' the secret and fool Cecelia and then 'fess up to all of it. But we sat there and Lola Bee started up on how come Cecelia would never give us the recipe. She got mad, I thought, and really pitched a fit. Well, Cecelia said something coy, something Cecelia-like and left the Visiting Room to get us some more iced tea. And Lola Bee looks at me and smiles and winks. It occurred to me she don't care about no recipe, she just loves the chase of it all. The game. I love that old woman way too much to take that away from her by spilling the beans."

Well, I'll be. Just never know about folks.

I walk to my car door and Imogene walks to hers. Before getting in, I call out, "So you know the secret, right?"

Imogene cackles and I don't care if she wakes up Boots or not. I join her.

As we get in our cars we say in unison, "Pickles!"

Chapter 32

Donna

"Mr. Jackson, I'll walk with you." I grab his arm and he stares at me with eyes that are blank and pitch black. They look like two bottomless pits, yet not deep enough for his sadness.

I keep thinking about my father at my mother's funeral. I remember holding onto his hand and looking up at his face. Sadness painted his face grey but he kept giving me a little fake smile. I knew he was trying.

It is natural for me to stay by Mr. Jackson's side as we walk up to the First Baptist Church's double doors. Belinda, Tracey, and Maggie are walking in front of us. Today we are Mr. Jackson's family.

Mr. Jackson stops me in the foyer. I look up at him but he looks down at the carpet and takes a deep breath. I can't imagine what he is feeling.

Maggie, Belinda and Tracey go on in to the sanctuary. "We forgot," Mr. Jackson whispers. "We gotta git back to the house."

"What did we forget?" I ask him.

He pauses again, looking at the carpet. "No matter, we just need to head back there 'fore we go to this here funeral."

"Okay." I squeeze his arm. Dear sweet man.

We start to turn around when Mark Kidwell approaches. His face is sensitive and stoic, perfect for a funeral director. I think about last night's antics with the cheese crackers and I give him a little grin. He returns it but it's so slight I'm sure Mr. Jackson missed it.

"Vern, are you ready to go in? The place is packed. Cecelia was loved." Mark speaks with such kindness and familiarity.

Mr. Jackson nods, apparently forgetting about whatever it is we forgot. We walk to the doors that are still closed.

"Now Vern, I tried to do everything just like Cecelia wanted it, per her instructions. But I want you to peek in and see if I missed something and I'll fix it before you go in."

Again, Mr. Jackson nods. His eyes are still black holes of despair.

Mark cracks open the door and Mr. Jackson leans over and looks. I hear a little gasp and he leans back, a bit off kilter. I'm still holding on, so I help him steady himself. Mark closes the door. "Vern, what is it? Did we miss something?" Mark is ready to jump into action.

Mr. Jackson looks at me, eyes watering. "The flowers." He looks at Mark. "It's a garden in there. Just like Sissy would've liked it."

"Well, is there anything wrong then?" Mark asks.

"It's just...well...Sissy loved flowers. I always gave her flowers on the big event days like birthdays and such. Sometimes I'd make a chicken coop mess of the dates. One time I went to the school cafeteria and walked in the kitchen with yellow roses and I just hollered, 'It's my Sissy's big day!' That evening I glanced at the calendar and saw her birthday already happened two days before. She didn't say a thing."

A tear comes down his cheek as he chuckles. I might just lose it.

"So I pert near had a heart attack thinkin' bout the flowers today. I wanted her to have a bunch, but no one sent any to the house. I was just telling Donna Gail that I forgot the roses I picked for Sissy this morning. And then I look in there. I didn't know…" Tears spill and he takes a handkerchief out of his suit pocket, wipes his eyes, and then blows his nose. I drop his arm.

Mark touches Mr. Jackson. "Vern, nobody sends flowers to the house. Most of the time they just send arrangements to the funeral home and we handle 'em all. I heard this morning that Gloria's is all sold out of big arrangements."

"Well, I'll be." Mr. Jackson grins at me and it is the sweetest look I've ever experienced.

"So you ready?" Mark asks.

"As I'll ever be." Mr. Jackson holds his arm out and I take it. The church is packed and I feel on the spot. Everyone is looking at me. I know they're actually looking at Mr. Jackson, but once again, I wonder if anyone is thinking about how much weight I've gained in twenty-five years.

We sit in the front row. Tracey is beside me, with Belinda and Maggie next to her. Cecelia's closed casket is just a few feet away. Mr. Jackson told us she wanted everyone to see her in 'memory's eye' not all stiff and laid out.

I hate funerals. Of course, this is the only second one I've ever been to. I feel a chill up my spine as it occurs to me that I sat in this exact place at the first funeral, next to my father. My dad arranged to be cremated and left instructions for no funeral. Probably so I wouldn't have to sit here again. And now here I am.

Suzanne Bolder, the mayor's wife, goes up to the front and starts singing the hymn, *In the Garden*. I remember this song. A picture flashes through my mind of the three of us all trying to sing the alto part as we sat in the back row. We were teenagers and decided we'd be a girl group with me playing piano and all of us singing. That idea didn't last long; I don't remember why.

Tracey leans forward and Belinda pulls her back. Why can't she just let the girl alone? Belinda didn't say a word to me this morning when we put the sandwiches together. Complete silence and that's fine by me. I'm sore from that stupid fight. I can't believe it happened. I shouldn't have called that sheriff. But I'm not going to apologize until she starts treating me decently. Which will be never. I can't wait to get out of here and back to my real world.

Suzanne ends her song and Tanya Snyder walks up to the piano. I remember Tanya. I think she was a few years ahead of us. She's gained some weight, too. I grin at that.

Tanya starts playing *How Great Thou Art*. She is really good. A twinge of guilt strikes me. I hated to say no when Mr. Jackson asked me to play today. But I don't play the piano anymore. I just can't.

Tanya's song ends and Ted Bellinger comes up to the pulpit. I haven't seen him in forever. Maggie glances over at me and I glance at Belinda. We all smile. Ted was captain of the basketball team when we were in school. We all loved him from afar.

Maggie leans over Belinda's lap and whispers to both of us, "I forgot to tell you. Ted lives here on a ranch outside town. He's never married."

Belinda and I turn our heads and I can tell we're both checking him out. No, he's not my type. Too tall cowboy-looking. Not that I should be picky. He has thick dark hair but his cowboy hat has left a crease around his head. He looks nervous and takes a deep breath and lets it all out at once. Wonder if Cecelia taught him that? He's holding a piece of paper that's quivering in his hands. He looks out at all of us but then focuses above our heads. He speaks to the ceiling.

"*Why Did the Cowboy Cry Into His Boots?* A poem by Cecelia May Jackson."

I look over at Maggie and she is looking at me. Belinda's hand goes to her mouth to muffle a giggle.

Tracey whispers, "What is it, Mommy? What's funny?"

"Nothing." Belinda looks toward the ceiling and swallows her laughter.

Ted is not a public speaker but he does have a deep drawl that is perfect for what he's reading. It's obvious to me he either hates the poem or hates being in front of all of us. Maybe both. He continues:

"No one knew old Buck Webster's horse,
Could kick up his hoofs with such great force (Ted pauses)
Of nature.
But Buck knew he was in deep doo-doo,
When old Salty made a dirt-kicking move (pause)
To hit him."

Ted starts again but all I hear is a squeak. He reaches and pulls out a glass of water hidden under the pulpit and takes a drink. I can't look at Belinda or Maggie. I can feel their bodies shaking in silent laughter.

"Buck was in the middle of a long cow run,
Herding cattle here and there despite the heat of
The scorching, orange sun, (Ted pauses again)
A great orb."

I hear some giggles throughout the sanctuary behind us. I smile. I have to control myself. Mr. Jackson is sitting right next to me.

"He had just set off to find a little doggie,
When Salty saw a snake in the grass and made like an old fogy (an exaggerated pause)
Who was scared."

The church is silent, but I have a feeling it's the quiet before the storm.

Ted Bellinger clears his throat and looks down at us as if he is going to continue. But then he says in his deep Texas drawl, "I'm not sure what happened next. That's the end of the poem. She wrote in here for me to put those pauses in."

Mrs. Friesen's cackle leads the way and the whole church joins in. I can't help myself but giggle too. Belinda laughs wildly and lets out a couple of imprisoned snorts. I look over and Mr. Jackson is smiling.

The new preacher, Pastor Ben, comes up and motions for Ted to sit down. Ted looks like he doesn't know if the laughter is about the poem or him.

We all quiet down and Pastor Ben speaks. "Cecelia chose that reading for this occasion," he announces amid more laughs. "She requested that after Ted read her poem, I should read the following: 'For years, I have been angling to be invited to a real Cowboy poet convention. Never was. So, I said to myself, hey, the only captive audience you'll ever really get for your poetry might just have to be your funeral. So, here we are.'"

Pastor Ben pauses for more laughter to die down and keeps reading. "'And here's to all those cowboys around Texas that inspired me! May all of you, cowboys or not, poets or not, never stop dreaming just cause someone might not believe your dream.'"

Scattered applause meets the end of Cecelia's note.

Pastor Ben continues, "Now I'd like to ask anyone who has a memory or story of Cecelia and would like to share it to stand up where you are and speak loudly."

It occurs to me that Pastor Ben doesn't stutter or stumble when he's in front of a crowd.

And it doesn't take long for the testimonials to begin. A woman who worked with her in the school cafeteria tells how Cecelia was all about cooking until the kids came. And then she was all about the kids. Brother Joe's widow, who came in from Austin for the funeral, stands up and talks about how Cecelia made her laugh and feel like a woman, not just a pastor's wife. The next person to stand up is Tommy Duncan, the pastor from Arizona, and the football player I liked during sophomore year at Boots High. Maggie reaches over and squeezes my hand and Belinda winks at me. I just shake my head in amusement.

Tommy is probably around forty-five now, and looking nothing like I remember. The tall slender football player is a short stocky fellow with visible scars on his face. "Mrs. Jackson worked for forty-four years at Boots' Elementary, but never taught in a classroom. Her lessons came when while she spooned out mashed potatoes and saw one of us with tears or a black eye. That's when she taught." I can tell Tommy is a preacher. "She influenced me for God. I didn't follow Jesus when I lived in Boots. Never saw the need. But when I left Boots, I realized I needed something the world just didn't have to offer. In college I realized the lunch lady back in Boots provided for me the directions to what I needed – or rather, whom I needed. I wrote a letter to Cecelia years back and thanked her for being a woman who served me green beans and life lessons at the same time."

I would not want to follow that. I feel a lump in my throat. I wonder if he's married. I look over at Maggie and she reads my thoughts and leans over, "He's married with five children."

I think no one will follow him, but then I hear the voice of Lola

Bee Turner. I turn around to see her. "Cecelia Jackson was one of my best friends in the world. Helped me out during some tough times. But I admired, more than anything, her ability to cook. Her pea salad and her cobblers and I've never tasted fried chicken like hers. She could put together a meal in less time than you could say lickity-split! She was a marvel in the kitchen and I will miss her. However, I must add right now that I think it is a crying shame that after today we will never again be able to have a Jackson tuna fish sandwich here in Boots. It's wrong, is what it is. That's all I got to say."

Belinda sighs and I see her roll her eyes. I look at Maggie and she is as uncomfortable as I am. A loud voice saves us. Mrs. Friesen, who happens to be sitting on the opposite side of the church than Mrs. Turner, stands and belts out, "Lola Bee, you knew Cecelia. She loved these three as her own young'uns."

I stretch my neck to see Wilbur Friesen sitting beside her. It's my first glimpse of him in twenty-five years. Besides the white hair, he looks the same. Of course, he can't talk now. Maybe that's why he is eyeing his wife with such venom.

Imogene continues, "Simple. So they get the tuna fish and that's that!"

Mrs. Turner stands up again and matches Mrs. Friesen's volume, "That's that? I am not through fighting, Imogene! Little towns everywhere are just disappearing. Being bought up by huge stores that sell light bulbs and snack crackers on the same aisle! We will not become one of those. Boots should mean more to each of you than that! And having some ex-Boots city slickers take our recipe is just the beginning!"

Pastor Ben pipes up, "Ladies, I believe we might want to take up this conversation another time. A more appropriate time..."

"Listen, Pastor Ben, you're a good new preacher and all, but

Cecelia wouldn't mind us being open and honest right here at her funeral," Mrs. Turner says.

Mrs. Friesen nods her head in agreement. "She would've gotten a kick out of it."

Several more voices enter the fray and soon nondescript mumbling fills the church. I want to escape. Pastor Ben raises his hands but not everyone quiets down.

And then Mr. Jackson stands up beside me. Everyone stops talking. He takes small steps and walks up to the pulpit. Pastor Ben steps aside. He's gripping his white handkerchief and by watching his hands, I know he is trembling. He turns to the crowd and I see a man who has died himself, in many ways.

"I love my Sissy. I sure enough always will. She made me laugh and she made me cry. She made me so angry I spit nails and she confused me sometimes I didn't know up from down. Most of all, she made me think about Jesus. She helped me look for Him in places like a new rosebud, right 'fore it opens. And in a sale at Stewart's Hardware Store." He pauses and then adds, "And in a darn-tooting silly poem about some herd on a range."

He stops and lets out a muffled cry. My heart drops.

"I say all this just to tell you one thing. After fifty-three years with this woman, many, many things she said and did are still a big mystery to me. Why did she give the recipe away to ladies who don't live here? I don't know. She did though and it was hers to do with it as she darn well pleased. One thing I do know is that my best friend is gone, and I am lost without her."

Mr. Jackson steps away from the pulpit and Ted Bellinger is suddenly there and walks him back to his seat by me. I grab his hand and he takes it.

Pastor Ben approaches the pulpit again. He looks up to speak and his eyes are shining. "The first time I saw Mrs. Jackson was at the Frontiers Day's high school dance. She danced with Vern and her face lit up with fun. She started doing the Charleston in the middle of some modern song. Now I am a dyed in the wool Baptist, and I don't care too much for dancing, but if I ever have a wife, I want to dance with her looking at me like Mrs. Jackson looked at Vern that night. Cecelia May Jackson was an extraordinary woman. She affected all who crossed her path. That is evident. So today, although we are sad and struck with grief, today, Cecelia celebrates. She is in the presence of the Lord and King."

Here we go. The sermon part of the presentation. I want to check out and think about something else but I can't. I owe it to Cecelia to listen to one last sermon in her honor.

"If you could ask her right now to come back to be with us, she would say no. The reason is clear. She is just beginning to explore what she lived her life for. God pictured her for His purposes even long before seventy-six years ago. In her teens, she made a decision to follow God and join with Him in the purposes for her life.

"Philippians 1:6 says, 'He who began a good work in you will carry it on to completion.' Our Lord God has completed the work He laid out for Mrs. Jackson. Imagine a marathon runner breaking the tape in the Olympics. The crowd goes crazy with applause as he finishes his race and receives his medal. Last Monday, Mrs. Jackson received her reward. The angels went crazy, as well as others who were waiting for her. And I bet you, I just bet you, she is celebrating right now. And she is dancing with her Master with a face lit up with fun."

Pastor Ben pauses and then adds, "If you want what Mrs. Jackson had, she would be the first to tell you that she experienced not an 'it,' but a 'Him.' She was in a relationship with Jesus Christ, who gave her the personality, the bit of mystery, the incredible abilities...all that made her Cecelia. And today, Jesus wants to do the same for you. He now yearns for you to let Him start the work He has for you or complete the work He has. If you have never met Him, all you must do to begin an incredible relationship with Him is admit that you are a sinner and believe He died on the cross for your sins. Accept the gracious gift He has for you and turn your life over to Him.

"And if you have met Him, but turned away for whatever reason, be it shame or anger or doubt, you must know that He loves you and has never left you. Never. He wants to have you turn back to Him and live an abundant life of joy and peace. All you have to do is humble yourself and ask. Let's pray."

I bow my head but in my own act of rebellion, I don't close my eyes like a good little girl Baptist. *I won't let your fairy tales rule my life, Cecelia. I won't do it.* I glance beside me and Tracey's folded her little hands and closed her eyes. Belinda stares straight ahead, angry as usual.

When I look at Maggie, I'm surprised. Her eyes are open and her head isn't bowed. She's looking straight up with a smile on her face. This just can't get any weirder.

The cemetery service is short and lovely. Boots Cemetery is at the edge of town right below the mountains. Cecelia chose a grave with a beautiful view of the B Mountain. It's a pretty spot. As per Cecelia's request, a violin and guitar play two worship songs. Mrs. Friesen and Mrs. Turner read Psalms. And then Cecelia May Jackson's funeral is at an end.

Pastor Ben makes the announcement for the meal at the Jackson home and everyone starts walking to their cars. I walk by Mr. Jackson and grab his arm. He leans into me a bit and we make our way among the town people, all of us in silence.

Pastor Ben comes up on the other side of Mr. Jackson and whispers something to him I can't hear. Mr. Jackson stops cold and

I let his arm go. He grabs Ben's hand and shakes it hard. I see a grimace on Pastor Ben's face.

"Pastor Ben," Mr. Jackson fiercely whispers, "Good judgment comes from experience, and a lot of that comes from bad judgment." He pauses, and then declares, "You will never be known again as the 'new preacher.' I will see to it, I tell you what."

He walks away and I don't move but smile at Ben. He whispers to me, "Our Lord works in mysterious ways."

I giggle and then hear Mr. Jackson's voice, "Why is there a Wind Storm, Texas police car here?"

Chapter 33

Maggie

Father, what is going on?

Belinda seemed softened somehow at the service. One minute I'm walking with her away from Cecelia's grave, I'm full of hope that we can really talk, and the next minute she spits out a dirty word and starts running.

"Mama! Where are you going?" Tracey runs after her and Belinda stops and turns.

"No. You stay here. Find Imogene right now." She says this with gritted teeth. I don't understand. Then I see a police car on the street. A tall man is standing beside the car looking at the crowd. Belinda is heading to her car, which is out in the parking lot on the outside of the cemetery.

Father, oh no. Is she running?

Donna is by my side. "Maggie, he's going to be

looking for Belinda." She looks toward the policeman.

"You don't know that. Do you? Donna?"

She walks away and nears Vern. He is heading for the policeman.

Imogene comes up to me with Lola Bee by her side. "Did Belinda leave, Maggie?"

"Yes, she went to her car." I point towards Belinda who is now getting into her car.

"Where's Tracey?"

"She tried to go with Belinda but Belinda told her to find you."

We all look around trying to spot the eight-year-old but I don't see her anywhere.

"There she is," Lola Bee chimes in.

Tracey is back at Cecelia's grave, sitting by it.

"I'll go get her," I offer and walk that way. I stop and look back. "Does anyone know why the policeman is here and why Belinda is running off?" As I ask this, the answer sounds obvious.

Imogene gives me an intent look. "Yes, I do. Now you go get Tracey and be quick about it." She grabs Lola Bee by the arm and starts speed wobbling to the officer.

I get to Tracey and she's crying. "Tracey, sweetie, we have to go."

"Nana left me, and now Mama is leaving."

I kneel beside her. "No Tracey, your mom isn't going anywhere without you." *Father, she isn't, is she?* "We have to leave now." I reach for her hands and pull her up as gently as I can. Tracey stands and buries her head into my stomach, crying.

When we turn back to go to the car, I see that most of the crowd has left. Just a few people here and there, talking. And Vern and Donna are talking to the sheriff. Imogene and Lola Bee are almost to him. Belinda's car is gone. What in the world? I start walking toward the crowd to see what's up and Tracey jerks my hand. I look down and I see her scared. Completely frozen. "What is it, Tracey?"

She lifts a finger but keeps it close to her chest. And she points. "Mr. Hank."

"Who, sweetie?"

She breaks off from me and runs back to Cecelia's grave.

Oh God, help. I look over and I see the sheriff, apparently Mr. Hank, pointing at me, or at Tracey? I decide to let Tracey be and see what in the world is happening.

"I just want to ask Miss Kite some questions, that's all." He's smiling and I don't trust him at all. Tracey has good instincts. "Hello, I'm Henry Hood." He extends his hand.

Something stirs in me so I don't take it. "What's going on here?"

"It seems like this here policeman has come to see Belinda all the way from Wind Storm, Texas. I just told him I don't know where she went. Do you, Maggie?" Imogene says this loudly. A little too loudly.

"I don't." That's the truth.

"We don't know where she is so you just go back to East Texas where you came from." Lola Bee is almost in the man's face.

"I'd back up if I were you, Ma'am." He's still smiling but his eyes are getting dark; it looks like they're on fire, too. "Maybe if you told me where Miss Kite is staying, well, then I'd leave you alone."

"I'm going to the house." Vern turns around and starts walking. Donna follows without saying a word.

I grab her arm and whisper, "Donna, what is happening? Does this have anything to do with the money?"

Donna looks at me with guilt all over her. "I'm sorry." She rushes to catch up with Vern.

Oh no, Jesus, no. I look back and Lola Bee and Imogene are both standing close to that sheriff. He's leaning back but not stepping back.

"And you better just watch yourself, Sonny," Lola Bee growls at him.

"You ain't in East Texas anymore, Toto," Imogene cackles as she and Lola Bee turn to go to their car.

The sheriff gets into his car but is staring over at Tracey.

"Imogene, can I ride with you?" She nods and I turn to go get Belinda's daughter, still sitting by Cecelia's grave, her knees hugging her chest. I kneel down beside her and I think of when she was crying yesterday after Belinda's outburst. This poor kid.

"Tracey, I've got you now. You stay with me until we find your mom, okay?" She stands up still quivering from her sobbing. My heart breaks for her. We walk to Imogene's and I glance over at that sheriff. He's staring at us. Then he jumps in his car and peels out.

Chapter 34

Belinda

This car don't go fast enough for me. Wish I owned a sports car that could hit 150. I'm weaving through Boots as fast as I can to get to the interstate. Not much traffic. Course ever'body and their dog is at the cemetery. Coulters actually shut down for the funeral.

I glide onto the interstate and I'm home free. If I know Vern and Imogene, they'll corner Hank for a good ten minutes. So I got time.

I didn't bring my clothes but I don't need 'em. I got enough money to set up shop in Mexico for a spell and get a job cooking. I can do this. I glance in the rear view mirror and no one is behind me. I'm free.

Something catches my eye in the back seat. I look back and see a doll sitting there. It's Tracey's. I'll mail it to her. This is the best decision. She's gonna have a life that she deserves. Imogene will be mad at me for a while, but then she'll see this is the best for all of us. It is.

I feel a jab in my heart like someone kicked me. No, this is what I need to do. This is what I have to do. I'm speeding but I don't care. Can't see anyone for miles. At last, I'm totally free. I see lights in my rear view mirror. Red and blue. Darnitt. I shouldn't be speeding. Getting a ticket is the last thing I need. But what if it's him? Oh God no, it can't be Hank.

I speed up. What am I doing? *God, help me. Yes, I'm asking You. Help!* My Accord can't outrun the police car. He's on my tail. I slow down. It's him. It's Hank. I pull over and I get out. Maybe if I run, another car will see me. I take off.

"Belinda!" He's chasing me. I feel his hands on me and I'm on the ground, dirt in my face. He turns me over and sits on me.

"Ow!" The familiar sting of his hand still hurts. "Stop it, Hank. Please."

"Don't you ever learn, Bee? You can't leave me until I give you permission. And I haven't given it yet. You're going back with me to Wind Storm and guess what? I'll give you a choice. Prison for being a thief or a job as my little slut just like it's always been." He leans down and puts his face close to mine. "I think I'll know what you choose."

I spit in his face. "Prison sounds great!"

He punches me hard. I close my eyes. I deserve this.

Chapter 35

Maggie

"Imogene, do you have a solution to this problem?" From the back seat, I try to say it delicately. Tracey is smart as a whip.

Imogene looks at Lola Bee. "I don't know. But we'll see."

"You know, old heifer, she would've loved to be right in the middle of this," Lola Bee says this looking out the window.

"Are you talking about Nana?" Tracey has the littlest voice I've ever heard.

Imogene replies, "You betcha your red hair we are, little'un." She glances toward the back seat and winks at Tracey.

Apparently, they have a plan. *Father protect Bee and may Your will be done. And stop that man.* Before we get to Cecelia's neighborhood, Imogene takes a turn towards town. And then she stops at the railroad track for a full thirty seconds even though there isn't any train. Imogene giggles and goes over the tracks slowly.

"Woman, we need to get there, you know that, right?"

"Oh, hush up Lola Bee. I'm doing exactly what we talked about."

"A head start doesn't mean time for a full Bahamas cruise."

"What do you know about cruises?" Imogene asks.

"That ain't the point and you know it. Let's get on with it."

"What?" I don't understand and no one is telling me anything.

Lola Bee's phone rings. "Okay? Do you see him? Okay." She hangs up and turns to Imogene. "He just hit the interstate so let's go. Hot diggity, I'm going to make a few calls." Lola punches in some numbers. "Hello? Operation Sissy is on. Repeat, Operation Sissy is on." She makes two more calls and the end of the second one she punches the off button and giggles. Imogene joins her with that cackling laugh. I look over at Tracey and she's smiling at me.

"What's so funny?" she asks.

"I don't know." I squeeze her hand.

"Ya'll will see in just a few minutes," Imogene announces.

Lola Bee's phone rings. "Turner here." She giggles. "I'm sorry, I was giggling. What did you say?"

"Don't waste time woman," Imogene tells her.

"Just a second," Lola Bee says into the phone and then looks up. "If you would stop talking to me I could hear what the next step is. Can you do that?"

"I'm not the one giggling and missing what could be vital instructions."

"Why do you have to take the fun outta everything?"

"Me? My middle name is fun, you old heifer."

"Stop it, you two," I plead. "What did they say on the phone?"

Lola Bee puts the phone back to her ear. "Sorry about that.

What did you say, Vern?"

Vern? He's in on this, too? It's his wife's funeral.

"Gotcha. This is Turner. Over and out."

"He's faster than we thought. He's already out a ways. Let's hit it, girl."

Lola Bee and Imogene laugh together and look ahead. If I ask they won't say anything so I don't. I am a bit nervous, though, thinking that we might be heading to tangle with a man who is armed. Father, guide us.

We take a left on Main Street, Boots' main drag. We pass the Post Office, the Dairy Queen, and Bell's Cafe and we drive onto the interstate. It was only a couple of days ago that I drove this route ogling every building on this street to see how it had changed. Now I'm driving in a car with two crazy women and a heartbroken child chasing a policeman. It seems as if I've been back in Boots for years. It seems like I never left.

"Imogene, aren't you speeding a bit?" It feels fast and even though we are on a freeway with no one in sight, I am nervous. I lean over the front seat to look at the speedometer. "90 miles an hour? Imogene, maybe you should slow down a bit."

Lola Bee answers me. "Maggie May, just sit back and enjoy the ride. Imogene knows what she's doing."

"There they are," Imogene says. I look ahead and see Vern's Lincoln. Wilbur and Donna are with him. Wilbur turns around and gives us a thumbs up. Imogene blows a kiss his way. "I love that man."

"Oh, get a room," Lola Bee says and then punctuates it with a giggle. Again, the two old women start laughing.

I look behind us and see that traffic is approaching. "Here comes a car." I say, trying to be helpful in a little way.

"Here comes a bunch," Lola Bee offers.

I turn back and can't believe my eyes. It seems in just a moment, dozens of cars have joined us. It's even weirder because they are all coming two by twos, using both lanes of the freeway. But when the first two cars get to us, they slow a bit and don't try to pass us. I look in the first car and see Pastor Ben sitting with Ted Bellinger. Mark Kildwell drives the car beside them. His wife and Mabel Worthers are with him.

It's my turn to laugh. "Am I part of a posse?"

Lola Bee and Imogene cackle at the same time. "This is the west, you know," Lola Bee says. Her phone rings. "Turner. Yep, okey-doke." She hangs up. "Vern can see them just ahead. It don't look good."

"Pass the word, then," Imogene tells her.

"I am! Just give me a second," Lola Bee makes a call. "Operation Sissy is on full alert. I repeat full alert." She pauses. "Yes, that's what that means Mark." She hangs up. "I tell you that mortician is funny and does his job well, but sometimes he just don't get it."

"Did you tell him the code, Lola Bee?"

"No, Imogene, that was somebody else's job."

"If he don't know the code, then how can you expect him to get it?" She over pronounces the t's like she always does when she is perturbed.

Vern is slowing down and pulls off the freeway. I see now that the sheriff has pulled over Belinda and has put her face against the top of his car and is putting handcuffs on her. *Oh Father please be with us and help us.* I look down at Tracey and I cover her eyes. "Why are you doing that?" She says as she tries to wiggle out.

Imogene pulls over parallel to Vern and Pastor Ben pulls over next to us. Imogene looks back at me. "Maggie, Tracey gets to see this. Let her go."

I don't agree but I comply. We get out and I follow Imogene and

Lola Bee to where Vern, Donna, and Wilbur are standing, about ten feet away from the sheriff and Belinda. Tracey comes up beside me and grabs my hand.

The sheriff eyes us and the burgeoning crowd. I look back and it seems half the town of Boots is joining us. I see Mrs. Morris and Alana Ortega standing together. Mark, Cathy and Mabel stand together. Suzzane Bolder who sang at the funeral is standing by the Boots mayor, Ken Bolder. Lots of other folks I don't know gather.

I look back and Belinda turns around. I gasp. Her face is bruised and a little blood is on her check.

"Mommy?" I reach down and pull Tracey to me.

Pastor Ben and Ted Bellinger walk out in front of us. "Let's beat the pulp out of him." Ted says to Ben.

"Absolutely," Pastor Ben responds.

"I don't think so." The sheriff pulls his gun out. He points it to the ground, but he's made his point.

I pull Tracey behind me.

"Hold on, boys." Vern walks between them.

"I don't know what you have in mind, folks, but this is a matter of law, so you just need to go on home." The sheriff jerks Belinda back from the car by her handcuffs. She lets out an "Ow!" Tracey releases my hand and starts to run up, but Vern catches her.

"Let go of my mom!" She yells, her red ponytail flying behind her. I take her from Vern.

Belinda sees Tracey and looks around at all of us. She doesn't say anything. Just hangs her head and looks at the ground. Her chest is heaving.

"Your mom is a criminal wanted by the good people of Wind Storm, Tracey. I am taking her away." He says it in such a snide manner.

Father, get him. Get him!

Vern takes a step toward the sheriff. "Listen, son, I know you are the law in your little town but we got the law of Boots with us." He looks back at the crowd and a man joins us in front. He is tall and Hispanic with a big bushy mustache.

"Good afternoon, Sheriff. I'm Manuel Gonzales, the Sheriff of Boots. Why don't we be civil about all this? First, put your gun away. There's going to be no more violence today."

"I don't know how you run your city, Sheriff, but it looks a little like a yellow-bellied chicken might. You had to bring all these people with you?"

I watch Sheriff Gonzales and he forms a little grin on his face. "May I see the warrant for her arrest?"

Hank doesn't say anything for a minute. "I don't have it with me, but if you check the Wind Storm records you'll find one."

"No warrant, no valid arrest Sheriff. You know that, don't you?"

Belinda is still looking at the ground. The fight I've seen in her is gone. She looks defeated and shamed.

"I don't know what you're getting at, but this lady is going with me." He jerks on her handcuffs again and Belinda glances up long enough for me to see her wincing in pain.

"Her face tells me you probably made time to read her rights. You beat this woman?" Gonzales takes a step toward the sheriff.

The sheriff points his gun at Gonzales. *Oh, God in the name of Jesus stop him.* "You need to just back up and mind your own business."

Imogene steps forward. "She is my business."

"And mine." Vern joins Imogene.

I hear the words, "Mine, too," repeated throughout the crowd. I look around amazed. I glance at Donna who has tears in her eyes. She steps forward and I join her. "She's our business."

Belinda looks up and around and then drops her head again.

"Listen, Henry Hood, we have something for you," Imogene says.

Vern holds up a piece of paper. "If you look at that you'll see a receipt through Western Union. We wired the $500 that Belinda took. You'll find it when you get back to Wind Storm."

Again, Belinda looks up in shock, I think, but drops her head again. Hank slips his gun back in his holster and puts his hand out. Vern walks up and gives it to him. Hood looks at the receipt and scoffs.

"So you just returned stolen goods. So what? She still needs to pay for what she did."

Imogene pipes up. "This is how it's gonna be, Mister. You let Belinda go and we will forget to tell your entire town about a certain affair you've been having. One that a sheriff going up for reelection, may not want publicized. One your wife maybe ain't privy to?"

The sheriff drops his hand away from Belinda's handcuffs. She doesn't move. He doesn't say anything. "It's my word against hers." He stands defiant with a look of arrogance. He thinks he's won? He has no idea who his opponents are.

Vern is shaking his head. "Son, I wouldn't bet on those odds if I were you. It's your word against every single one of us. You don't get that?" He turns to the crowd. "The wheel is turning but his hamster is dead."

Imogene cackles and says, "Now maybe you just take the handcuffs off and you skedaddle on home."

Hank looks at Gonzales. "I will have your badge over this. Blackmail is illegal."

I look at Sheriff Gonzales and he puts his hand on his gun. "This never happened. I think it might be your word against...ours." He looks at the crowd.

Hank starts cussing and kicks the dirt like a toddler. "What do you want with a useless tramp like this? She's a thief and a whore. And she's a horrible mama."

"No she's not!" Tracey yells and I have to hold on tighter.

Hank cusses some more and gets his keys and unlocks Belinda and takes off the cuffs. "She will never, ever have a place in Wind Storm!" He kicks Belinda into the dirt and she lands on her hands and knees.

Pastor Ben and Ted Bellinger get to Belinda at the same time to help her up.

For the first time in my life, I hear Vern Jackson yell. "Get your sorry excuse for a little boy outta here before I put my boot where the sun don't' shine and kick you back to East Texas! This little girl has a place with me. Right here in Boots."

"She has a place with me!" Imogene yells and Wilbur stands beside her nodding.

"She can always stay at my house. I got plenty of room," Lola Bee yells.

"She can move with me to Denver if she wants!" Donna yells through a broken voice.

I chime in. "Tucson is a great place for Belinda!"

And again I hear the domino calls of the people of Boots yelling that Belinda's place is with them.

I look at Belinda, who is standing between Pastor Ben and Ted Bellinger and I try to read her face. She is in shock and red-faced embarrassed. I think I see a softening around her eyes. *Do I, Father?*

Hank opens the door to his car when Belinda rushes from her place between Pastor Ben and Ted. She lifts her foot and kicks Hank hard in the behind and yells, "Never again!" Her voice is hoarse and loud and painful. Hank falls into the car door and his head hits the top of the car. He turns around and the look on his face is pure rage. He makes a fist but before he can swing, Pastor Ben and Ted rush him and throw him to the ground.

"Stop! Right now!" Manuel Gonzales is with them, ordering Ben and Ted to back off. They do and Hank stumbles up, hair messed and covered in dirt and gravel.

"Go back to your town, Hood." Manuel has his gun out, pointing toward the ground. His voice is threatening and I immediately resolve to never, ever cross the man. Hank says nothing but gets in his car and peels out. His car only causes a tiny stir of dust.

Cheers erupt through the crowd.

Imogene turns to face the town and yells, "Let's go eat a tuna sandwich in honor of Cecelia May Jackson!" More yells and chatting as people go back to their cars and start to leave.

Pastor Ben and Ted Bellinger surround Belinda and Pastor Ben asks her to ride with them. Wilbur points to Belinda's car and then himself.

"Wilbur will drive your car to the house, Belinda," Ted confirms.

"Mama, are you okay?" Tracey asks Belinda but her mom says nothing and turns to walk to Pastor Ben's truck. *Really, God? What is it going to take?*

As Belinda moves slowly toward Pastor Ben's car, she turns, "Vern? Imogene?" Her voice is scratchy. We turn to her. "How did you get the money out of my car?"

Vern looks at Imogene and Imogene looks at him. They say in unison, "We didn't."

Chapter 36

Belinda

I ain't never gonna believe that just happened. They did that for me. For me. Now, ever'thing is ruined. I sit between Ben and Ted and I feel awful. Humiliated. Angry. What were they thinking? Ted gives me a handkerchief to wipe blood off my face. My head is pounding. But I ain't gonna cry. What am I gonna do now? I need a minute to think.

Ben and Ted are quiet. Making a good impression on me. No need to talk. Not after what just happened. I want to sink into a bed and sleep. I can't even abandon my daughter right. And what did they mean by not getting the money? Does that mean it's still in my trunk?

They ain't got no idea who I am. Hank was right. I'm no good. And I don't want to stay in a town run by God people. In Wind Storm, I didn't know ever'body and they didn't know me. And the folks I did know weren't saints, that's for sure. I ain't gonna become religious just cause they tried to 'rescue' me. Their mistake - I didn't need their help.

We get to the Jacksons and I slip outta the truck after Ted. He offers me his hand and I take it to get down. I look at him and he's staring at me like some breakable china doll. I let go of his hand. He ain't got no idea who I am. But he sure is good-looking.

Ever'body is making their way into the house. A woman I don't know puts one arm around me, squeezes and keeps walking. I see an older couple look at me and grin. I wanna just disappear but I can't. I gotta be polite right now. I'll have a chance to leave again later.

Lola Bee comes up to me. "Belinda, you go upstairs into the middle bathroom and clean yourself up. Cecelia kept Ibuprofen up there, too. Then come down and eat something." She grins at me. I don't ever remember having Lola Bee grin at me. I don't know if I like it.

I go upstairs and stand in front of the bathroom mirror. I ache all over and there's a big bruise on my cheek. I open my mouth and see that Hank chipped one of my side teeth. Besides that, I'm okay. I wash my face, comb my hair, and take a bunch of Ibuprofen. Come on, Bee. Pull yourself together and get through today. Later tonight, you can leave.

I walk through the house with the crowd and go through the kitchen to the backyard. Card tables and a couple of long eight feet metal tables are set up. All sorts of food is ever'where. But the picnic table is reserved for platters of tuna fish sandwiches. An old woman that I don't know is sitting in the swing, despite the fact that folding chairs are ever'where. Some folks are walking through the arch to Vern's garden. It's absolutely beautiful back there and I see the sunflowers towering over all the other colors. For a moment, I sense they're calling out to me. I am losing it, for sure.

A light breeze crosses my face and it feels refreshing. It's a nice little wind, just enough to cool a face, but not strong enough to disturb the fixin's. Folks are bunching up in groups and, of course, Boots townspeople line up to self-serve the food. People keep coming up to me. I keep nodding at them to be polite and then I walk away. I look around to see Donna or Maggie but I don't see them anywhere.

I go back inside and I see Imogene and Lola Bee and their other cohorts Barbara and Maxine sitting at the Formica. They're laughing about something. Imogene catches my eye, but before she can say something, I walk out and down the hall to the Visiting Room. Just as I thought, this room is crowded with patches of people throughout, huddled in conversations. I hear Cecelia's name a couple of times. I walk over to the picture window. The curtains are open today and the sun is shining bright. Outside in the front yard, children play tag. Tracey is among them. I'm always amazed at her ability to be sad one moment and then carefree the next. Guess that's just childhood. I see Donna and Maggie to the side of the kids, standing close talking seriously. My ears are burning. I want to talk to Maggie. But I don't want to talk to Donna. Ever.

I turn away from the window and walk over to the corner by Cecelia's desk. It's open today, showing some of her notes and stacks of papers. And I see the picture of the four of us, the same one she sent Tracey, framed and sitting on the corner of her desk. I sigh. This is too much. I look up and see Vern and a man I don't know.

"Sweet girl, this is Bud Weaver, my oldest friend in the world."

Sweet girl. My heart hurts. I am not a sweet girl. I lean in and shake hands with Bud. He has kind eyes.

"Bud lost his wife, Margaret, five years ago. The four of us used to stay up late right here in this room playing forty-two 'til the wee hours of the night. Margaret fixed us banana pudding on some nights and Sissy made her peach cobbler on the others." He stops talking and blinks hard. "Bud lives in Tulsa by his kids now. I don't know what I'm going to do."

Vern looks at me when he says this, but it feels like he's looking past me into Cecelia's desk chair seeing her. I excuse myself and leave. I go through the kitchen again and to the back yard. Donna comes right up to me, a plate in her hand, full of goodies. Her mouth is full but her eyes are questioning me.

I just stare at her. She swallows hard and tries to smile. "This is wonderful, Belinda, you should eat something. It's been so long since I had great southern cooking."

I can't think of anything good to say to this woman.

She keeps talking. "The church service was a bit weird, but okay. I haven't been to church since I left Texas."

"Yep." I keep looking at her, thinking she's going to apologize for being such a weasel but she doesn't. She's acting as if nothing happened.

"It was like watching an old movie. Sweet, but please, that sermon? I just hate it when these old fashioned hellfire preachers think they can turn a funeral into a reason to play *Just as I Am* and have people walk the aisle, promising things they can never deliver." Donna takes a bite of fried okra.

I know she's right. This town is a backward pit stop. I have to leave here. "I'm going to look for Maggie."

"Suit yourself," Donna replies and bites into a piece of cornbread.

I walk through the house again and out to the front porch. Maggie's nowhere in sight so I sit on the front porch swing. I watch Tracey immerse herself in the freeze tag game.

"How are you doing?"

I look up and Maggie is standing there with that irritating compassionate look of hers. I don't say anything. Maybe she'll just leave. But I hope not.

She sits down beside me. "You won't believe what's going on in the kitchen, Bee. Imogene and her gang are actually sitting around a platter of tuna fish sandwiches, trying to taste their way to the secret. It's Cecelia's funeral, and they look like they're filming a cooking show."

I grin. Those old women are something else.

"I mean, come on, Belinda. It is just a sandwich. And yet, these old cronies are talking like it is some treasure of San Madre!"

"The treasure of San Madre?" I look at her. "Maggie, what exactly is the treasure of San Madre?"

"Some old movie where the treasure they found was a statue of a falcon or something."

"You're mixing up two Bogart movies. *The Treasure of the Sierra Madre* and *The Maltese Falcon*. Two totally different things."

"Well, you should go watch them. It's funny to see grown women so desperate to find something."

Desperate to find something. She's talking about me. Maybe not meaning to, but the phrase fits. What is going on with me? What am I going to do? My stomach hurts. Feels like cramping but maybe it's an ulcer from all my choices. A choice ulcer.

"Belinda? Talk to me."

I look at Maggie's face and I remember she's been through her own trauma the last week. But I don't care. It's good she can see what hurting feels like. Shame creeps up when I think about the cancer. "Leave me alone, right now, okay, Maggie?"

I go into the house and find my purse right by a hat rack near the front door. I pick it up and grab a piece of paper inside it. I glance at it.

"Belinda?" Maggie comes through the front door.

I storm into the kitchen.

"Belinda, what are you doing?" Maggie follows me.

"Listen up, ladies!" Their four heads pop up to attention. Each of them sits around the Formica with tuna fish sandwiches in their hands.

"It is just a recipe and this is Cecelia Jackson's funeral! And you know what? It just might hurt our feelings to hear you imply repeatedly that we are not good enough to have the keys to the kingdom of tuna fish. So, I have made a decision." I hold up the piece of paper.

"Belinda, that's not the…"

"…recipe, Maggie? Oh yes, it is! And I feel that these good women have proven to us that they deserve an end to their quest. I mean, someone in this world needs to find what they are looking for, right? Why not the Genteel Geezers of Boots Texas!"

"Well, I never…" Lola Bee gasped.

"Well, maybe you should, Lola Bee!" I toss it up in the air. I've never seen old women move so quick. All four practically stand up from their chairs to catch it, but it falls to the floor. I back up against Maggie and we move outta the way when I see elderly buttocks fly into the sky. I don't care anymore. Cecelia should never have given us the recipe in the first place. Imogene's faking anyway.

I turn and walk down the hall and head to my room. Maggie's following me. I can sense her right there. She slows down on the stairs but I keep moving and dart into my bedroom. I hear the unmistakable voice of Imogene as she cackles and then shouts, "Okay, anyone need a hip replacement? If not, let's get busy."

"Belinda, wait."

I slam the door in Maggie's face. She opens it immediately.

I sit on the bed. "Will you just leave me alone? Please?"

Silence fills the room as we stare each other down. Maggie plops down beside me. "No, I can't leave you alone." She crosses her arms.

I stare at the floor. "I'm grateful for what ever'one did. I am. Amazing, wasn't it?"

"Yes, absolutely."

"But to ask me to just change the way I am is useless. Ain't gonna happen."

"Who's asking you to change?"

I look at her. "Seriously, Maggie? That whole scene out there was to tell me to change my ways. Straighten up and fly right."

Maggie glares at me. "You are something else, Bee. What happened out on the freeway is not to get you to change, but to tell you that you are loved and accepted even if you *never* change. Don't you see that?"

I stand up and go to the window. From my vantage point, I can see the backyard and even down into the garden. People are everywhere. "Do you know what happened with the money? Did they take it out of my car or not?"

"You're going to have to ask Vern or Imogene. I have no idea."

I turn around to face her. "You don't know me really, Maggie. You don't know my pain. My justified anger. I know you've gone through cancer and I feel horrible for you, but I am not you. I am not strong enough to just look at my life and forget all the horrible moments and then smile happy and sing hymns."

She stands up and the bed is between us. "Belinda, I don't just smile happily and sing hymns. I cry and scream and get angry with God. He can take it because He loves me. I believe with all my heart that nothing happens to me that isn't sifted through His hands. That gives me hope."

"Can you really stand there and tell me you don't resent me at all?"

Maggie looks down at the bed and I know I'm right. She hates me but is putting on an act 'cause of church. She looks up at me. "Forgive me, Belinda."

"What?" I didn't expect that.

"I have resented you and Donna for years. I just couldn't let the whole Alan Deltan incident go. Even though I fell in love with Frank, a part of me was angry I didn't get to be a preacher's wife. I'm so sorry, Belinda. And yes, God told me to forgive and forget. He told me countless times. But I held on."

I don't know what I'm supposed to say so I just keep quiet.

"And I have to ask you for forgiveness for something else, too." She sits on the bed by the headboard, one leg beneath her. I see her breathe in deep like Cecelia taught us.

I'm curious. I sit at the foot of the bed and wait.

"Alan asked me to have sex with him countless times. When I said no, he would get so angry. Finally, I agreed I would sleep with him but only after we were engaged. Then he hit me. Two times. The first time it shocked me, but he started apologizing immediately so I let it go. I thought maybe I should pray for him more." She scoffs. "Praying didn't help. He hit me one more time. I should've warned you and I'm so sorry. I kept thinking when we got married and he started studying to be a preacher it would all change."

"Why didn't you tell us? Did you at least tell Cecelia?"

"I didn't tell anyone. I've never said anything about it until this moment." Her eyes fill up. "I'm so sorry Belinda. I've been judging you and resenting you and the whole time I've had this secret. I thought since I was 'good' nothing bad would happen to me. But you took Alan and then my husband decided not to be a preacher, and then the cancer. I put all that anger in this one place – resentment against you. It doesn't make sense but there it is. I'm so sorry."

"What did you do the second time he hit you, Maggie?"

"I hit him back."

I start giggling soft and then it comes out almost like Imogene's cackle. "Well, I'll be, Maggie May. That ain't in the Bible, right?" I keep laughing.

Maggie's smiling but doesn't laugh. "I should have told you."

I start knotting up the bedspread in my fingers. I look down and notice it's a dark forest green that's really striking. I didn't see that before. "You don't have to say sorry to me. I made my own bed and I had to lie in it. Simple as that." I look up at her and then glance back at the bedspread. We just sit for a few minutes.

"Belinda, you said Alan left you because of a dead baby."

My head jerks up at her. Why did I tell them? Suddenly, I'm so tired. I lay on my side at the foot of the bed. Maggie tosses me a pillow. I catch it and put it under my head. "So I did."

"What happened, Bee?"

"God gave me a baby and took it away. He punished me and gave me what I deserve and took away what I don't deserve. And I don't see love in it at all."

"Tell me."

I sigh and look at the ceiling. "Alan wanted to have a child so badly. When he wasn't hitting me, he was seducing me or taking me to doctors. All so he could have a son. His senior year of college, he got a job as a youth director at a small church in Abilene. No one knew, of course, about his temper. Ever'one loved him. He really knew the Bible and he knew how to talk to kids...." I breathe in deep and let it out slow.

"Belinda?" Maggie gently prods. "What happened?"

"He became friends with a youth director at a community church there in Abilene. A nice guy named Lan who was married to Brittany. They became our best friends. We saw them all the time. Brittany talked to me often, but I never really got close to her. She wasn't…well, like us, you know?"

Maggie nods, "I know."

"One night Alan came home from church…"

"What are you doing?"

I sat watching a Jimmy Stewart movie. I didn't move 'cause I knew that tone.

He kept going and said, 'What are you doing, fatty?'

"Alan, please leave me alone. Or why don't you sit and watch this movie with me?"

"Guess what, my darling wife? Guess what I just found out?"

I didn't look at him even though he stood directly in front of me. Alan turned to the TV and shut it off. "Alan, please."

"Lan and Brittany are pregnant."

I looked at him and then glanced at the floor. "That's wonderful for them, Alan."

"They've only been trying for two months. Two months. Seems she has been blessed by God, whereas you are some kind of barren shell. You know how that makes me feel?"

"Alan, please just leave me alone." I brought my knees up to my head and hugged them, trying to make myself smaller.

"I'm not going to leave you alone. You are my wife and you're going to give me a son!"

"It was pretty bad that time. He beat me worse than ever before. And then he…" My chest is heaving. I ain't gonna cry.

"What did he do?"

"He raped me." I look at Maggie and I feel the tears. They're sitting in my eyes and I try to blink them back. "And I can't believe I let him hurt me. I was so stupid."

"Belinda, you have nothing to feel guilty about. He's the one who raped you."

I sniff and breathe and a sardonic laugh escapes me. "Funny thing is, he never hit me again."

"Did you leave him?"

"No, I got pregnant." Tears come. After years of never crying, tears trickle down my face and I turn and bury my head in the pillow. I feel Maggie's hands on my head, stroking my hair. Maggie gets up and comes back with some tissue. I sit up to blow my nose. "He never touched me during the pregnancy. Not once. Those nine months were wonderful, Maggie. In fact, I thought that we actually had a chance at a real marriage. He treated me like he should - gentle and loving. We even laughed while we shopped for the nursery. The baby shower was one of the best days of my life. The entire church showed up. We celebrated with Lan and Brittany and we made so many plans. Alan looked proud and happy, like in high school. Remember when he preached that sermon about basketball and Jesus at that camp? So full of charisma."

Sadness covers Maggie's face as she says, "I remember."

"Lan and Brittany had a little boy named Gabriel. Healthy. Perfect. On April 7th, my baby came. Stillborn. Can you believe that, Maggie? Stillborn. I cried nonstop for hours. I held him in the hospital and they had to force me to let him go. And then I noticed no one cried with me. Alan left me. When I got home from the hospital, his stuff was gone and our bank account emptied. He quit his job at the church and moved. I ain't seen him since. And I ain't cried since then, neither."

Maggie reaches out and squeezes my hand. "I'm so sorry, Belinda."

I keep crying. My eyes are broken faucets that I can't turn off. I hate crying. I hate this.

"Did you give your baby a name?"

I blow my nose. "Yes. I named him Isaiah. He'd be twenty years old now." I stand up and throw my tissue away and get some more. I sit back down on the bed. "Cecelia was there when he was born."

"Really?" Maggie asks. "Of course. She always knew when we needed her."

"Cecelia helped me plan a little funeral. I don't remember anything about it, to be honest with you. I do remember this perfect shaped head and body. He just looked asleep. Cecelia held me and cried with me. She kept saying the same thing over and over."

"What did she say?"

"Belinda, God is here."

"She was right."

Anger flares up in me. "Was she, Maggie? How could God take away a life that hadn't even begun?"

"God can do anything He wants to, Belinda. And He usually doesn't tell us why." After a moment of silence, Maggie asks, "Did the church try to help you?"

"Actually, yes. They were quite nice and decent. But so many questioned me about Alan. I didn't have answers, at least none they wanted to hear. I think they blamed me for him leaving. So I left. I moved to Tyler and then later to Wind Storm. I gave up on God then. I don't want to live for someone who'd take my only chance of happiness. I slept around quite a bit after that. Nine years ago, I met a guy named Rick. I only slept with him once. Nine months later - Tracey. Makes no sense."

"Do you ever see Rick?"

"No. He was a truck driver passing through Tyler. He doesn't even know about Tracey." My body aches. I hurt all over but it feels good to hurt. It feels right to tell my oldest friend all of this. This is right.

"Belinda..." Maggie begins.

"What?"

"Belinda, can I pray for you? I don't want to turn you off but this is who I am and I love you, and..."

When she says this I don't feel any anger. But I don't know. "Maggie, God and I just don't work anymore. I left Him."

"I know. But He never left you."

"Then why did this happen?"

"I don't know." Maggie looks at me with uncertainty. "Can I pray?"

Why not? I'm tired of running. "Sure. Go ahead."

Maggie grabs my hand and bows her head. This is weird. It's been a while. "Lord, we don't know why You allowed little Isaiah to die. We don't know why You allowed Alan to treat Belinda so badly. But we know that Cecelia was right. You were there right beside Belinda. You are God and You love her. And You are right here now with her. You have never left. Lord, please heal these wounds. And please, God, let Belinda actually feel Your love. Thank You, Father. In Jesus' name, Amen."

I keep my head down with my eyes closed. Ever'thing in me says to let go, but I can't. I can't go back to Him.

I love you no matter what.

I hear a voice in my heart. No. I can't.

I cherish you, sweet girl. Come back to me.

The words bring more tears to my eyes. My heart is pounding.

Belinda, I am here.

It's time. It's time to run back to the only place I've even known peace of mind. My words come out with tears. "Lord, I'm sorry. Take me as I am." A sob from the pit of me comes up almost like I am throwing up. It scares me and yet, it is such a release. A flood of tears come. Maggie puts her arm around me and says nothing. Just lets me cry. Ever' time I think I'm about to stop, another wave hits me.

After a long time, I sit up straight and wipe my eyes. "Did I use the entire tissue box?" I look at Maggie and she's smiling at me. It's not a sanctimonious, holier-than-thou, smug grin. It's my old friend celebrating with me. I reach out and give the first hug I've given in a while.

A knock at the door startles me.

"Who is it?" Maggie calls.

"It's Tracey. Is my mom in there?"

I look at Maggie and my heart tries to jump out of my chest. Tracey? I whisper, "Oh, poor Tracey."

Maggie stands up. "I'll be downstairs watching the Geezers." She grins and rubs her eyes. It occurs to me she cried right along with me. Of course.

Tracey enters sheepishly and stands by the door leaning into it. "Mama, I'm sorry to bother you, but could I swim at Mrs. Friesen's later? She said she wanted me to come over and I won't be any trouble at all and I will be really good for her, I promise."

My heart breaks in two. How many years I done ignored this precious girl? How can I ever make it up to her? Lord, help! I see Tracey's green eyes and lovely red hair and I see myself years ago. I see myself trying to please my stepmother but never quite making it. I ache for Tracey. But I don't know how to treat her. I've made her an afterthought for nine years. Tracey's eyes are pleading with me to let her go swimming tonight. I ache for her.

But what do I do?

Lord, it's been a while and I ain't a good Mama. Help me put my life together. Help me love this little girl like I should. Like she deserves. Forgive me for all the hurt I've caused her.

"Mama?" Tracey questions me. She looks frightened. "Are you listening? I promise I won't be any trouble at all."

"Tracey, come here."

The red-headed little girl walks to the edge of the bed. She goes slowly, like she's expecting to be punished. Oh God, what have I done?

I reach out for her hand. Tracey takes it immediately. I draw her in, I pull her to my chest, and I hug her. She feels warm like a cookie out of the oven. Her hair is like a doll's hair. I stroke the red soft flames and I keep her close to me. I sniff. Tears have come again.

Tracey tilts her head back and looks into my eyes. "Mommy, are you okay?"

Mommy. The name I've loathed is suddenly filled with sweetness. Mommy, indeed. I pull Tracey out of my arms but I keep her close to look directly into my daughter's green eyes.

"Sweet Girl, I'm sorry." I've never used a pet name for my child. "I'm so sorry, Sweet Girl."

"For what, Mama?"

"I ain't done right. I ain't treated you like I should. I've been angry with God for a long time. And now, I made up with Him, I think. But while I was mad at God, I acted like I was mad at you. And I'm not."

I see my daughter through moisture. "Tracey, I love you." I ain't ever said those words.

A teardrop falls from Tracey's right eye.

"Oh, honey, please forgive me." I clutch Tracey and I hug her tightly. My daughter begins to weep into my chest. I have so much to make up for. It'll take the rest of my life.

I hear her tiny voice coming from my chest. "Mommy, did Jesus find you?"

"What?" I ask. I don't understand the question. "What do you mean, Tracey?"

"You know how Nana wrote me? She always told me to pray and ask Jesus to not stop looking for you. He found you, right?"

Oh Cecelia, thank you. What a wonderful old broad you were.

"Yes, Baby, He found me."

I feel the moisture of Tracey's tears and I like it. I like the smell of the eight-year-old red hair and the sound of the sweet little voice. I like the feeling of her hands on my back. Her skin is so smooth and pure. I'm overwhelmed with a love I didn't know I could feel. In a guest room of the Jackson home, I fall in love with my precious child Tracey. In the same room that Jesus found me.

Chapter 37

Donna

I am full of southern fried cooking and I still put on a bathing suit. It is a banner day in the world of Donna. The water is still like the night. Underwater lights on the pool walls cast a muted glow and I feel like I am dipping into a hidden Bahamas beach. When I went to the Bahamas five years ago, I didn't even put my toe in the water. I smile at this and go all the way under. I come up and shake my hair. I laugh. "I can't believe I let you two talk me into this."

Belinda and Maggie are leaning against the walls by the three feet marker. They're sitting on the pool's bottom, their heads and shoulders above water.

"You gotta love this, Donna," Maggie says and stretches out so her hair goes under while her face looks up to the sky.

I'm glad it's dark so no one around can see me. I hate bathing suits. I don't own one. But these two talked me into accepting an extra suit Mrs. Friesen owns. It is a bit large, though, and that makes me feel better. Somehow, it makes it easier for me to be comfortable enough to swim. Maggie and Belinda didn't say anything when I came out of Imogene's pool house, dressed in this, but Tracey looked up and said, "I like your bathing suit." I wonder if someone paid her to say that.

"This feels so great. I love being in a swimming pool at night." Belinda dives to the bottom of the deep and rises up to the top with a splash. Tracey, who is a fish, jumps on Belinda's back and they laugh as Belinda swims to the shallow end. I smile and once again wonder at the complete one-eighty change in their relationship. I guess Belinda came to her senses. She has been positively nice to me all evening. Weird. I don't trust it though.

Mrs. Friesen comes out of her house with Mrs. Turner. Each of them are holding glasses and are standing on Imogene's back porch.

"Can I get you ladies anything?" Mrs. Friesen calls.

"Imogene, they're swimming. What do you think they need? A glass of water?" Mrs. Turner snaps.

"Oh hush up, woman."

"But that reminds me," says Mrs. Turner, "I brought over some iced tea that you might like. You ladies want a glass?"

Tracey pipes up. "I want some."

All three of us yell, "No!"

Belinda adds, "She'll have water or milk." Then we look at each other and start laughing.

"We're great, thank you, Lola Bee!" Maggie calls.

"We're inside watching a Lifetime Movie about a woman who kills her husband 'cause she hates his cooking." Mrs. Friesen says.

"That could happen you know," Mrs. Turner retorts while they head back inside.

Maggie continues floating on her back. "I can't tell you how wonderful this feels."

It's a good idea and I lay on my back, too, knowing I won't sink cause of my tubby tummy. I look up to the dark sky and see it is speckled with the glittering stars of a Texas night. This is the sky of my childhood. Beautiful. This is a wonderful place to visit every twenty-five years, but I would never want to live here.

The funeral reception lasted for hours. People just stayed, talking. I enjoyed the food but wondered when everyone would leave. Belinda and Maggie showed up about an hour before folks started leaving. I could tell Belinda had been crying. She was close to Cecelia when we were kids. Probably finally hit her.

After the house and yard cleared out, Mrs. Turner led volunteers to clean up. Mrs. Friesen asked if we wanted to come over and swim. She'd invited Tracey and thought it might be a relaxing end to the day. When we left Cecelia's, Mr. Jackson sat at the Formica with his old friend Bud. They weren't saying a lot, just sitting like two friends who'd known each other forever.

"Watch, Mama!"

I look up and Tracey is flying off the diving board like a swan. Is she only eight?

"Yay! I give it a ten!" Belinda claps and yells.

What happened between the two of them? I stand up and wade over to Belinda and Maggie. They congregate near the five feet. Each are treading water even though they can both stand up. I join them and we keep watching Tracey do tricks off the board. She does a cannonball that gives amazing splash for such a little girl.

"Oh no you don't. You got me wet." Belinda starts swimming toward Tracey and Tracey starts giggling and swimming away.

"Is she a little tipsy?" I ask. "Or is she just really tired?"

"You should ask her," Maggie replies.

Once again, I feel like I've missed something. Belinda is actually having fun with her child. With all of us, actually.

"Belinda!" I yell. "Why are you so chipper?"

"Just a second," Belinda replies, as Tracey's giggles reach a hysterical peak. "I have a shark to catch first."

"Well, whatever it is," I say quietly to Maggie, "it is great for Tracey. Belinda is actually treating her like a mom should."

Maggie doesn't meet my gaze, but keeps looking towards the mother and daughter, smiling. Tracey climbs out of the pool squealing and heads back to the diving board. Belinda disappears under water.

Boo!" She screams. I jump, almost out of the water. Belinda is laughing along with Maggie.

"Belinda, what has gotten into you?" I ask.

"Mama!" Tracey calls. We all look over and she does a back flip.

"She is incredible, Belinda." Maggie says what I'm thinking.

"Yep, she is. No thanks to me, though. Her friend in Wind Storm had a pool and a swimming coach for a mama."

"If she keeps this up, she could go to the Olympics," I add.

Belinda doesn't respond but keeps eyeing her girl. Her eyes are shining with pride.

"Okay, I have to know," I interject.

Belinda looks at me and smiles. "What?"

"What? What happened between the two of you?"

Belinda exchanges smiles with Maggie. This is getting annoying. "Donna, I have something to tell you, and you probably won't like it."

"Okay," I say with a bunch of suspicion, "what is it?"

"First, I'm sorry about our fight."

"You should be. The way you attacked me…"

"Well, you called Hank and that ain't none of your business."

"Whatever, Belinda."

Belinda takes a deep breath. "I'm sorry, Donna."

Water under the bridge. "I am, too. And why in the world would I not like you apologizing?"

"Well, that's not what you won't like." Belinda pauses. "I have run back to Jesus." Belinda grins like a silly clown on drugs. I have no grin for her.

"What?" I ask looking between Maggie and Belinda.

"I have realized that it is time for me to stop running from the Lord. He was the answer for me then, and He is still the answer."

A pang of betrayal strikes my heart. I look at the radiance on Belinda's face. I am happy for her. I am. But I'm angry, too. I can't say anything.

"Donna, maybe you should come back to the Lord, too."

I recognize this Belinda from our childhood. Always the most courageous, Belinda never hesitated talking about Jesus to anyone. I ignore the sudden burning in my chest. I'm sure it's all those baked beans I ate. I stand silent, conscious of Belinda and Maggie staring at me, waiting for an answer. Well, I have one, but they won't like it.

"Belinda, good for you," I respond. I try to put cheerfulness into my tone but it's not coming through. "I am glad if you think it's what you need for you and Tracey. I think it's wonderful you're treating your daughter like you should. For once."

A dig and I meant it. I look at Belinda, waiting for a jab back. Her smile has gone, but she's not saying anything. I try again.

"I mean you have been horrible to Tracey and to us this whole trip. And if Jesus is what makes you halfway decent to people well, great. Congratulations."

She looks down into the water with an expression of hurt. Good. She deserves a little of her own medicine. She looks up at me. "Donna, I been a fool. I don't think 'fore I speak, you know that, right? Just foolishness. I got a lot to learn. I'm sorry I was mean."

You're kidding me. She's apologizing again? "It's just who you are, Belinda. Don't apologize for who you are."

Maggie chimes in, "Donna, you tell her she's mean and a horrible mom and now she apologizes and that's how you respond?"

Holier-than-thou Maggie. "Look, you two. Just leave me alone, okay? I don't want to be a part of your little religious club. I live out there in the real world."

"You know we're going to pray for you though, right?" Belinda's tone is teasing and she comes up beside me and bumps me with her shoulder.

I grin. No need to get upset. I'm leaving in the morning. "Hey, whatever floats your boat," I respond.

"You know, I know a great church in Denver. It is a wonderfully casual place to worship. Maybe I could get you the number," Maggie pushes.

"Fine. Call me anytime. Maybe I'll check them out." Not in this lifetime.

"You know, I need to find a church," Belinda realizes. "Course, I need to find a home, too." She giggles.

"You can always come to Tucson. You and Tracey can stay with us until you get settled," Maggie counters.

I probably should offer her a place to stay in Denver. I would have this morning. But I don't want a 'Jesus Woman' living with me.

"We'll see," Belinda replies with a faraway look. "Who knows what the future holds?" A sly grin forms on her lips.

"You're different, I'll give you that," I observe.

"I feel I have this whole new life now, Donna. A do-over." Her eyes are gleaming. The joy is obvious, even in the half-light.

"Speaking of new life, Maggie, how are you feeling?" Belinda asks.

"I'm good. It's strange to have so many people know about this before Frank."

"You haven't called him?" I wonder.

Maggie grins. "Nope. I think I'm going to tell him at the airport. Or maybe when we get to the house. No, I'll probably just blurt it out when I see him." Maggie's grin disappears and she lets out a big sigh. "I don't know though."

"What's wrong?" Belinda asks.

It occurs to me that Maggie's future is an unsure as Belinda's. "Maggie, are you worried about the cancer?"

Maggie nods. "After battling cancer for so many years, here I am sick again. It's because I'm pregnant, I'm sure of it. Well, maybe not positive. But what hounds me is the thought of being pregnant and having cancer. What if I don't get to see this baby grow up? What if..." Maggie hesitates. "What if the baby doesn't grow up?"

Belinda speaks up. "Maggie, the entire time we talked in my bedroom you had this on your mind. I'm so sorry."

"It's going to be okay," I say, hoping I sound certain.

Maggie reaches for a towel on the side of the pool and wipes her nose.

"From all you've said about Frank, he'll be someone you can lean on, right?" Belinda asks.

Maggie nods. "Absolutely. Frank is the best man I know and I don't think he'll be anything but encouraging. But once he realizes my life might be in danger, well...I don't know what he'll say."

Belinda reaches over and puts her hand on Maggie's shoulder. "Maggie, your baby may die."

I erupt, "Belinda!"

She ignores me. "But she may live. And you might die or you may live. I ain't sure of nothing. But like Cecelia told me and you told me, Jesus is right here." She gently places her hand on Maggie's stomach. "And He loves you. If you hang on to that, you can get through."

I feel nauseous. My friend is in pain, but Belinda is giving her false, silly religious hope. Maggie needs practicality, not fairy tales. Before I offer my point of view, Maggie speaks up.

"You're right, Belinda. I just have to wait and see. And while I'm waiting, well, that will be a wonderful time to hang on to Christ with all my might. You'd think I'd be used to that, but every time is a challenge. I'm constantly in a battle to believe Christ and to trust His Word." She pauses. "And you said 'she?' Honey, I don't know how to birth anything but boys."

The both of them laugh. I reach over and give Maggie a quick hug. I care about my friend. But I don't care about this Jesus talk. I swim away and turn over to float on my back again. I hear the two of them chatting. I gaze at the sky, a beautiful painting that makes me relax. But for some reason, I have a headache. It's just this town, is what it is. Boots is a place of Christians who love to talk about Jesus. Denver is a place for accountants to visit museums and see plays and discuss world affairs with friends and fall in love. William is a memory, but I'll find somebody else. Maybe Stuart? Probably not. But soon I'll be back in my own place, away from this gorgeous ebony canvas in the sky, but also apart from the incessant, conservative view points and endless make believe religious stories.

Tracey has joined Belinda and Maggie. "Watch, Mama. I'll make a whirlpool." I swim to the side and we all watch the eight-year-old. Splashing through the water in a circle, Tracey laughs and jumps and tries to run as fast as she can. Soon the water follows her and creates a force of its own.

Oh Cecelia. I remember in this very pool. "Remember when we did that?" I ask.

"Yes," Belinda and Maggie reply in unison.

"Do you remember when Cecelia saved you from drowning, Donna?" Margie asks.

"I remember quite well." I respond, envisioning that day clearly. "Right here in this pool."

Maggie puts her hand out in the middle of the three of us. "Remember this?"

Belinda places it on top.

I hesitate. "I'm not a Jesus Girl anymore, Maggie."

"How 'bout friends?" Maggie answers, smiling at me.

"How about cheesy?" I reply, laughing.

"Come on, Donna. We grew up and survived and here we are back again in the same place. Not many people get to celebrate the cyclical achievements of their lives," Belinda argues.

She has a point. As absolutely cynical as I feel, the Hallmark moment is not lost on me.

"Okay." I put my hand on top of Belinda's.

"Friends!"

We look over and see Tracey's whirlpool gain strength. I look at my childhood friends, the girls who saw me through so much. "It's been a while, but we can still make a whirlpool, can't we?"

"Absolutely!" Maggie starts swimming and Belinda and I follow our way to Tracey. Soon the rushing water is in full force and squeals and giggles join the growing current. As we plod around in a circle, Maggie calls "Belinda, do you feel good about leaving those old ladies the recipe?"

Belinda shouts back, dashing through the water, "I didn't give them the secret. I gave them a fake list of ingredients!"

"What?" Maggie and I yell together.

"Well, then what's the secret?" I call.

"It's in the pickles. Cecelia always makes her own pickles. So the secret is in the recipe for that. Which I asked Vern for and which he gave to me. You guys really didn't notice that?"

"No!" We yell simultaneously.

"Goes to show you. Cecelia loved a little mystery," Belinda responds.

"And poetry," I add.

Tracey, still leaping through the water, looks at her mom, "Can I have one of Nana's cowboy poems? They're pretty good."

We laugh and just as she did years ago, Maggie yells, "Now!"

Three forty-two-year-old women and an eight-year-old girl turn into the rushing water of the whirlpool and begin the battle against the current.

Chapter 38

Maggie

His smile always cradles my heart. On my way to baggage claim, I scan every group, every individual standing as if they are waiting on someone. When I see his face, his smile goes right to my heart. I let my breath out even though I didn't know I was holding it. With Frank, I can share all of me. The fear of seeing Belinda and Donna again. The frustration with Belinda's behavior. The consternation at Donna. The joy in being with Vern and Imogene. The surprising encouragement from Lola Bee. And the ecstasy of watching my childhood friend come back to Jesus. I'm home.

"Hello, beautiful." Frank pulls me in and holds me. He smells of Stetson after-shave. My own little reminder of Texas here in Arizona. I'm married to that scent, and I'll never divorce it.

"I missed you so much." He tries to pull back but I cling to him. I can share all of me, but not yet. I dare not tell him of the new life inside me while we're surrounded by travelers, luggage and a frantic sense of urgency. I start crying. I don't want to cry here, but the tears come without permission.

"Maggie, what is it?" Frank pulls me from his chest and looks right into me. His eyes are hazel and compassionate. He leans in and kisses me softly on the lips.

"I love you so much, Frank."

"I love you, too. Is everything okay?"

I want to tell him, but not now. "I'm just happy to see you."

"What is that?" Frank points at a large package I'm carrying.

"It's a gift from Cecelia. Vern gave it to me this morning and said Cecelia wanted me to have it."

"Do you know what it is?"

"I'm sure it's a picture. Maybe one hung up in the Visiting Room."

"Give me your claim ticket and I'll get your bag." I hand Frank the picture to hold and I pull the ticket out of the side of my purse. We exchange ticket for package. I go to a row of chairs. Frank stands by the carousel watching suitcases go by. I watch him. *Thank you, Father. Prepare him.*

When we get in the car, I broach the subject. "Frank, it was an eye-opening couple of days. A lot of surprises."

"Did an old love of Cecelia's crash the service?" Frank laughs at his own attempt at a joke. "Or did the folks of Boots holler at each other and disrupt the funeral?" Again he chuckles.

"Well, actually Belinda and Donna were there. Cecelia left the tuna recipe to all of us."

"Oh honey, I'm sorry. Difficult for you, I'm sure. You've been so close to Cecelia."

"I got so angry, Frank. But I have to tell you that God used the two of them to show me how wrong I've been about Him. I am loved and cherished by God the same as Belinda and Donna. I've been so judgmental and I need to apologize to you, too, sweetie. I am so sorry I've wanted your walk with Jesus to look like mine. I'm so sorry that I've harped on 'good choices' instead of the grace and love of God."

Frank turns the car off before we've left the airport parking lot. "Wow. Honey, what a trip." He reaches out for my hand.

"So you forgive me? I've been so foolish."

He leans over for another kiss. "Sweetheart, I adore you. Of course, I forgive you."

"I have to tell you about Imogene and Lola Bee, too." By the time we reach home, I've given him all the highlights of my trip. Except for one.

In our driveway, Frank turns the car off and then grabs my hand. "It sounds like a pretty good time. You've buried that old hatchet?"

I squeeze his hand. "It's six feet under."

"Good." He releases my hand and opens his door. "We are ordering your favorite pizza tonight. A quiet night at home sound good?"

"Absolutely."

That evening the Hawaiian pizza tastes delicious and the banter between the boys brings me back to my world. At one point, I sit back and watch Jeremy and Michael as they debate the finer points of Triple A baseball and the Tucson Padres. They are beautiful, my sons. I enjoy watching their bodies and remembering how little they once were.

"Honey?"

I look at Frank. "Yes?"

"Mom, are you okay?" Michael asks.

"I'm fine. Why do you ask?"

"You're crying," Jeremy adds.

I realize they're right. I grab my napkin off my lap and wipe my face. I smile at the three faces gawking at me. "Just love you guys. And I miss Cecelia."

"To Nana." Jeremy raises his glass of coke and Frank and Michael follow suit.

"To Cecelia," I chime and we lean in and click glasses. "To Cecelia indeed."

After an hour of TV, Frank and I leave the boys to turn it off and we go upstairs to bed. Talking to each other as we prepare for bed has always been a precious habit. After our discussions, which are sometimes profound and sometimes silly, we curl up, pray and go to sleep. Or we curl up, pray and enjoy each other a while. Frank finishes brushing his teeth and then leans against the frame of our bathroom door. I'm sitting on the edge of the bed.

"You have me worried, honey. You aren't talking much and you're really weepy."

Tears are in my eyes. Shoot. "We need to talk, Frank."

He grabs a chair from the corner and pulls it to face me. He sits down and looks at me intently. "I'm listening."

I see his face and his forehead crinkled with dread. I know that look. "It's not cancer."

Visible relief smoothes out the crinkles on his face. "Well then, what is it?" His tone is much cheerier.

I can't talk. How can I tell him this? It's four words that will change his life forever, no matter the outcome. I rehearse the words in my mind, but they weigh too much. I can't lift them to speak.

"Maggie, whatever it is, we can handle it. We've gotten through a lot, don't you think?"

I nod, my lips super-glued to each other.

"So," Frank tries. "You want to tell me that...."

I use every ounce of my internal fortitude to rip my lips apart. "Frank, I am pregnant."

I've read novels where faces in shock were described as going white, but I've never seen this phenomenon until now. My darling husband stares at me, mouth open.

"Honey, I know this is a shock." I sigh and I feel better as if I've just given him the giant rock I've been carrying around. It's his turn to be tongue-tied.

I look at his face and I know he's processing. Twenty years with this man has taught me to leave him alone while he digests this.

"I am going to go to the bathroom and then brush my teeth. I'll be right back." *Father, please cover his mind with Your truth.* When I come back, Frank sits in the same place, motionless. "Frank, can we talk? Or do you want to wait until tomorrow?"

He comes out of his shock-induced coma and asks, "How long?"

"How long have I known or how long have I been pregnant?"

"Both."

"I found out the day Vern called. I just couldn't tell you. I needed time to absorb it, I guess. And I have been pregnant for eight weeks."

"Did the doctor say you could have a baby?"

"He said that women in remission from cancer have had babies before. He wants to watch me carefully and see what happens." I can't believe how calm I am. Thank you, Jesus. "But I fainted in Texas. And I bled a little bit."

Frank walks to me and sits beside me. He puts his hand on my stomach. "Are you okay?"

"I feel fine, now. I just overdid it with the excitement and emotion and making all that tuna. I'll call the doctor tomorrow and make an appointment and have him check me out."

"So how do you feel?" He asks as if it's a totally different question.

"I feel pregnant. I think. If I remember what pregnant feels like, that is. I'm tired and I'm scared most of the time. I'm forty-two!"

Frank grabs my hand, "Come here." I stand up and he pulls me onto his lap. "Let's pray."

He prays for wisdom and guidance and most of all protection and health. It is a simple prayer and one of the most passionate I've ever heard. After the amen, he looks at me. "Let's tell the boys and call Noah, too."

"Do you think we should, Frank? I mean, what if something happens?"

"It will happen to them, too, no matter if they know or not. So let's go tell them and pray as a family. Maggie, what can we do? We serve a God who knows the big picture. Let's take this one day at a time. But I believe it's vital that we tell our family and friends soon and let them pray for us and this baby."

"Frank, how in the world did I end up with such a wonderful man?" Tears again.

"I am pretty wonderful, aren't I?" His words come with a twinkle in his eye.

"I should have told you immediately. I am sorry."

"It's okay, baby. Have you done the math on this, though?"

"Yes." I know exactly what he's talking about. "When she graduates high school, I'll be sixty and you'll be sixty-five."

"We'll get good seats with our wheelchairs." As we laugh, Frank falls back on the bed with me in his arms.

"Frank!" I squeal in delight.

A look of horror comes over his face. "Maggie, I'm sorry. I wasn't thinking. The baby. Are you okay?"

We sit up together and I calm him. "Honey, I'm fine. I'm not going to break." We stand up together, still holding hands.

"Let's go down and pray with the boys." Frank leads me out.

"She'll be the most prayed over baby ever," I say, smiling.

"She?" Frank teasingly replies.

"Belinda got me thinking this might be a girl who'll grow up to be a strong young lady. Anyway, I am so outnumbered. I need reinforcements!"

As we leave the room to go downstairs, I glance again at the picture Cecelia gave me. It's sitting on the floor, leaning against the wall. I opened it before dinner and it is indeed, a picture from the Visiting Room. It's a painting of a valley filled with a lush green meadow crowned with a beautiful horizon showing the sunrise. Right in the middle of the meadow is a rose bush. Out of place, but gorgeous. When I first looked at it, I remembered Sister Loretta's words. *The pruning of rose bushes is a necessity to a season of growth and beauty. Don't fight the pruning. Forgive.*

Thank you God, for pruning. Whatever is next, I know You will have me.

The verse across the painting reads:

"For I know the plans I have for you," declares the Lord, "plans to prosper you and not to harm you, plans to give you hope and a future." Jeremiah 29:11.

Chapter 39

Donna

Three months have passed since Cecelia's funeral and the red rash on my heart still itches. No one knew how much Cecelia's death affected me and that's how I wanted it. But now, it's hard for me to bat away the grief. I feel like it's with me all the time. I am constantly sad. Work helps. When I go to the office, I try to leave what happened in Texas in my apartment. It stays here, too. Gina's asked questions but I've successfully told her very little.

Stuart comes by my office often. He walks in with his compassionate smile and his goofy grin and I hate it. I also love it. I'm thinking about him even more than before. I cut our conversations short. I think he may actually want to ask me out but I can't let him. No one wants a sad woman leeching onto him. A sad, fat woman would be worse.

Tonight is yet another night where I will stay at home, watch TV, and wait for bedtime. I look at the dishes stacked up in my kitchen sink. Usually, I love to clean. It is a release. Not now. I walk into my living room and sit on the couch. Tissues cover the floor. I have to get a trashcan. I stand up and the phone rings.

"Hello."

"Hey, it's Gina. How are you feeling?"

"Not great."

"Are you going to the hospital?"

"What? No. It's just a cold."

"You haven't missed three days in a row in years. We at the office are worried."

"Let them worry. I'll be back. If not tomorrow, then Monday."

"The Saint asked about you."

My heart takes off on a sprint. I don't say anything.

"Don't you want to know what he asked?"

"I have to go, Gina. I'll see you later." As she starts to talk, I hang up. My new best friend, Procrastination, will hang out with me tonight. I'll get to the dishes and laundry tomorrow. I reach for the remote and start surfing. Nothing is on. I click off and sit back, hugging a pillow to my chest.

Why did I go back there in the first place? William? What a joke.

Maggie and Belinda have emailed me several times and I try to keep it light but they keep using phrases that unnerve me. Bible phrases. Christian-ese. I made the right decision in walking away from the Christian life. It wasn't just about Dennis, but about how I want to live my life.

I don't fit in with the Christian world. I couldn't live up to their rules then and I can't now. It might be wonderful to have the kind of belief Maggie and Belinda have. But I can't. I won't. Right? I take the pillow and throw it across the room. *Leave me alone, God.*

Ice cream. That's what I need. I walk to the kitchen and get a pint from the freezer. With a spoon in my hand, I go back to the couch. Maybe I'll rent a movie. I set down the spoon and ice cream and go to my bedroom to get a blanket. When I walk in the room, I see the Bible on my dresser. I've been considering reading it but the Bible doesn't have anything to offer me. I am a successful urban woman. I don't need those Texas southern Bible crutches anymore.

I switch to sweats and get my blanket. Slippers would be the perfect final touch. It's almost September and it's getting chilly quickly this year. I go to my closet to find my slippers. I haven't worn them since last April.

As I thrash around my walk-in-closet trying to find my house shoes, I see the package I tossed aside when I got back from Texas. Mr. Jackson told me that Cecelia left instructions that I receive this certain picture when she died. I'm sure it's Scripture in a picture. It is obvious by the feel of it. It is medium-sized and shaped like a frame.

I bend down and pick it up and consider if I want to know what is inside. I threw it in my closet when I got home from Boots. I knew the verses would point directly at me. Cecelia used the Visiting Room pictures as a teaching tool and now I am a proud owner of one of those lessons.

They're only words. Can't hurt me. I pick up the picture and decide to see what Cecelia thinks my verse of the week should be. I tear the brown paper quickly. It is a black and white photograph of an old wooden door. The door connects to a partial wall of a weather beaten house, in the midst of a field of wheat. The words across the picture read:

"Here I am! I stand at the door and knock. If anyone hears my voice and opens the door,

I will come in and eat with that person, and they with me."
Revelation 3:20

I stand frozen and I read it again.

I can't do it. I just can't. Too much time has gone by. *God, I know You exist, but I just don't need You.* My throat feels tight. "I don't need You!" I croak aloud.

I throw the picture into the top of the closet on the back wall. I don't care where it lands. The frame hits a shoebox high atop other boxes and falls to the floor. The shoebox falls and its contents crash to the floor.

Silver dollars lay askew throughout my walk-in-closet. I stare at them. *Oh Cecelia.* I fall to the ground and fold in my body, hugging myself. Why did Mama leave? Why did Daddy die? Why did I let that jerk treat me that way?

Cecelia, you lied to me. I never fit in. Why didn't God send me a husband? Someone who really loves me?

The doorbell rings. I ignore it. Probably a neighbor wants sugar or a lost Chinese delivery guy needs directions. I am breathing hard. I pick up the silver dollars and put them back into the shoebox.

The doorbell rings again. Just leave, whoever you are.

I sit here in exhaustion. I stand up and shove the shoebox back onto a shelf. I find my slippers and head to the kitchen, my blanket and Cecelia's gift in hand.

With my foot, I open the trashcan.

I cannot do this. She was too good to me. Even if she told me fairy tales.

Instead, I lay it on the counter. I remember my ice cream. It's probably melted just enough to make it creamy and yummy.

I sit down on the couch and snuggle into my blanket. I grab the remote again to click and rent a movie. As I turn the TV on, the phone rings.

"Leave me alone, Gina." I don't move.

A voice breaks through the room, "You've reached Donna's house. Leave a message and I will get back to you."

The answering machine beeps.

"Hi Donna! This is Maggie. Are you there?"

I mute the TV.

"I just called to let you know that I'm fine and I just heard from Belinda. You won't believe what she's doing. You should call her. I also want to leave you the name and number of that church I told you about. It's called Faith Chapel. I hope you try it out, Donna. From what I hear, I'm sure you'll like it. I loved seeing you and I wish you'd return my calls. Let's not drift apart again; we have too much history, don't you think? Well, let me know. I love you, Donna, and I miss you. Call me. Oh, here's the phone number..."

After Maggie leaves the number, the phone clicks and the room goes silent.

Blah, blah, blah. I stare at the TV, not really seeing it. I make my decision. I can't go back. Why follow a God who would take away my parents and let me screw up my life with a man who claimed to lead others to God? I don't need this. My life is fine. I'll delete Maggie's message later. For now, a mindless movie. Maybe with a couple of car chases. I un-mute the TV and start trying to decide which movie to choose. I reach over and take the top off the ice cream pint. It's melted just enough.

The doorbell rings again. This time it's incessant and whoever is out there is bruising their finger pushing my buttons. And not just the door ringer. I mute the TV, throw off the blanket and stand up. This had better be a bleeding child or a long lost relative with money.

I look through the peephole and I can't make out who it is. Looks like a man with a bald head. "Who is it?" As soon as I say this, I put my fist in my mouth. You've got to be kidding.

"It's Stuart. From work."

I can't pretend I'm not here. He heard my voice. Oh please. I think about running to the bedroom to change and comb my hair. I don't have the energy. Oh well. I open the door. Stuart is wearing a button down lavender Oxford and some blue jeans. He stands there, smiling at me. I wait to see his eyes check me out and disapprove, but they remain focused on my face.

"Hi." I say. "You checking on me, too? I'll be back to work by Monday."

He shakes his head. "This is not a work call." He's not smiling. My insides melt. I wait for him to tell me why he is here, but he's not saying anything. Just staring.

"Okay," I say, "why are you here?"

"I want to ask you something."

My heart does a flip-flop. No way. "What is it?" I glance down and see a stain on my sweatshirt. Wonderful.

"Donna Dougans, I would like to see you socially."

"What?" Is he asking me out, or does he want to spot me across the room at a party? "I'm not sure what you are saying."

He swallows. Goodness gracious, he is nervous. Stuart the Saint is nervous in front of me? "I would like to ask you out on a date. Just you and me. Dating. I want to get to know you outside of the office with no shop talk, no accounting, and no numbers. I pick you up and I pay."

I now stand in silence. I hate that I'm wearing this stained sweatshirt. What am I supposed to say? This is not happening. I almost want to look behind me to see if he's talking to someone else.

"And there's something else," Stuart adds.

He looks down and I sense he checked me out. The stain. Oh

no, he saw the stain and now he's going to change his mind. "Go ahead," I say. Let's get this over with quickly.

"Um, well. My faith is very important to me and…"

What? His faith? I don't hear the last part of what he said.

"I'm sorry, your faith? Are you Jewish?"

"No. I follow Jesus."

I start to laugh. And then a good ole Imogene cackle comes out of me. Even as I continue to laugh, I know I'm being rude. Stuart is not laughing with me. I try to stop but it just keeps going. I expect him to leave, but he just stands there, waiting.

"I'm sorry, it's just. It's a long story." I try to muffle my giggles.

"It's okay. I just wanted to tell you that. Because I want our first date to be on Sunday morning. Church and lunch. What do you think?"

The laughter rolls out again but I quell it.

"Me?" It just comes out. "You want to go out with me?"

He looks surprised. "I'd be honored to go out with you. The question is 'Will you go out with me?'"

I don't know what to do. I really, really like this man. But I don't know.

"Can I call you tomorrow with an answer?" I need some time. I look into his eyes and it occurs to me he is standing there and this is actually happening. To me.

"Of course. I'll look forward to your call. I guess I'll go. Goodnight, Donna."

"Goodnight, Stuart." I watch him walk down the hall to the elevator and something occurs to me. "Stuart?"

He turns around. He's smiling. "Yep?"

"What's the name of the church?"

"Faith Chapel."

"Of course it is."

"What?" He cocks his head.

"Nothing. I'll call you tomorrow."

He gets on the elevator and I come in and close the door. I look up. "Cecelia! Stop pushing me." I laugh. It's just weird. I know immediately what I'll say to Stuart. Of course I do. But what will I wear? Should my hair be up or down? I walk to the couch and pick up the remote to turn the TV off. I'm going to try on clothes tonight so I can find the right outfit.

As I head to the bedroom, I glance down and see that my ice cream is melting. In fact, it's overflowing. I don't care. It's just dessert. I'll clean it up later.

Chapter 40

Belinda

The most important aspect of food, besides a delicious taste, is making sure it looks scrumptious. I take pride in ever' plate, be it beef wellington or a top-secret-recipe special. I cut the tasty tuna sandwich in half and put a store-bought pickle beside it with one olive. I like the combination. 'Course my "piece that can't be resisted," or something like that in French, is the little Texas flag I plant into the sandwich. Gives it somewhat of a cowboy flair. I add the same creativity to twelve plates.

"Mama, can we take Melissa and Janis to church tonight?" I look over and Tracey is standing there, her little apron looking too big for her, but cute as a bug anyway.

"Yep, honey." I put six plates on a tray.

"Can we pick them up?" She comes over to me and puts her hands out.

"If their mothers don't mind, we'll go and pick 'em up on our way." I put three plates on a smaller tray and put it into Tracey's arms.

"Mama, they both think you are the best helper at church."

"Why, thank them kindly for me, okay? Now, I need to think about what I'm doing."

"Mama, table one needs more ice tea."

"After you deliver that tray, fill up their glasses. Ain't you big enough to do that?"

"Can I?"

"Yes. Go."

I watch her leave the kitchen carrying her tray carefully. I put the other three plates on another tray. I think I can balance both of them. I glance through the kitchen window and see Tracey deliver the tray and then go get the pitcher of tea and carefully take it to table one.

"Here's some more tea for you." My precious daughter says. She's wearing her hair up in a ponytail with green butterfly barrettes neatly pinned on the sides of her face.

"Well, if it isn't the little scarlet headed beauty of Boots, Texas!" Ted Bellinger says this loud enough that I think everyone hears him.

Bobby Lou Milton, the barber of Boots sits across from him and says, "Ted, are you going deaf? Why do you feel the need to yell every darn tooting thing these days?"

Innocently Tracey responds, "He's showing off for my mother." With that, she turns and takes the pitcher back to the stand.

Laughter rings across the room. I glance at Ted's face and

then turn around to get the trays. His face is the color of freshly ripe Texas tomatoes.

As I round the corner out of the kitchen, I hear Imogene's cackle followed by, "I wish I were a matchmaker, Ted. I would try to help you. But last matchmaking I did was between me and my husband and God love him, we're still wondering if we're gonna make another year. Wilbur used to say matchmaking is as dangerous as being a rooster in a henhouse after sundown."

"Well, why aren't you yelling, preacher?" Lola Bee calls over to Preacher Ben. "Don't you like our newest citizen a bit, too?"

I look over at Ben. It's his turn to blush. Ben and Ted flirt with me ever chance they can. Ted came out and asked me to go to the Frontier Day's dance with him. Two men who both love Jesus. And two men I don't know if I can handle. At least not like I should. So I told Ted no and I pay neither of them no mind 'cept to smile and be polite, even if my heart flits about like a firefly when one of them is near.

The future is Yours, Jesus. Right now, You're the man in my life. Still feels weird.

The small café buzzes with people chatting about life in Boots and life beyond the TV set. An eclectic variety of tables and chairs fill the room. Some chairs slide easily under the tables while others sit by themselves so folks can relax and drink coffee or a soda and visit. A couple of leather sofas are off in one corner.

I enter the room carrying a platter.

"Here we go!" I yell. "Freshly made tuna fish sandwiches for anyone who'll pay."

"Bring it on!" calls Pastor Ben who is eating today with the Methodist preacher Ed Barkley.

"Today I will figure it out." Barbara Harry comments to Maxine Massey. The ladies raised quite a storm over being tricked by me.

I often hear Lola Bee, who today is sitting with her three cohorts, comment, "On Cecelia's funeral day, no less!"

I told the four ladies I'd given them the original recipe and I challenged them to figure out the secret. I threw down a Texas gauntlet, so to speak. Barbara, Maxine, Lola Bee and Imogene often come to our little café to try to figure out the mystery. Of course, when no one else is looking I get a wink from Imogene. She could be an Oscar-winning actor. Saturdays at lunch, the Boots Tuna Fish Club assembles. The four detectives resemble Sherlock himself as they nibble and make notes, taste and discuss.

At their first meeting, I looked at the foursome and laughed, "As long as the recipe is back in Boots, does the secret really matter, heifers?" And it is. The Jackson tuna fish sandwich is officially a part of the town again.

After the funeral, I looked in the trunk of my car and found the red bag, completely full of the $495 I stole plus the $100 that old lady at the Gas and Go gave me. I asked Vern and Imogene to go to the Visiting Room and I handed the bag to them.

"I ain't proud of what I did. So I owe you both an apology." I said. "This is yours."

"We done talked it over and we want you and Tracey to have that money." Imogene said.

"I can't accept that. I have a lot to make right in my life and giving you this money is the first step."

Vern wasn't having it. "You take this money and start a new life. Use it for Tracey. Sissy woulda wanted this, so if you give it back you're disrespecting her memory."

"Yes." Imogene agreed.

I took the money and I went back to Wind Storm. I rented a U-Haul in Tyler and packed up the few belongings Tracey and

I owned. No one bothered us. I never even saw Hank but I didn't have one ounce of fear. A new power in me provided more courage than I ever had. It was a good time to think and to take some time actually talking to Tracey.

I planned to go to Tyler and start over, but Tracey kept telling me we should live in Boots. Didn't feel right at first, but then I figured it was time I listened to the scooter 'cause she tends to know a lot. I decided to try to get a job at Boots Elementary where Cecelia worked. When I told Tracey the plan, she hugged me and squealed. That night she started praying God would give us a house near Vern and Imogene. I wrote Imogene and asked if I could stay with her until I got enough money together to rent a place. I knew it would be a bit of a struggle but I felt a new sense of adventure in my way of thinking. So I welcomed the challenge. But a week after I sent the letter, I got a long distance phone call from Vern.

"Listen here, Miss Belinda, I just talked to Imogene and if you and that young'un plan on coming back to this one horse town I got you a prop-o-sition."

"What's the proposition, Vern?"

"Well, I tell you what. Sissy always wanted us to start our own little café. Just never was the time and we never had the direction from God. But I done prayed and talked with the Man upstairs about all this and I figure if you come back to ole' Boots it would be just about the right time. I will fund the operation, and you and that little red haired gal of yours can run it. What do you say?"

I lost my breath when I heard his idea. Sounded too good to be true. "Vern, I don't know. I'm a good cook, but I honestly don't know if I can run a restaurant, even a small one. Not right now in my life, that's for sure."

"Whenever Sissy talked about you in a kitchen, she'd imply that you were pert near as good as she was. You will do fine, thank you very much!" Vern replied. "And I can help a little here and there. I know that Ted Bellinger is good with accounting and numbers and such. He'll help us with the higher math 'til we can hire a bookkeeper."

"I'll think about it, Vern."

"Don't think, just do. This house is way too big for me so you and Tracey just move on in. Just come home, Bee and don't worry about the money, just come home."

Just come home, Bee and don't worry about the money.

I hung up the phone and started crying, thinking of that old lady at the Gas and Go. On the drive back to Boots, I stopped at that same filling station and asked for the old lady who wore the long apron. A young man told me she only worked every once in a while and today she was at home. So I left her a note and sealed it up with a $100 bill.

To the old woman with the floor length apron,

You helped my daughter and me a couple of weeks ago and gave us $100. You said God told you to tell me to go home and not worry about the money. Thank you. You were right. I am going home with my girl and I am at peace. Here's $100 so you can give it to someone else God puts in your path. May our Lord bless you as you blessed me.

Bee

Now I'm in charge of a sweet café in the heart of Boots where the Old Munn's pharmacy used to be when I was little. It's been vacant for several years so Vern said he got a good price on it.

We named it "Sissy's Visiting Room." It took six months to get it all fixed up, but when we had the grand opening, pert near the whole town showed up. Imogene and Lola Bee came in first before everyone else. When they walked in, Imogene started crying. "It's perfect. Looks like the Visiting Room."

"Are you going to put Scripture up, Belinda?" Lola Bee asked.

"No. It didn't seem right to recreate what Cecelia took years to build. So we're going to line the walls with pictures of Boots' residents."

"I have the first one!" Vern walked in and went directly to the main wall. In the center of it, he put up a nail and hung a picture of he and Cecelia's wedding photograph.

We ask anyone who buys a lunch and lives in Boots if they would like to add to the wall a nicely framed photograph of themselves or someone in their family. As the smiling faces went up, our café became more and more popular. Only one frame contained a piece of art and a verse. The one Cecelia left to me.

Against a painting of a great orange orchard just before harvest, the words read:

"I will repay you for the years the locusts have eaten..." Joel 2:25

"Richard, what are you doing here?" yells Imogene when the bell rings, signaling an entrance.

"I'm checking out the competition. It is my duty." The owner of Bells café speaks dryly and makes everyone chuckle. "So competition, let me have a tuna fish on white."

"Coming up, Mr. Bell," I spar right back and head toward the kitchen. I reach up to scratch my neck and remember again that my hair is tied up in a neatly pinned bun, displaying the reddish brown hair I'm allowing to grow back.

We offer more lunch items than the tuna fish sandwich but seems Saturdays is when we sell mostly tuna. I'm experimenting with some recipes and of course, I offer my chicken fried steak on Fridays. It's been a big hit. Vern agreed that we would only be open for lunch. I missed too much of Tracey's life and so I work as a teacher's aide in her class three mornings a week. I'm amazed at how much I like her. She's funny and smart and she's got herself a huge heart.

I am happy. For the first time in my life, I feel complete joy. Who knew it would be back here in Boots? Ever'body knows ever'one's business, for sure. But if they didn't, I might have ended up in the back seat of Hank's cruiser, with a black eye.

And though some folks eye the nicotine patch on my arm with a bit of judgment pushing up their eyebrows, I will take the bad with the good. I just look at Tracey and I know I'm doing the right thing.

The bell rings again and in walks my partner in crime, the owner himself.

"Vern!" everyone calls and I think of that old TV show, *Cheers*.

I peek through my window and I see Vern is doing something he loves, walking from table to table greeting and grinning.

I hear Ben talking to him. "Mr. Jackson, you look downright happy today."

"I'll tell you, Pastor Ben, putting one foot in front of the other is easier today than yesterday. All I can hope is that tomorrow it might be even easier."

"This café is the talk of the town, Vern," the Methodist preacher remarks.

"Ed, I thank you. Seems God still has work for this old cuss to do. But I have to tell you it's mostly due to that young 'un in the kitchen. She works harder than a cow with no udders."

The pastor chuckles and Vern keeps making his rounds. "Well lookie here – if it ain't the Boots Tuna Fish Club."

"Vern Jackson, how are you?" Barbara Harry says in her southern drawl. A couple of widows in town, including Barbara, look at Vern these days like a cat looking at catnip.

"I am finer than frog hair, Barbara."

"What are you holding in the envelope?" Lola Bee asks with her nose sticking up in the air. She can smell somebody else's business at three paces.

"Woman, if he wants you to know, he'll tell you," Imogene snarls. "Wilbur used to say everyday 'How come Lola Bee is so all fire interested in everybody else's business'?"

"Imogene, I am not talking to you, hag."

Maxine's sweet voice pipes up, "Isn't it a beautiful day?"

"Ladies, I will show you exactly what's in this here envelope directly."

I walk out of the kitchen and almost run into Vern. "Hello, partner." I give him a huge smile.

"Sweet Girl, I am the deliverer of good news today. Just call me John the Baptist."

"Hey Ed, too bad there's no John the Methodist, huh?" Ted Bellinger calls, a little too loudly. The Methodist pastor just grins.

"What is it, Grandpa?" Tracey's underneath Vern's arm giving him a squeeze. It wasn't long after we moved in that he asked her to call him Grandpa. She looks at him with wonder in her eyes and he teases her and gives her lollipops when he thinks I'm not looking. I love the man.

"Tracey darling, just wait one second." He nods at me to finish what I'm doing so I take the tray of sandwiches to Table Seven and then over to Richard Bell. I put the tray on the counter and nod back at him.

Vern turns to talk to everyone in the café. "Ya'll listen up, you hear? Don't let me interrupt you spending all sorts of money in here, but I got some news and a pretty picture to show!"

All eyes turn and the place gets quiet. I put my hands on Tracey's shoulders and wait to see what Vern is so excited about.

"Seems like somebody is having a birthday this week and wanted us to share in the fun. Over in Tucson, Maggie Curry Shanks is celebrating the one-year-old birthday of her baby girl. And everybody is healthy as a West Texas horse!" The small crowd hoots and hollers. Not everyone here knows Maggie but Boots folks celebrate the notion of celebrating.

Imogene calls out, "So you have a picture of the birthday girl?"

"He just said he did, Imogene. You should get your hearing checked," Lola Bee fires.

"Ladies, I believe a pretty photograph of a darling baby will brighten everyone's lunch." Barbara says with impeccable diction.

"Well of course, she's pretty, Barbara, she's a baby," Lola Bee is cranky as always.

"Lola Bee, hush up and let the man speak!" Imogene yells.

"Isn't this sandwich good?" Maxine quietly offers.

"Grandpa, show us!" Tracey yells.

I talk to Maggie at least once a week so I feel I know this little one already. The newborn photos were priceless, but nothing compares to the chubby cheeks of a one-year-old.

"Okay, I will," Vern says. "And I must let you all know that related or not, this little gal is the spitting image of somebody I knew and loved."

"Billy Lou?" Ted yells.

"No baby is that ugly, Ted!" Richard Bell cracks.

Billy Lou looks offended, but of course, he's not. He loves the attention.

"Here is the eight by ten she sent and I figure we put it up on the wall as soon as we can. What do you think, partner?" Vern looks at me.

"Absolutely." I reply. "Let's see her."

Vern pulls out the photo and holds it up high so everyone can see. Except one little girl.

"Grandpa, I can't see. Let me see." As oohs and aahs reserved for shower presents and pictures of adorable babies spread throughout the café, Vern brings down the photo and shows Tracey.

"She's pretty, huh Mama?" Tracey looks up at me and I nod and give her a squeeze.

Thank you, Lord. Maggie's baby girl, Cecelia, is a picture of loveliness.

THE END

Robbie Iobst

Robbie Iobst is a transplanted Texan, award-winning speaker and author. Her nonfiction work includes the devotional *Joy Dance* as well as numerous articles, including eight credits in the *Chicken Soup for the Soul* series. Robbie lives in Centennial, Colorado with her husband and son. *Cecelia Jackson's Last Chance* is her debut novel.

For Further information, discussion questions,
playlist, and more please visit:

WWW.WRITTEN-WORLD.COM

CPSIA information can be obtained at www.ICGtesting.com
Printed in the USA
LVOW05s1404030114

367946LV00005B/60/P